VEIL
OF
SHADOWS

FAE OF WOODLANDS & WILD
BOOK 2

KRISTA STREET

WELCOME TO THE FAE LANDS

Veil of Shadows is book two in the *Fae of Woodlands & Wild* trilogy, which is a slow-burn, fae fantasy romance.

This book takes place in the fae lands of Krista Street's *Supernatural World*. Although Krista's other fantasy and paranormal romance books also feature the fae lands, the *Fae of Woodlands & Wild* trilogy is entirely separate so may be read before or after her previous series.

THE

SILTEN

Nelive Sea CONTINENT

GLOSSARY

Kingdoms of the Silten Continent

Faewood – southeast kingdom, colors are turquoise, white, and dark brown. Elowen's kingdom. Magic is elemental.

Ironcrest – southwest kingdom, colors are silver, magenta, and dark orange. Magic is sensory.

Mistvale – northwest kingdom, colors are bright yellow, dark purple, and deep red. Magic is mental.

Stonewild – northeast kingdom, colors are forest green, gold, and sapphire blue. Jax's kingdom. Magic is shifting.

Seas of the fae lands

Adriastic Sea – the ocean to the west of the Nolus continent and to the east of the Silten continent.

Brashier Sea – the most northern ocean in the fae lands, large icebergs often present.

Nelive Sea – the ocean to the west of the Silten continent.

Tala Sea – the ocean to the south of the Solis continent.

Fae races

Silten fae – the Silten fae reside on a continent surrounded by ocean. Silten fae have numerous subspecies. The Silten species that is considered most powerful are the *siltenites*. Siltenites have bodies like humans, pointed ears, and varying skin and hair shades. The other Silten fae subspecies are called *wildlings*. Wildlings have primitive Old Wood magic, which connects them to aspects in nature. Wildlings typically have animalistic features: horns, scales, hooves, and tails, yet are often as intelligent as siltenites. Wildlings that don't reside in cities, usually live in underground dens, hollow logs, or wooded forests. Their ages vary based upon their subspecies, but siltenites live thousands of years.

Solis fae – the Solis fae reside on the icy, most northern continent of the fae lands planet. Solis fae have silvery white hair, crystalline blue eyes, and wings. They typically live for thousands of years.

Nolus fae – the Nolus fae reside on the central continent. They often have various shades of colorful hair, pointy teeth, glowing skin, and otherworldly strength. They typically live two to three hundred years, but royal Nolus fae live for thousands of years.

Lochen fae – the Lochen fae reside on a southern continent, islands, and in the seas throughout the fae lands. They can morph into fish-like creatures, similar to mermaids, but they can also walk on two legs and live on land. There are subspecies of Lochen fae who live in freshwater rivers, lakes, and ponds. The Lochen fae typically have green eyes and varying skin shades and hair colors.

Silten Fae Species

Beemi – a small wildling fae with yellow eyes that lives in the Wood. More animal than fae, with less intelligence than other wildlings.

Cerlikan – a small wildling fae with large eyes and a furry body. Highly intelligent and capable of language. They live in dens in the Wood and have an intricate community in which their chatter often fills the Wood with sound.

Dressel – a wildling fae with a bony head.

Fusterill – a huge monstrous wildling fae, with the strength of a giant.

Grundle – a wildling fae species who commonly works in serving jobs if they live in cities. They have hard scales on the backs of their body, furry eyebrows, and stubby fingers tipped in claws. They also molt like reptiles.

Half-breed – half-breeds are Silten fae of siltenite and wildling descent. They are able to procreate at a faster rate than siltenites, and some half-breeds are magically powerful. Because of this, procreating among siltenites and wildlings is against the law. Half-breeds that do come into existence are shunned in the Silten culture.

Iloseep – a wildling fae similar to a large rat with an excellent sense of smell.

Ramifin – a wildling fae with hooves who walks on two legs. Has a snout like a horse, but is able to speak and has high intelligence.

Siltenite – Elowen's species, considered the superior species among the Silten fae due to their appearance being most similar to the Nolus, Solis, and Lochen fae, and their ability to harbor and wield powerful magic. The siltenites have human-like bodies and a varied range of hair, eye, and skin color. They usually live thousands of years.

Wildling fae – fae of the Silten continent who aren't siltenites. Each wildling species has some animalistic trait or feature. Intelligence along with language abilities vary among the wildlings.

Yewen – a wildling with a long trunk that they often use to play music. Most yewens are musically adept.

Fae Terms

Barimum – a unit of speed used by ships.

Calling – the term used when Elowen travels to the Veiled Between to interact with the semelees.

Full season – equivalent of one year.

House – each kingdom has ten noble Houses that oversea land, businesses, and fae within their kingdom. House nobles are very wealthy and hold a considerable amount of power.

Kingsfae – the law of the land in the four kingdoms, similar to police, and commanded by the kings.

Lady – a noble title for a female fairy.

Lorafin – a female siltenite who possesses rare magic. Lorafins can venture to the Veiled Between. This is where the semelees reside.

Lordling – a noble title for a male fairy.

Salopas – a fairy version of a bar with no serving staff. There is a bartender and magically enchanted trays that serve patrons.

Semelees – all-knowing shadow creatures that live in the Veiled Between. They control fate, and they are neither dead nor alive, yet they are able to be commanded by lorafins.

Veiled Between – a plane of space between universes

that is neither a realm of the living or the dead but rather an alternate reality in between.

Fae plants and food

Babbo tree – a tree with a very wide base and thick branches. It's a common tree on the Silten continent.

Barnbrambles – a thorny bush with spikes as sharp as needles.

Bolum – a creature that's part animal and part rock that lives in the Shadow Valley Desert of Stonewild. If fae fall into them, they're often eaten, although it takes the bolum weeks to digest them.

Cottonum – a plant similar to cotton.

Femeral bush – a bush in the Wood, with wide velvety leaves that hold a pungent scent.

Goldling tree – a magical tree whose golden leaves can create priceless metals and gems from simple rocks or bricks.

Leminai – a bright-green alcoholic drink common throughout the fae lands.

Saggerwire – a common shrub in the Shadow Valley Desert. The center of its leaves holds water.

Wintercrisp fern – a plant on Stonewild's royal crest and a leaf that symbolizes trust and strength.

Fae animals

Brommel stag – a stag or deer-like creature that can run so swiftly hardly any fae can hunt them.

Colantha – a large cat that resides in jungles.

Crowfy – a huge black feathered bird.

Dillemsill – a messenger bird whose magic allows it to travel instantaneously throughout the realm.

Domal – an animal similar to a horse but more intelligent.

Dracoons – small scaled creatures that can morph into large beasts when provoked. They can also breathe underwater and are often used as guard animals by the Silten. It's illegal to hunt them since they're rare.

Fimiquails – an elusive and exotic bird that's considered a delicacy.

Ice bear – a large bear with six-inch claws and a naturally white furry coat, which stands eight feet tall on two legs. An ice bear's coat can change color to match its surroundings.

Larpanoon – most feared animal on the Silten continent that roams the northern Wood. Its fangs can bite through steel, and its claws can shred through any magic.

Malingees – large animals that live in the Wood. They carry no scent, making tracking them near impossible.

Redbeaked hawks – giant birds that have low intelligence and can be ridden by small wildlings.

Ustorill – a wild animal that lives in the forest, similar to a boar.

PRONUNCIATION GUIDE

Names

Elowen – Ell-oh-when

Jax – Jacks

Adarian – Uh-dare-ee-uhn

Alleron – Al-err-on

Lillivel – Lill-ih-vell

King Paevin – Pay-vin

Mushil – Moo-sheel

Esopeel – S-oh-peel

Phillen – Fill-enn

Trivan – Triv-en

Lars - Larz

Bowan – Boe-en

Lander – Land-err

Saramel – Sarr-uh-mell

Cassim – Cass-imm

Mezzerack – Mezz-err-ack
Aerobelle – Air-oh-bell
Drachu – Draw-koo

Fae Races
Lochen – Lock-uhn
Nolus – Naw-luss
Silten – Sill-tun
Solis – Saw-liss

VEIL

OF

SHADOWS

CHAPTER 1

Phillen pulled back a hanging tapestry in the Stonewild palace's west tower, and a cool circular stairwell appeared. "Back we go, Elowen."

I curled my lip at him but stepped into the stairwell. He lumbered in after me, letting the tapestry fall back in place, then began to climb the stairs.

Begrudgingly, I followed.

The feel of the stairwell's rock interior, numerous steps, and dampness reminded me of the tunnel Jax had used to smuggle me into the palace nearly a week ago—a palace that Jax, or rather the Dark Raider, or more accurately, *Prince Adarian*, had apparently grown up in.

I trudged up the stairs behind the crown prince's personal guard and carefully held my arm so I didn't bump my self-inflicted injury. Each step felt like it brought me closer to death, but I followed Phillen because I had no choice.

"You should have just done as you were told, Elowen, and waited for him to free you." He glowered, an expression I could actually *see* since his mask was gone.

My eyes narrowed at Phillen, or perhaps I should start thinking of him as Nellip, since that was apparently his true name . . . lying bastard that he was.

On second thought, I would continue thinking of him as Phillen as a reminder of his betrayal. Of *all* of their betrayals.

I scoffed and shot back, "It was three *days*, you know. How was I to have known any of you would return? I thought you'd all left me to remain locked in that chambers indefinitely."

Phillen looked to the ceiling and took a deep breath as we continued to climb the stairs. "We only just returned today. By tonight, the prince would have found a way to free you. It's just that . . . things aren't as simple as they seem. He couldn't very well race to release you the second we stepped foot inside the palace. Fae would have noticed his abrupt absence." The guard glared at me over his shoulder. "So, if you'd just waited, instead of pulling that stunt to escape, things would have turned out much differently." He paused to face me, and since he was a step above me, he literally towered over me. "Speaking of which, do you know what would have happened if any of the serving staff had learned who the prince really is? Did you even think of that?"

My nostrils flared, and I curled my uninjured hand into a fist. Stars, I wanted to punch something. My voice turned syrupy when I replied, "Oh, I'm so sorry, did my desperate actions put you all in a delicate situation? Pardon me. How atrocious of me to even consider taking matters into my own hands."

Phillen harrumphed, his aura rising in agitation, then he began climbing the stairs again, not saying another word.

Our footsteps echoed around us as we trudged back to my suite—or rather my cage—on the third floor.

Nobody was about in this forgotten stairwell. I had a feeling Phillen had chosen this route intentionally since the Dark Raider and his notorious band of criminals all knew how angry I was. They were probably afraid I would shout their crimes to anyone who would listen, even though I'd promised not to reveal their identities.

I seethed at Phillen, which he studiously ignored, but if I didn't focus on my anger, I would likely burst into tears. Because now, my lifelong dream for freedom—when it had been on the brink of my reality nonetheless—had all come crashing down simply because I hadn't trusted Jax to free me and instead had broken out of the enchanted chambers on my own.

Yet they could hardly blame me for doing that. Jax had

promised to return with my guardian three days ago to loosen my collar so my lorafin magic could mostly be free. But he hadn't. He'd never returned, so naturally, I thought he'd abandoned me. There was no way I could have known they'd all been called away unexpectedly for an emergent meeting with House Graniteer.

Shoulders weighing down, I continued up the stairs behind the burly guard, still cradling my arm as I tried to rally my spirit, but my soul felt crushed. Defeated. Despair filled me so poignantly that I could barely breathe, yet I followed Phillen, only because I had no other choice.

Phillen faced me again when we reached the third floor. An open arched doorway revealed the floor's empty hall waiting behind him. "Why did you do it, Elowen?" Regret twisted his features, and I couldn't help but notice the fight seemed to have gone out of him. "Why did you try to escape? He *promised* to free you, and he always keeps his promises."

My collar vibrated when a churn of anxious nerves dipped my stomach into a swirling mess. "How could I have known that? I've known Jax less than two weeks, and all he's done is lie to me." I threw my uninjured hand up, and in the process, accidentally knocked my injured arm into the wall. Pain exploded up my limb. Gasping, I cradled my elbow.

Phillen winced. "Goddess, Elowen, I know you've claimed you don't need a healer, but you do."

Panting, I huffed at the brawny, auburn-haired siltenite. "I don't. I'll be fine in a few hours." I sneered and cradled my arm more. "So do with me as you will."

He sighed heavily and nodded down the hall. "I wish it didn't have to be this way, but I have no doubt the prince will be checking on you soon, and the last thing I want to be is the receiver of his temper if I don't do as he says, so onward, Lorafin. We're almost to your chambers."

PHILLEN LOCKED me back into my suite, and once the lock engaged, a pulse of magic emanated from it. Once more, that buzz of Jax's monumental power coated the lock, which meant none of my unlocking spells could undo it. Well, not unless I wanted to risk more injuries by traveling to the Veiled Between again and asking a semelee to lend me their power. But considering the state of my still-healing arm, which I was guessing had at least two broken bones, that currently wasn't an option.

Caged once more, I swung away from the door and stalked across the plush chamber while cradling my injury.

Despite the extravagant décor and magical enchantments that would see to my every need, inwardly, I raged. Howled. Cried. Just when I thought for certain I would *finally* be free, my dream had been ripped away from me. And once again, I was a prisoner in this damned room.

I kicked at the carpet and paced a few times. Since my arm was still entirely useless, I was stuck here until I fully healed and could figure out my next move.

I padded to the couch in the sitting area and sat gingerly, then studied my injury more. My hand and wrist were swollen. Purple squishy flesh made my fingers look like sausages, but my elbow didn't hurt as badly. Already, it was bending more normally, but bruises were still present, although they weren't nearly as severe as the bruises I suffered from when I'd been subjected to Jax's magic during his calling.

Shuddering, I shoved that memory aside.

I finally released my arm and lay back on the sofa to stare at the wall. I had no idea what to do now. My attempt at escaping had failed. I'd discovered the Dark Raider's wicked secret. My collar was still in place, and according to Guardian Alleron, would be indefinitely since he'd requested that it be forged that way. And worst of all, the dream I'd been pursuing my entire life, the ability to be free if I only did as my guardian said until my thirtieth birthday, had been shattered. Guardian Alleron had never intended to free me, but I wasn't even sure it mattered anymore because apparently Jax didn't either.

Worst of all, whether Jax had ever intended it to be so, I had a new guardian now—the crown prince of Stonewild Kingdom. Jax owned me. And if that wasn't bad enough, he was also as dishonest as Guardian Alleron. The Dark

Raider had told me so many lies. *So many.* And to think I'd once hoped we could be friends.

I scoffed. Truth be told, I'd wanted to be more than friends with him. Much more. My stupid virgin body had craved his touch despite who he was. I'd reacted so acutely to his scent and protectiveness. Ever since I'd met him, an electric spark of attraction had sizzled within me. Yet the male had only sought to use me. Just like every other male in my life.

You're such an imbecile, Elowen.

A teapot and a cup of tea suddenly materialized on the table in front of me, appearing from thin air. I started, my heart beating rapidly at the suite's magical gesture.

"Took me by surprise with that one," I murmured to the enchantment, then I figured a cup of tea might help, and it wasn't like I had anything else to do. "Thank you," I added with a grumble.

Leaning forward, I poured a cup of the steaming brew with my good hand, then added a hefty dose of sugar and milk. Out of nowhere, a plate of biscuits popped into existence, sitting right beside the tea.

A small smile lifted my lips. "You always think of everything, don't you?" I murmured to the chamber.

"I try to."

Jax's quiet response made me jump, and I swirled toward the sound of his voice, nearly spilling the hot tea in my lap.

The crown prince of Stonewild Kingdom stood near the bedchamber's arched entry. He leaned against the wall, wearing the same cobalt sweater and black slacks that he had earlier when he'd discovered me downstairs detained by his staff.

I studied his features despite my anger with him. I couldn't help it. For the first time since we'd met, he wasn't disguising himself, and I couldn't *not* notice.

Dark hair, curling slightly at the ends, draped across his forehead, and eyes so blue they reminded me of ocean waves, cresting in shades of navy and sapphire, regarded me intently. I could stare at his eyes all day. He had mesmerizing eyes, hypnotic in a way.

Snapping myself out of his innate ability to entrance me, I quickly assessed the rest of him. He had a defined jaw, something I'd seen hints of through his mask in the previous two weeks. And he had a strong nose that was slightly wider than what would be considered classically handsome yet only made him more ruggedly appealing. His lips were well-defined and slightly full, exactly as I remembered when I'd caught a brief glimpse of them after slapping him across the face in the Ustilly Mountains. Broad shoulders, a tall and strong physique, and an intimidating presence rounded out his allure.

The Dark Raider's unhidden appearance was breathtaking, and I hated to admit it, but he was an absolutely beautiful male. Yet, without his mask, it was almost like looking at a stranger. Although, all I had to do was stare into those swirling cerulean irises and inhale his scent, and I knew who he was.

But despite recognizing him on an intrinsic level, I didn't actually *know* him. Because one minute, he was Jax, the Dark Raider and savior of the poor throughout the continent. And the next, he was Prince Adarian, the crown prince of Stonewild Kingdom, who could be just as ruthless as his counterpart, considering he'd locked me back in this chamber.

One thing that I was certain of—this male was a wearer of two faces and a deceiver of us all.

I waved at the tea distractedly. "You summoned this?"

He shrugged. "I thought it may help."

He pushed away from the wall, and his soft footsteps prowled along the carpet as he approached me, yet I refused to acknowledge him further. Even so, he dropped onto one of the chairs across from me, and his focus settled on my injury. "I wanted to make sure you were all right."

I angled my upper body away from him, shielding my arm from view. Chest rising faster than I wanted to admit, I took a sip of tea. The cup rattled on the saucer when I set it back down.

"I'm just fine, Guardian Jax," I replied, a sheet of ice in my tone. "I couldn't be better, and how are you on this lovely evening?"

His nostrils flared, and he leveled me with a narrowed

stare. "Don't call me that. You know I have no desire to be your guardian."

"Yet you are now, aren't you?"

The muscle in his jaw began to tick. "Not by choice. Please, Elowen. Call me Jax, as you have been, at least when we're not in public."

I met his gaze straight on and unflinching. I brought the teacup to my mouth and took another sip. "But Jax isn't your name. Your real name is Adarian."

"I prefer Jax."

"Why?"

"Jax is a nickname used by those I consider my friends."

"And you want *me* to use it?"

"I do."

Snorting in disgust, I set the tea down and pushed it away. Just a few days ago, hope would have bloomed in my heart at hearing that. I'd wanted friendship with him too. Okay, more than friendship. *But now?* I seethed inwardly. No, I wanted nothing to do with him now.

I tilted my chin. "Do you make it a habit to lock up your *friends* and lie to them about who you really are?"

His throat bobbed in a swallow, but then the corner of his lips kicked up in a devastating smile. "No, you're the first."

But I didn't rise to his inviting humor. I couldn't.

Bravado fading, my shoulders slumped, and I hated

that my voice sounded broken when I asked, "What are you going to do with me?"

His humorous expression vanished, and he leaned forward, draping his elbows on his knees. When he replied, his voice was quiet and his eyes dim. "That is a very good question, Elowen."

I wrapped my uninjured arm around my middle. "I would never tell anyone your secret, Jax. I promise I won't. *Please*, just let me go."

He studied me again, his look so intense that my cheeks began to heat. Raw emotion blazed from him, but then he shook his head. "Even if you mean that and your intentions are purely honest, you and I both know that sometimes our choices aren't up to us."

"Are you truly that worried about a Mistvale fairy forcing me to reveal your secret?"

"I am."

"But what are the chances?" I threw my uninjured arm up. "They would have to suspect that I knew who the Dark Raider was, and what are the odds of that?"

He sighed. "They're slim, *very* slim, I know, but it's still a chance I can't take. Too many lives are at risk."

"Because you're protecting your *actual* friends, not me." A stinging pain clenched my chest that had nothing to do with my injuries, but it was the truth. Jax was protecting Phillen, Lars, Bowan, Trivan, and Lander. His loyalty didn't lie with me.

Jax winced. But instead of denying my accusation, he slowly stood and prowled around the coffee table to sit beside me. The couch dipped under his weight, and since he sat so close, his thigh pressed to mine. Heat soaked through my breeches. Goddess, he was warm, always *so* warm.

But I inched away, breaking our contact.

"May I see your arm?" he asked softly.

I cradled it closer to me. "No."

"Elowen. Please. Let me see how badly you're injured."

"And if I refuse?"

"Then . . . I'll respect your wishes if that's truly what you want, but I would greatly like to help you if I can."

He sounded sincere. *Dammit, why does he have to always sound sincere?* Reluctantly, I extended my limb and revealed the full extent of the collar's brutal dousing effects.

He inhaled a sharp breath. Gently, he ran his hand along the broken bones, but already I was mending. His touch didn't cause me searing agony. "What caused this?"

I gave him an annoyed look. "I'm sure you can guess."

His attention shifted to the gold collar encircling my throat. "You ventured to the Veiled Between again without permission?"

"Yes."

His nostrils flared, his attention still on my collar. "I

hate that thing." He said it so quietly that I almost didn't hear him. "I wish I knew how to get it off you."

"Me too."

For a moment, we stared at one another, and I could tell by his rising aura that his frustration was genuine. I imagined it was even more irksome for him to be met with a problem that he couldn't solve, considering who he was—the heir to an entire kingdom. Fae no doubt did as he demanded whenever he commanded them, and if there was something he desired, he was probably given it.

But now, he had me—a caged lorafin with her magic perpetually suppressed thanks to the collar, and there was nothing in this kingdom or the next that could change what Guardian Alleron had done to me as a child, even if Jax was the crown prince.

He scrubbed a hand over his face. "May I get you a healer? If nothing else, to provide a potion to minimize the pain while you heal?"

I shook my head. "I'm fine. Truly. I'm healing fast, and it doesn't hurt as much. Each minute that ticks by, it gets less. I should be back to normal soon."

He looked down, then interlocked his fingers. "I can't change your mind on this?"

"No. There's no need."

"Very well." Another moment of silence passed. The only sound I heard was the faint noise of the bells chiming in the capital. Late evening was approaching.

Out of nowhere, Jax asked quietly, "Why did you try to escape?"

I raised my eyebrows. "Three days ago, you promised to free me, but then you left and didn't come back. I thought you were never going to, so what choice did I have?"

He released an aggrieved sigh and raked a hand through his hair. "I can't even begin to tell you how sorry I am for that. I never intended to leave you that way. An emergency with the ten Houses arose. It was out of my control, but I *always* intended to free you that day because freedom is the very least that you deserve."

"Right, of course." I released a breath dramatically, and my earlier ire began to rise. "How horrible of me not to have known what was going on outside of these locked doors and to inherently know I could trust you completely when you lead such an honest life."

He growled. "Elowen, I'm *sorry*. I would have explained things better if I'd been able to."

"You couldn't have explained anything? Or asked someone else to? Instead, you just *left* me?" That stinging feeling of abandonment that always rose up in me, considering I'd been raised to believe that my mother had left me, rose sharply. But even though my guardian had murdered my mother, and she'd never actually left me to die in the Wood, that age-old response held.

Jax's nostrils flared. "There was no time for me to return, but I see now that I should have asked someone to explain things to you. It just . . . all came about quite unexpectedly, and I made a poor decision." He turned to face me more. "But even if I had found a way to let you know what was happening, I couldn't have promised anything, not even when I would be back with your guardian to loosen your collar. My life here . . ." He shoved a hand through his hair again, displacing the wavy locks and making a few stand on end. "It isn't as easy as it seems. I'm constantly watched even though I'm the heir, and if anyone knew I'd smuggled you in here, I'd have to explain myself."

"Well, they know now since I ran around the palace this morning."

"Yes, I'm aware. And the two servants who found you have probably already spread the news."

"So how will you explain *that*?"

"I've created a new narrative."

I rolled my eyes. "Of course you have. And who have you told your latest lie to? Your father? Your mother? All of the staff?"

"I haven't told my parents yet, but I'll have to, and I'm sure the council will also be curious once they hear you were injured." He tore a hand through his hair and frowned heavily. "I'll have to think of something to explain your actions because despite being the crown prince, I can't randomly abduct fae, break their arms, and not answer for it."

"They think you broke my arm?"

He shrugged. "Who's to say? The staff love gossiping."

"Such a pity," I replied sarcastically.

He growled. "For now, please play along while I sort things out. So if anyone asks, you're a fairy I met in Fosterton the other week who I took an interest in, and you agreed to visit Stonewild and only just arrived yesterday. Your injury is from a fall you took down the stairs, and you're here of your own free will."

"*Free will,* did you say?" I curled my fingers so tightly into my palms that my nails nearly sliced my skin.

Jax's swirling cobalt irises blazed. "I can understand your anger with me, but believe it or not, I never intended for you to discover who I was. I never intended for any of this. I just wanted the best for you, Elowen. And getting wrapped up with me isn't what's best for you." Pain abruptly sliced across his face. Regret too. He quickly looked away, but not before I saw genuine sorrow filling his expression.

My breath caught. He'd looked that way too, three days ago, when he asked if I wanted to be free, even if freedom meant saying goodbye to one another forever.

Chest heaving, I tried not to react to him, but that was impossible. I'd felt things too at the thought of never seeing him again. My response held no rational explanation. We were practically strangers, yet . . . something in me had felt on the verge of breaking when I knew we were to part ways.

I scoffed inwardly. I *hated* these strange reactions he elicited in me, hated even more the warring emotions that abruptly shifted through me, even at this moment when I was determined to hate him. Anger. Doubt. Anxiety. It was all a swirling mess, but once again, he sounded sincere, and he looked tormented by what had happened.

But is he? Goddess, I sighed inwardly. *This male is a master at deception. Who's to say this isn't an act too?*

I forced my fingers to relax, then made myself take another sip of tea. I wanted to believe him, but I no longer knew if I could. He was living a double life, and anyone with that kind of treachery was lying to someone at all times. There was nothing to say he wasn't lying to me right now.

Despite knowing that, and despite knowing he could just lie to me again, I found myself asking, "Who is he, anyway? The half-breed male with the antlers that you wanted me to find? Why is he so important? Why did you risk bringing me here just to find him?"

Jax's jaw locked so hard that the muscle jutted out. "I can't tell you."

"Why not?"

"Elowen," he said in a warning tone, "don't push this."

"Why? Are you afraid I'll learn something else I

shouldn't? Something to use against you, perhaps? Would it even matter at this point if I'm to be caged indefinitely?"

His eyes darkened, but he didn't reply.

I tapped my fingers on my thigh, and the urge to fidget grew as quickly as my rising temper. "Then who are your friends? The ones who are apparently guards or noble fae, yet accompany the Dark Raider on his raids? Will you at least tell me who Lander, Bowan, Trivan, Phillen, and Lars really are? I know those aren't their real names."

His jaw clenched. "No. The less you know, the better." He scratched the back of his neck, his movements quick and agitated. "Believe it or not, I'm trying to protect you. Just being associated with the Dark Raider puts you at risk."

I scoffed and abruptly stood. Pacing, I cradled my healing arm, then realized I no longer needed to, so I let it hang normally. "So not only are you breaking your promise to free me, but you're also refusing to tell me anything about the half-breed you seek or anything personal about your friends, yet you claim it's all for my well-being. Funny how this doesn't feel like that."

Standing, Jax stormed toward me, his eyes flashing ice and fire. "It *is* for your well-being, Elowen. Just being close to me puts you at risk. I'm the fucking *Dark Raider*, and if that ever came to light, and you were questioned . . ." Agony swirled in his eyes. "I care so fucking much about you. That's why I'm not telling you anything, and believe it or not, I'm beyond sorry that I've put you in this position. I never wanted this for you. I wanted—" He tore a hand through his hair.

Lips parting, I stared at him.

Such raw emotion blazed in his eyes that it threatened to cut me open, but he didn't continue. Instead, he blinked and looked away.

"Wanted what?"

He shook his head. "Nothing."

I planted my hands on my hips. "If all of that is true, and you really do care about me, then you would trust me not to tell anyone your secrets, and you would know that I'd have the sense to avoid Mistvale fae and that I'd have the decency to guard your identity as the Dark Raider. Because I know you're not evil, Jax. I've seen that. I *believe* that even if you've lied about so many other things that I know I can't trust you. But I do believe you want the best for those considered less than you. I would still protect your secret for the good of others, yet you still refuse to release me."

I held my breath while waiting and hoping that he'd change his mind.

His face fell. "Elowen . . . I *can't*. Phillen and Lars are right. No matter how infinitesimal the risk is of you being questioned by a Mistvale fairy, I can't risk it. It wouldn't be fair to them. But it *kills me* to do this to you." The energy rising from him was so potent, so visceral. Again, the sincerity of his words rang through the room.

A moment of doubt hit me. *Is what he's saying now the truth? Does he actually care about me too? Not just his friends? Even though nobody in my entire life has ever truly cared about me?* Tears threatened to fill my eyes, and hope wanted to fill my chest, but in my next breath, I took a step back.

What are you doing, Elowen? This male is keeping you his prisoner. Even if he claims he doesn't want to. Don't forget that.

Swallowing the thickness in my throat, I blinked the tears back. "Even if that's true, it doesn't change anything. You're still *choosing* to keep me as your prisoner indefinitely. You're essentially choosing your friends over me. So if that's the case, then leave me here if that's what you're so intent on doing. I'll survive just fine in this pretty new cage with its magical enchantments. I'm sure it'll keep me fed and sheltered, so if you ever need to call upon your lorafin again, Guardian Jax, I'll be ready and waiting."

His head snapped back as though I'd slapped him. "Elowen, I'm *not* your guardian. Not in that way. I don't own you. I'll never claim ownership over you."

For a moment, my breath stopped. His declaration sounded so heartfelt, so honest. *But isn't keeping me here owning me?*

I took another step back the second any softening

occurred within me, then snapped my spine upright. I would *not* fall for his pretty lies again. I would not believe Jax as I had my guardian. To my downfall, I'd believed that Guardian Alleron had wanted the best for me when he'd claimed such things, and that had turned out disastrously.

But Jax is nothing like Guardian Alleron. You've seen enough to know that.

I shoved that internal voice of reason down. I was so damned tired of being understanding to my abusers.

That stopped today.

Standing taller, I raised my chin. "Save your apologies, Jax. They mean nothing to me now. Because as much as you don't want to admit it or take ownership for what's happened, you *are* my new guardian, and I'm your newest possession. It's best that we both accept that for what it is."

CHAPTER 2

I sat on the bed of my massive bedroom chambers, nibbling on my fingernail. It'd been hours since Jax had left and locked me in here. I had no idea where he'd gone and when, or *if*, he was coming back. I hadn't asked. And there'd been no talk of allowing me free roam of the palace. Apparently, he was still concerned that I'd try to escape. Who knew if he'd ever trust me not to.

The only good thing about the time passing was that my injuries had fully healed. The punishments that my collar had inflicted upon my hand, wrist, and elbow during my breakout were gone. Once again, my tendons were sturdy and strong, my wrist bendable and supple, and my elbow fully functional.

If only I could fix my life as easily as my magic did my body.

Moonlight bled through the suite's frosted windows. It

was late. Nearing midnight, according to the clock, yet I couldn't sleep.

I fell back onto the bed, bouncing a couple of times on the mattress. I stared at the ceiling and wondered if Jax would supply me with a calendar. If I was to now be the crown prince's lorafin, crossing off a day each morning would give me something to do. Besides, I missed that routine. I missed marking a day away each morning when I woke up. But most of all, I missed working toward my dream.

I'd been counting the days until my thirtieth birthday for as long as I could remember, and I relished the habit, even if my thirtieth birthday no longer held any predestined meaning.

Still, it was something to do. Something I could control. And having control in my life had always been nonexistent, so I would take it in whatever form I got.

A soft knock came on the door.

I bolted upright, my eyes going wide as a shot of electricity tingled along my collar, but before I could call out, the handle was turning, and a slim female slipped over the threshold.

My collar vibrated violently, and my hand whipped to my throat. "Who are you?"

The female gave an apologetic smile and closed the door behind her. The ring of the magical bolt sliding into place filled the room, followed by a pulse of Jax's magic.

Once again, *everyone* seemed to have access to Jax's unlocking spell except for me.

Bristling, I readied myself for whatever was to come. Probably more conflict. Maybe orders. Definitely demands. Somebody always wanted something from me.

The slim female faced me, her back to the door, and I quickly took in her blond hair and brown eyes. She was a siltenite fairy, no wildling features, and she wore a simple yellow dress. Nothing about her attire screamed wealth, but she didn't look poor either. In fact, she appeared similar to me now that I wore plain pants and comfortable tops, thanks to my single shopping spree in Fosterton.

"I'm sorry." She wrung her hands, and her voice was soft and small, reminding me of a delicate bird. "I should have waited for your permission to enter, but it's late, and I've been in such a hurry to finish my evening work so I could get down here to this abandoned chambers, but I know we haven't been very respectful of your privacy. I should have considered that and waited for you to call out."

My eyes narrowed. "*We*? Do you work with Jax?"

She laughed softly and walked farther into the room, clasping her hands behind her. "Oh no, he's a friend of mine, or rather, a friend of my husband's. You've probably met him. His nickname's Phillen."

My eyes bulged. "You're married to Phillen?"

She dipped her head. "For the past sixty summers."

Understanding dawned. Phillen had mentioned once that he was married, and he'd been more agitated than Lars earlier today when I discovered the Dark Raider's identity. He warned Jax of the consequences of me knowing the truth of them, and if I recalled right, he said something about needing to keep their families protected.

I cocked my head. "Do you and Phillen have children?"

She nodded again and stepped closer to me until she was only a few strides from the bed. "We do. Only one, so far. The stars blessed us with a wee boy after many, *many* full seasons of trying to conceive. Cassim's three now." A wistful smile curved her lips.

"You have a toddler." I let out a breath. No wonder Phillen was so protective of his family and insistent that Jax not let me go. He had a wife and a small child he feared would be compromised if the Dark Raider's secret came to light.

"I'm Saramel, by the way."

Saramel. That name rang a bell, and when I recalled why, my eyes grew round. "You're the fairy Jax wished he'd asked to visit me when they'd been called away, so I could be told that my release was delayed."

"Yes, that would be me." She dipped into a curtsy. "I only wished that he had. It would have avoided the circumstance we're currently in."

Flustered, all I could do was nod.

Saramel nodded toward the sitting area. "It's well past supper time, but the prince told me you never summoned any food. Would you care to join me for a meal?"

"The prince is monitoring when I eat?"

A blush worked across her face. "He's . . . quite concerned about you."

I glanced at the clock. "But it's the middle of the night. We're to have a meal at midnight?"

She shrugged. "Better late than never."

I found myself rising to join her. I was hungry after all. I'd barely eaten anything in the past week, so I followed her into the sitting area and seated myself beside her on the couch.

Saramel offered me another tentative smile before she turned her attention upward. "Please bring us a tray of the chef's roasted hen, sautéed rice, fresh salad, steamed greens, and the three desserts that were on the menu tonight."

My eyes popped open, when not even a second later, an overflowing tray of Saramel's selections appeared before us on the coffee table.

Steam rose from the food along with fragrant scents. My mouth watered, as though having someone with me—even if Saramel was a complete stranger and perhaps wasn't here with innocent intentions—calmed some of the nerves firing along my limbs so I could actually eat without anxiety twisting my stomach into knots.

"The chef's hen is always superb." Saramel dished a bit of everything onto a plate and handed it to me.

I started at her thoughtfulness. "Thank you."

"Of course." She dished herself a plate too, then settled back before another shy smile lifted her lips. But she abruptly straightened. "Oh! I forgot about drinks. Does anything in particular sound appealing?"

I shrugged. "Um, no, whatever you prefer is fine."

She tilted her chin up again. "Will you also provide a pitcher of the sparkling fruit juice served tonight?"

A glass pitcher abruptly shimmered into existence. Tiny bubbles fizzled on its surface. Not even a second later, two glasses filled with ice cubes appeared beside it.

"Thank you, Chamber," Saramel called. "That shall be all for now."

An answering pulse of magic came from the walls before it calmed and went still once more.

Saramel hoisted the pitcher up and poured us each a glass, then handed one to me. "My son loves this juice. Cassim would drink this entire pitcher if I let him."

I smiled awkwardly and took a tentative sip. My eyes widened at the lemony taste with a hint of mint. "This is delicious."

Saramel picked up her plate, and we ate in companionable silence for a few minutes, each of us sampling the various dishes. Everything was flavorful and tender, and it was by far the best food I'd had in months. Before I knew it, I was halfway through my meal.

"This reminds me of the banquets I've attended at Faewood's court when the king would ask me to present for a calling," I said, breaking the quiet as I took another bite of the juicy hen.

"Do you herald from Faewood?" Saramel cocked her head.

I shrugged and wondered if Phillen or Jax had told her anything about me or if she was simply playing coy. "At the moment I do, but my guardian said I was born in Ironcrest."

"And your guardian is the fairy that's being kept in one of the prince's other chambers?"

My jaw snapped closed as I was once again reminded of my guardian's betrayal. "That would be the one. Have you seen him?"

She shook her head. "Oh no, the prince won't allow me to enter his chambers. He's too concerned about your guardian trying to escape, although Jax sought me out to come visit you so you wouldn't be left alone."

"He did?"

She forked some of the herbed rice and nodded. After swallowing, she added, "The prince said you've been mostly alone in here since they arrived back. He's very worried about you. Come to think of it, I don't think I've ever seen him this worried about anything. Well, except for

—" She abruptly cut herself off and forked another bite of rice. "Anyway, both he and Phillen insisted you weren't a violent fairy, so it would be safe if I came here alone to visit with you."

"Is that so?" My stomach dipped at that gesture and their accurate assessment of my character. While I had no qualms about defending myself from fae who wished me harm, Jax and Phillen were right that I would never intentionally hurt anyone, especially someone as benign as Saramel appeared. But her earlier pause when she was about to reveal someone else the prince had been worried about, that I was guessing she wasn't supposed to, made me curious. "Does Jax often ask you to provide his prisoners company?"

Saramel laughed. "Oh no. He never brings captives back here. In fact, you and your guardian are the first."

In other words, if Saramel was being truthful, whoever she was referring to *wasn't* another captive. I pushed my food away. "Has the prince said anything about what he plans to do with me?"

"He hasn't, but"—she frowned—"I have to admit that I've never seen him in a state like this. He's quite distraught about it all."

"Truly?" I wanted to believe her, but who was to say I could.

She nodded. "He's been pacing in the library most of the evening. Trivan and Bowan have been with him while

Lars and my husband stand watch at the door . . . you know, in case any curious staff come idling by wondering what the crown prince is doing wearing a path into the carpet. His father has also been looking for him. And that never helps matters."

My eyebrows rose. "He's avoiding the king?" It felt strange to say that, but it was true. The *king* of Stonewild Kingdom was Jax's father.

Saramel sighed. "He often avoids the king, and one can hardly blame him. Next summer, Prince Adarian is of age to wed, so the king and queen have been trying to arrange courtship dates for him when the approved and potential females come to visit. We have several in the palace right now."

I sat back, my stomach doing a strange, queasy flip. "Why would he avoid that?"

"Simple. He doesn't want to wed, especially since *who* he can wed is decided by his parents, but the king and queen are growing impatient and insist that he start courting his potential betroths. He'll be a hundred summers soon, so it's time for him to make a match. As you probably know, it's expected of crown princes at that age."

Another flutter of nerves coiled my stomach. "So he's to court other females while keeping me a prisoner." I strode to the unlit fireplace and crouched beside it. Rough bark met my fingertips when I tossed a few pieces of firewood into the hearth. I wasn't cold, but I suddenly needed something to do.

Saramel released a long sigh, then joined me, her slim body kneeling on the carpet beside me. "I'm sorry, Elowen, about what's been done to you. I know you haven't done anything that warrants being locked up, but the prince never intended for this to happen. You don't understand. He's been so distraught since—" She licked her lips and shook her head.

I again got the feeling she was referring to what she'd stopped herself from saying earlier. "What? Tell me."

But she just shook her head again. "It's not my story to tell, but please believe me that Jax didn't take your abduction lightly. He only became aware of you the other month, and he immediately set out to learn what he could of you and to find a way to use your magic."

Nostrils flaring, I went back to arranging wood in the fire. "I know. He told me. He's been stalking me for weeks and decided it was more moral to abduct me than to pay a slave guardian for my services, yet how Jax doesn't want to admit that he's now my *new* guardian is entirely ironic."

Her eyes dimmed, and something about the energy strumming in her aura made me pause. I stopped arranging the kindling and faced her.

Misery pulsed around her like a sad friend who never smiled. "Please just believe me, Elowen, when I tell you that Jax would *never* have taken you if he'd had another way."

My brow furrowed, and I thought again of the male he'd wanted me to find. The half-breed with antlers permanently curving from his temples. "Who's the male he asked me to seek? Why is he so important?"

Saramel shook her head. "Again, it's not my story to share."

I gripped her hand, my fingertips digging into her skin. "*Please*, Saramel. Someone needs to tell me, and Jax's never going to, from the sounds of it. But please, will you? Help me understand why I'm here. *Please*. I'm going crazy being trapped within these walls, but maybe if I could understand it, even support it . . ." I raised my shoulders. "Maybe then this wouldn't feel so awful."

She sucked in a sharp breath and looked over her shoulder toward the door. A moment ticked by, but all remained still. It was only her and me in this quiet chambers in the dead of night.

Facing me again, she lowered her voice. "If I tell you . . ."

"I won't tell a soul. I promise."

Another heartbeat of silence passed until finally, she nodded gravely. "All right, but only because I agree that your treatment is unfair. But you must agree to a bargain ensuring your silence. What I'm about to tell you can never leave this room."

CHAPTER 3

Saramel took another deep breath. "Do you agree to make a bargain, sealing us before the gods and goddesses?"

My brow furrowed. *A bargain.* They weren't to be taken lightly. Saramel and I would be bound by the gods, and if I broke the terms of our agreement, I would suffer their wrath. It was why Jax had refused to do a bargain with me, even though I'd begged for one so he would release me. His reasoning had been that if a Mistvale fairy commanded me to speak, despite my promise to remain silent, my life would become unbearable because of the gods' punishment. The gods, after all, wouldn't care *why* I'd spoken, only that I had.

But while Jax's logic wasn't wrong, if I truly wanted to know who the half-breed was that Jax sought, which would also explain what had brought me here, and this was the only way anyone would tell me, then so be it. I would risk it.

I squared my shoulders. "I'll agree to a bargain."

She held out her arm. "What's your full name?"

"Elowen Emerson. It's the name given to me by my guardian. And yours?"

"Saramel Highcrest." She clasped my forearm, and I gripped hers in return. She sat up straighter and took a deep breath. "Elowen Emerson, siltenite and lorafin of Faewood Kingdom, I hereby agree to a bargain that ensures I tell you the truth of the male half-breed who Prince Adarian, the crown prince of Stonewild Kingdom, used your lorafin powers to seek. In exchange for this information, you hereby promise never to reveal the information I'm about to tell you to any fae, creature, or entity of our realm or any other realm in any capacity unless Prince Adarian gives you permission to do so. However, if a fairy, creature, or entity already knows of the male half-breed who Prince Adarian seeks, then you may speak freely of him. And at any time, Prince Adarian has the ability to null this bargain between us if he chooses to do so, rendering it obsolete. Elowen Emerson, do you accept this bargain?"

Heart pounding, I licked my lips. The bargain seemed relatively simple. I wasn't to tell anyone about who Jax sought in any capacity, unless they already knew about the male. That meant I could speak of him to Jax and his friends. Saramel had left that loophole open for me. She'd also given me the loophole that if Jax gave me permission to speak of the male half-breed to others, then I was free to do so, or he could obliterate this bargain completely making neither of us subject to the gods' wrath. It was kind of her to give me that flexibility while also maintaining Jax's secret.

"Saramel Highcrest, siltenite of Stonewild Kingdom, I hereby accept your bargain."

A clang of magic shimmered around us, like an invisible drum banging, and I sucked in my breath when the bargain's mark seared into my skin like a hot brand.

I turned my wrist upward. A wintercrisp fern glowed brightly on my wrist's inner skin before it disappeared. Saramel rolled up her own sleeve. The same mark shone on her wrist before it vanished.

A *wintercrisp fern.* How fitting. It was the plant on Stonewild's crest and was a leaf that symbolized trust and strength. The gods and goddesses always loved their bargain marks to have greater meanings, so I wasn't surprised they'd chosen such a mark to seal me to this female in our promise.

Once the mark vanished and our skin was smooth once more, Saramel settled on the floor into a comfortable position. "Now that that's done . . ." She licked her lips. "The male the prince is looking for is his brother, his *only* sibling. His name is Bastian, and he went missing several months ago. Prince Adarian has been beside himself trying to find him. That's why he took you. His brother is the only family member who's never sought to use him or hurt him. He loves Bastian fiercely, and without him, the prince feels so lost. He was willing to go to any lengths to find him, even if that meant abducting you."

His brother? Stunned, I just sat there. *He has a* brother? *Who's a half-breed?*

For a brief moment, I thought of the night in Fosterton in which Jax had told me evasively of his past, of the abuse he survived. Surely, he hadn't been referring to his own family . . .

Stomach tumbling, I forced that thought away. "I didn't realize he had any siblings, and a half-breed none-theless."

"That's because nobody knows, apart from a select few."

I frowned heavily, because as far as I was aware, it was common knowledge that Prince Adarian was an only child. It didn't make any sense that he had a brother who was a half-breed. But Saramel had revealed the information so quickly. So easily. And the gods hadn't exacted instant revenge or struck her dead, which meant she wasn't lying.

She clasped her hands, and a moment of doubt crossed her features. "Jax will be so angry when he finds out I just told you that, but you deserve to know, and since you can't tell anyone unless you want to suffer severe punishment from the gods, I don't regret it."

"And you're not afraid of Jax punishing you?"

She shrugged. "Not really, and if you want to tell him that I told you, that's fine. I'm not going to hide it." A soft laugh parted her lips. "I'll probably get an earful and be put on extra kitchen duty for a week, but I can handle that."

"Kitchen duty? Do you work in the palace?"

"I do. My husband and I are both in serving positions. I work in the kitchen, helping to prepare feasts, and I also clean. That's what I was finishing up before I came here." She waved her hand. "But back to our bargain, the least you deserve is the reasoning behind your abduction. But more than that, I want you to understand the truth of what's going on here. The prince wouldn't have taken you unless he felt he had no other way to find his brother."

I sat back, the wood in the fireplace entirely forgotten. "But . . . *how* is his brother a half-breed?"

"Bastian is the king's illegitimate son. He was born five summers after Jax. And Bastian's mother is a *fireling wildling*."

"Can Bastian create fire?"

"He can. He's actually quite magical."

Frowning more, I let that information digest, then asked, "But if the king has a child around Jax's age . . . that means the king was unfaithful. The king's been married to the queen for centuries, hasn't he?"

"Yes, the entire royal family knows of the king's indiscretion. And because of the king's torrid affair, Bastian's existence is a closely guarded secret—a secret that Jax, my husband, and their friends strive to protect in order to keep Bastian safe. And it's a secret the king and queen keep to protect themselves."

I once again tried to fully comprehend what she was telling me. A king had bred with a wildling. And the child they'd created lived, and said child's royal heritage had managed to be kept a secret.

While I didn't know *how* a secret of that magnitude could be kept, I understood why they'd done so. Procreation between siltenites and wildlings was against the law. And when it occurred, their half-breed children were scorned and the parents were punished.

Because when siltenites and wildlings bred, occasionally they would produce a half-breed child who had just as much magic as a full-blooded siltenite—sometimes even more—yet also had the breeding capabilities of a wildling, making many siltenites fear a potential power shift if half-breeds grew more plentiful.

And because of that, an even stricter law had been put in place as well. It forbade all half-breeds from breeding amongst themselves.

Long ago, there'd been fear that if half-breeds were left unchecked, they would outnumber siltenites and take over the kingdoms. It was why siltenites had created the law forbidding half-breeds to bear children.

And if it was discovered a siltenite was coupling with a wildling, they were arrested, sometimes even imprisoned. On top of that, all half-breeds that were born were forced to consume sterile-inducing potions at a young age so they could never breed, and then, they were scorned by society —a further deterrent for anyone contemplating breaking the law.

But if two half-breeds had somehow managed to avoid the sterilization process and they had a child, the child and both parents were immediately executed. All four kingdoms had that law. It was one of the few unified kingdom laws, not unlike the law that allowed lorafins to be enslaved. Because if half-breeds reproduced, their children could potentially be magically superior while also being able to far outbreed any other race.

So for a *king* to have coupled with a wildling and then to have brought a half-breed child into the realm, knowing how egregious such an action was considered . . . That was entirely taboo.

Shaking my head, I finally said, "How in the realm did they manage to keep this all a secret?"

"The king and queen have enacted many bargains within their inner circle to keep the king's indiscretion from reaching the public. Many fae are sealed by those bargains, too afraid of the gods' wrath to speak of it."

"Then how are you able to tell me?"

"I haven't made a bargain about Bastian. The king and queen don't know that I'm aware."

My eyebrows shot up. "Jax told you freely?"

"He did. He's not bound by his parents' bargains. He refused to do one, and his parents couldn't very well execute or banish their only heir for refusing, so he's remained free to speak of Bastian, but Jax is also aware that if a fairy knows, that fairy is at risk, so Jax has only told a select few. Only me, his band, and very few others know of Bastian, and none of us would ever tell a soul."

"Yet you told me."

"Only because you deserve to know and agreed to a bargain."

I nibbled on my lip, then asked, "Do *any* siltenites outside of these walls know of the king's outlawed child?"

Her expression turned grim. "Only a trusted few, and again, all of them are bound by bargains. The king has ensured the news didn't travel." She twisted her hands together. "If the public learned that the king had coupled with a wildling, conceived an illegitimate half-breed child, and in doing so had broken a unified kingdom law—" She shuddered. "The council would have grounds for removing him from the throne. And once he was removed, the ten Houses would likely all be vying to take his place, which would result in an uprising among the nobles, perhaps even among the general public, leading to chaos in our kingdom."

"But despite the reason for secrecy, why did Jax need *me*? Bastian is still the king's son. Surely, a *king* could find him. Why did Jax need to take me when his father has unlimited resources?"

Saramel sighed again and drew her knees up. "That, Elowen, is the heart of the prince's problems. Despite being of the king's blood, Bastian has never been accepted or protected by him. When the king found out that the wildling he coupled with had become with child, he demanded she abort the baby, but she refused, thinking that once the king saw the child, he would undoubtedly change his mind. But once Bastian was born, the king called for Bastian to be executed, so his wildling mother took him and fled. For many summers, Bastian was in hiding, and by the time the king located him, his mother had wielded a plan. She had magical safeguards in place that would release upon Bastian's murder if the king executed him or hired anyone to do so. Word would spread of what the king had done, and the king would lose his throne. I'm not sure of all the details, but Bastian's mother didn't sit idle. She ensured no matter what, the king's secret would be revealed if any harm came to her son."

"Then why hasn't it been revealed if Bastian's gone missing? Surely, that's considered harm?"

Saramel shrugged. "There's been no harm from the king or queen or anyone they hired. The magic would enact only if that happened. Bastian's mother was very clever in her magic wielding. She left no loopholes for harm to come from the royal family."

"So all they know is that Bastian is missing, but his disappearance couldn't have had anything to do with Jax's parents. And since it didn't involve them, there was no way to know if Bastian was alive or dead."

"Correct, which is ultimately why Jax decided he needed you. He tried for months to locate his brother on his own. He hired trackers, consulted seers, prayed to the gods, everything. But every avenue he tried came to a dead end until he was told of *you*. Because a lorafin could find exactly where Bastian was and tell him if his brother still lived. The prince was guaranteed answers if he sought you."

I frowned, my eyebrows drawing together. She wasn't wrong. Only lorafins could speak with the semelees, and the semelees were all-knowing. They would undoubtedly know where Bastian was or if he'd died. Frowning more, I thought back to what the semelees had told me of him. *Something's not right.* I still didn't entirely understand what they'd meant by that.

Shaking that off, I asked, "But how did Jax ever learn that he had a half-brother if Bastian's mother fled with him upon birth?"

"It was by chance, actually. The prince overheard his parents speaking of him once, when the king and queen didn't realize he was in the same room with them. Bastian was already six summers old, and the prince sought him out, not stopping until he found him." Her eyes took on a faraway look. "Bastian and Adarian are quite similar in some ways, entirely opposite in others, but they quickly grew close, and they care deeply for one another. The prince has been, and likely always will be, fiercely protective of his brother. I'm sure that level of loyalty is also partly due to the fact that Bastian remains his only sibling. The queen hasn't been able to conceive again."

I sighed and scrubbed my hands along my cheeks. "I wish Jax had just told me all of this himself." Abducting me was an extreme measure, but if Jax felt he had no other choice . . . I sighed quietly. "Too bad he didn't mind paying slave guardians, then I could have simply done a calling for him and carried on as I'd been. Although, considering Guardian Alleron never planned to release me, perhaps that wouldn't have been a better alternative in the long run."

She smiled placatingly. "Oh, Elowen, don't lose hope. The prince truly wants to set things right with you. If there's a way, he'll find it."

I forced a nod, even though at this point, that seemed unlikely.

"Anyway." Saramel released her knees and sat cross-legged. "Now that we all know Bastian is alive and in Faewood, we at least have peace of mind that he hasn't passed to the afterlife."

"But *why* is Bastian in Faewood? And if Bastian and Jax are so close, why didn't Bastian tell Jax that he was going there?"

Her eyes dimmed. "I was hoping you would know that."

"I don't. The semelees only revealed where he was, not why he'd gone there, and their response to that initial question took them so long to answer—which is entirely unlike any calling I've ever done—that I didn't ask for more details." I shuddered when I recalled how they'd dragged me deeper into the Veiled Between after telling me where Bastian was. By that point, enough time had passed that Jax's magic had begun to take root in me. I didn't even know if I could have asked more questions of them. The collar had pulled on too much of Jax's power, leaving me in a perilous state.

Shaking that memory off, I focused on Bastian again. "Don't you think it's probable that Bastian simply decided to leave Stonewild of his own free will? Perhaps he got tired of his life here and opted for a change of scenery and wanted to explore the kingdoms?"

Saramel inclined her head. "If it were anyone but Bastian, that's probably what I would think too. It's what we all would have thought, but you have to understand how close Jax and Bastian are. They never go a day without speaking. Never. And they don't keep secrets from one another. It's entirely out of character for Bastian to up and disappear without telling anyone. Not to mention, he'd just started employment at a ship manufacturer that he was very excited about. And he'd begun courting a siltenite a few months prior who he was very enamored with, and her him, even if they could never have children. So for him to have left . . ." She sighed, then huffed. "It just doesn't make sense that he would disappear like that. If you knew Bastian, you would understand why Jax is so worried."

I mulled everything over again, then sat back, curling my legs beneath me. "So, now what? What's to become of me? Will I also be banished now that I know this information? Or kept caged here indefinitely? If Jax knows that Bastian is at the Centennial Matches, surely he's going to go to him, now that the emergency with House Graniteer is over. And where does that leave me? Stuck in the Stonewild palace forever?" I raised my arms, waving at the hidden chambers he'd put me in.

Saramel's eyebrows pinched together, and her mouth puckered. "I hope not, Elowen. But if it's any consolation, I think that's exactly what the prince is trying to figure out. I don't think he knows what to do with you, but I don't believe he wants that to be your fate."

CHAPTER 4

I paced in my chambers, alone once more now that Saramel had left. My thoughts whirled, moving as rapidly as my pacing feet. From what Saramel had told me, Jax was simply a desperate fairy trying to find the half-brother he loved so much and would do anything to locate. And after exhausting every possibility he could think of to find him, he abducted me as a last resort.

At the end of the room, I spun and walked back to the other side in hurried strides. Fragrant flowers abruptly appeared on a table I passed, filling the chamber in scents of lavender, honeysuckle, mayberry, and juniper. When anxiety coursed through me, it seemed the enchantment loved nothing more than to fill the space with calming scents.

But it did little to calm my turbulent thoughts. Because the entire reason Jax had taken me was because of *love*. I'd been right when I guessed his reasoning. Love was what drove the Dark Raider, not vengeance.

Huffing, I finally stopped and sat on the couch, my foot tapping on the soft carpet. And with as noble of a reason as that, I now firmly believed Jax would have released me as soon as he'd been able to. It would have been out of character for him to keep me any longer than necessary. Essentially, it was my mistrust that had landed me in my current position.

Grumbling, I threaded my hands through my hair, then fell back on the sofa. "If only I'd waited longer for him to return."

A pot of tea abruptly burst into existence on the table. I bolted upright, expecting to see Jax casually leaning against the wall again, but the chamber remained empty.

"Is tea your answer to everything?" I muttered.

A bouquet of two dozen yellow roses materialized beside the tea. I snorted. "You're not very original."

A hum of magic pulsed on the walls, and then a fluffy kitten appeared at my feet.

I melted when the tiny creature gave out several mewls. "A live creature? You summoned an actual *live creature* to soothe my anxiety?" Scooping it up, I cradled it in my lap.

A knock came on my door, and my spine straightened, my heart beginning to thump.

The door opened and closed, and then Jax appeared by the arched entryway.

I sagged back against the sofa. "Oh, it's only you."

Some of the pounding in my heart slowed, yet Saramel's words still swirled through my mind. Just hours ago, when Jax had stated I was to remain a prisoner here, I'd hated him. But now I knew about Bastian . . .

I pet the kitten more and nibbled on my lip. I had no idea how I felt anymore.

"I saw your light on under your door," he said hesitantly and took another step into the living area. Stopping, he frowned, then eyed the kitten. "Where did you get a kitten?"

"The enchantment gave him to me, but I have no idea from where."

"Ah, probably from the domal stables. The stable cat gave birth last month." He walked slowly toward me, his hands stuffed in his pockets. He still wore the same slacks and sweater as he had earlier. Even though it was the early hours of the morning, he obviously hadn't retired for the night either. "Since your light was on, I figured you also couldn't sleep?"

I sighed. "No."

He sat down on the couch beside me, and all I could do was stare at him. According to Saramel, he'd been pacing in the library because of me. He was that concerned about my fate.

But that wasn't the only reason I stared. It was still startling to see him undisguised and in normal clothes.

I quickly reverted my attention to the kitten and pet it more. Loud purrs emitted from its throat. "I thought you'd be in Faewood by now, searching for that half-breed."

"I thought I would be too, but such impromptu trips need to be explained, which means I can't leave until tomorrow."

"I see." I swallowed the thickness in my throat. I knew he planned to leave me behind until he could figure out what to do with me. But I couldn't help but wonder what waiting to leave for Faewood was doing to him. It'd been nearly four days since his calling.

"Did Saramel come to see you?" Jax interlocked his fingers, drawing my attention to his strong hands.

"She did."

He glanced at the coffee table, now devoid of the supper Saramel and I had shared. A heavy frown snagged his eyebrows together. "Did you not eat again?"

I dipped my chin and dropped a few kisses on the small kitten's head. "I did. Not a full meal, but I had some."

A low, discontented sound came from him. "You need to eat, Elowen. It's not good that you spend so many days not eating."

I started at the worry and protectiveness in his tone. Once again, it seemed *genuine*.

Slowly, he inched along the sofa until he sat closer to

me, then reached across the distance and scratched under the kitten's jaw. The feline closed its eyes and purred even more. "They usually like that spot."

The kitten turned over in my arms, tilting its head up to give Jax better access. I couldn't help but smile. "Yes, he does seem to like that."

"I'm going to have to return him to the stables soon. He still needs his mother's milk."

I cuddled the bundle of fur closer to me, my heart rate calming even more as the kitten's purrs continued. "How do you know it's a boy?"

"Because the stable cat's most recent litter was all boys. This little guy has three male siblings." His eyes dimmed slightly, and for the briefest moment, I wondered if he was thinking of his own brother.

I ran my fingers through the kitten's soft fur, and with a start, realized it was the first time I'd been in Jax's company since arriving here when anxiety over my future wasn't claiming me. It seemed the enchantment had gotten it right after all by delivering a kitten.

"Who designed this chamber?" I asked.

"I did."

My brow furrowed. "But why? It seems like pretty intricate magic to be left abandoned."

"Did Saramel tell you that detail too?"

My spine stiffened, and I said cautiously, "She did."

"Did she tell you the original reason I created it?"

"No, she didn't reveal that."

He sat back, leaving the kitten for me to pet, and rubbed at his own jaw. Jax cocked his head, and that intensity I was coming to associate with him made an appearance. "What else did Saramel tell you?"

My heart thumped again even though the kitten was rubbing into my palm.

"Not much," I said too quickly, getting a frown out of him. Rushing on, I added, "Just that she's Phillen's wife, they have a child, and that she was sent by you to keep me company. Oh, and she summoned food so I would eat."

"Is that all she revealed?"

"Why do you ask?" I arched an eyebrow. "Was she supposed to tell me more?"

He raked a hand through his hair. "No, I'm just surprised. Saramel loves to talk."

"Does she? I never would have guessed that." I brought the kitten to my mouth to give him a few kisses on the nose. "So, why are you here this time, Jax?"

A groove appeared between his eyes. "Like I said, I'm going back to Faewood tomorrow."

My hands began to shake. Before I dropped the kitten, I set him down, and the little guy ambled along the carpet until he found a loose string near the fireplace and began to bat it with his paw.

I cleared my throat and entwined my fingers together. "And I'm guessing that you want to leave me here, locked in this cage while you search for your—" I stopped myself even though Saramel had given me permission to tell Jax.

He arched an eyebrow. "Are you sure Saramel didn't tell you anything else?"

I smiled innocently, and perhaps it made me a horrible fairy, but it was nice to see him agitated for once about not knowing something. "Whatever do you mean?"

He huffed out a breath, but then his expression smoothed. "Anyway, since I'm leaving tomorrow, I was hoping to try something before I left. If you're willing." He pointed at my collar, his eyes locking on it. "I would like to command your guardian to release you from that to the best of his ability. It's long overdue, and the least I owe you. And if I can do that before I leave, I'll . . ." He frowned, the gesture so severe that it was practically a scowl. "Maybe I'll feel less guilty for everything that I've done to you, and maybe you'll have a more peaceful existence."

A peaceful existence. It felt as though an arrow pierced my heart, but perhaps that was the best I could hope for now. "You want to command my guardian when? Now? Tomorrow morning before you go?"

"Now, if you'll allow it." A sad smile tugged at his lips. "It's the middle of the night. Everyone's retired, no one's about, and it's private here. None of the servants know either of you are in these chambers. It seems like the perfect time and place to demand this of your guardian."

My breaths sped up, and I told myself it was from the

thought of my collar's debilitating magic being lifted, not from the intense way Jax was looking at me, and not from my fear of what a loosened collar could mean for my magic.

"But . . ." I sputtered. "I haven't prepared. What if I become unstable? I could destroy the palace. I could doom us all."

"You won't."

"How do you know? I could blow this place up."

He smirked slightly, a hint of amusement rolling into his expression. "Are you always this dramatic?"

"Dramatic?" I swatted him on the chest, then curled my fingers into my palm, horrified at what I'd just done, but Jax laughed.

"Such violence."

"I'm sorry. I wasn't thinking. I was . . . I mean, you were teasing me and—" I hastily ran a hand through my hair, smoothing the chestnut strands. "I'm sorry, my prince."

"Don't be. I quite enjoy this side of you."

"What side?"

"The side where you're acting like yourself, feeling comfortable in who you really are and not treating me like I'm a prince." He inched closer to me, and this time, my breath *did* stop. His eyes, which were always so intensely energized, sparkled as vividly as the sea, and the aura pulsing around him grew, commanding all of my attention.

His gaze fluttered to my collar, my hair, my face. I felt stripped raw in front of him.

A flash of something grew in his eyes, the same flare I'd seen in his expression so many other times. Hunger perhaps? Or . . . *want?* But it was gone in a blink. Whatever that look meant, similar to the times before, it'd disappeared as quickly as it started.

Voice low, he asked me in a hesitant tone, "Will you trust me, Elowen? Never in any of my studies or information I've acquired from the scholars I consulted have I found that without a collar a lorafin's magic is unstable. You may be surprised to find you're the same."

My eyebrows scrunched together as Jax's inherent spicy pine fragrance billowed around me. Stars and galaxy, the male always smelled so *good*.

"What if you're wrong?" I whispered.

"I doubt I'm wrong. If I had any concerns that I might be, I wouldn't try to reassure you." He inched even closer, his aura so warm and potent it wrapped around me. "Will you trust me?"

I could only stare at his beautiful irises, a dazzling display of bright blues and navy. I'd thought I'd been a fool to trust him at all after he locked me in this room, but he was once again showing me that he was trying to do what he thought was right. Trying to free me in the only way he knew how. It wasn't just trusting him to follow through with his promise. He was also requesting that I trust his judgment.

And I'd been wrong not to trust him before. It was ultimately *why* I was in my current position.

"Elowen?"

A stirring began in my belly, a swirling emotion that climbed up my chest and filled my heart with a swelling pulse that made me want to trust him. Want to believe him. Want to have faith that not everyone was out to hurt me. *But can I? And more importantly, should I?*

I'd blindly trusted my guardian, someone I thought had cared for me, and that had turned out disastrously.

My throat bobbed in a swallow, brushing against my collar. A hum of power vibrated from it, and Jax's attention shifted to my neck.

"Please, Elowen, please trust me."

"I—" My words caught in my throat. "I . . . I don't know if I can. Trusting others, for me, is . . . difficult."

His hopeful expression evaporated, and a flash of disappointment washed over his face. But in my next blink, his expression returned to that of the prince. Closed off, resolute, and impossible to read.

Jax was gone, and Prince Adarian had returned.

A swell of pain crashed through me, but it was too late. The moment between us had broken, and there was no getting it back. But it was probably for the best. Not trusting others meant I stayed safe.

The prince straightened, and his tone turned formal when he said, "If you're willing, I'd still like to try having your collar removed."

"And if you're wrong, and I become unstable?"

"I can always command Alleron to return the stifling power of that collar if needed, but I'm confident that won't be necessary."

I took a deep breath and looked away from him, to the little kitten. The tiny feline had fallen asleep, curled against the stone fireplace. He looked so small, so fragile. *Is that how I looked when Guardian Alleron took me from my mother in the Wood?*

I thought of my guardian, someone I'd trusted completely to keep his word, when I shouldn't have. Then I thought of Jax, a male who was terrifying on some levels but was also inherently . . . good. He was trying so hard to do what was right by me.

Perhaps I could at least trust that, even if I couldn't trust him completely.

I took a deep breath.

Swallowing, my throat bobbed against my collar once more, but I found myself nodding. "All right. Fine. I'll trust you about my collar. Let's try to lift its power."

JAX RETURNED the kitten to the stables and then came back to my chambers with my guardian in tow, except this time, Jax was once again dressed in disguise. A mask covered his face, hiding his identity from my guardian. The familiar black bandana draped over his features, concealing his nose, mouth, and jawline. Once again, only his dazzling cerulean eyes were visible.

I couldn't help but wonder how difficult it was to always keep track of who knew his identity and who didn't. Since I'd discovered the true male beneath the mask, Jax no longer had to hide from me, but if my guardian ever learned who he was and broke free, it could spell catastrophe.

Jax shoved him forward, and Guardian Alleron's lip curled at the Dark Raider. Mussed hair covered my guardian's head, and from the looks of it, Jax had likely pulled him from sleep.

The fairy lights were fully lit in the seating area, and those sparkling rays reflected off the hatred glittering in my guardian's eyes when he assessed me. Something told me he knew why he was here—his precious lorafin would finally be stolen from him.

My thoughts tumbled, and I crossed my arms protectively around myself. This was the male I'd once considered my father. My trusted guardian. The one who'd promised to free me if I only did as he asked until I reached thirty summers. The male I thought would then view me as his cherished daughter.

Yet, this was the male who murdered my mother, destroying the blood family I once had. And he'd lied to me about *everything*.

"Here's the adaptor." Jax tossed it to him, and a pulse of his Ironcrest magic lifted from Guardian Alleron.

My guardian gasped, then brought a hand to his throat. He grabbed the adaptor, lifting the metallic wand that held a magical gem embedded in it. "Are you wanting her to do another calling?" My former guardian's voice sounded raspy, as though his throat was raw from trying to scream through Jax's magic all day.

Jax's eyes narrowed. "No. I want you to remove that collar's hold on her to the best of your ability."

My guardian gaped. "But that's incredibly dangerous. Removing most of its magic from Elowen could render her unstable. It would be remiss of me not to warn you."

I twisted my hands, my fingers gripping painfully around each digit.

Jax scoffed. "And where did you acquire this vast knowledge about lorafins?"

"I've acquired my knowledge from knowing *her* for her entire life." Jax's eyes narrowed, but my guardian pushed on. "She was uncontrollable as a child. When she grew, her power grew with her to the point that she was a danger to those around her. If you knew what she did when she was five—"

I paled, just as Jax snarled, "You're saying she deserved to be collared as a *child*? All fae children have to learn to control themselves when their magic emerges. No other children are enslaved because of it."

Despite his vulnerable situation, Guardian Alleron puffed his chest up, his self-righteousness filling the room. "But she's not like others. It's why lorafins are allowed to be enslaved. You're going to doom us all by demanding this here and now. She'll destroy this house."

House. Guardian Alleron thought he was in Jax's home. He had no idea he was in Stonewild's palace. He still had no idea who Jax truly was.

But I did, and because of it, I would never be free.

"Don't do this, Dark Raider," my guardian hissed. "You're going to kill us all."

A flash of a distant memory surged in my thoughts. My tiny hands. Shadow creatures. Screams. Endless death.

"Oh stars, he's right." Heart racing, I knotted my fingers even tighter until they turned white. "We can't do this. Just leave my collar as it is. I'm not ready for it to be removed. I need to be fully prepared, and I'm not."

Jax closed the distance between us and placed his hands on my upper arms. "Don't listen to him, Elowen," he said gently. "Don't listen to any more of his lies."

Guardian Alleron scoffed. "It's true. She'll—"

Jax's magic speared through the air, right for my former guardian. Guardian Alleron open and closed his mouth. No sound came out. Once again, Ironcrest magic wove around him, robbing his voice. Lip curling, Guardian Alleron seethed at Jax.

"Elowen?" Jax said quietly to me.

I wrapped my arms around my middle even though Jax's hands now ran soothingly up and down my shoulders. "We shouldn't—"

"Elowen. *Please*. Trust me."

His plea was so quiet, so gentle, that my rapid breaths began to slow. I glanced between him and my former guardian, but the second my attention shifted to Guardian Alleron, Jax stepped in front of me, forcing my focus away from the male who raised me.

Swirling energy danced around the crown prince, and he slid his hands down my arms to entwine his hands with mine.

The feel of his rough palms sliding over my skin reminded me of so many things. The night he took me. The night he slept at my side, his arm looped around my middle before Lordling Neeble's attack. The day he slid those palms over me in the enchanted bath. His masked face and startling cerulean eyes only made those memories more acute since he now stood before me as the Dark Raider.

60

"I would never do anything to hurt you," he whispered. "Never."

I took a deep, steadying breath and met his eyes. A storm raged in his irises, the potent, vivid power of this male swirling through his aura.

Brow furrowing, I recalled every time he'd asked for my trust. The truth was, each time he'd asked me to trust him, his promise had held true.

Some of the tension in my shoulders eased, and the painful beat of my heart lessened.

I didn't know if I could trust him completely. Didn't know if he would ultimately abandon me, as so many others had, despite his concern that a Mistvale fairy might command me to reveal who the Dark Raider was, but in this task, I thought *maybe* I could believe him fully.

"Elowen?" he said gently.

Finally, I gave a single nod and hoped I wasn't making the biggest mistake of my life. "Okay, Jax. I'll trust you."

CHAPTER 5

A moment of lightness broke through the prince's aura. "Why don't you sit for this."

He led me to one of the plush chairs and then rounded on my former guardian. "You're to use the adaptor to permanently loosen the collar to the maximum of your ability."

Guardian Alleron opened his mouth, but no sound came out.

Jax growled, and a pulse of his magic puffed out of him around my guardian.

My guardian sucked in a breath when Jax's magic lifted a second time. "The collar is designed to never allow her to access the full capabilities of her powers," he said in a rush. "Nor is it designed to leave her indefinitely without its suppression. I can only do so much."

The sound of Jax's teeth grinding came from beneath

his mask. *"How long will the collar stay loose on her if you command it now?"* Jax's Mistvale magic coated his words, forcing an honest answer from the receiver of his question.

In a rush, my guardian said, "I honestly don't know, but my guess is a few weeks. A couple of months, at most. I'll have to wield my adaptor again at some point to ensure she stays free of its afflictions." He gave Jax a pointed look, but I caught the meaning of his words too.

If I wanted to remain free, Jax would have to keep my guardian alive. I would *never* be free of him. Not even in this.

From Jax's sharp inhale of breath, I knew in that moment he understood that I could never be rid of my guardian either. Not completely at least if I didn't want to suffer for the rest of my life with a full-blown working collar.

My shoulders slumped, and it felt as if my soul withered.

Still staring at my guardian, Jax said on a low growl, "Gods, you're a monster." I could have sworn he was seething beneath his mask. *"Do the best that you can. Tell the adaptor to keep her free for the maximum length of its ability."*

My former guardian's jaw worked, but Jax's magic took hold, and he was helpless to resist. It suddenly struck me that not once had my guardian spoken directly to me, only to Jax, reminding me of the command Jax had given to him days ago in the Ustilly Mountains on our ride to Stonewild. *You're never to speak to her again.*

My lips parted as the strength of Jax's magic struck me anew. *Days* had passed since that command, and his power still held.

Guardian Alleron faced me, his expression hard, intense, and resentful. But Jax's magic wouldn't allow him to delay. He ran his thumb swiftly over the adaptor in a series of taps, then whispered a few words.

I held my breath. Waiting. Watching. I was ready to pounce upon my magic and wrestle it into submission if I felt about to explode.

A wash of magic shimmered in the adaptor's gem. An answering pulse came from the stone at my throat. It warmed, more so than usual, then vibrated, and a light-weight feeling shimmered over my entire body.

The veil of my collar's magic, which always felt as though it suppressed me and caged me in, began to lift. It felt as if a heavy cloak was being removed from my innards. That weight upon weight of solid bricks that had been heaved upon my shoulders began to levitate upward until my shadowy lorafin magic soared beneath it, rising, flying, and existing almost entirely unchecked.

In another breath, the cloak disappeared, nearly vanishing from existence, and it struck me that Guardian Alleron had *never* loosened my collar's restrictions to this extent. Not even close.

My eyes widened when the freeing feeling flowed through me. I still felt the power of the collar, but it was farther away, as though it kept a watchful eye on me but wasn't hovering. Like a mother would do with a child, watching and remaining there, ready to pounce if needed, but giving the child the false sense of freedom and independence.

Despite the collar not being removed completely, I felt light. Airy. As though boulders of suppression had just . . . disappeared.

I waved a hand through the air. Magic crackled along my skin and along my fingertips. Power barreled down my limbs, *magnificent* power. I was tempted to test it, to see what I was capable of, but . . .

An image of fae screaming before me shot through my mind, the vivid details resurfacing of that horrid day all of those summers ago.

I quickly brought my hands back to my side.

Breaths coming faster, I waited. Waited for my magic to rise up and take over, exploding out of me and dooming us all.

The crown prince studied me, his gaze intense and focused. Steady puffs came from beneath his mask, as though he was breathing faster. "How do you feel?"

I searched for the word to describe this new sensation. Power hummed within me, but nothing could summarize this inexplicable feeling of my hope twisted with fear, so all I replied was, "Different."

"And your magic?"

"I don't know yet. I'm hesitant to try, just in case . . ."

He nodded. "Only do what you feel comfortable doing."

Slowly, I lifted my hand. I was careful, not doing anything jerky or unrestrained, but I didn't feel unstable. Not yet at least.

But the weightlessness that soared through my inner magic was unlike anything I'd ever experienced. I shook my head in wonder. I'd never known such a feeling. And feeling that, understanding it . . . my breath sucked in as the knowledge of how caged I'd been my entire life took root. *My guardian could have done this full seasons ago, at any time, but he never did.*

That knowledge penetrated my heart, shredding through the last remains of hope I'd harbored that my guardian had cared for me on some level, no matter how small.

But he didn't care for me. Not at all. He'd kept me completely caged. My only purpose had been to serve him, nothing more.

Knife-like pain stabbed me. For full seasons, he'd kept me confined, even during callings, if what I was currently feeling was any indication. It was no wonder I'd never been able to fully control the semelees. I'd *always* been suppressed.

But could I fully control the semelees now? That thought struck me like an arrow. *With my magic this free, could I command them completely?* My pulse thundered. If I could, then that would make me their queen.

My heart fluttered anew, and I ran my fingers along the cool metal at my throat. A faint vibration tingled along my fingertips, so faint that I barely felt it.

Swallowing the anxiety in my throat, I took a deep breath, then dipped into my body. I tentatively stoked my lorafin abilities. They swirled and rose, billowing along my limbs and coming to my aid immediately without the restricting collar pushing them down. I pulled on them more, something I hadn't done since I was a child, but only a small sting came from my collar. That was it—no further punishments were elicited. Magic rushed through me, just waiting to be used. Immense energy crackled along my nerves, yet a part of me was aware that it still wasn't the full extent of my abilities. Regardless, I felt *powerful*. Gasping, I quickly suppressed it.

"Stars Above."

"Elowen," Jax rasped. "Your eyes."

I palmed my cheeks and cocked my head.

"They're shining like emeralds."

I rose from the chair, and a throb of magic made my movements swift and strong. I felt capable and steady.

Power hummed along my limbs, and the darkness swirling inside me grew, making me feel as nimble as a colantha.

Across the chamber, near the door, hung a large mirror.

My eyes bulged when I saw my reflection. My usual green irises shone back at me, but they glittered in a way I'd never seen before, and I could practically see the magic crackling along my skin. A slight shimmer rose from my body, as though the magic inside me was so potent that it needed to continually release.

"Her aura is so—" My guardian shook his head, then cast Jax an accusing glare. "This wasn't a good idea."

"It was." Jax's attention remained on me. "The power of a lorafin is akin to the gods. Vibrant, mighty, and a sight to behold. This is to be expected."

For the briefest moment, I locked my gaze with his in the mirror, confusion strumming through me.

"It's what the scholar told me that I consulted," the prince replied, his smile so dazzling that for a moment, I couldn't breathe. "How are you feeling now?"

I lifted my arms and studied my limbs. Other than the strange feeling of my magic continually skidding over me, I felt like me, just . . . freer. "I feel good, like myself, I think."

But while I did indeed feel less caged, it also felt like something was missing. As though a final piece to the puzzle of my magic hadn't locked into place yet. That realization marred my hope. Perhaps I wouldn't be able to fully command the semelees after all.

"And you don't feel unstable?" Jax pushed.

I tested my magic again and dove my attention inward, just to see what would happen and to see if the first time had been a fluke.

My magic again rose readily, coming to me so easily, and the only effect of the collar was a very faint sting upon my neck. Nothing more. Heart pumping a bit harder, I waited for my darkness to rise. Waited for it to take over and render me unstable.

Seconds ticked by as I stood there in trepidation, ready to douse it if it began to erupt.

But my magic only hummed along my limbs, coursing through my veins like an old, familiar friend. I suppressed it anyway, still worried that at any moment, I would gush like a volcano, but my magic did as I commanded and relaxed when I told it to, halting the strange glow of my eyes and crackling power along my skin.

Relief flooded me. "I don't think I'm unstable." A fresh wash of betrayal fired through me, and I shot my guardian an accusing glare.

But Guardian Alleron didn't even flinch.

Jax nodded, and his eyes crinkled in the corners. "So it's as I suggested."

His meaning hit me so hard that I turned rigid. Jax had been right. Right all along. I wasn't unstable without the collar. What had happened to me when I was five was probably because of what Jax had implied. I'd been a *child*. Untrained. Immature. Scared.

Fresh hurt washed through me. To think that all of those summers, my guardian had used that knowledge against me, that he'd been lying all along . . .

Tears moistened my eyes. Tears of rage, tears of mourning, tears for the young girl who had spent full seasons hating herself for what she'd done, but most of all, they were tears of relief. Jax had insisted I could trust him, and he'd been right. Just like he'd been right the other times he begged me to believe in him. And the implications of that seared me to my soul.

Maybe I *could* trust Jax.

For a moment, I just breathed, not able to do anything else. Too many emotions had taken a hold of me, but when I finally felt sure that my voice wouldn't crack, I replied, "Thank you. For convincing me to do this."

A blast of raw emotion flared in Jax's eyes. He dipped his head in a bow. "It was my pleasure."

Guardian Alleron watched on, and as I stood there, I realized that my guardian's warning that I would be a danger to others was truly just another lie. One more deception that he'd concocted following a string of them. When I'd been young and had accidentally done that horrible act, I'd been a child—a young, untrained *child*. But he wielded that against me like a weapon and made me believe I would always be dangerous.

And while I *could* be dangerous without a collar, if I chose to be—which was the entire reason why lorafins were allowed to be slaves—I would never choose that. Jax and Phillen's assessment of my character was correct. I could never willingly hurt another for no reason.

I sliced my attention back to my guardian. The adaptor was still in his hand, hanging at his side, and the only acknowledgment he showed from my stinging glare was a bob of his throat.

"How could you?" I finally whispered to him as the aching pain of betrayal cut me open once more. I let him see all of the hurt that he'd caused me. "How could you?" I repeated. "For so many seasons . . . *how could you?*"

Silence was his only response, but in his eyes, there was no apology, no remorse, only hard indifference and accusation.

My breath caught in my throat, and I gripped the nearest chair to steady myself. The pain of his betrayal threatened to sever me in two and bowl me over, and in that moment, it nearly cleaved my heart.

This male, this *fairy* who'd known me longer than any other, had never acted as a father should. Guardian Alleron's professed caring had all been a show, a trick of the mind. He'd never loved me, much less cared for me.

And that realization finally burned through me completely. Any hope that I'd previously harbored that perhaps he cared for me on some level disintegrated. My magic crackled and rose, but I took deep breaths and reined it in even though my guardian's betrayal solidified that no one in my entire life had ever loved me. Not one soul.

And it struck me as I stood there in a forgotten chamber in the mighty Stonewild palace, that even with access to most of my power and magic—that, according to Jax, rivaled a god—I was still entirely and completely alone.

CHAPTER 6

"I think I should head to bed. It's been a long night." I still gripped the chair. Still stood there immobile. Emotions were running through me so rampantly that I could barely breathe, and I needed them to leave before I broke down.

Jax took a step toward me, his brow furrowing, but I stopped him with a raised hand.

"I'm fine," I said hastily. "I just . . . I'd like to go to bed."

His irises flashed, and his jaw snapped beneath his mask. His eyes shot daggers at my guardian, a flare of magic emitting from his aura, but Guardian Alleron continued looking entirely nonplussed.

"Please," I added when both of them still stood there.

Jax shifted his attention back to me, and he watched me for another second, but when I didn't falter, he dipped his head. "All right. If that's what you wish. Goodnight, Elowen."

He propelled my guardian to the door and into the hall, but at the threshold, Jax paused. I turned away, but I still felt his probing gaze. Questions swirled in his unspoken stare. Concern did too, but when I didn't say anything further, he finally took his leave, and the door closed behind him, locking in place.

And then it was just me, the quiet chambers, and my soul-shredding thoughts.

I walked stiffly to the frosted window, dim moonlight from outside barely penetrating it. I closed my eyes and breathed. I tried to dispel the pain coursing through me, but the depths of Guardian Alleron's betrayal went so deep. I felt weak because of it. Surely, anyone with any sense would know not to let such a despicable male's lies control them.

But no matter how hard I yearned to let this pain go, I couldn't stop from picturing the way he'd taught me as a child. His scoldings, but his praise too. He'd spent count-less hours teaching me, or finding tutors when he was unable to. When I'd been young and he'd been at my side, it felt as if he cared for me as a father should.

But now I saw it for what it truly was—it was time and energy spent on his investment, nothing more.

Jax had been right about him all along. I'd made Guardian Alleron a very wealthy fairy, so much so that King Paevin was considering making him one of the ten noble Houses in Faewood by removing another. Essentially, Guardian Alleron's time, praise, and false love had all been to better himself. Not because he genuinely loved me.

And stars and galaxy, did that *hurt*.

A knock came at my door, startling me.

When the door didn't open, I tentatively called out, "Who is it?"

"It's me." Jax's deep voice rang through the solid wood. "May I come in? Please?"

I twisted my hands together and quickly scrubbed at my eyes to ensure no tears had fallen. Once certain I'd gotten myself together again, I called, "Yes."

Jax opened the door, his frame so broad and tall that he filled the space. His mask and disguise were gone.

In a blink, he stepped over the threshold and closed the door behind him. "I wanted to check on you again, but I'm sorry, am I disturbing you?"

I blinked rapidly. "No, it's all right."

He took a tentative step toward me, and his aura was so potent that he seemed to fill the space. My own magic responded to his, dipping and swaying toward him, as though gravity called to it. Without my collar suppressing it, it practically flew to him.

I'd *never* felt anything like that.

Startled, I plastered myself to the window.

Jax's eyes glittered, and inky hair fell artfully across his forehead. He prowled closer, a predator to his core, yet his words were gentle when he asked, "Are you still feeling well?"

"Yes, I'm fine, my prince. You were right. I'm not going to destroy the palace, and I'm not unstable without the collar suppressing me. You don't need to worry."

He stood there, watching me, and once again, it felt as though he saw into me.

I quickly looked away and did my best to appear at ease and happy. "Did Guardian Alleron give you any troubles on the walk back to his chambers?"

"No." His frown deepened. "You're upset. Why?"

My breath stuttered out of me, and I flashed him a broad grin. "What are you talking about? I'm fine."

He inhaled. "I can *see* that you're not, but I can also smell it. Your scent is filled with pain."

My heart jumped, and any lingering doubt I'd had that he could scent emotions disappeared. "Is that a trait you got from your Ironcrest magic?"

"Yes, but my shifter magic too. Stags have a heightened sense of smell."

"Hmm, so you got double the sensory magic. Lucky you."

But my flippant reply did little to deter him. "Are you upset about your magic? Is it proving hard to control? Is that why you're unhappy?"

I nibbled on my lower lip and tried so hard to push down the pain I was feeling. "No."

"Then why, Elowen? Why are you sad?" He took a step closer to me, then another. Within seconds, he was only feet away. His scent clouded around me, filling my senses. A part of me wanted to lean toward him and wrap my arms around his toned waist and sink into his strength. I wanted to depend on someone. No, not someone—*him*. I wanted him to carry some of the heavy burden in my heart.

It was such a bizarre response to a male I'd known for such a short amount of time, so I snapped myself upright and kept my spine rigid. I reminded myself that Jax wasn't at fault for Guardian Alleron's betrayals, and therefore he didn't need to shoulder that burden. It was mine, and mine alone, to carry.

A slew of emotions flittered across the prince's face. He dipped his head and tentatively reached for me. "Let me help you, Elowen. You don't have to do this alone."

His quiet plea made another rush of weakness barrel through me. "Do you have mind-reading abilities too?" I quipped quietly.

A small smile curved his lips. "No, not yet at least."

My breaths came faster. "Well, you certainly have a knack for understanding how fae feel."

"I always have."

"Why is that?"

He shrugged. "I've spent most of my life observing others. In my line of work, it's needed if one's to survive."

I knew he meant his raids, not his princely duties, and I

remembered again how he always sat in the corner of establishments, with a clear view of the vicinity, whenever he was in public as the Dark Raider. He was constantly scanning the room, watching others, reading the situation.

I cocked my head. "Have there been many close calls where you were almost caught? Other than that time you already told me of where you *were* captured?"

"Why do I have the feeling you're trying to change the subject?"

Because I am.

His finger coasted over my cheek, the touch so fleeting that it felt as if I'd imagined it. "Tell me what's wrong."

His quiet demand, while not laced with a Mistvale command, broke through my resolve. A bubble of emotion clogged my throat, and tears began to fill my eyes. "It's Guardian Alleron."

His nostrils immediately flared. "What did he do?"

I scoffed quietly. "Nothing new. I just—" I looked down and interlocked my fingers, playing with each digit. "I just fully realized tonight that he's never cared for me. Ever. He's used me my entire life. What I thought was fatherly love was all a show. He never loved me. Never cared what happened to me. I was just a pawn for him to use." More tears welled in my eyes, and I tried valiantly to blink them back. "I mean, I knew that," I added in a rush, "when you made him speak the truth back at that campsite in the Ustilly Mountains, but

I don't think it fully sank in until just now. I kept hoping that I was wrong or that some part of him did care, but now . . ."

Jax released a breath. "Now you see him for who he really is, and it hurts."

"Yes." I laughed self-deprecatingly. "Does that make me stupid?"

His voice grew even softer. "No, Elowen, it doesn't make you stupid. It makes you fae. Anyone in your position would be feeling that way." He closed the distance between us completely, and pine and spice clouded around me, wrapping me up as though in a warm embrace. "He hurt you unforgivably. He doesn't deserve your tears, but you are justified in how you feel. Your pain is warranted for what he did."

His gentle words snapped something inside me. The dam that had been barely holding back my bruised heart burst. Tears flooded my eyes. They spilled in earnest down my cheeks despite me trying to hold them back.

"Will anybody ever love me?" I whispered. "Is something wrong with me, Jax?"

"Elowen," Jax groaned. In a blink, I was in his arms. "*Nothing* is wrong with you," he said so fiercely that his growl vibrated all the way to my bones.

He held me tightly, his arms like steel. It felt as though he was trying to stop the realm from hurting me, seeing me, torturing me.

And that simple act of kindness, his genuine act of concern, undid me completely.

I sobbed, my arms curling around his waist as wetness from my tears coated his chest. I cried so hard that I could barely breathe. I wept for the child who'd been used and caged. Wept for the young fairy who tried so hard to please the only male she ever had as family. Wept for the lorafin forced to wear a device that suppressed who she really was for her entire life. And wept for a blood family that she once had but had never known.

I cried it all out, and just when I thought I was done, I cried some more.

And through it all, the Dark Raider, the male feared by the most powerful and mighty fae on our continent, held me. Not once did he let go. And not once did his embrace falter as I broke down and revealed the extent of my bottomless pain.

But as the minutes passed and his embrace held firm, my tears slowly began to dry. Still, he held me. Warm, hard arms kept their grip around my waist. Hands moved up and down my back in soothing gestures. Aching words were whispered into my ear.

"He doesn't deserve you, Elowen. He never did. Someday you will see that and truly believe it. And someday you will see how magnificent you truly are."

His words were quiet, heartfelt, and I clung to them as

though they were the only thing that kept me from drowning.

I let him hold me, and I held him back just as hard. And as the minutes ticked by, I knew that Jax wasn't going to let me go, not until I wanted it, and something about that heartbreakingly intimate gesture made me melt against him completely.

"You deserve so much, Elowen," he whispered. "You deserve the realm, and by the gods, I wish I could give it to you."

We stood quietly, and eventually his soft words grew silent, and he simply cradled me.

His heart beat against my ear. His scent enveloped me. And something in me cracked open. The first tendrils of hope bled into my system. A belief kindled within me that perhaps this male felt more for me and genuinely cared more about me than my guardian ever had.

Silence surrounded us as the moonlight grew brighter through the windows, and for the first time in a long time, I didn't feel alone anymore. Not within Jax's arms. Not within his soothing embrace.

It hit me that the reality was, Jax was the only fairy I had now. He said he couldn't let me be free, not after I learned who he truly was, which meant in the days to come, he would always be at my side, at least to some capacity.

And for the first time, that thought of my new cage brought me comfort, not despair.

I sniffed, and even though my tears had dried completely, Jax's hands still drifted up and down my back, and a low, soothing sound hummed in his chest.

But I didn't pull back. Not yet. To feel another hold me like this . . . it was too hard to let that go, so for this one moment, I closed my eyes and allowed myself to enjoy it.

THE CLOCK STRUCK three in the morning by the time I finally pulled free, but despite holding me for who knew how long, Jax's arms tightened when I inched away, and then, as though catching himself, he released his grip.

"Thank you," I said, those simple words not doing justice for all he'd just done for me. I wiped at Jax's wet clothing and laughed softly. "I swear I normally don't cry like this."

He brushed a lock of hair behind my ear. "I don't mind."

I swallowed the ball of emotion clogging my throat and gazed up at him. The night sky pierced the window and highlighted the planes and angles of his features.

Fluttering feelings stole over my heart again, and as I gazed up at the Dark Raider, it struck me that I could still find happiness and meaning in my life, if only I chose to grasp it.

"Jax? I have a request."

He cocked his head. "What is it?"

"Take me with you to Faewood tomorrow."

His eyebrows shot up. "You want to come along?"

"Yes. I can help you find the male you're seeking. If needed, I can travel to the Veiled Between again to find his exact location, and—"

"No." Jax said the word so quickly, so fiercely. "I will *never* do that to you again."

"But . . . I want to help you."

His jaw worked, and the aura around him grew. "Elowen, I would rather die than see you again in the state my magic put you in."

"Even if it means that doing so finds the half-breed you're seeking? That it pinpoints *exactly* where he is?"

A stirring of magic billowed around him, radiating off his broad shoulders like waves in the sea. It lapped through the room, roll after roll of raw power. He sucked in a breath. "You know that I want to find him, rather desperately in fact, but after everything I've done to you . . ." He shook his head. "I can't do that."

My brow furrowed. "I could still help you. I know that area of Faewood better than you. I can still aid in finding him, even without my magic."

His gaze softened. "You truly *want* to help me?"

I somehow managed to nod, but when he looked at me like that, with his eyes smoldering in intensity and the potent magic inside him flooding the room, it was hard to think straight.

And stupidly, I found myself blurting out, "Saramel told me the male you're looking for is your half-brother. It makes me see things a bit differently."

A guarded expression fell over his face. "She told you that?"

"Don't worry. She bound me to secrecy in a bargain. I can never tell anyone what she told me without your permission unless they already know about Bastian too."

His brow furrowed. "Tell me exactly what bargain you agreed to."

I repeated it. Word for word. And when I finished, I lifted my shoulders. "As you can tell, she was thorough. Nevertheless, she said she would probably be put on extra kitchen duty for a week after you found out, but she thought me knowing was more important than any punishment you'd give her. But please, don't mistreat her. I begged her to tell me. If you want to take your anger out on anyone, it should be me."

He let out an aggrieved sigh, then placed his hands on his hips and looked toward the ceiling. "Damn. That female is always trying to do what she thinks is right even if it defies me."

"Which one can argue is an admirable trait. Please, Jax, don't punish her. She was just trying to—"

"I know. Don't worry. Her bargain covered what it needed to, and I won't order extra duties to be given to her. But believe it or not, that's not why I'm angry. I'm upset because I was trying to keep you out of this, as preposterous as that may seem, considering I've turned your life upside down, but I meant it when I said I wanted to free you after you located Bastian for me. I never meant for you to become involved in this any further." He frowned heavily, his aura dimming. "Being associated with me puts you at risk, Elowen, even though I want you—" He took a deep breath. "I don't want you at risk. You're safer away from me. It's why I've never told you anything."

I laughed softly. "It's a bit late for that now. I know too much."

He sighed heavily, so heavily that I couldn't help but wonder if there was something deeper going on regarding his concern for me. "I know. Trust me, I know."

"What's done is done, Jax. I'll always know that you're the Dark Raider, and now I also know about your secret brother. Why not let me help you since I can? Keeping me here doesn't benefit either of us."

His eyes glowed slightly as an unreadable expression covered his face. "You truly want to join us and help me find him?"

"I do, and I have an advantage, considering what I am."

His nostrils flared. "I *won't* see you put in that position again." The absolute steel in his voice made my stomach flip, and the storm in his eyes grew, but a moment of pain filled them too. "Elowen, I'm so sorry. I never meant to compromise everything in your life."

"I know, but it's not like returning to Emerson Estate with Guardian Alleron would be any better, even if that was an option." I pointed at my collar. "If this is to stay on me forever, my freedom will always be restricted to some extent, so I might as well do something useful and good, and if I can't leave to forge my own life because of my collar and what I now know . . ." I shrugged. "I'm trying to find the best path forward from here, and helping you seems like that option."

"Elowen . . ."

"No." I raised a hand. "Don't feel sorry for me, Jax. I'm a lorafin, just like Bastian is a half-breed. We'll never be treated like other siltenites. Perhaps, this is the best I can hope for, and the last thing I want is anyone's pity."

Magic vibrated off him. "I'd so love to find whoever created that collar for you and send them to the afterlife." His attention dropped to the gem at my throat.

A shiver ran through me. The ruthlessness of the Dark Raider was commanding his expression once more.

Trying to make light of it, I replied flippantly, "Good luck, since apparently Guardian Alleron doesn't even know who the fairy is." Self-consciously, I traced my fingers along the confining piece of jewelry. Power pulsed from the gem, but it didn't zap me, not like it used to.

Jax's brow furrowed. "My brother is caged like you, not by magic, but by birth. He's never been able to live a normal, *free* life either, thanks to what he is."

An aching feeling overtook me, so much so that I placed a hand on my stomach when my magic tried to rise. "I know. Saramel told me about that too, about how his mother fled with him, and how your father had wanted him executed, and how it was only by chance that you found him."

His lips twitched in a sardonic smile. "Is there anything Saramel *didn't* tell you?"

I bit my cheek to keep from smiling. "I still don't know where your nickname comes from."

He smirked. "I'm sure she'll happily tell you if you ask."

I laughed, unable to help it. His smile stayed, and given his lightening mood, I said again, "Please, take me with you."

"Do you know what you're asking? You'll have to play the part, pretend like we're only there for fun."

"I can do that."

"And you'll have to learn our ways, call us by our actual names. You can no longer refer to me as Jax."

"Of course, Prince Adarian." I bowed mockingly.

His lips twitched again, and for the briefest moment, a tender look stole over his face. "You really want to do this?"

"I do.

"All right. If it's what you wish."

A moment of carefreeness hit my heart. "Is there anything I need to do to prepare?"

"Not really. Pack whatever you like, but no need to bring your pile of rulibs. You can keep those safely here."

"All right, packing won't take long since I don't have much."

A fleeting emotion stole over his face. "No, you don't have much, but you deserve so much more, Elowen." Before I could respond, he stepped back. "It's late. We should both turn in, but I'll come for you in the morning. Until then, good night."

I watched him leave, and when the door shut behind him, the magical bolt sliding into place, that sound didn't depress me because a new sense of purpose filled me. A purpose that I truly wanted to fulfill.

I would find Bastian.

I would uncover the truth of why he'd fled from his brother and what was keeping him in Faewood.

Because tomorrow was the first day of the rest of my new life, and for once, that thought didn't fill me with sorrow—it filled me with joy.

CHAPTER 7

Morning sunlight bathed my chambers in soft light while
noises from Jaggedston carried through the thick panes.
The palace had been built high up, overlooking the city. I'd
learned that much from my wild run through the palace.
But while sounds from the city did carry through the
windows, they were faint. Faint enough that when I'd first
arrived, I hadn't been able to distinguish them.

The bells, though, weren't quiet. Every morning and
well into the evening, the bells rang on the hour, letting the
Stonewild fae know the time as they carried on with their
busy lives. Considering the last toll I heard had been ten
rings, I assumed Jax would be arriving soon, even if we'd
been up until the wee hours of the morning.

Despite our late night, I'd woken early, too energized to
truly sleep. Consequently, I'd been dressed for hours.
Black breeches covered my legs, and I'd chosen the last

remaining top purchased in Fosterton that I hadn't worn yet. The blood-red long-sleeve garment was fitted throughout, except for the sleeve cuffs, which flared around my wrists. The cinched cut highlighted my waist, and the square neckline revealed a hint of cleavage.

Of my new clothing, it was the most revealing, yet it was nothing compared to the seductive gowns Guardian Alleron had forced me to wear. But the crimson color felt appropriate. Daring in a way. After all, it wasn't the norm for an abducted female to join her captor and his gang of masked bandits on their quest to find his missing half-breed brother.

Too keyed up to sit still, I paced in my chambers, braiding my hair in the process. Once finished, I had a long, smooth braid down my back. Lillivel would have been aghast if she saw it. It was nothing like the intricate creations she'd woven through my hair, but it was the best I could do on my own.

I spared a glance at the frosted window, and my brow furrowed. "Where is he?" I whispered under my breath. The crown prince of Stonewild was indeed taking his time.

I turned and paced the other way across the chambers' soft carpet.

A quiet knock abruptly came at the door, and my heart jumped into my throat.

"Finally." I grabbed my bag and hurried to greet the crown prince.

The door cracked open, and I was about to call a greeting to Jax when a male I'd never seen before sauntered into the room.

I froze, my feet planting to the center of the chamber.

The male was tall and lean, an easy smile readily forming on his lips. Light-brown eyes regarded me from a handsome face, and thick mahogany hair covered his head.

"Before you panic," he said, his tone low and deep as he raised his hands in a non-threatening manner, "I'm one of the prince's friends, but we haven't met yet, so no need to scream or faint or zap me with that powerful magic of yours, or whatever it is you're considering doing."

Magic indeed surged through my body, but some of the pounding in my chest slowed. I still clutched my bag protectively to my abdomen, as though the canvas sack would offer any protection from a male who truly intended to do me harm.

"Who are you?" I asked warily.

Once the door was firmly closed behind him, he dipped into a bow, the movement practiced and smooth. It hinted at a lifetime of court duties. "Lordling Alexander Maysin Pruveen Graniteer of House Graniteer at your service, but please, call me Alec. Everyone else does, including Jax."

I loosened my claw-like fingers around my bag. The fact that he knew Jax's nickname, when only his raider friends called him that, had to mean that Alec was one of them. But then my brow pinched. *House Graniteer*. Something about that rang a bell, and then I remembered whatever had pulled Jax away for three days had to do with that House.

"And what brings you here today, Alec?"

Alec's smile widened, and his aura carried a sense of playfulness that had me relaxing my grip on my bag entirely. "Jax asked me to fetch you. He had to attend a council meeting this morning, and it's running longer than expected. At the moment, he's unable to leave, so he thought it made a good opportunity for your face to be seen in the palace more than the, um"—he covered his mouth, as though attempting to hide a smile—"the one time you were seen out of these chambers yesterday. He figured if the servants and nobles saw you about, with someone of such esteemed bloodline as myself, then they would be less inclined to ask questions, especially if you begin turning up at court events with us in the future. I am known, after all, for being quite appealing to the lovely females in our realm."

Court events with them in the future? So Jax wasn't going to keep me locked in these chambers every time we returned here. He truly was going to give me the best chance at freedom that I had in my new life with him.

I smiled tentatively. "Well, you know, in my defense, I had no idea you were all leaving for three days. If I'd known, I never would have tried to escape, and then you wouldn't be here having to save face among the servants."

He chuckled. "True, but since we can't undo what's been done, I hope you'll accept my company this morning?"

"I suppose I could do that. Does that mean I don't need this yet?" I indicated my packed bag.

"Correct, you can leave that here. We'll retrieve it before we depart."

He made a move to head toward the door, but I stopped him, knowing once we stepped foot into the hall, I would have to watch what I said. "Alec, you're a member of the House that had the emergency the other day, aren't you?"

He sighed. "I'm afraid I am."

"May I ask what happened?"

"Stars . . . but it was a most unfortunate situation. Our northern lands had been plundered by the Lochen. An entire city had been seized, and Jax was needed, since I'm sure you can understand how useful his magic is in such situations. Thankfully, he and other powerful House nobles were able to restore order."

I tried to imagine what those three days had been like for them, because if Jax's magic had been utilized, there'd likely been fighting. "Does everyone know that Jax can wield magic from all four kingdoms? Before meeting him, I had no idea that any royal in any kingdom had that kind of ability."

Alec laughed. "You would be surprised what the royals keep hushed throughout the kingdoms, but to answer your question, no, most don't know what Jax is capable of. He doesn't flaunt his magic. If anything, he keeps it hidden, and he never uses his Mistvale magic unless it's absolutely necessary."

"Why is that?"

"As you know, being able to wield magic from all four kingdoms is exceptionally rare. Once his magic began to manifest, his parents grew concerned. If word spreads that they bred such a powerful child, one likely capable of overpowering every other noble or royal on the continent, some may view him as threatening. The king and queen were concerned that an assassin would be sent to murder their sole heir. Therefore, they kept his magic a secret. Most don't know of all that he's capable of, although it's common knowledge that he's a stag shifter."

My brow furrowed, but I nodded. "That's why I had no idea about him. The royal family has kept his powerful magic concealed."

"Indeed. The royal family, especially in this kingdom, is *very* good at keeping secrets." His expression turned grim, and I wondered if he was thinking about Bastian.

Not wanting to test the bargain's ability to let me speak

of the prince's half-brother, I switched subjects. "Is everything back in order now on the northern coast?"

Alec grinned, revealing a mouthful of perfectly straight white teeth. "Oh yes, the city has been restored, and the Lochen who tried to steal our goods and cause egregious mayhem have been driven back to the sea. All is well once again. Until the next time, that is." He laughed lightly.

Cocking my head, I tried to contemplate what other princely duties arose last minute like that for Jax. Truth be told, I had no idea. "Anyway, if we're to be wandering about the palace this morning, does that mean the trip to Faewood is delayed?"

"Only slightly. We're still doing that too, just a bit later than planned, thanks to this dastardly meeting." The noble held out his arm, his chivalrous offer hard to refuse. "Shall we? I would love to show you more of the palace, Elowen. Let me lead the way."

I KEPT my hand looped around Alec's arm as we strolled down a wide hall. Mosaic tiles covered the floor in this area of the palace's north tower. Large bouquets of fresh flowers, carefully arranged in blue vases, dotted each table between windows. Fresh air swirled around us, and I inhaled deeply, loving the scent of roses and junipers.

We were two hours into our stroll, yet I was enjoying

every minute of it. I was still slightly breathless from the long climb up the tower's stairs, but the warm breeze swirling through the open windows and the bright sunshine streaming onto the patterned floor made the entire climb worth it.

"Then what happened after Nellip tripped?" I asked, still breathy as I smiled up at Alec.

The noble grinned. It was an expression I was quickly learning he wore regularly. "Probably what you would expect. Entirely intoxicated, Nellip fell down the stairs, staying unconscious the entire flight down. The prince, in a similar state, tried to break his fall . . . even though Nellip's job as his personal guard is to keep him safe at all times. But no matter, Prince Adarian tried anyway, but all that did was make him join his guard in their tumble."

I laughed softly, picturing it.

Flashing me another wide smile, Alec continued, "The two of them landed in a heap on the bottom landing, Nellip entirely oblivious, and the prince moaning in pain. And to top it all off, a stone sculpture of Queen Rashelle— a gift from the Nolus king many full seasons ago— promptly fell from the table they'd rolled into. It smashed on the top of Jax's head and gave him a lovely cut that sliced him open just above his ear."

I laughed, but even though Alec's stories had all been light and fun, I had come to learn one important matter.

All of the Dark Raider band's nicknames were similar to their real names but spelled roughly backward.

Alec had also informed me I must *always* use their real names when in public or where others might hear. A part of me warmed when he'd told me that. They obviously trusted me enough not to reveal that secret.

I raised my eyebrows. "And this unfortunate accident down the stairs was all because you were trying to out-drink one another?"

"Correct."

"How . . . dashing."

A twinkle filled his eyes. "I never said we had brains at that age. Brawn? Indeed." He puffed his chest up. "But brains? No, none at all. In that department, we were severely lacking."

"But you all recovered, obviously."

"With horrendous hangovers, yes. Although, when the queen learned of our drinking game, the broken statue, and a deep gash on the sole heir, well . . ." He winced. "That didn't go over so well. I'm afraid Nellip was banished from the palace. It was only after three months of the prince begging his mother to allow him to return that the queen finally relented. Nellip has never once drunk on the job again."

I wrinkled my brow and thought back to the inns we'd stayed in during our travel to Stonewild's palace. That wasn't entirely true . . .

Alec's smile turned cheeky. "Well, not in any *official* capacity, that is." He waggled his eyebrows.

I laughed anew, the sound ringing down the hall.

Two wildling servants walking by us in the long corridor gave each other knowing looks before dipping their heads together and whispering. They scurried away, but not before I caught a few words.

". . . I heard the prince had a guest staying in the palace. Nobody knew who she was, though, until yesterday."

It was only when they reached the end of the hall that I drifted closer to Alec and whispered in his ear, "You weren't kidding when you said that news travels fast through these walls. I've only been walking with you for two hours, and it seems as though all of the servants already know who I am."

Alec turned to face me, but I'd leaned so close to him that our lips almost brushed.

I quickly pulled back, but all he did was lean closer, his own lips pressing against my ear. "And that, dear Elowen, is entirely the point of this little wander. By nightfall, your presence within these walls will already be seen as old, boring news. They'll likely think you're another conquest of mine who's succumbed to my charms and is entirely helpless to resist my appeal."

I scoffed in amusement. "If only that were true."

He brought a hand to his chest. "Are you saying it's not?"

His aghast look had me giggling again, and he nudged me playfully. The noble slipped his arm around my shoulders, steadying me as we both laughed like children until a throat cleared loudly from behind us.

Sobering, I peered over Alec's shoulder.

Jax stood only feet away with his arms crossed.

My jaw dropped. Jax's casual sweater and pants from last night were long gone. Instead, he wore official royal attire in Stonewild colors. Dark navy slacks and a navy jacket, both made of fine wool, covered his frame. Gold buttons trailed up the jacket's middle all the way to his throat, and embellishments in cobalt blue, gold, and shades of green decorated his shoulder straps. A long forest-green cape was clasped around his throat, and the gold stitching along its edges was bright enough to reflect the sun.

He looked magnetic. Important. *Regal.* And in that moment, I felt the social differences between us so sharply that it felt as if a knife pierced the space between us.

But if the Stonewild prince noticed my response, he didn't comment. Instead, his attention fixated entirely on Alec.

"Having a nice tour?" the crown prince asked, his tone brisk.

Alec, still grinning, immediately bowed to the prince, even though his arm stayed around me. "Your Highness."

Jax's gaze dropped to where Alec was touching me before shifting upward. A rising pulse flickered in his aura, so subtle that I would have missed it if not for his close proximity. "Ready to go, then?"

Alec smiled cheekily. "Of course, and it's about time. I thought we'd never leave." He tugged me closer, but I barely reacted. I'd gotten used to Alec's frequent touches and teasing flirtations. It didn't actually seem to hold any meaning. "And I did as you asked, my prince. I've been showing the lovely Elowen all over the palace, loudly telling our foreign visitor of our kingdom's magnificent history and anecdotes."

"Which apparently consists of stories from our youth involving drinking games." Jax's nostrils flared. "You've outdone yourself, Alec. Even I heard a few whisperings on my search through the halls trying to find you two."

My eyebrows shot up. "You've been looking for us?"

"I have." Jax's gaze remained on his friend. "Lordling Graniteer seems to have forgotten that the ship we're taking departs at two, and it's already well past one, so we should be on our way."

"Ship?" I repeated. "We're taking a *ship* back to Faewood?"

Both males ignored me as Alec sighed loudly. "Oh galaxy, you're right, I did forget, but no matter." Alec ushered me forward, brushing past Jax in the process. The prince's arm stiffened when we swept by him. "We'll still make it. It's not like it would depart without you anyway, my prince. Come on then, the southern kingdom awaits."

CHAPTER 8

Outside, on the palace steps, I waited with Alec, Trivan, Lars, Phillen, and the prince for our ride to the wharf. Lander and Bowan were staying behind. The two of them would tend to Guardian Alleron as needed because while I'd been given freedom in my new life, my guardian had not. He was to remain a prisoner of Jax's indefinitely, from the sounds of it.

A salty breeze drifted through the air as we waited for the enchanted carpet to pick us up. At least none of the nobles had to hide. As Alec had explained to me on our walk down here, Jax had told the king and council that he and several of his lordling friends wanted to attend the Final Match selections in Faewood before the Centennial Matches officially began.

Considering most of the nobility throughout the Silten

continent were traveling to the Matches for at least a few days in the coming weeks, nobody thought anything of it, making it the perfect excuse to return to Faewood. And it also meant that neither Jax nor his friends and guards had to wear disguises since all of them were attending the Matches as themselves.

Consequently, Jax stood tall and proud, his jaw tight and his shoulders stiff. He was the portrait of royal disdain, and he'd been like that since he found Alec and me in the north tower.

I tried not to be bothered by the fact that we'd barely spoken. But ever since he found us, Jax had been distant. Cold, even. It was so different from the raw emotions we shared in the early hours of the morning, and I was reminded again that the prince wore many faces.

Taking a deep breath, I tried not to let that bother me. Instead, I shifted my attention to the city. The view was magnificent, and for the first time, I was able to see it entirely.

Jaggedston had been built on stone cliffs, overlooking the coast. The permanent presence of salt in the air permeated the breeze, and since the palace was perched high on the rocky terrain, the city spread out before us. The buildings and winding streets drifted all the way to the distant cliff's edge, where the capital stopped abruptly above the plunging ocean shore.

Crashing waves from the Adriastic Sea pummeled the

black sand at the cliff's base, sending foamy spray splashing onto the beach's ebony pebbles.

Farther down the shore, the huge wharf waited. In the distance, at least a dozen ships were docked at the port, some with sails raised, others waiting idly.

"Why are we traveling by sea?" I asked Alec just as our enchanted carpet flew around the corner toward us.

"Nobility often travels by ship, carriage, or enchanted carpet." Alec nudged me. "Is it any different in Faewood?"

I shrugged. "I'm honestly unsure. I'm not well versed in Faewood royalty or nobility even though I've met the king a few times."

Alec cocked his head. "Regardless, what about you, lovely Elowen? Do you enjoy traveling by sea?"

I lifted my shoulders once more. "I've never been on a ship, so I have no idea, but I'd just assumed, considering you're all stag shifters, that we'd travel by land, and you'd all run, or—" I stopped myself. "Wait, are *you* a stag shifter? Or something else?"

Jax, standing a few feet away, gave us a side-eye. He rocked back slightly on his heels, and a muscle began to tick in his jaw.

Alec chuckled and leaned closer to me, waggling his eyebrows. "That would be telling."

I groaned. "Not you too. The prince also loves to keep me guessing."

"Does he?" Alec raised an eyebrow in the prince's

direction, then slipped an arm around my waist, getting a squeak out of me. The muscle in Jax's jaw ticked even more. "You'll have to tell me more about *what else* the prince doesn't tell you."

I rolled my eyes but couldn't keep the smile from my voice just as the gliding enchanted carpet reached us. "Well, that would be a bit hard, considering I *don't know* what he's not telling me."

Alec's sharp laughter rang through the air, and Jax said in a clipped tone, "The carpet's here. Get on."

I jumped at the anger in the prince's voice, but Alec's lazy grin only grew.

Trivan leaped onto the carpet first, flashing a smirk to a group of females who walked by on the street outside of the palace gates. But their attention wasn't on the nobles. It was on Jax, and they seemed to be walking much slower than necessary, and more than a few smoothed their hair down their backs and glanced demurely over their shoulders.

But the prince didn't so much as look in their direction, and considering the females in Fosterton had acted just as besotted, I could only guess this was the norm for him.

Still . . . my stomach tightened.

"Elowen?" Jax's soft question had my attention snapping to him.

He stood atop the carpet, the wind ruffling his dark

hair. Sapphire eyes blazed into me, and my pulse tripled its beat.

"May I give you a hand up?" Jax began to extend his arm, but Alec leaped onto the carpet.

"No need to exert yourself, my prince. I can help." Outstretching his own hand, Alec asked, "Elowen? Can I assist?"

Jax's fingers curled into his palms, and another flicker of his aura washed over me, similar to what I'd felt in the north tower. Stiffly, the prince gave both of us his back and said something to a palace guard.

I eyed the prince, then Alec. I knew something was at play here, but for the life of me, I didn't know what.

I lifted my chin. "Thank you, Lordling Graniteer, but I'm just fine on my own." I placed my foot on the wavering rug and ignored Alec, which didn't seem to bother the noble in the least since he just grinned and clasped his hands behind his back.

The enchanted carpet only dipped an inch when I put my full weight on it, but I was still thankful for my breeches. They made moving so much easier than when I'd been made to wear gowns. If not for the stretchy pants, I probably would have been forced to accept Alec's help.

I surveyed the large traveling carpet. "Where should I sit? Is here okay?" Before I could claim a spot near the side, Alec *tsked,* and his hands encircled my waist. He lifted me to the center, and it was only when I was positioned right beside him that he let go.

I sucked in a breath at the abrupt shift in my movement. "Was that necessary?"

Alec grinned. "This is a much better spot for you, don't you think? And until the day comes when you tell me not to touch you, yes, it was necessary."

I was about to reply, but the prince growled, "Alec? Sit."

"Ah, of course." The noble elegantly lowered himself to the carpet, not even glancing toward the prince's glare.

Brow furrowing, I awkwardly settled myself beside Alec as Trivan, Lars, and Phillen watched on with a mixture of amused expressions. Trivan even snickered.

I snapped my spine straighter, and Alec slipped his arm around my waist again. "The ride can be cold with the wind, and being so close to the ocean. The sea's breeze can be quite chilled," he offered by way of explanation. "I'll help keep you warm."

I sighed but didn't bother replying. At least, I managed one last glance at the palace before the carpet careened around the curved drive.

Tall black stone palace walls soared several stories above street level of the king's residence. Flags in Stonewild colors flapped on the top of every tower, and glimmering onyx shingles soaked up the sunlight. But even as we flew toward the city center, the palace remained visible given its impressive height. It looked exactly as I'd been told it would—dark, oppressive, and entirely intimidating with its powerful aura.

It was so different from Faewood's palace. Black instead of white. Imposing instead of serene. Cold instead of warm. I couldn't help but wonder which Stonewild king had commissioned its design.

"Have you not seen the palace before?" Alec's quiet question snapped my attention back to him. "You look as though you're seeing it for the first time."

I tucked a strand of hair behind my ear. "Well, it is actually. When I first arrived, I wasn't allowed to . . ." I stopped myself, realizing we were in public, and I had to watch what I said. "I mean, I never really got a good look at it before."

The prince glanced over his shoulder at me, and for the briefest moment, our gazes collided.

But whatever I thought I would see in his expression—camaraderie, a subtle knowing, even a conspiratorial smirk—*something* to indicate that he too remembered all that we'd shared . . . it wasn't there. His face remained blank, any emotion he felt impossible to read.

My chest locked, as though my breaths refused to release. I didn't understand how the prince could be so aloof after the way he'd held me in the wee hours of the morning. He'd embraced me. Consoled me. Cared for me.

His hands had traveled up and down my back, so soothing and gentle.

But his behavior now . . .

A stinging sensation filled my chest, but I tried to brush it off. *He has a lot on his mind. His brother's missing after all. Maybe that's the reason for his sudden distance.*

I angled myself away from the prince and firmly focused on the passing streets. Wind blew over my cheeks as we flew onward, which whipped strands of hair around my face despite the braid I'd woven. I continually pushed my hair back, but I didn't mind, even though Alec was right that the breeze was chilled.

But being cold with my hair flying everywhere was so much better than being locked in the palace or paraded around Faewood at Guardian Alleron's side. Everything about this was better.

Alec leaned closer to me. "That shop is known for its custom jewelry." He pointed toward a large two-story building. The store's glass display was filled with gems and sparkling stones. "And that one"—his finger shifted toward a bakery on the corner—"makes the best honeybuns this side of the continent."

Doughy scents carried on the breeze, and I couldn't help but recall the honeybuns Lars had warmed for us in the Ustilly Mountains. I wondered if that bakery was where he'd gotten them.

Alec pointed out a few more landmarks, divulging

details of each's history and purpose. Every time he did, he leaned close to me, brushing against my side and effectively wrapping me in his ocean-breeze scent. I could have been imagining it, but each time we touched, the crown prince appeared to grow tenser and more rigid.

I cleared my throat and asked Alec, "Have you lived in Jaggedston your entire life?"

Alec nodded. "Indeed. As a member of House Graniteer, it's required, although we do have a few country homes in other parts of the kingdom, the northern section being one of them."

"Was that where the Lochen raid recently occurred?"

"It was. Our House watches over that city. Because of that, my family spends most of the summer up north. Despite the cold northern climate, it's truly beautiful, and summers are quite pleasant." Grinning, he added, "Perhaps I'll get to show it to you one day."

I couldn't help my smirk. "Has anyone ever told you that you're a shameless flirt?"

Behind us, Trivan laughed, and Phillen brought a hand to his mouth to cough. Even Lars appeared to be holding back a smile.

But the prince didn't move a muscle.

Alec's grin strengthened. "I might have been told that a time or two."

The noble once again brushed his chest against my side, then he returned to explaining what all of the buildings and shops were that we passed. Oftentimes, he leaned directly into my space to do so, filling my head with his scent and completely distracting me since I couldn't remember any male ever touching me so freely.

I wasn't sure how I felt about it. Alec was a shameless flirt, obviously. But I didn't think he meant any disrespect. Half the time, he didn't even seem aware of his close proximity.

But he was still a male who'd taken many liberties with me today, and I had a feeling if I wasn't so starved for a close connection with other fae, I might have been annoyed by it. But since he was the first siltenite I'd ever met who seemed to genuinely enjoy my company and enjoy being affectionate with me, I decided that I rather liked it. Something about his easy, coquettish nature warmed me.

The carpet moved quickly, so Alec couldn't tell me more than a sentence or two about each location that we passed. I didn't learn much history, but I still soaked up every detail.

Just as we reached a busy intersection, in which dozens of new shops lined the streets, the prince glanced over his shoulder. "Brace yourself. We're going to climb."

The carpet abruptly lifted upward, climbing at a sharp angle until we soared over the buildings and shops. We didn't level out until we reached an altitude high above everything.

I gasped, my lips parting as I took in the vast view. Pastel clouds drifted above us, the wharf now in a straight line only miles away. Wind continued to blow across my cheeks, sharper and fiercer, but I was glad the prince didn't enact his elemental magic. This high up, I felt alive and free, and it was marveling that we were allowed to travel above the roads.

My gaze collided again with Jax's. He was watching me, his stone-like expression cracking. For the briefest moment, the intensity of his focus was so consuming that my breath was trapped in my throat.

He looked positively . . . hungry.

Eyes hooded, the prince's attention dipped as he took in my flushed cheeks. A small smile curved his lips, but then Alec leaned closer to me, and the prince's smile disappeared.

Alec pointed north. "And that section of the city is where the ten Houses reside. You can see it much more clearly from up here. Each estate has nearly as much land as the prince's residence."

I tried to focus on what Alec was telling me, but my attention wanted to drift to Jax. "Where did you say it was?"

"Just there." Alec pointed again. "It's hard to miss."

I finally spotted the large section of the city that revealed ten monstrous estates, and my eyebrows shot up. Alec hadn't been jesting. It *was* hard to miss.

Each estate had manicured gardens, fountains, and pristine landscaping. All of the ten noble Houses sat on sprawling parcels of land, spreading northward toward the Wood, and some only stopped when they reached the coast.

Each residence held a stone castle, although all of the castles were slightly different colors and had unique architecture, but each residence had opulent spires and elegant towers. One even had a moat.

None of them were as grand as the palace, or had quite as much land, nor were as forbidding with black exteriors, but the ten Houses were nothing to scoff at.

"They're all so beautiful," I whispered. While Emerson Estate was also magnificent in its own way, it was nothing compared to these.

Alec inclined his head. "Most of the House castles are centuries old, some even dating back to just after the Elvish wars. My House has been in existence for nearly eight hundred summers, and we've managed to hold onto it that entire time."

"Truly? But House heads change so frequently."

"Exactly. It's a matter of pride in my family that we've maintained our status for so long. In fact, my grandfather built that residence after demolishing the previous, stating it was too small for our great name."

"So much history," I murmured.

Nodding, Alec settled back, propping his arms behind

him. "As you know, the Houses were established in most of the kingdoms as soon as we regained control of our lands following the wars. It was a time of great celebration and strategic power struggles. I wasn't alive back then, obviously, so I just consider myself lucky to have been born into a line that has such fortuitous roots."

Alec kept up his commentary for the rest of the carpet ride to the wharf, pointing out the ship we were to travel on as we grew nearer. It was the grandest of those docked. Navy sails billowed from its great mast, and pristine planks scoured its deck. Each sail displayed the king's crest: a shield with stag antlers, wintercrisp ferns surrounding it, and blazing gold borders.

"That's quite a ship." I glanced at Jax again, but he remained facing forward. He hadn't once looked at me since Alec had begun telling me of the Houses.

Alec nodded in agreement. "The royal family often travels by sea when venturing to Faewood, so of course, they like to travel in style. They also travel around the northern coast, through the Brashier Sea, when going to Mistvale, so it needs to be a strong ship to survive the northern ocean." Alec shrugged. "Since it's easier to pass distance over water versus land, ships often make for a faster journey to the various kingdoms even though brommel stag shifters can travel faster than a boat." He waggled his eyebrows. "But alas, it's considered of poor taste for the royal family to present to another kingdom in their animal form. The king's demanded we all travel by ship, enchanted carpet, or carriage when doing so in a royal capacity."

My stomach clenched when I pictured Jax and his friends running as stags throughout the kingdoms when they did their raids. I couldn't help but wonder what the king would do if he knew his son spent a considerable amount of time in his animal form while in the other kingdoms.

I glanced at Jax again. I'd never seen him in his shifted form even though I'd seen everyone else in their animal shapes. I couldn't help but wonder how large he would be and what color his stag fur was. Black, was my best guess, but I didn't know for certain.

We reached the ship only minutes later, gliding down at a steep angle, the enchantment holding us in place like phantom steel bands. The carpet stopped just above the ship's deck, hovering a finger's length above it.

A sharp, cold wind from the north billowed the sails, and I finally stepped off the carpet and stood on the ship. The others did the same, and then the carpet lifted and cruised away, flying high in the sky on its way back to the palace.

"Your Highness." One of the crew members rushed forward, dressed in attire similar to what the staff wore at the palace. He held out a tray of flutes filled with champagne.

Jax offered the servant a polite nod, then took one of the flutes. Once Jax was served, the crew member brought the tray to everyone else.

I took one as well, and the second I took a sip, cool liquid flooded my mouth. My nose scrunched up as the fizzy bubbles made me want to sneeze.

Alec grinned as he watched me, then drank from his glass too.

I eyed the prince again, wondering anew if he would remain this distant throughout the entire trip to Faewood, but before I could ask Alec if this was Jax's normal behavior when he was in his princely role, a male's shout cut through the wind from across the deck.

"Your Highness!" On the other side of the ship, a male sauntered toward us. Given his opulent uniform, I assumed he was the captain.

The captain sashayed toward Jax and then clasped the prince's forearm, shaking it in a formal greeting before bowing. "It's a true pleasure to have you on board, my prince."

"Thank you, Captain Mezzerack," Jax replied, his tone crisp.

Other fae, not crew, moved in around us from across the deck, and with a start, I realized there were many other noble siltenites also on board.

I did a quick count as I took another sip of champagne. There were around twenty other siltenites present. And given that all of them were dressed in gowns and fine apparel, I knew they were either members of the ten Houses or nobility of high standing.

A quick survey of their clothing soon revealed they were House members. On the sleeves of the oldest fae males were crests signifying which Houses they belonged too. The same crests hung from pendants around the females' necks.

My heartbeat picked up. Every single fairy on this ship was of noble standing. Every single one except me.

I counted three Houses from Stonewild, yet I didn't know their House names or what magic they possessed. But of the group, there was an older male and an older female. Four younger females also accompanied them, who I could only presume were their daughters or nieces. The second group held an old male and six young females—another father and his daughters or nieces, I was guessing—and the last was an older female with five younger females.

Frowning, I assessed them more. The ship was literally crawling with young females. None of them appeared old, and all of them were gazing at Jax with stars in their eyes. And it hit me very suddenly who they likely were.

"Are all of these females potential betroths for the prince?" I whispered to Alec.

He inclined his head as the captain continued

speaking boisterously to Jax. "Indeed they are. How did you know that?"

I made a noncommittal noise. "Just a guess. Saramel told me he's to be wed next summer."

"Unfortunately." Alec shrugged. "The prince isn't keen on the idea, but royal protocol and all can't be ignored. And seeing a third of the potential betroths are all right here, I have a feeling the queen arranged this. She's been trying for months to get his courtships going, and she likely knew the prince wouldn't be able to avoid the females she and the king have chosen on a ship."

I smiled, but it was strained. "How . . . resourceful of her."

"Indeed. The queen can be quite single-minded when she decides she wants something."

I took another sip of champagne, not wanting to delve much thought into what the queen had in store for her son.

The captain took a step back from Jax and waved toward the sails. "Now that everyone's on board, we shall make haste to Faewood Kingdom." He turned his attention to the other siltenites. "I do hope you enjoy the journey."

The nobles raised their glasses, some murmuring pleasantries while the females continued giving Jax moon eyes.

Jax merely smiled tightly and took another sip of champagne.

The captain barked several orders at the crew, and within minutes, the anchor was lifted, the sails were billowing, magic shimmered in the air, and the ship headed toward the sea.

A fairy with an air element stood at the stern of the ship. He whipped his hands through the air, and a huge gust of wind abruptly propelled the ship faster forward.

I cast the prince another glance, but several of the females from the Houses had encircled him. They peppered him with questions about what he hoped to see at the Matches.

Jax's jaw remained tight, but he spoke with all of them, answering politely, and even laughed a few times.

A pang cut through my stomach so sharply that for a moment, I couldn't breathe.

Turning away, I discarded my champagne glass to a nearby servant, then placed my hands on the ship's railing. I watched as Stonewild grew smaller the farther we sped out to sea, and I wondered if I would ever consider that land my home.

Since Jax planned to keep me forever, thanks to my uncovering their identities, that meant I would inevitably be returning to Stonewild's capital.

Perhaps I would inhabit the enchanted chambers for the rest of my days. Or maybe Jax would move me somewhere else in the palace, in which I could move more freely from my chambers. All in all, I had no idea what the coming summers would bring, but I knew my fate lay along this northern coast.

Because whatever was ultimately decided, Jaggedston was where I lived now, which meant that come next summer, I would have to watch when Jax wed another.

My fingers curled around the railing so tightly my knuckles turned white. I closed my eyes and took a deep breath. I needed to remember why I was here. I'd wanted to help Jax. I'd *requested* this.

Which meant that I needed to stop these strange reactions that Jax elicited in me and force myself not to care when he laughed or touched other females.

I needed to accept my fate for what it was—I was to be owned by him, and he was to marry another.

CHAPTER 9

The ship's bow sliced through the waves of the Adriastic Sea as we headed out to the open ocean. Churning sprays of seafoam burst across the bow of the ship, raining everyone nearby in a salty mist. The captain led the prince away from us, gesturing to the sails and mystical engravings carved into most of the ship's surfaces, protection magic from the sounds of it, as he strutted about the deck.

From what I could hear, the captain had requested the prince accompany him on a tour now that we were underway, and honestly, I couldn't fault the captain for bragging. The ship was clearly one of the newer vessels in the royal fleet. It cut through the water like a knife, and every surface of its deck and masts looked shiny and new.

Most of the House females trailed along behind the prince and captain, hanging onto every word that Jax said. Phillen and Lars followed too, but Trivan was nowhere to be seen. However, after doing another count of the retreating siltenites, I quickly realized two of the younger House females were also missing, and I figured those two hadn't set their sights on the prince after all.

"How long will this journey take?" I asked Alec as Jax and the captain strolled across the deck, farther down the portside.

Alec leaned his elbows on the railing and shrugged. "Two days, give or take a few hours."

I raised my eyebrows. "That's fast."

"It certainly is, Gorgeous."

My eyebrows rose even higher. "*Gorgeous?*"

His lips curved in a teasing smile. "It's a good nickname, don't you think? Perhaps that's what we should call you."

"I thought"—I lowered my voice so nobody could hear —"Newole would be more fitting. It's what Phillen called me once." I thought back to when the burly guard had first said it in Fosterton. At that time, it'd confused me since I had no idea how their nicknames were formed or why he would call me that.

Alec sighed. "Ah, that would be par for the course, but that's so absurdly boring."

I laughed, then shivered when a gust of cold wind hit me. I wished I'd worn warmer clothing. Now that we were truly out at sea, the breeze was biting.

"You're freezing." Alec clucked his tongue. "How

remiss of me." He pulled his cloak off and draped it over my shoulders.

Warmth flooded me, and in the same beat, Jax's head snapped in our direction from farther down the ship.

"My prince?" one of the young females called to Jax, her voice carrying on the wind. "Isn't it fascinating that only twelve crew members are needed to run this entire ship? And to think their fairy with an air element is able to propel the ship if the breeze isn't sufficing. It's just incredible, don't you think?" She continued gushing and placed a hand on his forearm.

Jax's lips curved in a gracious smile. "Indeed, Lady Aerobelle."

I cleared my throat and pulled Alec's cloak tighter around me. "Does, uh, the prince like ship tours?"

Alec laughed lightly. "Doubtful. He's only doing it to appease the captain. Captain Mezzerack loves the attention the prince always gives him, and he'll bend over backward for our heir. It can be quite amusing to watch. Of course, obedience is required of a captain on a royal ship when anyone in the royal family demands it, but Captain Mezzerack moves even faster to fulfill the prince's wishes. Faster even than for the king."

Jax and the captain moved toward the stern, and the females eagerly followed. I tried not to watch and instead pulled the cloak tighter to fend off the salty sprays propelling us away from the shore. Already, the coast was barely visible.

In the back of the ship, Jax continued to stroll easily behind the captain, his legs dipping and swaying to accommodate the rolling vessel. The females moved just as easily, and I was reminded of how physically agile shifters were.

"Are most of the royal Houses in Stonewild stag shifters?" I asked Alec.

"Most, but not all." He waved toward the female Jax had spoken with earlier, the one he called Aerobelle. "Lady Aerobelle of House Dallinger is a wolf shifter, as are the rest in her House. Another of the ten Houses are colantha shifters, and one is a cave bear, and then there's the dragon House, but the rest are all stags." Straightening, he brushed a lock of windswept hair from my face. "You truly are beautiful, do you know that, Gorgeous? Out here, with the sun on your face, your beauty is captivating. I can't remember the last time a female enthralled me quite like you have."

I started at his abrupt change of subject but just shrugged. "It's my lorafin magic, my lordling. That's what's captivated you. Nothing more. The way you're reacting to me is why my guardian was able to sell me for such a high price."

He waggled his eyebrows. "You would be worth every rulib."

I sighed but couldn't help a light laugh. "And once

again, you're a shameless flirt. You could kill a fairy with how charming you are."

His grin returned. "Some consider it my greatest attribute."

"Is that so? I have a feeling all of the females with broken hearts that you've left in your wake wouldn't agree."

"Who said their hearts are broken? They may be very intact."

I snorted in amusement. "Which would be even worse as that implies you've given them false hope and are still leading them on."

"Ouch." He brought a hand to his chest. "Do you always call fae out like this?"

I shrugged and batted my eyelashes. "Just playing along, my lordling."

His eyes flickered with mischief. "What I would give to take you in my arms right now." He made a show of stepping closer and pretending to embrace me.

Laughing, I slapped him away.

A loud chuckle reverberated through him, and he dropped his hands. I was about to comment further, but the energy from the back of the vessel soared.

I swirled around, my thoughts racing that something had gone wrong with the ship, but I surveyed the deck, and nothing seemed amiss. But my sweep of the pristine boards and tall mast had me realizing that quite a few crew members and fae from the noble Houses were watching Alec and me. Some cast us knowing smiles, others pressed their lips together before returning their attention to the sea, but that powerful energy I'd initially detected still strummed from the stern even though the ship sailed just fine.

Craning my head, I searched for where the energy came from.

But only Jax and the captain stood in the back. Jax's midnight hair ruffled in the wind as they slowly made their way along the starboard side. Jax walked stiffly and glanced everywhere the captain waved, but surges of palpable energy rose from him.

With a start, I realized the energy was coming from *Jax*.

The females continued to trail behind them, but they'd put more distance between themselves and the prince, some even wincing when his potent magic hit them. Phillen and Lars were no exception. They stayed stoic, following as well, but even though both guards rested their hands casually on their sheathed swords, every time Jax's aura crashed into them, their jaws ground together.

The captain, however, merely grimaced and continued his tour, even when Jax's aura rose like the growing ocean swells, cresting right over him.

With a tight smile, Captain Mezzerack waved at the mast. "And have you noticed the threading in the sails, my prince? We used steel woven fibers that can hold a thousand stone per inch. Even our air elemental fairy's power cannot snap those threads."

"How interesting." The prince dipped his head. "Tell me, how fast has this vessel been clocked?"

The captain beamed. "At full throttle, she travels at fifty-two *barimums*."

The prince raised his eyebrows. "That's fast."

"Indeed, the fastest in the royal fleet."

Frowning, I gazed up at Alec. "What's going on with the prince? He's been acting aloof all morning, and now he's having power surges. And if I didn't know better, I would say that he doesn't even like you from how he's been behaving, yet you're supposed to be good friends, right?"

Alec grinned, his smile growing broader with every second that passed. "Why, it's quite simple, Elowen. He's jealous."

My head snapped back. "Jealous? Of what?"

"You and me."

My eyes felt as though they popped out of my skull. "You and me? What in the realm are you talking about?"

Alec leaned his forearms on the railing, still grinning. "I didn't believe it when the others told me that they thought the prince had fallen for you, so I decided to find out for myself, and alas, how right they are."

I could only stare at him. My stomach was doing strange flips over and over, making it impossible to speak.

Alec continued, seeming to take my silence as encouragement to embellish his theory. "I knew the best way to find out if what they were claiming was true was to flirt mercilessly with you. And while the prince knows that I am indeed a shameless flirt, I've gone a bit over the top with you. But if he'd actually developed feelings for you, I knew he would react. And if he hadn't—" He shrugged. "Then he wouldn't care, but lo and behold, the boys were all right. The prince looks on the verge of losing his mind, which means, I fear our prince is smitten with you, Elowen."

My flipping stomach didn't stop, but I somehow managed to get out, "So . . . you're *not* usually this flirtatious?"

He laughed. "I'm definitely a flirt, but no, I'm normally not quite this bad."

"And the prince typically doesn't look at you with murder in his gaze?"

"No, actually, this is a first for us, and dare I say, once he admits to how he feels for you, I'll likely have to come clean and apologize about my dastardly behavior to make him jealous."

"But, he, I mean, he's going to . . ." I gestured to the females trailing behind him. "He's to marry one of them. How could he have feelings for me?"

"Hmm, indeed. 'Tis most unfortunate, but he's only to marry because his parents are demanding it. Royal protocol requires him to marry a female of royal birth or noble standing, but that doesn't mean he can't *enjoy you* until then." He waggled his eyebrows suggestively.

"Enjoy me. Until then." My mouth opened and closed like a fish, and my cheeks heated. I slapped him on the chest, my ire rising, but Alec merely rubbed where I'd hit him, and his grin grew. "You're saying I should be his mistress?"

He laughed and slipped an arm around my waist, then leaned closer to my ear to whisper, "If you would like, I have a feeling he wouldn't object." He pulled back and straightened his lapels. "Anyway, on that note, as much as I hate to leave you, I best go below. I have to meet with Trivan to discuss a few things to come." He winked. "Come find me if you get bored. We can continue driving the prince crazy if you're so inclined."

Before I could say anything further, he strolled away, his walk easy despite the rolling vessel. At the back of the ship, Jax watched his friend retreat with narrowed eyes.

Swirling away so I couldn't see either of them, I tried to calm my breathing. Alone with only the sea before me, I leaned against the ship's railing and gazed at the turbulent water. Still reeling, I tried to understand the full meaning of what Alec was claiming.

Jax has feelings for me? Yet he was to marry another.

I darted a glance toward the back again. Jax's energy was still palpable, surging toward me regularly, but I did my best to ignore it. It was quickly becoming apparent that our journey back to Faewood was going to be entirely different from our travel to Stonewild. Jax was no longer traveling as the Dark Raider. His more relaxed demeanor was gone. On this trip, he was every inch the royal, and according to Alec, he had feelings for me. *Me!*

I nibbled on my lip just as a spray of salty seawater misted across my face. That strange flipping motion returned in my stomach, and I couldn't tell if it was from the beginnings of seasickness or the mind-blowing claim Alec had just dropped on me.

I gazed down at the water and could have sworn a face stared up at me, but the Lochen fairy was there and then gone so quickly that I wasn't sure if I'd imagined it. But it was common knowledge that the Lochen fae trailed ships just to ensure the land-dwellers meant them no harm.

"Stars Above," I whispered to myself.

Another spray misted over my face when the ship plunged down a wave's trough. Using the feeling to distract me and stop my turbulent thoughts, I closed my eyes. The ship rose and fell beneath me like an undulating carpet, and refreshing splashes of ocean water settled over me like a fine veil. I was still cold, but at least Alec had left his cloak with me, so I let myself enjoy the moment, getting lost in the rhythmic feel. If nothing else, it helped to distract me from Alec's ridiculous claim.

"Have you traveled much by sea?" Jax's quiet question had my eyes snapping open.

The crown prince stood right beside me, somehow having masked his aura on his approach. He leaned against the railing only a foot to my right, and for once, his energy had calmed.

Behind him, Lars and Phillen stood a respectful distance away, but the captain was long gone, and the following females were back with their families, although more than a few watched us from afar.

Apparently, the tour was over, which left me relatively alone with a prince who Alec claimed had feelings for me.

I straightened and wondered how long I'd been standing idly while he'd observed me. "Um, no, my prince. Actually, this is my first time. I've never been on a ship before." I avoided the urge to fidget, but Alec's words kept pounding through my head.

Jax's attention swept over my face, his eyes hooded. "Ever?" He arched an eyebrow, then cast a look at Alec's cloak slung around me. I could have sworn his jaw tightened.

I shrugged. "Performing a calling at sea would prove difficult, and since my entire existence and reason for traveling was to perform callings for my guardian, our travels always remained on land, so no, I've never been on a ship."

His eyes darkened. "Of course."

I shifted my attention away from the hypnotizing

waves and cocked my head. "Alec said he had to speak with Trivan about what's to come. Is something specific going to happen?" I glanced around, but other than the fawning House females standing on the other side of the deck, watching our every move, nobody was paying us any attention. And from the distance the females stood, I doubted they'd overheard me. Besides, I was desperate to keep our conversation away from what Alec had just dropped on me. A mistress. *Me.* And to Jax nonetheless.

Despite our relative privacy, a shimmer of magic abruptly fell around us. The ocean spray misting across my face stopped, and the rolling waves grew silent. My fingers automatically reached out, but I encountered a solid wall of air.

"If we're to have this conversation here, it's probably best to keep it private." Jax's tone and demeanor didn't change, and it hit me that he'd just cast a silencing Shield around us to stop anyone from overhearing our conversation. Yet he'd done it while keeping the same expression and posture. It would appear to others as though nothing had changed.

Stars and galaxy, the absolute power of this male . . .

Despite knowing the precaution was necessary, I couldn't stop from saying, "You're quite good at leading a double life, aren't you?" *And does that double life also include harboring feelings for me you're too hesitant to voice?* Of course, I kept that question to myself.

He shrugged. "I've had some practice."

My stomach coiled, and I was reminded of the many masks he wore.

"But to answer your earlier question, Trivan and Alec are planning out which Finals we should watch, to maximize our time searching for Bastian while making it appear as though we're only there for fun. In case anyone asks what our plans are, we'll have a believable agenda outlined."

My brow furrowed, and it struck me that it was smart to keep his plans so close to the truth. It was harder for one to get caught up in lies if the truth and lie were near the same. "And at the council meeting this morning, was my presence in the palace brought up at all?"

He dipped his head. "It was, by one councilor."

Heart thumping, I gripped the railing again. "And how did you explain my presence to them?"

"Similar to what I told you. I told her that I met you during my recent hunt in Fosterton, and that I invited you back to the palace with me."

"Hunt?"

"It's an excuse I often use when I disappear for days, weeks, and on occasion, months at a time. Didn't you know? The boys and I are all avid hunters, and of course, my guards always have to accompany me. We often disappear in the kingdoms to hunt game, and it can be quite dangerous." His smile turned devious. "Hunting has been our favorite hobby for many full seasons."

"Hunting is how you explain your time away when you're conducting raids?" My eyebrows shot up. "And nobody's ever questioned that? But you don't return with any wild game, do you?"

"On the contrary, we always return with several kills."

My jaw dropped. "But . . . you didn't hunt anything while I was with you."

"No, *I* didn't, but Alec and Quinn conducted an actual hunt while we were *visiting* with you. They had a dozen fimiquails for us to share with the chef when we made our official appearance last week."

"Quinn? Who's he?"

"You haven't met him yet."

"Oh . . . I forgot there's still one more in your group, but *fimiquails*? Where in the realm did they get fimi-quails?" The elusive and exotic bird was considered a deli-cacy and very hard to find. The birds were similar to dillemsills in that they could disappear. Frowning, I ran my finger along my collar, and a wash of its magic pulsed through me despite its repressed state.

Jax cocked an eyebrow. "Quinn harbors Mistvale magic in addition to shifter power. His magic is particu-larly helpful when hunting elusive animals." The prince's gaze dropped and lingered on my collar. "Is it bothering you?"

I started, taking a second to understand the abrupt subject change. "Are you referring to my collar?"

A pulse of energy swirled around him. "I've noticed you've been tugging at it."

"No, it's not bothering me. It's just a nervous habit."

"You're nervous?"

"No, I mean . . . it's just a habit."

His eyes glittered, their endless depths threatening to pull me in despite my better judgment telling me to tread with caution around this contradictory male, but before I could say anything further, a bell rang on the ship.

"Fine fae of Stonewild Kingdom, lunch is being served below," a crew member called and then bowed toward the prince. "Please join Prince Adarian for a relaxing afternoon and evening as we venture south to the exciting Match Finals."

CHAPTER 10

I followed the prince below, and it quickly became apparent that the midafternoon meal was a grand production. It was held in the ship's impressive dining hall. Sconces lit the walls, Stonewild banners hung from the ceiling, vases of freshly cut flowers perfumed the air, and large windows allowed one a clear view of the sea.

When Jax escorted me into the hall, the ship rocked gently beneath our feet. A large table sat in the center of the room, thirty chairs around it. Elegant candles lit the table's center, magic suspending them to hover midair so they were never knocked over when the ship rolled.

Most on board were already present, and Alec and Trivan were in a lively discussion with those who had beaten us down here. One thing I noticed immediately—everyone was dressed regally. All except me.

Around the table, each House family wore their

House crest somewhere on their clothing. On the males it was either on their sleeves, across a silk sash, or on the tassel of their shoulders. Wherever it might be, the crest was there if one only looked. The females were no different. All of them wore jewelry, mostly pendants with their crests proudly displayed in a gem's center, but their crests were also visible on their rings.

These were the elite fae of Stonewild. House nobles nonetheless, and I was a slave dressed in black breeches and a simple crimson top.

My footsteps slowed, and a wash of embarrassment flowed through me when several turned to assess me, but Jax clasped my hand and threaded his fingers through mine. "You belong here just as much as any of them do," he said so quietly that I knew only I heard him.

He squeezed me, and given his comment, it was as if he'd known exactly what I was thinking. His knack to always be so in-tune to those around him once again astonished me.

Taking a deep breath, I continued walking at his side and did my best to hold my chin high, but the feel of him holding my hand, for everyone to see, had Alec's words pounding through my head again.

I fear our prince is smitten with you.

Aerobelle Dallinger's attention snapped to Jax and me the second we reached the table. A wolf's head was ringed in gold metal on her pendant, the small token proudly displayed between her breasts.

She beamed, all eyes for Jax, as though I wasn't even there. "Prince Adarian, we've all been eagerly awaiting you."

The other females perked up too, but smiles began to falter when they realized, one by one, that Jax was still holding my hand. Aerobelle at last seemed to realize the same. Her previous snub of me turned to a haughty glare.

Despite that, everyone made a show of welcoming their prince, calling out boisterously, letting me know the leminai and wine were already flowing.

"Prince Adarian!" one of the fathers called. He gave me a curious side-eye, but nobody asked my name or paid further attention to me. "I've been eager to hear your thoughts on the Osterland Exchange, recently solidified between Faewood and Mistvale."

"Ah, yes, that was an interesting agreement." Jax inclined his head. "It seems the mines between the two kingdoms are now sharing diagonal tunnels beneath the borders, something never done before, but first I would like everyone introduced to my guest, Lady Elowen." Jax gestured toward me, his eyes sparkling in cerulean shades in the fairy lights. "Elowen will be joining me to watch the Finals in her kingdom."

"Is that so?" Lady Aerobelle's nostrils flared delicately. "How kind of you to show a commoner such grace. Was she awarded a grant by the palace? To attend at your side? I've heard our dear Queen Rashelle has been organizing more charity events and grants for those beneath us."

My jaw tightened, and it took everything in me not to scowl at her.

A few strained smiles followed Aerobelle's stinging comments, but more than one murmured their agreement of the queen's generosity.

But Jax's gaze turned icy. "No, Lady Aerobelle, Elowen is not here on a grant. I personally requested that she join me."

The female's eyes flashed wide, her cheeks turning rosy, but everyone else dipped their chins at last in my direction and finally muttered a greeting.

But it was obvious they only did so because of the prince. If he hadn't been at my side, none of them would have even looked at me.

Another female called out, one from the cave bear family, "Is Queen Rashelle aware that your guest has joined us?" Her tone was one decibel short of biting.

Jax gave her a devastating smile, but when he replied, his voice dripped with venom. "She isn't, Lady Penepee. Believe it or not, I'm a grown male who doesn't run to his mother to ask permission of everything."

A few of the House fae laughed, but Aerobelle's and Penepee's gazes turned glacial when they assessed me again.

I stiffened, but focused my attention away.

"Please everyone, have a seat," a servant called from the corner. "Lunch is about to be served."

House crests flashed in the lights as everyone began to sit around the massive table. One House had a snarling jungle cat—a colantha—on their crest, the other a massive bear. And House Dallinger all wore their wolves.

I paused, not moving since I had no idea where I should sit—if anywhere—since I wasn't of noble blood, but Jax propelled me to the front of the table and pulled out a chair at the head of it. Two chairs sat side by side, facing everyone.

"Lady Elowen," he said softly. "I would be honored to seat you at my side."

My chest warmed even though Aerobelle leaned closer to Penepee and whispered something in her ear. Both snapped their napkins over their laps, their auras rising.

I quickly took my seat, but a flash of my temper simmered within me when even more of the House females began to glance at me with either angry or speculative looks. It was as though they were truly beginning to realize that the prince either had taken me as a mistress or planned to.

Even though Jax and I were far from anything like that, magic crackled inside me. I might have been born of commoners, but one thing was becoming entirely apparent to me. I had better manners than most of the fae here. And I wasn't about to let them humiliate me.

Taking a deep breath, I called upon my seasons of lessons under my tutors and the playacting I'd done over the summers. This certainly wasn't the first time I'd been in the presence of arrogant nobility, and I wasn't going to let them run me off.

"Thank you, my prince," I said softly to Jax.

He sat beside me, giving me a side-eye and an encouraging smile when my back straightened and my chin lifted.

But when he shifted, and his thigh brushed against mine in the process, a genuine flush of heat washed over me.

Two servants rushed forward from where they stood by the wall and held out decanters for the prince to choose from.

"The Ironcrest wine," Jax told them.

They bowed and quickly fled to grab more bottles.

"They announced before you arrived what the main course will be, my prince," an older female called from the cave bear House. "Sea lobster, which is one of your favorites, is it not?"

Jax dipped his head. "Indeed, it is."

"And did you know that my daughter, Lucille, is a master in the kitchen?" The older female beamed at a willowy blond female, who gave the prince a sultry smile. "Why, I bet Lucille would love to cook for you one night.

You wouldn't regret it after you've tasted her creations, and she's a master at preparing sea lobster."

Lucille's lips flashed scarlet in the lights when she nibbled on her lower lip. "Any time you would like it, my prince, I would be happy to serve you."

My fingers tightened in my lap at her blatant come-on, but beneath the table, Jax's hand settled on my thigh. I nearly jumped when the heavy weight and warmth of him touched me. But just as quickly, he removed his hand.

"I'm sure our chefs could be tasked with something such as that. No need to exert yourself," he answered easily.

Lucille's eyes widened, but it was her only reaction to his slight.

Across the table, Alec caught my eye and winked. I wouldn't have been surprised if he next mouthed, *I told you so.*

Flustered, I hastily spread my napkin over my lap.

Wine began being poured by the servants, everyone's goblets getting filled, and I used the distraction to study the nobles present even more.

Since the families on board this ship weren't of stag origins, I couldn't help but wonder if the queen was favoring those Houses for her son's wedding. It wouldn't surprise me, since it was rumored that mixing powerful shifter blood could result in stronger offspring. Or perhaps they felt that mixing shifter Houses would form better alliances among the nobility.

Whatever the case, similar to most of the females, the males had also donned their House rings on the third finger of their right hand. The aqua gems were the same cut and color for each house since they were all Stonewild fae, but the animal prints upon them reflected their unique shifter magic.

"Elowen, was it?" Lady Aerobelle called from farther down the table.

I glanced her way, just as Jax corrected, "Lady Elowen." He reached for his wine glass and gave her a pointed look.

Her lips pursed, and she regarded me with a barely concealed sneer. "Is she truly a lady if she's not of noble birth?"

"She's a lorafin," Jax replied easily, his tone deceptively calm given the flickering in his aura. "She's more powerful than any female here, and if that doesn't demand respect, I don't know what does."

"You're a lorafin?" Aerobelle looked down her nose at me. "I didn't know any existed."

"Well, now you do," I replied and reached for my wine. My gaze didn't drop as she stared at me.

"So *that's* why the prince has you here." Her look turned smug. "You must be very useful to him."

Her subtle hint that the prince was merely using me

smacked me in the face, but before I could bite back with a sharp retort, the same older male who'd spoken with Jax when we first entered the room cleared his throat.

"Now, tell me, my prince, what else do you know of the Osterland Exchange?" He leaned forward, obviously eager to speak of it more with the prince.

Plates began getting filled as Jax was pulled into a discussion with the older male.

Several of the others began talking about the Ironcrest Ball, set to take place after the Matches. Like the Centennial Matches, the ball only occurred every hundred summers, and most on the continent were looking forward to it.

While I was curious to hear about previous Ironcrest Balls held throughout the centuries, I paid more attention to Jax's conversation. I was tempted to tell both of them that the Osterland Exchange had resulted because of *me*. Lordlings Himil and Messepire had only signed the document because of the king's promise to use his lorafin, but I didn't bother declaring that.

Boasting of such a thing would only make me look desperate for approval or would be proof that Jax was only keeping me at his side because I was *useful*.

Instead, I began to eat and sip my wine between bites.

Everyone else dug in too, and my gaze darted to Alec. He'd changed for the meal into a navy coat with an emerald sash. A ring graced his finger as well, showing a rack of antlers stretching across the gemstone. So he *was* a stag shifter.

"What a delightful trip it's been so far," Alec called jovially when a lull happened in the conversation. "And, Lady Elowen, it's truly lovely that you could join us. I'm sure your knowledge of Faewood will be needed while we attend the Matches."

Jax's nostrils flared in his direction, but I inclined my head at Alec. "I would be more than happy to show you around my home kingdom and share what I know."

I took another sip of wine, but my pulse thrummed more in my neck. Jax's aura had kicked up again, even more so when Alec gave me a sultry smirk, and I truly realized that Alec was right—the prince was not happy about his friend's flirtations.

"And do you think a similar exchange could take place between the other kingdoms?" the older male asked Jax again, apparently determined to keep his conversation going with the prince about the Osterland Exchange. "Perhaps between Stonewild and Faewood? Or Ironcrest and Mistvale? The waterfalls in Ironcrest harbor so much magic. Imagine if a river was diverted to allow such magic to be used in the other kingdoms. The possibilities would be endless."

The conversation carried on, and Jax sat stiffly. He ate bites as he was able to, but most of the time he was answering questions of those around him or thwarting off more flirtatious comments. And he kept getting roped into conversation with the older male who was so fascinated with the kingdoms sharing goods that he practically dominated Jax's attention.

It wasn't lost on me that Jax's sea lobster remained barely eaten.

But even though this was the midday meal, everyone seemed more interested in littering the prince with questions and vying for his attention than enjoying the succulent food.

Everyone also peppered Jax with questions about his expected nuptials next summer, as well as his plans for the upcoming Matches. And one of the females boldly asked if he'd chosen his date yet for the upcoming Ironcrest Ball.

"No, I haven't," was all the prince replied to that intrusive question.

Yet several of the females seemed to take that as affirmation that I *wasn't* a true threat.

I could be his mistress, but not his date for the Ironcrest Ball. And certainly not his wife.

Yet from the occasional verbal daggers that were thrown my way, I knew that many of the females in this room wouldn't allow me to be a mistress to the prince in any capacity, not when she became his wife at least.

It was humiliating, in a way, but I kept my posture up and made myself hold my chin high.

I ate slowly and quietly as Jax took each House in

stride, dividing his attention between them and somehow managing to pacify each.

Throughout it all, it struck me again what was expected of him. Jax was the crown prince of Stonewild. He not only had a name to uphold, but he also had to ensure power stayed balanced in his kingdom. Each House wanted to be the biggest, strongest, and wealthiest, but all of them were needed to keep our society running smoothly.

Since the noble Houses owned most of the land, businesses, and farms throughout the kingdoms, squabbles among the Houses were common, and it typically fell on the throne to listen to disputes and ultimately act as the judge. And watching Jax now, I realized how much rested on his shoulders. He listened patiently to each House as they shared their woes and successes, his demeanor formal. But with how stiff his body position was, I wondered if these conversations took a toll on him.

Because the only time I'd seen Jax alive and looking free had been when he was acting as the Dark Raider.

I cocked my head as a horrid thought struck me. Perhaps I wasn't the only one who'd been living in a cage. Because from what I was seeing, Jax was also leashed even if his chain was dipped in gold and studded with jewels.

He caught my eye just as dessert was being served, and for the briefest moment, his mask dropped. He smiled slightly, his eyes softening, and it struck me that none of these nobles knew that the eyes of the Dark Raider were peering back at them. Especially not when they revealed where their latest shipments were coming from or what the other Houses were reporting about goods arriving via the sea.

Each detail they shared gave Jax more information on where to conduct his next raid from those who'd taken more than they should or deceived the less fortunate in the process. Stonewild fae weren't immune from his raids. Jax exacted his revenge in all of the kingdoms.

It took everything in me to keep my expression neutral when all of the Houses, tripping over themselves to win favor with their prince, spewed that information to him so easily. They had no idea that it was *he* who was stealing everything out from under them if he deemed their House unworthy.

And it also made me realize what a dangerous game Jax was playing. If it was ever discovered that he was the Dark Raider, I knew to the deepest part of my soul that not even his royal name would save him.

CHAPTER 11

We sailed into port after two days at sea, and the energy from my kingdom could be felt even on the open water.

A buzzing sense of excitement filled the air, wafting out to greet us the closer we got to land. The Centennial Matches were only held every hundred summers, and some fae had been training for them just as long.

Others were hoping to qualify based upon their intrinsic magic, and some tried out simply so they could boast that they had. But only those truly skilled in magic, combat, and athletic performance were allowed to compete. And while each winner of every competition was awarded medals and rulibs, it was every competitor's dream to win the overall competition and be declared the supreme winner of the Centennial Matches. Doing so would ultimately result in receiving a noble title, a large parcel of land, and more rulibs than most fae could ever dream of.

As the royal ship drifted to shore, the wind whipped around us. On the deck beside me, Jax stood in his usual princely attire, and Alec and Trivan were dressed just as finely. Even his guards, Phillen and Lars, looked dashing.

I was similarly dressed, and a silky gown billowed around my legs as the sea air whistled through the masts. Jax had brought the dress to my chambers this morning, an apology in his eyes before he asked me to wear it.

But since I was traveling with the royal party, I wasn't surprised by the request. I was now expected to dress the part, just as he had to.

"But I won't force you," Jax had added gently when he showed me the gown. "However, such formality is usually expected when meeting with the king."

I'd taken the dress, letting the forest-green silky material slip through my fingers. Part of Jax's royal duties included seeing King Paevin today, and if I wanted to join them, wearing anything less grand would be considered exceptionally rude.

"Of course, I'll wear it. I would have expected nothing less." The gown had thin shoulder straps and minimal bulk in the skirts. It wouldn't be too hot and would be easy enough to move in. Somehow, Jax had chosen the perfect gown for me. It was regal yet comfortable and was nothing like the gowns my guardian had chosen. "Where did you get it?"

He'd raked a hand through his hair and, if I hadn't known better, looked slightly unsure. "I had it sewn for you in Jaggedston, just the other day when you learned I was the prince. I knew I wouldn't be able to free you, and I didn't know if you would choose to attend formal engagements with me or not, but I hoped that you would eventually, so I had it sewn just in case."

He hoped that I would?

Those words still rang through my ears as I watched my kingdom grow closer as the ship sailed toward port, and they reminded me of what Alec had claimed. The prince still hadn't said anything to me about these supposed feelings he harbored, and the impossibility of any future with him kept my lips sealed as well. Even if he did want me, I still wasn't sure how I felt about being his mistress.

My attention slid to the noble females standing on the deck. Most of them were also watching the approaching wharf. They'd grown less boisterous following the luncheon on our first day at sea but had been no less cruel.

Several times in the previous two days, I'd been cornered when I'd been alone. All of them had found a way to talk to me privately in one form or another. Some had asked incessant questions about the prince to learn what he liked or ways to entrance him. Others had dropped subtle passive-aggressive comments about how inept I was or found ways to remind me that I would never be anything but an enslaved lorafin.

Regardless, I couldn't wait to never see any of them again.

But despite whatever was growing between Jax and me, I also knew that ultimately, he would still have to wed one of them, and if not someone on this ship, then another.

My stomach tightened, so I hastily inhaled the salty air to distract myself. Clearing my throat, I tried to dispel the ridiculous course of lightning that sped through my veins every time I thought of Jax's future.

We finally reached the wharf, and the ship's crew threw long, thick ropes to the workers on the docks. Salty air whipped around us, and the nobles who accompanied us on the trip were already gushing over what they planned to see.

Jax gripped the side of the ship and scanned the crowd on shore. Fae had formed into small groups, watching us from below. It wasn't every day that a royal from another kingdom visited, and the ship's elegant sails shining with Stonewild's crest could be seen for miles from the coast.

A crew member bowed to Jax, then gestured toward two enchanted carpets that flew to us from land. "Your carpets shall be here momentarily, Your Highness."

The carpets reached the ship and lowered themselves to a comfortable height on the deck. Crew members took all of our luggage and began piling it onto the second, smaller carpet until everything was secured. I couldn't help but wonder if some of those trunks carried more dresses for me to wear during my time in Faewood Kingdom.

But unlike when Guardian Alleron demanded that I wear such finery, I didn't feel forced to with Jax. He'd said I had a choice, and some might think me stupid for believing him, but I knew his words had rung true.

Captain Mezzerack hurried forward once the crew finished the task. "Your Highness, your luggage is ready, so you may be off whenever you desire. And might I say that it was my honor to transport you to Faewood for this momentous occasion." The captain bowed, and the sunlight caught on the tips of his pointed ears.

Jax inclined his head. "Thank you for the safe passage. I'll be sure to mention to my father how accommodating you were."

The captain beamed. "You're too kind."

Jax stepped onto the awaiting carpet, Phillen and Lars following closely at his sides. Trivan hopped on next, followed by Alec.

When all of the males were on board, Alec leaned down and offered me his hand. "Elowen, may I do the honor of assisting you."

Since everyone was watching, I automatically fell into the role I'd been groomed to play my entire life. Smiling, I took his hand and made a show of stepping onto the carpet.

I felt, rather than saw, Jax watching. When I glanced at

the prince, his lips were pressed together, his gaze glued to where Alec and I held hands.

My throat grew dry, and I licked my lips.

The other noble Houses watched on, all of them waving and calling to their prince to enjoy the Matches. More than a few of the females stared at me enviously or spitefully. Throughout it all, Alec stayed close to my side, but I didn't mind. The ocean breeze was cool, my dress thin, and the large male sheltered me from any further scornful looks.

Jax eyed us briefly again, then turned stoically. The crown prince of Stonewild stood before me. Regal. Resolute. And entirely foreboding. His public mask had fallen into place again, and he whispered a command to the carpet.

The enchanted carpet lifted beneath us and glided over the ship's railing. We sailed effortlessly over the docks, and all of the spectators below cheered.

Jax waved to them, his lips curving in a stiff smile. The cheers grew. He kept up the act until we passed the spectators and began flying over the port's shops and homes, then he dropped his hand.

"How are the other nobles getting to the Matches?" I whispered to Alec.

He shrugged. "Probably a carpet or carriage, but that's not our concern now. We only have one purpose for this visit."

To find Bastian.

Jax's aura swelled, no doubt overhearing us, but his attention fixated on the distant Wood, growing closer with every second that passed. Rolling hills waited just behind it, and the vast distance to Leafton spread out before us.

Jax stood tall, his shoulders back. Tension radiated from him, and I had a feeling his entire focus was now pinpointed on finding his brother.

"It's best if everyone has a seat," he called over his shoulder.

We all sat down on the carpet, and the crown prince kneeled on his haunches, then whispered another command. The carpet took off, leaving the small seaside city behind us in a blur of speed. Despite the capital being over a hundred miles inland from the coast, from how fast we were traveling, we would be there within the hour.

Wind rushed over my cheeks, and the familiar sights and sounds of the Wood ahead made my heart soar.

When we reached the Wood, instead of the enchanted carpet dipping down to the Wood's road, Jax commanded it to stay aloft, and we grazed the tops of the trees.

My jaw dropped at seeing the Wood from this angle. Trees burst from the top of the Wood's canopy, and leaves of brilliant shades filled my view in an endless carpet of color. Wildlings peered up at us from the top branches, some of their eyes glowing when they beheld the prince at the carpet's edge.

"Are we going to stay this high up the entire way?" I asked.

Alec winked. "Enjoy traveling with a royal while you can, Elowen. It isn't often he pulls this kind of rank in a foreign kingdom."

Any joy I'd felt at flying so high diminished. Jax was trying to get to the Matches as quickly as possible and was doing so in a way that other fae weren't allowed to. Normally, one had to travel along the road, but as the crown prince, the rules didn't apply to him. Like King Paevin, he could travel where he wanted, when he wanted, as he wanted.

"Does he not normally travel like this?" I leaned closer to Alec since Jax seemed lost in thought as he stared straight ahead.

Alec shook his head. "He will if his father's with him, but believe it or not, Jax doesn't like to flaunt his royal status. We usually travel as others do. Granted, we have nicer carpets to choose from and usually the best domals, but our prince doesn't boast of his privilege. Not usually, at least." The tall fairy gave his friend a worried glance.

I hesitantly inched forward on the carpet until I sat closer to Jax. Before I considered what I was doing, I laid a hand on his arm.

The prince's entire body tensed, and he glanced my way. Blazing emotion shone in his eyes, like swirling stars circling in our magical galaxy.

"We'll find him, Jax. We won't rest until we do." Beneath my palm, his bicep felt warm and hard. A tingle shot up my arm.

"It's been over five *days* since you saw him in the Veiled Between, Elowen. Who's to say if he's even—"

I squeezed him. "I know, but we'll find him. We will."

The aura around the prince grew. He glanced at my hand again, and some of the lines around his eyes smoothed. For the first time since stepping onto the carpet, the tension radiating from him lessened. "Do you know anything else about where Bastian could be? Any details? Any specific location? Anything more than what you told me previously?"

I furrowed my brow as I thought back to what the semelees had shown me. "He was in a building, maybe a barn? The floor was dirt, and I remember seeing hay."

"A barn." He shook his head. "There have got to be dozens of those at the Matches."

"There are." I cocked my head, then my eyes widened. "Wait, I remember watching the wildlings a few weeks ago setting up the equipment. They were erecting a barn near the arena where one of the competitions will be held." I closed my eyes, picturing again what the semelees had revealed. My hope grew when another key detail came to me. I opened my eyes to find Jax watching me intently, his gaze focused on my mouth.

I released my lower lip, not realizing I'd been nibbling

it. "I think we should start with the barns directly around the Matches, specifically the newer ones. When they showed me Bastian, if I recall correctly, the wooden planks behind him looked freshly constructed."

A new lightness shone in the prince's eyes. For the first time that morning, a small smile curved his lips. "Then that's where we'll start."

THE PALACE CAME into view not long later. It was a dazzling display rising from the Wood as the pale-green sky shone clear and cloudless. Everyone's attention focused on the royal structure, but I couldn't help but look southward, toward Emerson Estate.

My former guardian's estate lay only a few miles from the palace. Its gray stone exterior, with blue and green vines crawling up the sides, was visible from this high up.

That's a cage I will never inhabit again.

But I couldn't help but think of Lillivel and wonder where she was. Without me to dote on and Guardian Alleron absent, I wondered if she even had a job any more. Perhaps she ended up like Mushil and had been fired. Whatever the case, seeing my former home made me realize that such a life was now far, far behind me.

Tears threatened to sting my eyes as I thought of the fae who'd been kind to me. I knew I'd likely never see them again, and not wanting to think about that, I shifted my attention to the palace.

Soaring peaks from the castle's turrets and spires grew larger the closer we flew to it. Smooth white stone walls covered its entire exterior. Banners in turquoise and white, bordered with dark-brown accents, hung from the windows.

The opulent white structure was so different from Stonewild palace's black monstrosity.

My stomach clenched when I remembered the last time I'd set eyes upon this place. It'd been the night of my abduction following the three callings I'd done for the king. That was the night Jax had come into my life.

I glanced at him, but his attention hadn't wavered from what lay ahead. As before, when I'd been watching the Matches being set up by the wildlings, the grounds were awash in activity, except now, all of the structures were built and only minor construction appeared to be underway.

A full-sized arena, with a sandy floor and tiered seating, waited just west of the palace. The last time I'd seen that, the wildlings had been devising ways to move the sand as Lillivel and I had observed them from afar.

A pang filled me when I thought again of my attendant, but the carpet abruptly headed east, toward a maze that had been cut into the Wood. The new sights helped to distract me once more. Solid walls, netting, and obstacles could be seen from above. But some of the maze was covered, rendering the inside entirely dark.

Other structures had also been built. The large lake, north of the castle, now had soaring platforms surrounding it. Hoops were suspended in the air over the water, held by magic, and within the lake, a few fins cut through its surface.

I shivered, thinking what creatures had been shipped in from the Adriastic Sea to fill those waters.

Forcing my attention away from the splendor and impressive structures, I began to search for barns.

Jax and his friends did the same. All of us shielded our eyes from the bright sun as the enchanted carpet sped toward the activity.

"There's one." I pointed southwest of the palace to a newly erected barn. Outside of it, corrals with simple fences held dozens of domals and other creatures from the Wood. A large roar abruptly cut through the morning sky.

"Stars Above. Do they have a *larpanoon* fenced in by the domals?" Alec gave a soft laugh. "Fools. If that thing gets loose, it'll eat all of the domals for breakfast, and then all of the nearby fae for lunch."

"Hopefully it won't be as bad as the last Centennial Matches." Trivan snickered. "One of those got loose and attacked several nobles from Ironcrest, nearly killed them and would have if one of them hadn't been so powerful. He took the creature's eyesight, allowing them a few moments to get away. If he hadn't, they would have all died."

I glanced at the huge larpanoon. It roamed in a lone pen near the domals, who all appeared skittish and continually whinnied.

The creature was generally only found in the northern Wood. It had powerful low hunches, tall withers, and long whiskers on its snout. Razor-sharp teeth hung from its gums. It generally inhabited caves in the rocky terrain of the Clawfur Mountain range in Mistvale. Occasionally, however, larpanoons would wander into northern villages and terrorize fae.

Larpanoons were some of the most feared creatures on our continent, and for good reason. Their teeth were not only sharp enough to cut through steel, but they were coated in a deadly venom, and their claws could rip through any magic. Even powerful fae with superior Shielding abilities, were no match for the fierce creatures.

"Smart move to remove its eyesight," I murmured, "although I dread to think what games the king has in store for any fae arrogant enough to battle one. What do you think they're going to do with it?" I angled my head toward the males.

Phillen shrugged. "That, Elowen, is what I'm wondering as well. I wouldn't mind sticking around to see what your king has planned for the poor fae who end up in the arena with that thing."

Trivan muttered a similar sentiment, and even Alec looked intrigued, but Jax didn't even glance toward the corrals. All of his focus had zeroed in on the barn.

From the intent way he was studying it, I couldn't help but wonder if he was trying to distinguish who the fae were walking around the outside perimeter. We were still too far away to see anyone clearly, but I didn't spot any half-breeds with antlers.

"Are we going straight to that barn?" I asked Jax.

He frowned, then sighed heavily. His hand cut through his dark hair in an irritated stab. "We can't. I have to make an appearance at the palace first to see the king. Since I'm here, attending as a royal, certain expectations are required of me, but the second I can get away, we'll head there."

"What do you want me to do?"

He shifted to face me, and his brow furrowed. Sunlight sparkled in his cerulean irises, and for the first time since we boarded the carpet, his gaze softened. "That depends entirely upon you. I won't ask you to do anything you're uncomfortable with, but considering that you know the king, and he is quite fond of you, that could prove problematic."

I angled my head upward. "What's your plan?"

"Well, I had an idea." He leaned down and whispered it in my ear. My eyes grew rounder with every word he uttered. Straightening, he gazed down at me, his look intent and slightly . . . wild. Once again, that savage emotion clouded around him. "It's up to you, but are you willing?"

My heart pounded as I was again reminded of what Alec had told me, but I managed to nod. "I can do that."

A slow-spreading grin emerged on his face, yet all I could do was wonder how much harder this would make things come next summer.

CHAPTER 12

Jax landed the carpet in a small clearing just north of the palace. A Faewood attendant rushed forward, bowing deeply to Jax. "Shall I have your luggage delivered to your usual spot in Leafton?"

Jax handed him several rulibs. "Indeed. Thank you."

The attendant bowed and began to roll up the carpet we'd ridden on. Laughter carried to us on the wind. Other fae glided toward us from along the Wood's road, more spectators no doubt here to enjoy the upcoming Finals.

"Ready for what's to come?" Jax held out his hand to me, his palm large and inviting. A moment of hesitation filled me, especially when his eyes grew hooded and his voice dipped to a husky whisper. "You don't have to, but if you're willing, this will explain why you're now with me and why you'll stay with me. Nobody will question this, and the king won't be able to find a price that I would agree on to release you."

Behind us, Alec smirked. And for good reason.

"I'm willing. It's fine." I took a deep breath and entwined my fingers with Jax's.

The second our skin made contact, a flash of *something* filled the prince's eyes, and my magic surged, rushing toward him and wanting to join with him.

My breath sucked in, but in my next blink, that strange energy between us calmed, simmering to a more normal level.

Stars Above.

It wasn't the first time I'd felt such a thing, and that wild look in Jax's eyes had made an appearance more than once. But it was always so brief. I still had no idea what to make of it.

Holding me firmly, the prince tugged me toward him. Heat from his side crawled up my body, and my core clenched. *Gods and Goddesses, don't make a fool of yourself, Elowen.*

The prince curled me into his side, the satin gown easily moving and swaying to accommodate the gesture.

Another party of siltenites landed in the clearing, wealthy fae from the looks of it, and the attendant rushed to help them, giving us a moment of unobserved privacy.

A flare of magic puffed from Jax, and since it was similar to what I'd felt on the ship, I knew he'd just cast a silencing Shield. "We'll see the king first, pay our respects, then we'll search the grounds."

Everyone in the group dipped their heads.

The six of us stepped away from the clearing, Jax leading the way. His hand held mine firmly, his grip pleasantly smooth. Within minutes, we were striding toward the palace.

Banging sounds came in the distance as well as the scent of magic being cast. With the Matches only weeks away, it appeared the king had called in siltenites to help complete the final touches of construction after all. Just west of us, a female siltenite stood near several wildlings. Her hands wove through the air, and a large turquoise banner lifted under her magic.

I smirked and wondered if Lillivel was also watching. My assistant had said it would be smarter to hire siltenites with telekinetic magic, and she'd been right. The main construction was now complete, only cosmetic displays being added, and from the looks of it, even those minor details would be finished by nightfall.

Neither Jax, Trivan, or Alec paid the Matches much attention. They seemed intent on assessing the distant barns. Only Lars and Phillen continually scanned the area, their guarding duties taking center stage.

Automatically, I fell into the role I was asked to play and stepped even closer to Jax.

His breath hitched when I grazed his side, but when I

glanced up at him, he continued striding forward, his hand securely wrapped around mine.

We ambled along the palace's expansive lawn. Several servants gaped when they spotted us, and I had no doubt a few recognized me.

We didn't ask for help, though. Since it wasn't the first time Jax had visited the Faewood Kingdom palace, he knew where the entrances were and made a show of escorting me. When we dipped past the fountains and opulent gardens, he slipped his arm around my waist and drew me even closer before leaning down to nuzzle my neck.

My breath caught. In a blink, my heart was pattering so quickly I felt lightheaded even though Jax had explained to me on the carpet that this was all for show. These actions meant nothing. Jax was now my new guardian in the eyes of the Faewood throne. But not only that, he was also my new lover. It was the ploy he'd come up with to trick the king. King Paevin knew that I'd been abducted. He'd sent Lordling Neeble as a backup to secure me if Guardian Alleron failed. Only thing, the king had no idea what had become of me since my guardian had never returned and neither had Lordling Neeble.

But while my guardian was currently locked within Stonewild's palace, Lordling Neeble and his party were all dead and buried deep within the Ustilly Mountains. And considering they were all under feet of mountainous soil, I had a feeling their remains would never be found, effectively leaving King Paevin in the dark as to what had happened to them.

Consequently, Jax had taken it upon himself to create a new narrative, similar to what he'd done with his parents and his kingdom's council. Since I'd been seen with the Dark Raider in Stonewild, he decided to let that work to his advantage and say that he saved me from the ruthless brute in Fosterton while he was there on his hunt.

If asked, I was to say that the prince had learned of my abduction and that he paid the Dark Raider handsomely to release me. Now that he'd bought me and had me secured, he was my rightful new guardian per siltenite law. Even King Paevin couldn't refute that.

Although, Jax had taken it upon himself to add another twist. In the time since he'd rescued me, he'd also become my lover, and I'd grown infatuated with him. Unlike Guardian Alleron, who I obeyed due to law and the fatherly love I'd once felt for him, with Jax, I obeyed due to lust.

And Jax felt the same.

In other words, no payment the king could offer would have Jax selling me back to Faewood.

I had to admit, it was a good plan. But the way my body was genuinely reacting to Jax's close presence was another matter entirely. And Alec's claim that the prince actually had feelings for me began to feel more real with every step we took. *Because if he truly didn't, would he have spun this tale?*

Memories of Jax's attentive touches in the palace's bath following his calling and the soothing caresses the night my collar had been loosened reared in my mind. He'd acted so caring toward me on a number of occasions. And sometimes, the way he stared at me . . .

At times, he looked positively *hungry*.

But I quickly shoved those thoughts away. Speculating now on what all of that could mean, could very well end in disaster if I grew too distracted. Not to mention, Jax was to eventually marry another. Even if I did desire him, and even if he desired me, in a full season's time, it would have to end because I would *not* be his mistress. I'd thought about it repeatedly during the past few days, and such a future wasn't what I wished for myself.

We rounded the final turn to the front of the palace, and Jax whispered, "Put your arm around me, darling. If we're going to convince the king, you have to play the part."

His husky endearment had goosebumps sprouting along every inch of my skin, and a quickening in my belly had my insides flipping.

My magic stirred, writhing inside me at the feel of his aura brushing around mine. A faint sting came from my collar, but it was trivial and made ignoring it easy. Yet it wasn't lost on me that it was the umpteenth time my magic had reacted in such a way to Jax. It was almost as though my lorafin powers had a mind of their own when the prince was near.

Embarrassment heated my cheeks, but I did as the prince requested. I curled my arm around his toned waist, my fingers grazing the side of his abdomen.

A very low, contented purr came from his throat, so brief that it could have been a trick of the wind.

Lars and Phillen marched at our sides, their focus honed into everything around us. But none of the wildlings approached us, probably because Jax sauntered toward the palace stairs as though he owned the place.

The second the royal guards spotted him, they bowed deeply and opened the large doors. Silent white stone swung outward as they murmured a greeting to the foreign royal.

Wildling servants quickly stood to attention when Jax and I climbed the steps and walked inside the palace's grand entryway. Soaring walls, hanging tapestries, and an elegant crystal chandelier suspended with magic greeted us.

"Good morning, Prince Adarian." The same ramifin wildling who had led me through the corridors only a few weeks ago to perform three callings for King Paevin bowed deeply to Jax. He wore the same attire as before—brown trousers and a turquoise top with white buttons. When he straightened, his gaze slid to me. Eyes popping, he exclaimed, "Lady Elowen!"

I dipped my head. "Good morning."

"Is that really you?" The wildling gaped, then stuttered, "The king, he's been . . . he's been very concerned about you. We've received devastating news about your guardian, but as for Lordling Neeble, we . . . I mean, we'd hoped he'd eventually rescue you, but he hasn't returned either."

"Lordling Neeble?" I cocked my head innocently. "I didn't realize the lordling had been sent to find me, but as for my guardian . . ." I shuddered. "It is absolutely *horrible* what's happened to him. I haven't seen him since Lemos. Not since the Dark Raider . . ." I brought a hand to my mouth as a soft sob escaped me.

"Is your guardian all right, Lady Elowen?" the servant asked, genuine worry in his voice.

I shook my head rapidly. "I don't know. In Lemos, he rescued me from the Dark Raider, but when we were escaping through the Wood . . ." A tremble racked my entire body, and Jax growled.

Shielding me from the servant, Jax said, "I would ask that you not upset my lady. That entire experience has been quite traumatic for her."

The servant's eyes widened. "Oh, of course, I meant no disrespect, Your Highness. I was simply surprised to see her since no one's seen or heard from her, and we received such devastating news about—"

Another growl from Jax cut him off. In a glacial tone, the prince added, "The only one who rescued her was *me*, and Elowen's abduction has left her with nightmares and harrowing memories. I would advise you not to bring it up again."

The servant immediately bowed. "Of course. My sincerest apologies, my prince. Please, follow me."

The servant set off down the hall, and the six of us followed. I made sure to stay locked in Jax's arm, sniffling along the way.

The aura around Jax soared as I stayed glued to his side. Leaning down, he nipped the skin along my neck. "You're doing brilliantly."

My lungs seized when his teeth grazed my skin.

We stayed in our close embrace the entire time we followed the servant, and a flurry of whispers erupted from the staff we passed.

But even though this was all an act, and even though I was pretending to be distraught at what I'd experienced, the exact opposite was actually occurring inside me. A flame of heat erupted in my core. *Goddess.* Embarrassment surged through me that Jax's touches and nips were arousing me, after pretending to be sick with distraught about my abduction nonetheless.

Jax's nostrils flared, and my embarrassment turned to mortification since he probably scented my arousal.

Trivan snickered behind us, and Alec coughed. Only Lars and Phillen retained their composure, but I still wanted to sink through the floor.

But even though my heart was thundering, I stayed plastered to Jax's side the entire way and was thankful for my former guardian's charades. Acting was like breathing to me since I'd played so many roles in my lifetime. This was simply another one that I automatically fell into.

We rounded another corner, and the familiar chambers where the king accepted guests appeared.

"If you would be so kind as to wait here, I shall let the king know you've arrived." The wildling stepped aside to give us room to enter the chambers.

"Thank you." Jax tugged me with him, his touch blatantly possessive to anyone watching.

Mutely, I followed since my tongue was currently refusing to work.

The servant bowed again, then left, leaving the six of us alone to wait for the king.

The vast sitting area was filled with decadent couches, chairs, and chaise lounges. A breathtaking view of the palace gardens spread out before the windows. Magic shimmered around the windowpanes, keeping the outside noise at bay. A tray filled with sweets and savories sat on a nearby table.

Jax helped himself to one of the petite pies and popped it into his mouth. When I went to grab a piece of chocolate for myself, though, his fingers snatched it before I could.

"Allow me."

My eyes widened when he brought the chocolate to my mouth. "But . . . the king and staff aren't here to see this," I whispered quietly under my breath.

His eyes only darkened as he settled the chocolate against my lower lip. "I don't like breaking my roles once I'm in them." He pushed the sweet more against my lip, and I opened my mouth.

Slowly, he slid the chocolate inside, and my tongue flicked against it.

His aura grew, swelling around him to a palpable level as he watched my lips, his gaze once again *hungry*.

I sank my teeth into the chocolate and bit off a small bite. His eyes never left my mouth as I chewed and swallowed it.

He brought the remaining chocolate to his own mouth, and watching his lips close around it—around something that had just touched my tongue—created a mortifying stirring in my core.

Alec coughed again, and Trivan wasn't even trying to hide his smirk, but Lars pointed to the map above the fireplace. "Why does the king have a framed map of the Solis continent and not our continent?"

Thankful for the distraction, I was about to comment

to the guard that I'd once wondered the exact same thing, but then the king's booming voice called from the doorway, "Prince Adarian! Such a pleasure to have you join us for the Matches in my kingdom." The king bustled toward us. "I hear you just arrived, and—" He stopped short. "Elowen?"

It struck me that it was quite possibly the first time the king had ever said my name aloud. Normally, he referred to me as *the girl* or something else that was equally abhorrent.

The king glanced between the two of us, his eyes widening even more. "I don't understand. What are you doing with the prince?"

"Your Majesty," the servant said from behind him, rushing into the room. "I tried to tell you—"

"Leave us," the king said dismissively, waving him away, and the servant exited the chambers, shutting the doors behind him.

Trivan bowed to King Paevin. "Prince Adarian is Elowen's new guardian, my king."

All of the males automatically dipped into bows, and I curtsied. Yet despite those gestures, Jax's arm around me never faltered.

When we straightened, the king opened and closed his mouth, but no words came out. Wide eyed, he assessed all of us again.

"What in the realm are you talking about?" he finally

blurted. "Last I heard, she'd been rescued by her guardian in Lemos, only to have the Dark Raider attack them in the Wood. All of the guardian's hired hands returned in the days following that botched rescue, stating they didn't remember much after waking upon the Wood's road, only that they believed the Dark Raider was behind it." He huffed. "But her guardian never returned, and neither did *you*." He turned his attention on me.

I shuddered and curled into Jax. His arm tightened around me.

The king's brow furrowed. "Explain if you would. *How* are you with Prince Adarian of all fae?"

"He . . ." I sniffed again. "The Dark Raider took both of us. Like you said, my guardian tried to rescue me, but in the Wood . . ." Another sob lifted my chest, and I brought a hand to my mouth to stifle the sound.

"The prince bought her from the Dark Raider," Trivan said with authority in his voice. "My prince learned of her abduction from those who saw her with the Dark Raider, and he bartered for her release. And it's a lucky thing that he did. She was in rough shape when we finally got her away from that dastardly male."

"*Bought* her?" The king's gaze immediately settled on Jax. "You bought her from the Dark Raider? You actually gave that mongrel rulibs?"

"I did," Jax replied easily. "He had her in Stonewild

when the exchange occurred. I saw it as my duty given what soil they were on."

The king's cheeks turned ruddy. "But how . . . how could such a thing happen? We've been searching for her since the day she was taken. Her guardian went off first thing the next morning even though he was injured. And I sent multiple hunting parties to secure the borders throughout my kingdom, just to ensure her safe venture home. All of those parties didn't find anything except for Lordling Neeble's group. He sent a dillemsill as soon as he located her, but nobody's heard from him since. Have you heard any word?"

"Lordling Neeble?" Jax arched an eyebrow, his face a portrait of innocence. "I'm afraid I have no idea who that is."

"My king, I fear the Dark Raider still has my guardian," I said in a small voice, "but I don't know how he fairs. As for Lordling Neeble . . ." I lifted my shoulders. "I didn't realize other parties had been sent to search for me as well, but I never saw him."

"You didn't?"

I shook my head. "Are you sure he said that he'd found me? Perhaps he was mistaken?"

The king frowned. "Granted, it was the middle of the night when that dillemsill arrived, but the message said he was positive he'd found you." He harrumphed. "And the rest of you?" the king demanded of Jax and his friends.

"Do you know where her guardian or Lordling Neeble are?"

One by one, they shook their heads, their faces filled with looks of genuine confusion and bafflement. It appeared I wasn't the only gifted actor in the group.

The king huffed. "I'll have to assume the Dark Raider still holds Guardian Alleron, which doesn't bode well for him I'm afraid. But as for Lordling Neeble, we can only hope for his safe return eventually." Taking another deep breath, the king placed his hands on his hips. "But as for the matter at hand, I'm in your debt for returning my lorafin to me safely, Prince Adarian. I shall of course pay you for her. I just thank the stars you were able to secure her release." He held out his hand to me, his face expectant.

A flash of panic flipped my stomach, but before I could say anything, Jax replied in a cold tone, "She's not for sale. I bought her, and I've ensured she's stayed safe, unlike what occurred here in Faewood. Under siltenite law, that means she's *mine.*"

My eyes widened at the possessiveness that one word exuded, but I quickly schooled my expression into contrition.

"Yours?" the king arched an eyebrow in amusement, but then his mouth tightened when Jax's expression didn't relent. "Surely, she doesn't wish to live in Stonewild. Faewood is her home."

The prince's expression turned into unrelenting stone. "No, she won't be living in Faewood. Elowen's mine now."

"But, she's—"

"King Paevin," I said in a rush, "I'm honored that you went to such endeavors to try to ensure my safety, but I can assure you that I'm perfectly safe now that I'm in Stonewild and free of the Dark Raider, and I can assure you that I'm most content even if it's a new kingdom." I gazed up at the prince and pulled my bottom lip suggestively into my mouth. "The prince has become more than just my guardian. I'm very happy to stay with him."

A satisfied grin emerged on Jax's face, his earlier ire vanishing. He leaned down and kissed my neck, and his scent clouded around me.

My entire body shivered, and I just hoped Jax didn't know that such a response wasn't an act.

The crown prince placed another kiss on my neck, his lips lingering before he lifted his head, almost regretfully.

Heart pounding, I somehow managed to understand the prince's next words.

"The feeling's mutual, as you can see, Your Majesty." His voice was slightly husky, his eyes hooded when he looked at me. "No price could tear her from my side." His grip around my waist tightened. "Lady Elowen is absolutely fine and perfectly content to stay mine." The weight of his words hung in the air as his attention stayed locked on my face. "I consider myself very lucky to have acquired such a treasure. I can understand your envy however, Your Majesty, but I do hope you will respect our common law."

The king's jaw muscle began to tick. "But she was a lorafin of *my* kingdom."

"And now she's a lorafin of *mine*." Jax's gaze cut to the king. Malice dripped in Jax's tone, and his immediate reply only made the king's cheeks redden further. "As I said, I do hope you respect our common law."

The king's nostrils flared, and his eyes turned to beady slits. The energy around him grew, and the temperature in the room dropped. It grew so cold from his air elemental magic, that for a moment, I could see my breath.

My heartrate sped up, and I thought for certain the king was going to explode in a fit of rage. But some of the crimson color finally leeched from his skin. Another moment passed by, and the room warmed again.

Finally, the king dipped his head, even if the movement looked forced. "Very well, but if you should ever tire of her, I do hope you shall give me precedence to buy her back."

I stiffened, and the heat from Jax's side climbed. "I shall indeed keep that in mind."

A warring emotion passed between the two royals, and I held my breath as I waited to see if the king would do anything else.

Thankfully, he didn't and instead gestured to the sofas. "Please sit," he said stiffly.

Plenty of sweets and savories still waited on the tray sitting on the table. The king snapped his fingers at the servants in the corner. "Bring my finest port."

The wildlings bowed and rushed to do his bidding.

WE SPENT the next hour with the king, engaging in pleasantries and a few political discussions. The entire time, Jax kept me close, his arm locked around my waist. His fingers continually ran up and down my side, brushing the bottom of my breast at times. His skimming motions were entirely distracting and embarrassingly arousing. One would never guess that internally he was probably raging that we were wasting so much time here versus searching for Bastian. But the prince was a master at deception. Outwardly, he seemed perfectly content to engage in conversation while driving me mad with lust.

Several times, I completely lost track of what was being discussed. Jax's fingers and the hardness from his thigh commanded all of my attention, and I had to remind myself that even if he did desire me, this was still an act.

Thankfully, nobody seemed interested in a caged lorafin's opinion anyway, not even when Jax tried to pull me into the discussion, asking my thoughts and feelings about matters. Each time he did, I opened my mouth to reply, my mind scrambling with what they'd recently said, but it was all for naught. The king merely waved his hand dismissively and stated such things were best kept between the males.

I bristled inwardly at that, even though I wasn't surprised.

After the necessary formalities of a royal visiting another kingdom were completed, King Paevin finally stood. "Well, I'm sure you're eager to be on your way."

If you only knew. I pushed to standing, and Jax's fingers curled into my side, heat filling his aura.

The king waved toward the door. "Enjoy the Matches, and do let me know if you need anything during your stay."

Jax bowed. "Thank you, Your Majesty. I appreciate your generosity, but we shall try not to be a burden. We'll be staying at my private residence in Leafton."

The king grunted. "As you wish."

The others bowed as well, and I somehow managed a curtsy.

"Elowen?" Jax gestured toward the door, keeping his arm firmly anchored around me.

I leaned into him, my breasts squashing against his hard chest.

His breath sucked in, and a low sound came from his throat. His fingers curled even more around me, his touch hot and possessive. It didn't have the ownership upon it that I always felt with my former guardian, but something else clung to his touch, something that made my breath catch and my insides turn molten.

The king watched us when we passed, his attention dipping to our close proximity, and Goddess, he even inhaled, making me wonder just how potent my arousal had become. But at least it played into the game Jax and I had woven.

Still, I had to remind myself on our walk back to the main doors that even though Jax's touches showed the realm that he was my new guardian and lover, I knew that underneath it all, he was simply playing his part, even if he did desire me on some level.

And a part of me *did* wonder if there was some genuineness to his acts as Alec had claimed. Because every time the king had looked at me with envy, Jax's side had pressed closer to mine, as though shielding me.

And every time the king had approached the subject during the past hour, of perhaps using me as his lorafin once more, the aura around Jax had swelled to a feverish pitch.

Throughout it all, Jax's decision had held firm, keeping the king at bay. One thing I knew for certain, he'd made it clear to the king and anyone watching that in no unspoken terms, I was his and his alone.

And more than once, that *hadn't* felt like an act, making me wonder if a part of Jax truly did view me as his.

CHAPTER 13

"That seemed to go well." Alec sauntered along the paved walkway outside of the palace. Bright sunlight shone down on us as we crossed the lawn, and a few pastel clouds had formed in the sky, but it was still mostly clear. "Even I believed you two have spent time between the sheets. If I didn't know better, I dare say I would be jealous." He waggled his eyebrows at me, and I had the strongest urge to roll my eyes at him.

"Alec, calm yourself," the prince said tightly even though Phillen snorted, Trivan snickered, and even Lars muffled a laugh. "You are not to flirt with Elowen anymore. It would blow our cover."

"Of course, my prince." Alec fell into a deep, mocking bow. "I agree. We must take our roles *very* seriously." The Graniteer House noble winked subtly at me, and I *really* wanted to roll my eyes at that gesture but managed to refrain myself.

The prince glanced my way, but the earlier irritation he'd worn around his friend had faded.

"And, Elowen," Alec continued. "Why the scent of your lust was enough to fill the room back there. I daresay you had the king completely fooled. You almost had *me* fooled." He released a low whistle. "I must say, you're quite good at acting. Because it was an act, correct?"

A blazing blush bloomed in my cheeks just as the prince growled at his friend.

"Yes, of course it was," I replied a tad defensively. "I mean, I've always taken my roles quite seriously too."

Trivan barked out a laugh, and their teasing was growing so insufferable that I tried to put some distance between Jax and me, just to fend off my embarrassment, but his arm tightened, refusing to let me do so.

"Enough," Jax said to his friends. "Elowen and I need to stay in our roles the entire time we're here. She doesn't need to be constantly teased about it."

My eyebrows shot up. "The *entire* time?"

Jax's lips curved in a satisfied smile. "The first lesson you have to learn if you're to be working with the Dark Raider is that we never break our roles. We stay in them until we return to Stonewild. Always."

"But you're not the Dark Raider here," I said beneath my breath. "You're the prince."

He shrugged. "It's only a technicality on this visit. What I'm doing here has nothing to do with princely duties. We're to stay in our roles."

"You actually mean the *entire* time?" I licked my lips. "Even at night?"

"Yes." Fractured sunlight twinkled in his eyes when he cast me an assessing look, as though gauging my reaction.

"But . . ." I sputtered. "It could take days or even *weeks* to find Bastian."

"True. Will that be a problem for you?"

I tried to picture what being Jax's supposed lover for an extended length of time could mean. Constant touches. Frequent, heated glances. Occasional kisses and caresses. And, Goddess, possibly even a shared chamber at night.

It was essentially foreplay for, well, possibly days on end.

Kill me now.

"Um, no, that will be fine, my prince." Somehow, I managed not to groan. If I was as aroused as I was now, after only an hour of play acting, I couldn't even imagine what I would be like by the time we left.

"Elowen?" He leaned closer again, and his nose brushed along my ear as his scent billowed around me. "Are you sure?"

I snapped my spine upright. I hadn't realized what I signed up for when I agreed to this, but I managed to get out, "Yes, my prince. It'll be okay."

"You two reek of lust, you know that, right?" Trivan called from behind us.

Jax cast him an irritated look.

Trivan held up his hands in surrender, yet a cheeky grin emerged on his face. "I was simply pointing it out as a way to tell you that you're doing a *fantastic* job in your roles."

Alec sighed again. "And here I thought I stood a chance at becoming Elowen's lover after our time together in the palace and ship."

Jax cut him a look so hard, it could have punched through Alec's jaw. "Alec. Enough."

Alec bowed again but even more dramatically.

The charged atmosphere around us grew so energized, that by the time we reached the outward part of the Matches, more than a few siltenites were openly staring at us. I told myself it was because I was plastered to the side of a foreign crown prince, and it wasn't actually *me* they were looking at. But when several nostrils flared as we sauntered past, I couldn't help but wonder just how potent my arousal truly was.

"Someone please kill me by week's end," I mumbled under my breath.

Jax's fingers tightened at my waist. "It would be a pity to partake in such a violent act with a female as lovely as you," he whispered. "I fear I would never get over it."

His comment sounded teasing but the slight heaviness in it gave me pause.

I shook my head. Surely, I was being delusional. Jax would whole heartedly get over my passing if such a tragedy did ensue, even if he did want me as his mistress. Obviously, the roles we decided to play were impairing my judgment. It was best I remembered *why* we were actually here and not get lost to the sensations the crown prince was provoking in me.

My thoughts returned to Ladies Aerobelle, Penepee, and Lucille on the ship. In only a full season's time, one of them could be his wife. Unlike everything Jax and I were doing, which was temporary.

We kept walking toward the Matches, and the sights grew closer.

"There's a new barn just over there," I whispered and pointed subtly to the structure I'd spotted atop the enchanted carpet.

Jax angled us that way, but everyone still kept their attention on the events, our destination not entirely obvious.

Corralled domals whinnied in the distance, and another roar cut through the sky when the larpanoon let loose another bellow. Most of the fae wandering around the enclosures were in pairs or small groups, and thankfully, the fearsome beast garnered most of their attention.

But whenever someone did happen to glance our way, a flurry of whispered comments followed.

"Isn't that the crown prince of Stonewild?" someone muttered under their breath.

"It is. I heard he might be here to watch the Finals."

"But who's with him?" another hissed.

"Probably his current lover. Look how close they're walking."

"I heard he's to marry soon," another whispered. "That poor female. She'll be thrown out like yesterday's trash in no time."

I stiffened when that comment swirled toward me on the breeze as we grew closer to the barn.

"Does this look familiar to what the semelees showed you?" Jax asked me quietly.

I studied the dark-wood siding and peaked roofline. "Not the exterior, no. They never showed me that."

"Let's go inside." Jax angled us toward the main door.

Two wildlings stood near it with large forks. They were spearing hay and tossing it onto a small wagon.

When we passed, they stopped and bowed at Jax. Others did the same when we drifted by them. The entire time, Jax either ignored them or dipped his head, and it struck me that this was who Jax truly was. He might be the Dark Raider at night or during clandestine endeavors, but in reality, he was the heir to Stonewild's throne.

The truth of that struck me so completely that I nearly stumbled.

"Are you all right?" Jax pressed a kiss to my temple, and a tizzy of whispers erupted following that gesture.

I shivered and forced a nod.

We wandered into the barn, the rest of our group following, and Jax's touches continued as we all pretended to look around and admire the domals. They were some of the largest I'd ever seen, and I wondered what events they would be used for at the Matches.

The aura around Jax swelled as we ventured down the aisles. So far, only stalls had greeted us, and certainly not anyone who looked like his brother.

I leaned up and pressed a kiss to Jax's neck. His step faltered, but he quickly corrected himself when I whispered, "Sorry, I was just trying to get closer to your ear so I could tell you that this is likely the wrong barn."

He squeezed my hip. "All right. Let's walk the length of it and search for more."

His pulse throbbed in his neck, and even though he was masking his worry in his expression, I could feel it since I stood so close to him. The end of the barn neared, and crashing disappointment rose from him in swells.

We ventured outside again and went to a barn farther west, but after searching that one too, we once again came up empty handed.

"There's another one over there." Lars pointed subtly toward it.

We strode through the crowds, admiring everything we passed, but when we reached the third barn, nothing about it showed any hint of Bastian being there either. So far, each barn had simply held stalls with animals, and that was it.

Worry grew in Jax's aura, and I knew that he was thinking of the time that'd passed since his calling. Bastian could literally be anywhere now.

"The damn Lochen," he whispered under his breath. "If they hadn't . . ." But he cut himself off, as though realizing complaining about things he had no control over was pointless.

We were about to leave the fourth barn we'd checked, dismay evident in the prince's energy, when I spotted a door with a large room closed off in the barn's corner. I stopped, effectively halting the prince with me.

"What do you suppose that is?" I angled my head toward it.

Jax's eyes narrowed, and his pace increased. He seemed to realize his eagerness two steps into it, though, because he slowed.

Only a handful of other siltenites were in the barn, and none of them were paying us any attention, yet Jax still kept his pace controlled.

The door neared, and the more I studied the enclosure, the more I realized that a sizeable room lay behind it.

When we reached it, I subtly brushed my fingers over the handle. "It's locked." Before anyone could reply, I whispered one of the many unlocking spells I'd mastered. The words flowed effortlessly out of me, not even a hint of rattling coming from my collar in its new relaxed state.

The door clicked the second the final word left my lips.

Alec snorted quietly. "You fit right in, Elowen."

I gave him a side-eye but couldn't stop my smile.

Jax turned the handle, and we all sauntered into the room casually as though it was part of our self-guided tour.

Inside, my eyes widened at what it held.

A dozen beds, bolted to the walls and stacked three on top of each other—all the way to the ceiling—waited before us. On the far wall, domal equipment and saddles waited, but it was obvious a group of employees likely slept here. A few of the beds even had rumpled sheets.

Energy spiraled out of the crown prince, and before I could say anything, Jax had the door closed and locked behind us.

Everyone kicked into action. All of the males went to each bed. Jax even bounded up several of the bunks to reach the top ones. He brought the sheets to his nose, then the pillows, going from one bed to the next.

My jaw dropped. It hit me that he was *scenting* for his brother.

All of the other males were doing the same, going to each bed and sniffing, their stag senses kicking in.

"Here!" Jax hissed. He'd stopped at the middle set of beds, his face going white when he lifted the pillow from the mattress. "This smells like Bastian. Elowen was right. He's been here, and recently too."

A moment of relief hit me that we found a clue as to where his brother had been, and that he was still *here*, but just as quickly, I wondered why that was and what had happened to Bastian to make him run from his only brother in the first place.

CHAPTER 14

The second Jax and his friends knew that Bastian had been sleeping in the barn recently, they turned the entire sleeping quarters and storage room upside down looking for more clues. Their movements were quick, efficient, and methodical. It was obvious they'd conducted work like this before.

"Nothing, my prince," Phillen finally said when the last storage trunk had been emptied before being carefully restowed. One would never have known it'd been rifled through from how carefully each item was returned to its precise location. "Only that bed smells of him."

"And from the faintness of it, it's been two days since he slept here." Jax raked a hand through his hair. Potent spikes of magic billowed in his aura. "This doesn't make any sense. He slept here recently, but nothing else in this room belongs to him. And the biggest question remains unanswered. *Why* is he even here? He never showed any interest in the Centennial Matches or competitions before."

Phillen laid a hand on Jax's shoulder. "We can figure those answers out later, but remember that he likely *is* here. Somewhere. We'll find him."

"But if he hasn't been here in two days, he could be anywhere now," Trivan countered.

"He's right." I stepped closer to Jax. "I'll travel to the Veiled Between again. It's the only way to know for certain. I can try to demand better answers from the semelees." But I twisted my hands. I'd done Jax's calling less than a week ago, and oftentimes, the semelees wouldn't answer me if I pressed them again on the same subject too quickly. They could be finicky like that. It was why I had to wait so long between callings if it was for the same fairy.

Jax's lips pressed into a thin line. "No."

"But if I go again, I might—"

"I said *no.*"

I inched closer to his side, and my gown flowed around me. "But if we can't find anything else to explain where he currently is, and he doesn't return here, then what choice do we have? We're at a dead end."

A muscle pumped in the prince's jaw, and his eyes darkened into chips of ice. "No, Elowen. I'm never doing that to you again. We'll find him another way." A fearful look passed over his face, and I wasn't sure if it was from remembering the state I'd been in after his calling or if it was due to the reality that Bastian might never be found.

"Is there any way you could travel to the Veiled Between and *not* do a calling?" Alec crossed his arms, his eyes assessing. "You know, go there looking for yourself so you're not affected by another's magic?"

I fingered my collar. "Honestly, I don't know. Every time I tried previously, I was never able to because of this." I tapped on the gem. "It always punished me. And this collar's always prohibited me from using my magic to my full extent, which would be required if I wanted to do a calling of my own. But now that it's loosened . . ." I shrugged. "It's still doubtful, but I suppose I won't know for certain unless I try."

Jax's eyebrows shot up. "Are you telling me you've never gone to the Veiled Between for yourself before?"

I shook my head.

His nostrils flared, and a dangerous seep of power swelled in his aura. "You're telling me that your former guardian only ever allowed you to use your magic for himself? He never allowed you to do anything for your own good? Not even before that collar was put on?"

"I mean, I have traveled there alone, not in a calling, but that was when I was young and my powers first emerged. Those ventures were allowed so I could learn my magic, but I wasn't strong enough then or knowledgeable enough to ask the semelees anything."

Jax stabbed another hand through his hair. "That total and complete selfish arsehole."

Trivan cocked an eyebrow. "How many times have you tried to venture to the Veiled Between for your own benefit?"

My cheeks flushed. "I only do so now when it's truly needed." I thought back to what I'd done when Jax had initially abducted me and I'd needed to delay them, or when I'd done it to break through his locking spell in the palace. "But each time, it takes a great toll on me because of the collar's punishment, and I'm never able to stay in the Veiled Between for long. The collar would likely kill me if I tried to do that."

Alec put his hands on his hips. "Perhaps you can do a calling on your own now that your collar's not so tight. Maybe you should try it, to see if you can locate Bastian without Jax's magic hurting you."

A slow smile spread across my lips. "I can certainly try." But then my smile dimmed. "Although, I don't know how agreeable the semelees will be. Oftentimes, when I ask them the same questions too closely together, they ignore me. I usually have to wait several weeks before pressing them for more details."

"Ignore you?" Lars's eyebrows shot up. "But you're a lorafin. I thought they had to obey you?"

"If I was their queen, they would, but they still consider me a princess, so . . ." I raised my shoulders. "They sometimes won't respond to me."

"That doesn't bode well." Phillen crossed his arms. "What have your scholars told you, Jax, about lorafins with collars? Do you think Elowen could do her own calling now? Maybe later when the time has passed and the semelees will answer her?"

Jax's brows folded together, a groove appearing between them. "Lorafins in the history books haven't worn collars. Elowen's unique in this aspect."

"Right, but like Elowen said, we don't know what she's capable of now since it's loosened." Trivan grinned wickedly. "Which means there's only one way to find out."

"And if that doesn't work, perhaps you could do a calling for one of us, Elowen?" Alec asked. "We're not as magical as Jax, so you shouldn't be as affected. Could you ask the semelees about Bastian for one of us instead? Would that work?"

I sighed. "With enough time passing, yes, I could try that. But it wouldn't work if I did it right now. They can't be fooled even if I'm there and channeling another fairy's magic. They likely still won't answer since it's the same question so soon to the last time I asked."

Trivan cocked an eyebrow upward. "How much time will it take for them to answer that question again?"

"Usually, at least two weeks before they'll consider answering the same question again."

"In that case, in a week's time, you could use my magic for a calling," Lars offered. "I'm generally considered the least magical in the group."

"That'll still hurt her," Jax growled. "You may not be as strong as me, but you're no weakling, Lars."

"But he's not nearly as strong as you," I countered. "None of your friends wield magic like you do, Jax. Nobody's magic will hurt me like yours did."

He winced, and I immediately regretted my comment. But instead of agreeing with me, he took a deep breath and then shook his head. "No."

My eyebrows shot up. "No? Seriously? Don't you want to find your brother?"

His nostrils flared. "Of course, I do. But we've only just started searching, and you've never been unaffected by a calling, right?"

My throat bobbed, brushing against my collar when I swallowed. "Well . . . no, but I can still try doing one for *me*. That'll likely not leave me injured."

"But will that leave you weakened?"

"It . . . well, I suppose . . ." My brow furrowed. "Honestly, I don't know. All of this is new to me."

"Exactly. You have no idea what state you'll be in."

I glared at him because even though I hated to admit it, he made very good points. Since I wasn't a queen to the semelees, I didn't have complete control of them. As a princess, it was common for them to deny me answers on the same subject, or if I ventured to the Veiled Between too quickly for the same fairy to ask a new question, they often denied me too. It was why I could typically only do one to two callings a month for the same fairy. The semelees wouldn't allow anything more than that.

I'd always been grateful for that limitation in a way. It'd kept me from being mercilessly used, again and again, by the same fae. But now . . . for the first time I was wishing the semelees *didn't* have that stipulation.

Holding himself in a rigid line, Jax said in his princely tone, "My official answer is no. Elowen is not to hurt herself for us again, especially if there's no guarantee we'd even get any further answers."

All of the males eyed one another, nodding accept-ingly, and Trivan even bumped Alec, giving him an *I told you so* look.

And in that covert gesture, I couldn't help but wonder if Jax's complete inability to even consider having me harmed again stemmed from the feelings Alec claimed he'd developed for me.

A flush ran through my body, and it took me a moment to realize what it was.

I felt warm. Because to Jax, I had worth. He actually cared about my well-being.

The flush in my body grew because maybe Alec was

right. Maybe Jax truly *did* care for me more than he was letting on.

Or maybe Jax would have had that reaction for any fairy who he felt was innocent of deserving the punishment a calling could inflict.

Some of the warmth in me diffused, and I opened my mouth to tell Jax that while I appreciated that he cared, the fact remained that I would ultimately recover from any pain inflicted on me. And more than that, for the first time *I* was choosing to do a calling. I wanted to find Bastian too, and in roughly a week's time, enough days would have passed for me to venture to the Veiled Between again to ask of his brother. The semelees would likely answer at that point.

But just as those words formed on my lips, voices came from outside of the room.

Everyone fell silent.

But the voices soon drifted past.

Trivan moved closer to the door and listened. "It's just another group enjoying the excitement of the upcoming Matches."

I released a sigh of relief, but it was enough of a reminder that we needed to get out of here and carry on searching for Bastian.

"What would you like to do, my prince?" Lars dipped his head toward Jax, the red in his hair glowing like fire in the lights.

"I want eyes kept on this barn at all times in case he returns. When are the others arriving?"

"End of the week." Alec glanced toward a clock on the wall.

I placed my hands on my hips, my palms sliding along the gown's slippery surface. "Others? What others?"

Trivan shook his head, and a lock of blond hair curled around his forehead. "Did you really think Lander and Bowan would stay behind indefinitely, Little Lorafin?"

I raised my shoulders. "Um . . . yes? I thought they were caring for Guardian Alleron?"

Trivan laughed. "They'll leave him food and water, just enough so he'll survive. Your former guardian can fend for himself in his locked chamber while we're gone."

My jaw dropped. Locked chamber. Food and water. They were treating him worse than a dog. But I didn't comment. I no longer felt any pity for my former guardian.

"We often travel in two groups," Alec explained. "It's the same on raids. We never all leave at the same time. Sooner or later, someone would notice, and while we do our best to keep our raids hidden, sometimes the Dark Raider's presence becomes known. It would be trouble-some if anyone began to connect that our presence is always missing in court when those raids occur."

I cocked my head. "But even if you leave in different groups, your presence is still missing during a raid, isn't it?"

Jax nodded. "True, but a few of us make a point to

venture back and forth from court, so at least some of us are seen around the time our raids occur. Doing so has resulted in nobody suspecting us."

I realized once again how deep Jax's crimes went against the powerful Houses and nobles of our kingdoms.

"But back to the matter at hand." Jax turned to his friends. "Trivan, you take watch in the Wood. Alec, Phillen, and Lars, you're coming with me." He stepped closer to my side and entwined his fingers through mine. The feel of him halted my breath, and I had to remind myself this was part of our playacting. He was my supposed lover after all.

"And me?" I said, my words breathier than I wanted to admit.

Dazzling blue irises raked over my face. "I thought that was obvious. You don't leave my side."

"Ever?"

He leaned down and ran the tip of his nose up my throat. A myriad of shivers tingled down my spine.

"No, Elowen, not ever. You stay with me . . . where you belong."

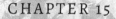

CHAPTER 15

We waited until nobody was in the nearby barn aisle before slipping through the door and relocking it. But once we were outside and back out in the open, we made a show of taking our time wandering through the many corrals to look at the animals.

The entire time, though, Trivan was subtly scoping out the surrounding Wood. A few minutes ticked by before he drifted closer to the prince.

"East of here, about a hundred paces. There's a large pine with good coverage. I can climb it and stay aloft until someone can take my place. It should offer a clear view of all of the barn doors."

Jax's head barely dipped in reply.

Pretending as though we were admiring all of the venues, we drifted back to the Wood to wander along a wildling trail. Trivan fell behind us, and the next time I looked over my shoulder, he'd disappeared.

"He's gone already?" I whispered, then leaned closer to Jax when another group of siltenites passed us on the path. Several nodded and murmured pleasantries.

"He's likely already at the top of that tree," he replied quietly.

My eyes bulged. "That fast?"

When he replied, his voice held a smile in it, "Yes, Little Lorafin, that fast."

Sunlight poked through the Wood's canopy, growing brighter as the sounds of the Match Finals carried on the wind. Cheers, boos, and roars erupted from a stadium north of us.

Alec hooked his thumb toward the noise. "Should we check out the stadium? Perhaps he's working there."

"Good idea. Keep your eyes peeled," Jax said under his breath when we emerged from the Wood.

Ahead, the huge stadium waited as the distant roars and cheers continued. In the distance, the white stone palace glittered in the sunlight, and even farther away, Leafton, Faewood's capital, waited.

The capital's buildings and shops soared above the Wood. Similar to Lemos, Leafton had been constructed with nature instead of destroying it. Trees, vines, and shrubs intermixed with the sprawling acres of roads, buildings, and shops. And like Jaggedston, an entire area of the capital had been dedicated to the lush manors of the ten Houses.

Applause broke out from the crowd within the stadium as we marched toward it. The huge circular structure soared to four stories, and a bright sky shone down on the open design since it didn't have a roof.

"What do you suppose is happening within there right now?" I asked as we approached the entrance. At the arched doorway leading in, a wildling was collecting entry fees.

"Most likely hand-to-hand combat or races," Phillen replied. "At the previous Centennial Matches, those were the most popular activities in these kinds of stadiums."

Jax dug several rulibs from his pocket and gave it to the wildling. It was more than needed. Admittance only required a quarter of a rulib per fairy, and when the light caught on the extravagant jewels studded in Jax's cuff, the wildling's head lifted.

He muttered a sound of surprise and then fell into a low bow, his hooves scraping across the grass. "Prince Adarian, such an honor."

Jax inclined his head. "May I ask where the best view is in the stadium? I would be willing to pay extra for it."

"No need, no need at all. The king has instructed us to give the best seats to all visiting royals. I have several areas reserved for fae such as you, and it would be my honor to show you, my prince."

Jax's expression stayed cool, his only reply a slight nod of his head. As I'd witnessed several times already, the crown prince of Stonewild Kingdom emerged, his freer counterpart, the Dark Raider, gone.

The wildling called another employee to take his place at the door, then he led us up several flights of stairs as the crowd continued their jubilant cries from their seats. I still hadn't seen anything worthwhile since the stairwell was entirely encased within stone, but when the wildling finally stopped at the second landing and led us through a small maze of corridors, my eyes widened when the first glimpse of the arena floor hit me.

A vast open area, filled with sand and obstacles, spread out before us. Several competitors were fighting, each trying to win and guarantee their spot in the Centennial Matches.

Jax's hand closed over mine, startling me from the scene. He pulled me closer to his side, and I remembered I was supposed to be his lover.

I slipped my arm around his waist as the wildling led us out onto a dais perched high above the arena floor. It projected slightly outward and sloped down at the perfect angle to allow us an unobstructed view. It also gave us clear glimpses of most of the crowd, even those seated higher above us.

"I hope this will do, my prince." The wildling bowed.

"Indeed. Thank you." Jax gave him several more rulibs. "Those are for you to keep. I insist."

The wildling's broad smile grew. He dipped into another bow and then scurried off.

Alone in the relatively private dais, Jax pulled me to the plush seating. Everywhere else in the arena, the seats were made of stone or wood, but here on the dais, the stone seating was covered in thick cushions and fluffy pillows. Elegant tables already filled with fruits and sparkling drinks waited, as though ready for whichever royal arrived, and it struck me how quickly such a structure and its amenities had been erected once the Mistvale spellcasters had arrived. It was truly marveling.

Jax lowered himself to the middle seat, his guards standing stoically behind him while Alec lounged on the chair near the railing. I began to lower myself to sit beside Jax, but before I could, he *tsked* and pulled me onto his lap.

I fell onto him, my breath huffing out of me and my stomach flipping.

Nearby, several siltenites leaned into each other, whispering and pointing toward us. They weren't even trying to hide that they were talking about us.

"Are you comfortable, my love?" Jax leaned down and nipped at my neck.

My entire body flushed. "Um, yes, my prince."

His hand drifted around my waist, and the bottom of

his fingers skated upward and almost touched the lower portion of my breast.

I wasn't sure if he even knew how close he'd come to touching me so intimately, but an answering pulse of longing throbbed in my core.

"Lean back. I won't break." He settled me against him, his firm chest strangely comfortable against my side.

Still, it took a few minutes to relax. I'd never sat this closely with any male before, not even when instructed to by Guardian Alleron when he'd asked me to charm males he was trying to seduce with my power.

I thought for certain I wouldn't be able to relax with so many eyes on us, but Jax began making soft lulling motions with his hand. He ran his strong fingers up and down my back in circular strokes. The caresses were soothing and arousing simultaneously.

Stars and galaxy.

For the briefest moment, I closed my eyes. Tingles shot up my arms, and I allowed myself to enjoy his caressing touch, but just as fast, I whipped my eyes open and reminded myself we weren't alone.

Tittering came from nearby. Several females were watching us and whispered behind cupped hands.

Snapping out of my reverie, I scanned the crowd, realizing the others were already subtly doing the same.

Everyone was covert about it, either angling in their

seats or pretending to stretch when they turned, but I quickly joined in and searched the crowd as best I could.

I looked for antlers, a clearly defining feature that no siltenite would have. But everywhere I looked in the crowd, it was either pure siltenites or pure wildlings only. No half-breeds.

My hope dimmed, but I thought back to the group of half-breeds I'd seen traveling in the Wood when Jax had still held me as a captive. And I'd seen a second group of half-breeds too after Guardian Alleron had rescued me in Lemos.

Multiple groups of half-breeds had ventured here. I was sure of it, so there had to be other half-breeds somewhere. We just had to find them. Because where there was one half-breed, there were usually others. It was no secret they tended to stick together, their outcast status bonding them.

"No sign of anyone interesting," Alec commented, his remark obscure enough that it wouldn't draw any attention if anyone overheard.

"Could be too early to tell," Jax replied just as evasively.

Minutes later, the competitors fighting on the arena floor finished their battle. Cheers rose from the crowd as they shuffled off the sandy arena, and for a brief moment, the floor was empty.

A group of wildlings ran out to change the props.

They moved so quickly that it was only minutes before the entire arena looked like a new venue. What had previously been a sandy floor with several walled obstacles in its vicinity was now a maze of hoops, low-lying barbed spikes, and enchanted weapons that randomly shot out spells.

Spectators leaned forward eagerly in their seats as the next round of potential competitors walked onto the arena's floor.

Jax stiffened beneath me just as my spine snapped upright.

The entire group of new competitors were half-breeds. All of them.

Murmurs erupted in the crowd as everyone took notice. Several siltenites near us began to boo, those behind us voicing their displeasure just as fast.

A low growl erupted from Jax, his friends having similar responses.

All of the half-breeds had animalistic features in one way or another. Three had hoofed feet, two had whiskers, one had wings, and half of them had exteriors that were fur or scales instead of bare skin, yet all of them wore clothes.

But no antlers.

I sagged against Jax, and for once, his wandering hands stopped. Disappointment swelled in his aura so potently it robbed my breath. Unconsciously, I shifted closer to him, wanting to give him comfort. The second I realized what

I'd done, I stiffened, but Jax's arm locked around me, and he kept me close.

Alec leaned over to the prince and whispered, "Now this is interesting. Do you think he traveled here because friends of his came to compete?"

Jax frowned. "Could be, but I hadn't heard of any half-breeds he knew having an interest in the Matches."

"Do you recognize any of them?" I asked the prince quietly.

He subtly shook his head. "No, none of them."

Some of the booing crowd had quieted, and thankfully, a few cheered in encouragement. But the majority's reaction was typical of our society. Most despised the half-breeds because of the threat they posed to siltenites, but there were groups of fae who championed for them. Nobody could deny that the half-breeds were shunned and treated as lesser, even more so than wildlings, and it took bravery to speak up against it since those who did were often shunned too.

I nibbled on my lip. That strange kinship I felt toward them resurfaced. Like me, half-breeds were *other*, but the belief that half-breeds should be eliminated ran deep in our culture, unlike the reverence a lorafin received. Our society despised them so much that it was a miracle King Paevin had allowed them to compete at all.

A siltenite walked out onto the arena floor, his gestures grand as he waved his arms in dramatic fashion. "Fine fae of our four kingdoms," he boomed from a magical device, "our next competition shall require the competitors to remain in the fray as they battle unseen attacks. Those left standing, shall proceed to the next round. Let the battle begin!"

The spectators cheered just as the arena erupted in a display of magical traps and obstacles.

Where there had been sand only moments ago, pillars burst from the floor, knocking one of the competitors off his feet. The other devices activated as well. The hoops soared through the air, forcing the half-breeds to leap through them or be knocked over.

Demobilizing spells shot from the weapons, freezing anybody they touched. One of the half-breeds froze mid-step when a spell hit him, as though paralyzed. A flying hoop knocked him off his feet a second later, but he quickly recovered, shaking off the spell and leaping back into action. But he hadn't even gone two feet before a boulder tumbled out of a trap door and rolled right over him.

My breath sucked in. Even from the distance, a sickening crunch reached my ears. The boulder rolled to a stop, and the half-breed lay unmoving. Two wildlings rushed out to drag him off the floor.

Just as fast, a shimmer of magic billowed in the air, and then new wildlings burst through small doors mid-way up the arena's interior walls. They flew atop large redbeaked hawks, the giant birds soaring through the air while the wildling riders shot at the competitors with poisoned darts.

One half-breed took a dart in the shoulder. She was unconscious before she hit the floor.

The remaining half-breeds fought valiantly, some even using a combination of weapons and their own magic to fend off the attacks.

One of the competitors wove his own illusion, and my breath sucked in. A snapping beast of fangs and claws appeared out of nowhere. A redbeaked hawk shrieked and dove off course, knocking its wildling rider off as the illusion engulfed the wildling in a single gulp.

The illusion's magic fizzled out of existence, and the crowd gasped, but the wildling landed harmlessly on the floor, falling right through the illusion. Everyone laughed. But a second later, when the same half-breed with illusion magic took a poisoned dart to the shoulder, the dart barely penetrated him. He pulled it out and threw it onto the floor before another illusion emerged from his magic.

The crowd's easy laugh gave way to terrified gasps.

"And that is why they fear them." The prince's comment was said so quietly under his breath that I almost didn't hear him. But he was right.

A half-breed powerful enough to wield illusions and also be immune to poisonous darts that could barely penetrate his tough exterior was indeed threatening to a siltenite.

My eyes stayed glued to that particular half-breed as the competition wore on. He was tall, powerfully built with broad shoulders like a siltenite, but he had a partial snout, and his entire body shimmered with stone-like scales. On top of that, compared to the others, he had superior magic. He moved quickly, ducking and fending off anything the arena threw at him. Magic perpetually clouded around him, creating a shimmering dome.

Lars whistled softly in surprise behind us, then said, "Is that a . . . Shield?"

"It is." Phillen's brow furrowed, and shock barreled through me.

Shields could only be wielded by powerful siltenites, and even then, it took a higher level of magic and training to accomplish such a task. But given this half-breed's talent, he was just as skilled as any siltenite, if not more.

The competitors carried on, showing off their skills to the judges who sat on a similar dais to us across the arena's floor.

When the fighting and sparring finally ended, an eruption of magical numbers appeared hovering above the arena floor.

Not surprisingly, the half-bred who'd woven illusions had received the highest marks.

Cheers rose from the crowd, but whisperings began just as fast. The words that I caught weren't flattering . . .

"They should all be locked up," one hissed.

"Disgraceful. They should be banned from the kingdoms," another sniveled.

"Executed is what I say," a third sneered. "They all should be killed at birth."

Shock billowed through me at the blatant hatred swimming through the crowd. I sank back into Jax, but as sickened as I was at hearing such comments, I also wasn't surprised. This was what siltenites feared most—a half-breed who could easily outwit them, outmagic them, outbreed them, and in the end . . . kill them.

WE STAYED in the arena for the rest of the afternoon, hoping to catch a glimpse of Bastian. And it soon became apparent, due to the number of half-breeds appearing in the Finals, that the Centennial Matches would indeed have siltenites and half-breeds competing this time around.

"This is the first time that's ever happened in our history," Alec said.

I scrunched my eyebrows together. "Why do you suppose King Paevin is allowing them to compete? No king has ever allowed that."

Jax frowned. "I've been wondering that too. I've never heard of him championing half-breed rights. Have you?" he asked Alec.

The noble shook his head. "If anything, I thought he despised them from what my father's told me."

The prince's frown grew. "I was under the same impression."

I nibbled on my lip and mulled that over, but I was as baffled as Jax and the others were as to why admission requirements had abruptly changed in the Matches.

But from what we saw, it was evident the half-breeds were worthy competitors. More than a few were as magically strong as siltenites, and it could be argued that some were even stronger.

One half-breed with *dressel* ancestry, given her tusks and bony head, had even vanished during her competition, only to reappear at the other end of the stadium. An audible gasp had erupted through the crowd, moving like a tidal wave through the stadium, when she'd done that. She'd actually *mistphased*, a magical marvel that was usually only seen among Solis fae.

The sun was dipping toward the horizon when the Finals for the day at last came to an end. Disappointment clouded around the prince.

Bastian had never appeared.

Jax shifted subtly beneath me. "We should get going," he said quietly into my ear. "He's obviously not going to show here."

The prince's scent clouded around me, the pine and spicy fragrance going straight to my head.

Nodding, I stood, and the others did the same. Several muffled conversations reached my ears as the siltenites sitting near us spotted us leaving. From their curious stares and blatant questions that were loud enough to carry on the wind, it soon became apparent that more than one was wondering who I was.

But while the prince kept a firm grip on me the entire walk out of the arena, I could tell that his thoughts were scattered since he never even glanced toward them. A troubled frown had descended over his features.

I wasn't surprised. Not only had we not found his brother here, but Bastian's actions made no sense based off what I'd learned of him. Because if his brother had indeed come here to compete in the Matches or support his friends or find employment or simply watch the Matches for enjoyment, he would have told Jax that. He wouldn't have disappeared so mysteriously and certainly not months prior. There was nothing logical about it, especially since Jax and Bastian were so close.

Once free of the stadium, Jax's attention shifted back toward the barn, and then the tall pine in the Wood. None of us could see Trivan, but we all knew he was there.

"Alec?" Jax nodded toward the Wood. "Do you want to take Trivan's spot and tell him to meet us at the inn?"

Alec dipped his head. "I was waiting for you to ask that."

The noble jogged off while Lars and Phillen remained at the prince's side.

Jax approached one of the wildling staff. "Are there any enchanted carpets available?"

The wildling bowed. "Of course, Prince Adarian. I'll have one summoned immediately."

We didn't have to wait long. A moment later, a large enchanted carpet raced toward us, flying only feet above the ground.

When the carpet glided to a stop, the wildling bowed. "Your ride, my prince."

Jax nodded in thanks. Lars and Phillen hopped onto the carpet first, one standing at the front, the other at the back. Jax stepped on next, then offered me his hand. The gesture seemed entirely automatic given the haunted expression and faraway look he wore.

I took his outstretched hand, nibbling on my lip, then seated myself beside the prince at the carpet's center.

Jax muttered a command, and the carpet took off.

Wind whipped through my hair, and as though entirely unaware of what he was doing, Jax wove a cloud of his air elemental magic around us, and the wind halted. Once again, it was as though he did the gesture without even being aware of it.

My brow puckered in concern as I studied Jax's profile. Ever since it'd become apparent that hundreds, perhaps even thousands, of half-breeds were present at the Matches, the aura around Jax had steadily pulsed.

I couldn't help but wonder if he feared his brother had intentionally left him with no plans to ever return to Stonewild. That perhaps he'd packed up in the middle of the night with a group of half-breed friends, and he feared that his older brother wouldn't support whatever decision had driven him to do that.

"We'll find him." I squeezed the prince's hand.

Jax started, his expression momentarily clearing. His gaze dropped to where our fingers were entwined, and I realized I'd initiated our touch, not him.

Irises that were an endless blue met mine, and the swirling fear in them made my heart clench. "I hope so, Elowen. I really do."

"We will." But even to my ears, the words rang hollow because a part of me was starting to wonder if his brother even wanted to be found.

If Bastian had left in such a clandestine manner without any word to his family, perhaps he'd chosen to leave Jax behind.

And given the prince's expression, once again morphing into one of hurt and betrayal, I was beginning to wonder if he was reaching the same conclusion.

CHAPTER 16

The carpet took us to a large inn, located in the heart of Leafton. The prince made a show of our arrival, his earlier concern for his brother entirely masked as he nuzzled my neck when we entered the establishment. His affectionate gesture made it hard to breathe. I was barely able to appreciate the inn's grand entryway with soaring ceilings and twisting vines crawling up the stone walls.

Several inn employees stood at attention, checking in guests, but Jax didn't halt and instead strode straight toward the salopas on the ground floor, my hand firmly in his grip. His guards kept pace several steps behind us. Violin music from enchanted instruments played near the salopas entrance and filled the air with beautiful chords.

The prince led me toward a corner booth. The light grew dimmer, the brightness of the entryway falling behind us as he wove us deeper into the drinking establishment.

Even though Leafton had been my home for the past season, while Emerson Estate was being constructed, I was still relatively new to living in the capital. I didn't know many of the entertainment venues or how to traverse the winding streets of its inner city. Even so, I tried not to look like a gawking spectator.

At the booth, Jax tugged me in with him, and he didn't stop until he had a clear view of the entire room. With his side pressed firmly to mine, he finally settled while Phillen and Lars stood at attention at each end of the U-shaped booth, not sitting.

"Why are we here?" I asked the prince quietly. I could have sworn that the prince mentioned something about staying at his private residence, not an inn.

"This is where we'll stay. The Silver Hand is where my residence is. My parents own a suite here." Jax raised his hand to signal the barkeep. She nodded briskly in return. "And this salopas is where we typically frequent when we're visiting Faewood. It's easy to drink as much as we want since it's attached to the inn." He gestured toward the elegant bar to our left. Behind it, hovering shelves held decadent bottles and a plethora of alcoholic choices. The shelves were constantly moving, shifting up, to the side, and down as though in time with the music. A huge mirror waited behind them, and I caught sight of my flushed cheeks and excited eyes.

Stars Above. Have I ever looked so alive?

The lone bartender working in the salopas grabbed various bottles, throwing them and twirling them in the air as she made our drinks. The free entertainment garnered a few claps and thrown rulibs in her bowl from those sitting at the long bar.

All the while, enchanted trays waited nearby for her to deposit drinks, which quickly glided away to serve the patrons already seated.

The establishment was only half full, the evening still an hour away, but I had a feeling by tonight this place would be packed.

"Is this where we're meeting the others?" I asked.

Jax dipped his head and pressed a kiss along my throat. Goosebumps broke out across my skin as he whispered, "We'll meet them upstairs. We're simply here to make an appearance and be seen. That's all. It would be unusual for me not to do this, and since we do our best to keep our activity as close to normal as possible, that's why we're here. But after a drink, we'll head up."

The feel of his lips on my skin was so distracting that I couldn't reply. I managed a strangled murmur, but my head didn't clear until he pulled away.

When my wits finally returned, I realized we were being watched. More than a dozen patrons weren't even trying to hide their curious stares, and I knew that the prince had just done that intimate gesture to draw even more attention. He wanted our presence here known, and he wanted to be seen in public with only me and his guards while the others remained hidden. Everything he did was smoke and mirrors and a game of deception.

None of this is real. I firmly needed to remember that, but then Alec's claim again swirled through my mind.

Our drinks floated toward us a minute later, but the last thing I needed was alcohol. I was ready to jump out of my skin after all of the touches the prince had given me today, and adding alcohol to my system would only add fuel to the fire. I felt ready to combust. Explode. I was so ripe with wanting that I feared every male in the establishment could smell my arousal, and alcohol would make me completely lose my inhibitions.

The prince stiffened when several passing wildling males stared at me a bit too long. One of them was an *iloseep*. His nose twitched, and his eyes turned to slits. His species was known for their sense of smell.

The tray carrying our drinks landed on the table, but just as our drinks floated to our place settings, a dillemsill appeared in a puff of magic, standing right in the center of the table.

I jumped.

"Prince Adarian of Stonewild Kingdom, you have a message," it chirped.

Jax frowned, but he picked up the small bird with purple feathers and a long yellow furry tail, then brought it to his ear. The bird chirped its message, and Jax's mouth tightened.

Once the message had been conveyed, Jax set it down. "Thank you." He inclined his head.

The bird bowed, then began to spin, moving like a mini tornado, and in a puff of magic, it disappeared and traveled back to wherever it'd originated from.

I eyed my drink but didn't touch it. "Is everything okay?"

He picked up his ale and downed half of it in one swallow. "Everything's fine." But his jaw muscle ticked, and his eyes turned into chips of ice.

"Was it about . . ." I let my words hang, hoping he would know I was asking about Bastian.

But the prince shook his head. "No, it was just a message from my mother."

"Oh." I frowned and picked up my drink, my fingers curling around the cool green beverage.

"It seems someone reported to her that I was more attentive to *you* on the ship than the House females, and my mother felt the need to reprimand me and remind me she expects me to take one of them to the Ironcrest Ball after the Matches."

"*Oh*." I quickly guzzled a large gulp of my leminai. "Does that mean she's . . . angry?"

His lips turned upward in a brittle smile. "How my mother feels about what I choose to do is irrelevant."

"But is it?" My fingers curled even tighter around my glass, and I downed more of my beverage as I was once again faced with the reality of the prince's future. He was to marry another. Whether he liked it or not. And the most I could ever be was his mistress.

"Yes, it is," he replied in a clipped tone.

I started at his harsh words, and for some reason, irritation rose in me. Maybe it was because he was avoiding the inevitable. Or maybe it was because he wasn't being honest with himself about what would undoubtedly happen next summer. Or maybe it was because I was reminded that I had never been considered worthy of anything but performing callings in my life and certainly would never be considered worthy of marrying a prince.

Whatever the case, I quickly finished my beverage. "Are you done?" I asked a bit sharper than I intended to.

The prince set his drink down. He still had a quarter of it remaining. "No, but I can be. Are you ready to go?"

"Yes."

I slid out of the booth, nearly swaying when I was upright. As I feared earlier, the alcohol I drank was going straight to my head. And it hadn't helped that I practically slammed it.

Despite knowing that the drink was likely impairing my judgment, I couldn't stop the irrational annoyance stoking my insides like a flame, which only made me angrier, then embarrassed, then angry again.

Frustration stole through me that I couldn't control my reactions to the prince or change what his future held or alter the path in life I'd been given.

It didn't help that we hadn't found his brother yet, which meant I would have to continue this charade at his side for who knew how long, even if he did have *feelings* for me. It was insufferable since I was ready to straddle the prince at this very second, but nothing could ever come of it.

The prince joined me at the table's edge. He towered over me and inhaled, his nostrils flaring sharply. "Elowen, tell me what's the matter."

I shook my head and forced myself to take a deep breath, yet the alcohol kept burning through my veins. "It's nothing. I'm just tired. It's been a long day, and I think it's hitting me."

His frown deepened, but he drained the rest of his beverage in one gulp, then nodded at his guards. "Let's go."

The four of us headed back toward the attached inn, and Jax took the lead, his hand once again clasped over mine.

We wove through the dim salopas, out into the grand entryway, then past the inn's magical lift that would take us up flights of stairs on a levitating platform.

Jax led me to a back staircase, and the old spiral stairs groaned under our weight as we trudged up three stories.

I was winded by the time he reached the top floor, but Jax didn't slow.

He went to the door at the hall's end, and with a start I realized it was the largest suite. We were on the top floor, and none of the other rooms had a double-doored entry.

The lock clicked when he hovered his finger above it.

I canted my head. "I take it, this is your residence."

"It is."

"But is this normal? To have a private residence at an inn?"

The prince shrugged. "My father always liked this inn, so when he requested to purchase their nicest suite, they obliged."

"I'm sure the fact that he's a foreign king had nothing to do with their decision."

His brow furrowed. "My father has no qualms about taking what he wants and using his status to do so."

Phillen cleared his throat from behind us. "But the fact that we can use the inn's kitchens is a nice perk. All you have to do is summon food from the inn, and it appears."

Lars nodded. "I have to agree with Phillen on that one. Cooking has never been my favorite pastime."

Jax opened the door and pulled me inside. The double doors had opened to a grand entryway with polished stone flooring, paneled walls, and glittering fairy lights. Just beyond the entryway was a vast sitting area. A large kitchen waited to the side of it, and several hallways branched off in other directions farther down the hall. The halls were long, and I figured those led to multiple sleeping chambers in this massive apartment.

"Will my chambers be down there?" I asked, pointing toward the hall.

"Yes, but—"

I didn't wait for the prince to reply. I fled from his sight, and a quick perusal of the rooms showed they were nearly identical. I figured it didn't matter which one I took, so I closed the door behind me on the second one down and quickly flopped onto the bed.

Alcohol still swam through my system, and even though it was only mid-evening, my eyes drooped, so much so, that within minutes, I was asleep.

I AWOKE the next day to a knock on my door. Lars opened it cautiously and peered inside. "Elowen? It's time to get up. We need to get moving."

Sunlight streamed in through the windows. It was bright enough that I knew it wasn't sunrise, but it was still early.

"Okay," I somehow managed, and he closed the door.

My head pounded, and I cursed the leminai I'd

consumed at a much faster rate than I should have, but I did as requested and forced myself to get up.

Someone had placed my bag inside my chosen chambers. It sat atop a large chest that hadn't been in that spot last night. Someone had obviously brought the chest in too. Cocking my head, I opened it.

My eyes widened when I beheld all of the fine clothing. Dresses similar to the green one I still wore from yesterday were carefully packed, but there were other clothes too. Fine slacks, decadent sweaters, loose yet fashionable tops. It was as though an entire mini wardrobe had been crafted for me, but considering we didn't know how long we'd be in Leafton searching for Bastian, I wasn't surprised.

If I was the crown prince's lover, others would expect to see me in a different stunning outfit each day.

Sighing, I chose a pair of slacks and one of the flowing tops. It was crafted from luxurious material, yet once on, it flowed over me like water. Smooth and comfortable.

Some of the ire I'd felt last night lessened. This outfit was befitting a mistress to the crown prince, yet it was also comfortable, and I liked it.

Once dressed, I made my way to the large living area. Everyone was already present.

Tentatively, I met Jax's eye. His expression was guarded, entirely unreadable. "Thank you for the clothes. They're beautiful."

His eyebrows rose. "You like them?"

"I do."

A devastating smile appeared on his face, and my insides quickened.

To cover up my reaction, I hastily turned away and grabbed some of the food on the counter, then helped myself to a cup of tea.

"First Match Final starts right at eight." Phillen glanced at the clock. "Best be on our way soon."

I hastily finished the meal, then we all set out again.

FIVE DAYS PASSED of Jax and I playacting at being lovers, attending the Match Finals, watching the competitions, and searching for Bastian.

But no matter where we looked, we couldn't find him.

I'd told Jax repeatedly that I could venture to the Veiled Between again to ask about Bastian, but the prince still adamantly refused. His concern for my well-being was bordering on crazy.

He wanted desperately to find his brother, yet he refused to even consider putting me in harm's way, even if I did a calling for one of his friends that meant I wouldn't be hurt as badly. Apparently, just the possibility of me being hurt wasn't acceptable.

Jax's extreme protectiveness made no sense to me

whatsoever. I'd been hurt monstrously throughout my lifetime due to callings, yet I'd always survived. I healed quickly, and I'd proven that I was resilient, yet the prince looked positively murderous at the thought of further harm coming to me at his request.

So I finally stopped offering to venture to the Veiled Between. Instead, I helped the others as we kept looking for Bastian while waiting for Lander and Bowan to arrive at the week's end.

Trivan and Alec traded places regularly as they perpetually kept eyes on the barn, but there was still no sign of Jax's brother.

By the end of day five, even their determination looked strained. I was guessing that had something to do with the number of pine needles that both Trivan and Alec had to pull from their arses and hair every time they returned from a shift in that tree.

Also not surprisingly, after five days, the mood in our group had diminished.

Trivan, Lars, Phillen, Jax, and I trudged up the stairs, back to Jax's suite in Leafton near the end of the week. Alec was once again in the tree, watching over the barn even though each day that passed, it seemed less and less likely that Bastian would ever return to it.

Phillen clapped the prince on the back when we reached the top of the stairs. "At least the others are arriving tonight. With more eyes and bodies, we'll have a better chance at finding him."

Jax didn't bother replying but instead strode down the hall to the double doors. I followed behind him. It was now second nature to stay at his side after so many days of pretending we were together.

Yet behind the closed doors of his suite, it was another matter. I refused to share a chambers with the prince at night. And since I was careful to cleanse my chambers each morning of my clothes and scent, none of the inn staff were whispering that we didn't share a bed.

Well, at least, as far as we could tell.

Grumbling, the prince hovered his finger over the door's lock, his mood even fouler than it was this morning, and I had the strangest urge to go to him and try to offer comfort, but the second my feet stepped into the suite's entryway, I drew up short.

Bowan, Lander, and another male I didn't know stood in the room. And all of them were dressed in black with head bandanas in place. The only thing missing were their masks.

Since it was the first time I'd ever seen Lander and Bowan without their masks on, it took me a minute to recognize them. But Lander had always had darker-brown skin than Bowan, and his hair was longer too. And when Bowan's earring flashed in the light, it was easier for me to tell who was who. It helped that the males had different eye colors as well. Where Bowan's eyes were green, Lander's were brown.

But the new male was someone I could have sworn I'd never seen before. He had light-blue eyes, and a hint of silver-streaked dark hair peeked out from under his bandana. But he didn't appear old. He looked young, with high cheekbones and firm lips. I studied his unusual hair and wondered if he had distant Solis ancestry.

I had a feeling this was Quinn, the remaining member of their band I hadn't met yet. But I didn't have time to contemplate that further because Bowan jumped forward to greet us.

"Finally, they've arrived." An amused smile slid across Bowan's face, and I blinked. I'd never seen his grin before, but it was just as wide as I always assumed it would be.

The newcomer's attention drifted to me, and his piercing light-blue eyes looked me over. "Are you going to properly introduce us?"

Bowan laughed. "Oh, right. That's Elowen, the lorafin we were telling you about."

The male inclined his head. "I'm Quinn."

"I kind of figured. It's a pleasure to meet you." I nearly dipped into a curtsy, my age-old response when meeting new fae, but I stopped myself at the last moment.

Lander, not surprisingly, remained entirely impassive despite Bowan's enthusiasm. His dark-brown skin shone in the fairy lights, and he didn't smile. He merely crossed his arms and leveled Jax with a pointed stare, then said in his monotone voice, "About time. We've been waiting."

Jax scowled and firmly closed the door behind us, then cast a solid wall of air around everyone to ensure our conversation remained private. "Why are you all dressed for a raid?"

Bowan rubbed his hands together, his eyes glittering. "We just got word before we left Stonewild that the shipment we've been tracking in Ampum is on the move again. It's passing through just north of here in Possyrose Forest. If we go tonight, we can intercept it."

"Seriously?" Excitement filled Trivan's tone, and a sly grin spread across his face. "We've been trying to get that shipment for months." He waggled his eyebrows. "When do we go?"

"You're going to conduct a raid *tonight*?" I hissed, then drew up short just as fast. *Ampum? Shipment? Why does that ring a bell?* I could have sworn I'd heard something about it before, and then it hit me. My eyes widened even more. I *had* heard of it. The day I'd done three callings for King Paevin, I overheard lordlings from Faewood's ten Houses discussing it as I walked by a room they'd been visiting in. They'd been saying they were worried the Dark Raider was pursuing it. "Wait, you're going after that shipment with gold bars?"

Lander's brow furrowed. "How do you know about that?"

I waved a hand dismissively. "I overheard some lordlings talking about it several weeks ago in Faewood's palace. But is that safe? To go now when we're supposed to be finding Bastian?"

Jax's nostrils flared, and his hand pressed to my lower back. My body immediately responded, but I tried to suppress the rush of awareness that slid through me. "I agree with Elowen. That's not why we're here, even if I do covet that gold. What about Bastian? Any news on your end?"

"Still no sign of him in Stonewild," Bowan replied. "None up north either."

Lander's fingers drummed against his thighs. "Tonight is the most advantageous time for this raid, Jax. It's the only opportunity we've had in months."

A muscle began to tick in the prince's jaw. "If we go now, that would require leaving Elowen here. Alone. Not to mention, you both know how I feel about attempting a raid last minute."

"She's a big girl. She'll be fine. Just don't get captured and interrogated by anyone." Bowan winked at me, then turned to Jax. "And I know you don't like last-minute changes considering the risk, but if we can pull this off, the payoff will be worth it."

Jax's scowl grew, but since he didn't shoot them down immediately, he seemed to be considering it.

My heart raced, thinking of what they were contemplating doing tonight. Just as fast, I chastised myself. They'd been doing raids for full seasons. Who was I to worry if an impromptu raid was a good idea or not?

Jax finally sighed, and his aura practically pulsed with power, but from his concerned look my way, I knew he was worried about leaving me by myself.

I offered him a reassuring smile. Well, as reassuring as I could muster considering I was suddenly worried about all of them. "I'll be fine. Don't worry about me. Like Bowan said, I'm a big girl."

He arched an eyebrow. "You're sure?"

"Yes, I'll be fine."

"All right." He nodded curtly, and it struck me that he *trusted* me.

A tingling sense of warmth bloomed through me. Jax trusted me not to run, never once questioning if I would, and strangely . . . I liked that. Oddly, it was a pleasant feeling, gratifying actually. Even though I'd been doing my best to keep him at arm's length all week, when we weren't pretending to be lovers in public, I couldn't deny that his trust pleased me.

Is this why he's always asking me to trust him? Does he feel similar in the times I've extended my trust? Those thoughts made me pause.

"You'll stay hidden from others?" Jax asked me, his eyebrows raising.

I knew his concern was about Mistvale fae. As unlikely

as it was that I would ever be captured or interrogated by one, it was the entire reason he'd refused to let me be free.

I nodded. "I'll stay hidden. You don't need to worry. No Mistvale fairy will capture me."

His gaze dipped to my mouth, so briefly that I nearly missed the flare in his eyes. Hunger filled them, and the heat of it hit me right in my center.

He'd been giving me looks like that all week. Each time, I grew flushed, and at this point, I was ready to combust. But just as fast, Jax was pulling black clothing from one of his bags and issuing orders.

"You'll have to change back into normal clothes," he told Bowan, Lander, and Quinn. "We can't leave looking like that since fae in the city will see you. You'll have to change into your raider attire once we reach the forest."

"We can actually leave like this," Quinn replied. "Nobody will see us."

Jax cocked his head. "How so? I can't cast an illusion over us. Fae may knock into us on the street. And you know we don't glamour ourselves when our presence is already known in a city, just in case the glamour fails."

"We're not going on the street. We don't need illusions or glamours. We're going to travel using these." Bowan opened his palm to reveal several tiny keys.

The keys glittered like metallic stardust, and my eyes widened. Stepping closer, I had the strongest urge to touch them but managed to refrain.

"What are those?" I asked curiously.

"Portal keys." Bowan nodded toward Quinn. "He brought them along."

Jax's brow furrowed, and he planted his hands on his hips, giving Quinn a heavy look. "Where did you get portal keys?"

Quinn smiled slyly. "From Drachu."

Jax's eyebrows shot up. "Drachu? The Lochen fae king?"

Quinn shrugged. "He lost a bet, and I don't feel the least bit guilty about it. After his raid on our northern coast last week, he deserved to lose all of these."

Jax gave him a resigned look, his sigh following. "Do I want to know the backstory of how that encounter with Drachu happened?"

Quinn grinned wickedly. "Probably not."

I eyed the keys again, my interest growing. "What exactly are those?"

"Portal keys are forged in the *other* realm," Quinn explained. "Yet some fae in our realm have also acquired them."

I cocked my head. "What do they do?"

Quinn pinched one between his two fingers. The key was tiny. "They allow one to magically transport instantaneously, like the Solis fae who can mistphase."

My brows shot up. "You're jesting."

Bowan laughed. "He's not. We've had these before, but

not this many." He inclined his head toward a jar on the table that was full of them.

My jaw dropped. "You won *all* of those in a bet?"

Quinn smirked. "What can I say. I'm good at weighing my odds."

Bowan laughed and clapped him on the back. "Normally, we don't have this many portal keys at once, but since Quinn is well . . . *Quinn* . . ." He shrugged. "At the moment, we do."

The prince placed his hands on his hips, and a small smile tugged on his lips. My breath caught. He'd gotten changed in the time I'd been talking to the other males, and he looked exactly as he had the night he'd taken me.

He glanced at me, only his eyes visible, and damn my traitorous body, but a pool of desire flared in my core.

His voice dipped, taking on a husky tone, his eyes never leaving mine when he said, "You'll be okay?" I nodded again, and he added, "If nothing else, those keys will help make this raid in Possyrose Forest faster and more discreet. Shall we then?" he asked the others.

Quinn placed a key in his pocket, then closed his fist around another. He held his free hand out. "Lander? I know you've always wanted to hold hands with me."

Lander didn't even crack a smile, but he linked hands with Quinn. The others quickly followed, Lars and Phillen too, until all seven of them were in physical contact with one another.

"Alec's going to be so jealous that he missed this." Trivan snickered.

"Where is Alec?" Bowan asked.

"In a tree," Phillen replied. "It's a long story," he added when Lander, Bowan, and Quinn all shared confused looks.

"Are you sure you'll be all right?" Jax asked me again, his gaze still boring into mine.

All I could manage was another nod. Stars and galaxy, what this male did to my insides . . .

Bowan winked at me. "See you soon, Little Lorafin."

"Try not to get into trouble," Trivan added.

"Open key for thou I ask, I need a door for this new task." Quinn finished muttering the strange words, and in a blur of magic, they disappeared.

CHAPTER 17

One moment, the seven males were in the royal's private residence, and the next, they were gone.

I didn't know how long it would be before they returned, but I knew it would be late since it was already evening.

My stomach flipped, thinking of what could happen. They could get caught, or worse, killed. But then I reminded myself that they did raids like this all of the time, and it was silly to fret.

To distract myself, I perched on the window's ledge to look outside. Fae filled the streets since the Matches had brought in so many crowds, but my thoughts still turned to where Jax and his friends had just landed. *Possyrose Forest.* That was miles from here.

Sighing, I spun away from the window and flopped onto the couch. Above, the ceiling stared back at me, and I realized it was the first time since the prince had taken me that I was by myself and not locked inside a chamber. It was almost as if I was . . . free.

That thought hit me so hard, that my breath caught. I stood and toiled around the room, a laugh bubbling out of my lips. I could do whatever I wanted at the moment. If I wanted to draw a bath and soak in it for hours until they returned, I could. If I wanted to summon the inn staff and ask them to bring me up a meal of whatever I chose, I could. If I wanted to hang my head out the window and stare at all of the crowds the Matches had summoned, I could.

A tiny smile grew on my lips. Jax trusted me to stay with them because I wasn't a true prisoner anymore. *Stars Above, I can do whatever I want. Well, not quite . . .*

I'd promised to remain hidden after all, which meant I couldn't let any fae in Leafton see me, but my magic was mostly free now, meaning I could wield nearly any spell.

My eyes widened. My tutors had given me a very thorough education when I'd been young, and that education had included complex illusion spells that most fae could never master without Mistvale power. But I was a lorafin. My magic wasn't born of the kingdoms, and I wasn't caged by where I'd been birthed in the realm. My magic was *other*. More powerful, and I was capable of spells others weren't.

My pulse thrummed when that heady realization hit me.

As an adult, I'd never tried wielding an illusion spell before, since my magic had always been caged by my collar, but now . . .

I rubbed my finger along my collar, and the cool familiar metal doused my spirits slightly. I might be free of my guardian and this collar's suffocating hold, but I was still irrevocably chained to it. It would never come off.

Still, at the moment, I didn't feel like I had any walls holding me prisoner. And if I *was* able to cast an illusion spell over myself, I *could* leave these walls and still remain hidden. Nobody would be able to see me in Leafton, which meant I could still keep my promise to Jax to stay out of harm's way and prevent the incredibly unlikely chance of being captured by a Mistvale fairy.

That thought hit me like a million volts of lightning, and my collar vibrated subtly. Just as fast, it occurred to me that while I could be traipsing through the capital, Jax would be enacting a dangerous raid.

A stirring of anxiety skated along my limbs at the risks Jax and the others would be facing tonight.

Right. Decision made. There's no way I can stay here and stew about that. I'm going out. Alone.

I CHANGED into simple black breeches and opted for the purple sweater I'd grown to love. Even though nobody would be able to see my clothing, I wanted to feel comfortable.

Once fully dressed, I slipped into black boots and draped a scarf over my hair to help alleviate any chill the evening brought. Then I went to the mirror, faced it, and closed my eyes.

I pulled on a strong stream of my magic and whispered an illusion spell. The amount of magic it took to wield the spell cascaded over me, but my magic rose steadily within me given my loosened collar until the amount of magic needed was filled.

Holding my breath, I opened my eyes.

Nothing stared back at me in the mirror.

I gave an excited yelp, then turned left and right just to be sure. But my illusion had worked. I was *entirely* invisible.

The spell would hold for at least a few hours, which meant I had most of the evening to enjoy myself and my newfound freedom.

Nearly skipping in excitement, I left the suite. In the hall, the doors clicked shut, locking as they did so. I ran my fingers along the curved door handle. I didn't have a key to reopen it, nor Jax's fingerprint to trigger the magical lock, but I did know several trusted unlocking spells.

Sure enough, when I whispered one to test it, the lock

unclicked immediately. A smug feeling swept through me that my childhood lessons were coming in handier than I'd ever thought possible.

Giddiness seeped through my veins, and this time I did skip down the hall toward the circular stairs. I hurried down them until I reached street level.

I had to wait until the inn staff opened the door for a siltenite entering from outside, but at the first opportunity, I slipped past them. Once free of the inn's elegant entryway, I was truly on my own in the capital.

I inhaled deeply when the fragrant evening air hit me.

The smell of roasted meats filtered out from several food stands down on the street corner. Scents of casting magic from the inn's mechanics that kept the building cool even in the heat of summer tickled my nose. And laughter from a small child who passed by as she held her mother's hand rang through my ears.

The sounds of the city hummed around me, and I didn't think I'd ever heard anything so blissfully poignant.

My grin grew as worries about Jax and the others slipped away.

I wandered down the street, completely uninhibited. Since nobody could see me, I was entirely free. Nobody asked me who I was. Nobody asked where I was going. Nobody even so much as glanced in my direction, and for the first time *ever* when in public, Guardian Alleron's guards didn't accompany me.

I was truly alone among the masses.

I spent the next hour dipping in and out of shops and weaving my way through the crowds. I wasn't able to buy anything, but just looking and browsing was enough. Everything was so new to me, but I wasn't worried about getting lost, since I kept a close eye on each turn and street that I followed. I'd always had a good sense of direction, so I knew I would find my way back.

I finally stopped at the Venapearl Fountains near the city's center. I'd visited them once before with Guardian Alleron when he'd taken me into the capital to perform a calling for one of the rich businessfae who preferred living among the city bustle versus the sprawling countryside.

But the fountains were even more beautiful in the evening light. Glittering streams of water shot into the air, and music came from magically projected devices sitting at its base. The fountains were huge, encompassing an entire city block, and the water changed color with each spurt from its jets.

Pink, yellow, green, and glittering blue water streamed and wove together. The show was not only pleasing to watch but hypnotic. The music made me want to dance and sway, reminding me of the last time I had the opportunity to be so uninhibited. Memories of dancing back in Fosterton when Jax had been the Dark Raider flitted across my thoughts.

My insides immediately clenched, and I wondered

again what Jax was doing at this very moment. Even worse, I wondered if he was still safe.

Knowing those thoughts would lead nowhere good, I forced myself to sit on a nearby bench and enjoy the dazzling fountain as stars begin to twinkle in the growing twilight.

I'd just settled back, deciding to stay until the sun truly descended, when the sound of clanking metal sounded behind me.

Shifting metallic armor, spelled with protection enchantments, clinked quietly as two kingsfae strolled around the corner on their nightly patrol. Fae parted in the streets to give them way. Many dipped their heads respectfully, but just as many scurried out of sight.

I stiffened when they drew near, which was silly. I was not only invisible, but I still wore my collar. I was still indentured to a guardian, but it didn't stop the shiver of unease that slithered through me. The supernatural courts had deemed me unsafe to the general public, and here I was, in public unattended, with a loosened collar that gave me immensely stronger magic than I'd ever been awarded previously.

Folding my hands in my lap, I sat quietly and reminded myself they couldn't see me.

The kingsfae drifted closer, then stopped only a stone's throw to my side. My heartbeat ticked steadily upward, and it took actual concentration not to alert them to my presence.

Instead, I focused on my breathing as the sun continued its downward journey, the moons glowing brighter. I fixated on that calming sight. Anything to keep my nerves steady and my aura from spiking.

The two kingsfae dipped their heads together, talking quietly. A few words drifted my way.

"He'll end up in the supernatural prison." One of them chuckled. "Deserves nothing less."

The second laughed too. "He'll probably get sentenced to the maximum-security section on the Nolus continent. He'll be lucky if he's ever released. I hope he enjoys those shifting walls." He shuffled his feet, making his armor clink again. "Did you hear about the female caught in Ironcrest last week? She was smuggling baby *dracoons* to the Lochen. Got fined a thousand rulibs and sentenced to a full season in Ironcrest's refinement ward." He snorted. "Sounds like too light of a sentence to me. She should have gotten at least five full seasons in prison for that crime."

"I heard she heralds from one of Ironcrest's ten Houses, and that's why she got off easy."

The other kingsfae spat on the ground. "Getting off easy like that just because of family ties is a load of domal dung in my opinion."

"Aye, you and me both agree on that."

I finally started to relax. It sounded as though they

were discussing criminals who had recently been apprehended. Nothing more. The two didn't even know I was there as they carried on with their mundane discussion about recent arrests. It was as though they were merely passing the time until their shifts ended.

Considering this area of the capital usually saw little criminal activity, I couldn't blame them for spending the remainder of their worktime enjoying the fountains while they chatted.

Settling back, I allowed my attention to drift again. The stars had truly begun to shine, and Jeulic's pulsing aura lit up around it. It was still visible in the night sky, and near the horizon, the faint glow of another planet that hadn't been in the sky in the previous weeks began to pulse. My smile grew as the tiny speck of Daphnis's aura shone faintly.

But just as true relaxation began to seep into my pores, two words caught my attention, snapping my attention entirely away from the distant planet.

"What?" one hissed. "Did you just hear that? The Dark Raider's seasons on the run is likely coming to an end tonight."

The other brought a hand to his ear. "I thought I was hearing things."

I stiffened, and magic instantly buzzed through my system, creating the slightest sting along my neck. But I hastily checked my illusion to ensure it was still intact and then subtly used my loosened magic to amplify the sounds around me.

Both kingsfae hunched forward, fingers pressing to their ears. It was only then I realized they wore tiny devices inserted into their ear canals, and whatever they were listening to was likely being communicated to them by other kingsfae at this very second.

Eyes widening, they turned to one another, and their voices dropped to a whisper. They spoke so quietly that if not for my loosened collar, I never would have heard them.

"It can't be," the first said. "They know where the Dark Raider will be tonight? How in the realm do you suppose they know that? He's been eluding us for full seasons."

"I don't know, but sounds like it was a direct order from King Paevin. And he's calling for all kingsfae in the area closest to Possyrose Forest to take action."

"But how would the king know?"

The second shrugged. "No idea, but I'm sure the Raider's arrest would beat this." The kingsfae scoffed and gestured to the quiet fountains. "Of course, the one night I'm not on patrol in the Wood is when the biggest arrest of the century is about to happen."

My heart felt as though it'd stopped. *Oh, stars and galaxy.*

As discreetly as possible, I stood from the bench and began weaving my way through the small crowd mingling around the fountain. I moved carefully, so as not to bump anyone and alert the kingsfae to their lapse in security.

But the second I was out of the kingsfae's sight, I sprinted.

Wind blew over my cheeks as I made my way as fast as I could back to the inn.

No, no, no. Jax couldn't be caught. None of them could be. My heart twisted when I remembered Saramel, and Phillen's young son, Cassim. Jax's entire band would be executed if the kingsfae apprehended them. Not even Jax's noble status would save them, even if it went down as the scandal of the century.

I had to get to him. Somehow, I had to warn him. *But how?*

The solution hit me the moment I careened around the corner. I would have to use one of those keys that Quinn had snagged from the Lochen king.

It was the only way I would get there in time.

CHAPTER 18

I was breathless by the time I reached the inn, but I didn't stop. I shed my illusion the second nobody was looking, then I sprinted up the stairs two at a time, darting down the hall and into Jax's private suite at breakneck speed.

And once I was in his chambers, I nearly collided with the wall since I ran so fast to the jar that Quinn had produced earlier and left behind.

I fumbled with it, knocking it over in my haste to collect a key. The jar clunked to the side, thankfully not shattering, but a waterfall of keys spilled over the table's edge and scattered all over the floor, going everywhere.

"Shite!" Fingers shaking, I crouched and snatched a single key off the floor, not bothering to pick up the rest.

Slow your breathing, Elowen. Don't panic. If you mess this up, Jax and all of his friends are dead.

I sagged against the wall, clutching the key to my chest as I heaved in shallow gulps. I just thanked the galaxy I'd been paying attention when they'd all left. The words I'd heard Quinn use to activate this peculiar magic flowed out of my lips as I concentrated completely on where I wanted to go.

"Open key for thou I ask, I need a door for this new task."

The realm vanished around me, and a void opened up beneath me.

I fell into nothingness.

Yelping, I held onto the key tightly as the realm spiraled around me, pulling me every which way. Panic threatened to close my throat. *Jax. Possyrose Forest. Take me right to where Jax is. Please!*

My breath rushed out of me when I abruptly materialized, my feet hitting solid ground. I teetered, my balance off, but I managed to stay upright. I stood on moist soil with trees towering above me.

The key I'd been clutching fizzled out of existence, and it hit me that in my haste to find Jax, I'd forgotten to grab more keys, and apparently, I needed another key for the transfer back.

Double shite!

Darkness filled my vision. The trees blocked most of the moonlight. I spun around.

"Jax?" I hissed, panic making my voice breathy.

"Elowen?" Jax's shocked call came from close by. "Fuck," he growled. "What are you doing here?"

Before I could reply, hands grabbed me and were forcing me down. His scent hit me simultaneously, pine and spice. I nearly cried in relief that he was still free.

Six other sets of surprised eyes met mine. His entire band was still free, but the rage in Jax's aura quickly doused whatever relief was coursing through me, but the reminder of *why* I was here hit me just as fast.

"What in all the realms, Elowen?" Jax snarled. "Did you use one of those keys to get here?"

A large bush covering us rustled slightly from his agitated movements, and my grin disappeared.

I gripped Jax's forearms tightly. "We need to get out of here. The kingsfae are coming for you. They know you're here. That's why I've come. To *warn* you."

Dark eyebrows snapped together under his scarfed head, and he glanced quickly at Lander before growling at me, "What? How do you know that?"

"I heard two kingsfae speaking near the Venapearl Fountains—"

"You were at the Venapearl Fountains?" His voice rose slightly.

"Yes, but"—I frantically shook my head—"I wasn't running. And I wasn't stupid. I hid myself under an illusion. I just wanted to enjoy my freedom." I shook my head again. "But that's *not important* right now. We need to get out of here!"

Phillen crawled along the soil to be closer to us, his large body barely rustling the leaves. "The shipment is only minutes away. What in the realm is going on, Jax?"

"You're not listening," I hissed. "We need to leave. *Now!*"

Jax's gaze cut to mine, and something swirled in his irises, an understanding, a connection . . . Something that I couldn't entirely name, but a swift current of energy passed between us.

He gave a curt nod. "Retreat. Now," he called quietly to the others.

Trivan cursed softly under his breath, but nobody questioned their prince's order. Everyone immediately began slithering through the forest, moving so quietly and low to the ground that they were nearly undetectable.

I did my best to keep up and stay just as concealed, but more than once, Jax pulled me along, quickening my movements while keeping me partially covered with his body.

When we were roughly fifty paces away from where they'd been hiding, the sound of distant wagon wheels carried through the air.

Jax stiffened. He tugged me closer, then raised his hand in a silent gesture.

Everyone stopped, and in a blink, Jax was on top of me,

shielding me completely since my purple sweater was easier to spot than their attire.

Several of the others cast envious glances toward the approaching shipment, and I second-guessed if I'd made the right decision. They were about to watch their night's raid pass by, and I could only imagine the disappointment coursing through their systems.

Another moment of doubt hit me. *Goddess, I hope I didn't mishear what the kingsfae were saying.* My guardian had always admonished me, making me second-guess everything and making me feel that I constantly misunderstood things. That age-old insecurity reared, and I had the strongest urge to bite my fingernail.

Above me, Jax grew entirely still, his body hot and heavy. Nobody moved or made a sound.

I wanted to wring my hands. I wanted to apologize. *Nothing* was happening. The shipment was merely rolling by in several wagons. No kingsfae were about. Nothing seemed amiss.

Oh Goddess. What have I done?

But just when I was about to whisper that I was so sorry and had been mistaken, a burst of kingsfae atop domals abruptly appeared through the trees as if coming out of nowhere.

My eyes widened to saucers, and I clamped my lips closed to avoid making a sound. Jax turned entirely rigid, and in my next breath, he whispered a spell. Thick illusion magic from his Mistvale power cloaked all of us, hiding us completely, and a silencing Shield followed it.

The authorities spanned out. They must have been hidden underneath a powerful Shielding spell that they'd only just released. It was the only thing I could think of that would hide them for so long, but it wasn't simple magic. A Shielding spell like that—if it didn't come from one's own magic—required potions carefully guarded by the authorities that were made by spellcasters from Mistvale and Ironcrest kingdoms using combined power. I'd heard such potions took months to properly produce, yet I wasn't surprised if the kingsfae had drunk them to hide themselves.

One of the kingsfae glanced our way, but his gaze skimmed right over us, and I thanked the complexity of Jax's magic. If not for that, despite the band's dark attire, we likely would have been spotted.

Three dozen kingsfae atop domals trotted around the shipment. Swords were drawn, shields were held ready, and magic cascaded around them.

My hands fisted as the extent of the kingsfae's might hit me. Magical devices glowed from within their ear canals, and I realized it was the same device the kingsfae had worn at the fountains. I knew those devices could be used for communicating, but something else I remembered registered in my mind. Something about those devices also preventing anyone with Mistvale magic from commanding them. Jax had once told me, if he was caught again, he wouldn't be able to use his magic to command them again and escape twice.

"Any sign of them?" one of the kingsfae called.

"No, Commander."

The commander snarled. "Enact the dome. He's not getting away this time."

One of the kingsfae threw something in the air, and a dome of magic burst into existence. It fell around the dozens of kingsfae, shimmering slightly in the darkness.

My eyes widened even more. I'd heard of the kingsfae's protective magic over the seasons. It was a common tactical measure. Anyone who touched that dome was instantly paralyzed for several hours. The power it commanded was so intricate, so potent, that few were able to withstand its wrath.

Despite my heart feeling about to burst, Jax remained unmoving. His body was as still as stone, and I questioned if he was even breathing. Everyone else was just as silent despite Jax's Shield containing our sounds.

The commander glanced at a female beside him. "Sheralynn, scan the area."

The female's eyes narrowed, and a swell of magic emitted from her. She scanned the perimeter, likely using sight sensory Ironcrest magic. Since the kingsfae employed by each kingdom could herald from any of the four kingdoms, their combined gifts made them uniquely formidable.

"Risalto," the commander called to another. "Tell me what you hear."

A male nudged his domal forward, then he closed his eyes, and a puff of magic radiated from him.

A brief moment of panic hit me when I realized that Jax's illusion magic and Shield could hide us from sight and sound, likely masking us from the kingsfae with the sight and sound sensory magic, but Jax couldn't hide our touch.

I held my breath as the female continued to scan the area. A moment passed as she carried over the Wood, her eyes tracking over everything slowly. Deliberately.

And at the same time, the second kingsfae continued to listen.

Stars Above. It felt as though my heart was going to leap out of my chest.

"Nothing," Risalto finally replied, opening his eyes. "If they're here, they're entirely unmoving."

"Agreed," the female said, and her magic died around her. "I see nothing unusual."

I released a relieved breath.

The commander seethed. "But the king insisted they would attack *here*. How am I to tell the king he was wrong?"

Jax tensed, the slightest tightening of his muscles.

I stilled. *How does the king know that?*

"I'm sorry, Commander," the female replied. "But I sense nothing."

Several of the kingsfae swirled their domals around, all of them surveying the Wood.

"Stay close to the wagons," the commander finally called. "We don't leave until this shipment reaches port. Perhaps the king made an error about the location, but that doesn't mean the Dark Raider won't be somewhere along this route."

My heart thundered when another kingsfae kicked his domal to move deeper into the Wood, heading our way. He lifted his nose and inhaled.

Oh Goddess. The kingsfae was *so* close that if Jax hadn't moved his band when he had, the domal would have been trampling us at this very moment.

The domal pranced closer, its breath huffing with every step. Closer. *Closer.*

The kingsfae stopped only four paces away. He scanned the area. Watching. Waiting. If he moved any closer, his domal would hit Jax's air Shield.

"Berryl!" the commander called. "We're leaving."

At last, the kingsfae whirled his mount and joined the others, yet it felt as though I'd lost a full season off my life in that moment. Trembling, I forced my breaths to remain silent as Jax's body remained as unyielding as stone atop me.

Finally, the wagons and kingsfae pushed onward. All of the kingsfae pulled out potions from their supplies and ingested them. One after another disappeared from view.

Nobody in our group moved a muscle. Not even when they'd left the area and the sounds of the wagon wheels faded. Even then, nobody said a thing as Jax's illusion spell and Shield stayed in place.

Minutes later, when the shipment was long gone and the bird song had returned to the Wood, Jax's magic at last dispelled.

He lifted himself from me completely, my back going cold in the wind when he eased himself away and to the side.

The prince lifted his hand and made several silent movements with his fingers. In a blink, Lars had a portal key in his hand, and everyone grabbed onto one another.

Phillen's large hand enclosed my forearm, and I could have sworn his aura was trembling as he gave me a squeeze.

Lars began to whisper the spell to activate the key, and it hit me that nobody was touching Jax.

"Jax?" I called quietly and reached for him.

But he inched away even more. "Go," he whispered quietly.

Wildness filled me, and I frantically grabbed for him, yet he pulled even farther away. "What are you doing?"

He shook his head and maneuvered to the balls of his feet, body still low to the ground. "I want to track them for a bit, to see what I can learn. They shouldn't have known we were here. Go."

Lars finished muttering the portal key's spell, and the realm fell out from beneath me. The last thing I saw were Jax's blazing sapphire eyes as the forest disappeared around us.

CHAPTER 19

I landed on unsteady legs in Jax's suite, the others materializing beside me just as fast. Tension filled the room the second I was able to make sense of who I was with.

Everyone was present and dressed entirely in black: Phillen, Lars, Trivan, Bowan, Lander, and Quinn. All except Jax.

"How in the realm did you know they were going to be there?" Before I could reply, Phillen had me in a suffocating hug, his arms nearly crushing me he held me so tightly. "If we'd been captured, my family—" He swallowed thickly, and I absentmindedly patted his shoulder.

The others joined in, most of them thanking me, but I twisted my hands and glanced at the clock. Already, minutes had passed, and there was no sign of Jax.

I clasped my shaking hands together. "How is Jax going to get back?"

Trivan's brow furrowed. "Jax is a tricky bastard. He'll find a way."

I gazed at all of them as they ripped their masks and bandanas off one after the other.

"How in the realm did the kingsfae know we would be there?" Lars whispered, a troubled look on his face.

"They shouldn't have." Lander scowled heavily.

They quickly fell into discussion about how their planned raid could have been leaked, or if one of them could have made a mistake unknowingly, allowing someone to overhear them.

At one point, Lander pulled a bottle of leminai out from one of the side cupboards and poured drinks for everyone. Given the trembling hands that took them, I knew they were as shaken as me at what had almost occurred.

But when nobody asked of Jax, not once, I finally threw my hands up. "Aren't any of you worried about him?"

Frowning, Lander poured a glass of bright-green liquid for me and forced it into my hand. "Drink this, Elowen. It'll help calm your nerves."

I drank it all in one swallow, but despite its potent effect, I began to pace. I moved back and forth, back and forth. At least half an hour went by as the others drank and spoke in murmured tones about the absolute strangeness of what had just occurred in Possyrose Forest. A few times,

Trivan glanced up at me, his gaze suspicious, his aura questioning. I had no idea if Trivan suspected it was me who had ratted them out to the kingsfae, but from his growing distrust I suspected he might.

"You're going to wear a path into the floor," Bowan finally called with a forced smile on his face. "Sit and have another drink, Elowen."

"I can't. I don't know how all of you can pretend to be so relaxed when—"

A flash of magic came from beside me, and the prince appeared.

"Jax!" I nearly choked.

He appeared from out of nowhere. Obviously, he'd had a backup portal key with him, and the second he was solid and whole, I almost flung my arms around him. Almost. Somehow, I stopped myself before the urge overtook me.

Jax, however, roughly ripped his mask off, then grabbed a hold of my shoulders. His aura pounded through the room, making me flinch. Sizzling blue irises met mine. "You're okay?"

All I could do was nod.

A look of relief filled his face, and amazement filled his aura. "How, Elowen? *How* did you know they would be there?"

Tremors wracked my frame. Now that Jax was here and safe, the buzzing energy that had been cascading through me began to fade. Shivers took its place. "I . . . I heard two kingsfae talking near the fountains. It was pure luck that I did. They knew you were going to be in Possyrose Forest tonight and finally be caught. They said the *king* had known."

He scrubbed a hand over his face. "How in the realm did the king know?"

The troubled expressions on all of his friends grew.

"Anyone have any ideas?" Jax bit out.

One by one, they all shook their heads, but Trivan cast me another scathing glare.

"What did you find from tracking them?" Lander asked, his eyes narrowing. "Anything?"

Jax raked a hand through his hair, finally letting go of me completely. "No. The kingsfae were entirely silent as they traveled with the shipment since that potion clouded them. I followed for a bit, but when it became obvious I wasn't going to hear anything they said, I came back." He turned seething eyes on Bowan and Lander. "Where did you get the information about the shipment?"

"I . . ." Bowan gulped, his throat working. He shoved both hands into his hair. "A fairy in Jaggedston was talking about it at Wolfbane Salopas. Do you think we were set up? Do you think he knows I'm a raider? Shite, shite, shite."

"Exactly," Jax snarled. "And *this* is why I don't like

last-minute raids. That information was not vetted enough."

Trivan scowled. "But how did *King Paevin* know? That lazy arsehole is always the last to know of anything we do, unless someone he knows told him." His gaze slid to me again.

My lips parted, his accusation making a rush of pain fire through me. "It wasn't me."

"Trivan," Jax growled. "Elowen wouldn't do that. The truth of the matter is that we were too eager. We *shouldn't* have gone tonight."

"Do you really think Elowen's behind this?" Lander's eyebrows slanted together as he assessed Trivan. "Wouldn't spies be more likely? She didn't even know we were going there until a few hours ago."

Trivan shrugged. "A few hours is all that's needed to alert the kingsfae."

Jax growled again and said in a warning tone, "Trivan . . ."

Phillen scoffed, coming to my aid too. "Elowen warned us about them. Didn't she? Why would she have been the one to give up our location when she ultimately saved us?"

"To gain our trust?" Trivan replied. "So she could trick us again in the future."

It felt like someone stabbed me in the heart.

"Triv," Lars said, his voice taking on an edge. "Don't. It's not her."

"They're right, it wasn't me," I said more adamantly.

But the lean blond crossed his arms. "Prove it."

I shrank back, but just as fast, a tidal wave of power emitted from Jax.

"Trivan. Stop it," Jax growled. "It's not Elowen. She didn't betray us. She wouldn't do that."

But Trivan shook his head. "How do you know? None of us really even know her."

Lars frowned, but he didn't disagree. Jax, though, was in Trivan's face in two strides.

"It wasn't her," he snarled.

Trivan's nostrils flared just as fast. "Just because you want to stick your cock in her doesn't mean she's—"

A ferocious snarl tore from Jax, and in a blink he had Trivan pinned to the wall and punched him in the stomach. Hard.

The blond doubled over.

My jaw dropped just as Phillen winced.

Trivan wheezed, eyeing me again before giving Jax a murderous glare. "Command her, Jax. *Command* her to tell the truth."

I paled.

Jax had told me once that he never used his Mistvale magic on fae unless they were truly vile. He'd called that aspect of his magic evil, yet Trivan had just asked him to use it on *me*.

"Watch yourself." Jax shoved him against the wall

again. "I'd advise you to choose your next words very carefully, *friend*."

But Trivan's suspicions seemed to speed through the group. Phillen, who'd always seemed to be on my side previously, cast me an apprehensive look. Lars did too, and even Bowan's jovial smile disappeared, and Quinn's entire focus centered on me.

"Maybe you should, Jax, just to put everyone's mind at ease," Lander finally offered. "I'm not saying I doubt her, but if you did, then we'd all know for certain."

"I'm not doing that to her!" Jax roared.

But I took a step forward, my heart cracking that none of these males felt I was trustworthy, even though I tried to tell myself it was only natural to suspect me. They'd all known each other for full seasons and trusted one another explicitly. Of course, they would suspect me.

"It's okay." I licked my lips, my throat suddenly dry. "If it helps and stops everyone from fighting, you can command me, Jax."

Trivan's eyebrows rose, and a fleeting sense of doubt crossed over his features.

Jax shoved Trivan against the wall one last time, then faced me. "I won't do that to you."

"Just do it," Trivan snarled from behind him. "In fact, do it on all of us. Make sure nobody in this room has turned on us."

Quinn's eyes narrowed, a heavy frown descending

upon his face. "You think one of your brothers would do that?"

Lars shook his head. "Really, Triv . . . this is low, even for you."

But Trivan just shrugged. "Then prove me wrong."

Jax glowered at him, but the fact that everyone seemed okay with being commanded by Jax's Mistvale magic seemed to put him more at ease to command me. If he did it to everyone, he wasn't singling me out. Still, he raised his eyebrows at me, his expression full of remorse.

"It's fine," I said, answering his silent question. "Despite what Trivan thinks, I'm not a liar."

"All right." Jax took a deep breath, and magic speared the air. "*Did anyone in this room tell the king or kingsfae where we would be tonight?*"

Potent, fiery power spiraled into me, and my lips moved of their own accord before I could even consider what was happening. "No."

"No."

"No."

One by one, everyone replied, and each fairy had the same answer. No.

"*Has anyone betrayed our identities or whereabouts to anyone outside of our group?*"

Another resounding round of *Nos* came through the room.

Satisfied, Jax calmed his magic.

Phillen slugged Trivan in the shoulder as soon as everyone was free of Jax's magical grip. "See, you big louse. Nobody here's a traitor, not even Elowen. I knew my wife was right about her."

Trivan's attention slid my way, and perhaps he felt the pain ripping through my aura, or perhaps he cowed because of Jax's menacing expression, but he finally dipped his head and had the decency to look sheepish. "All right, fine. But she knew where we were tonight. How could I not wonder?"

The prince stepped closer to me, and it almost felt as though he was shielding me from any further suspicions, not that anyone could suspect me after being subjected to Jax's magic.

Fingers tapping against his thigh, Jax said, "Until we figure out how the king learned of our whereabouts, we *won't* be attempting a raid again unless we're certain it's safe. Now, what does everyone know?"

They all sat in a circle around the table, regularly passing the bottle of leminai around. And whatever bad feelings had sprouted between Jax and Trivan melted away as the alcohol flowed.

The seven of them huddled together, their conversation moving rapid fire. Tentatively, I sat beside Bowan, and when none of them tried to hide anything they were discussing from me, it struck me that they obviously trusted me enough now to speak freely, even if Trivan had momentarily doubted me.

The hurt I'd initially felt about that lessened the initial sting.

Jax finally leaned back from the group and stated, "You know the drill now. Lay low. We go dark. We won't be able to provide anything for the poor for several months. Not until we learn more about how the king knew of our whereabouts. Quinn?" He glanced at the newest male. "I'll need your ears everywhere."

Quinn nodded solemnly, then dipped his head at me. "By the way, I'm in your debt, Elowen. You stopped all of us from being caught tonight."

"We're all in your debt," Bowan agreed, and a small smile emerged on his face.

Phillen cocked his head. "How did you reach us so fast anyway? I never asked."

I shrugged and gestured to the jar Quinn had brought. "I stole one of those portal keys."

Trivan laughed, seemingly completely over his earlier suspicions of me. "A criminal in the making. How fitting."

"How did you know how to use it?" Lars asked, the redhead's question almost sounding shy.

I raised my shoulders again. "I paid attention when Quinn used his. I remembered what he said."

Bowan laughed. "*Definitely* a criminal in the making."

Trivan cocked an eyebrow. "That takes balls, Elowen. I have to say, I think I really like you, even if I thought the worst of you an hour ago."

But Jax scowled at me. "I don't want you risking yourself for us again."

I arched an eyebrow. "I'm in this up to my neck at this point. I figure I'm either all in, or I'm not."

Phillen stroked his beard, nodding. Some of the panic he'd emitted earlier had lessened, and he was now looking at me with pride in his eyes. "Saramel said she had a good feeling about you, and my wife is rarely wrong."

Bowan snorted. "Saramel's always had you wrapped around her little finger, Phil, but she's right. You get my vote, too, Newole." He clapped me on the shoulder, and his hand was so heavy that I nearly fell forward in my seat.

"Stars, sorry about that," he said gruffly, and then he tried to straighten me, which got even more awkward.

"Bowan," Jax growled. "Hands off." A ring of authority carried in his tone.

A surprised look passed over Bowan's face, but a knowing look passed between Trivan and Phillen.

I glanced at all of them, and I wondered who it was that told Alec the prince had feelings for me. I was betting it was either Trivan or Phillen, considering the subtle look between them I just witnessed, not to mention Trivan's rather crude comment earlier . . .

But despite that, it hit me that for the first time, all of them were looking at me with respect and . . . friendship.

A feeling of hope swelled in my chest. Never in my entire life had I ever been a part of a group. I'd always been alone, an outcast, a slave. *Other*. But in this moment, I felt like maybe I was one of them. And that I was *choosing* to be one of their group. I'd never chosen anything for myself before. Ever.

A lump formed in my throat, and I knew if I didn't get my emotions under control, I was going to do something incredibly embarrassing, like burst into tears.

Before I could thoroughly humiliate myself, Quinn tipped his head toward Jax. "I'll be off then."

"See you soon, brother," Jax replied.

Quinn's entire body abruptly puffed out of existence and drifted into dark shadows. His inky form hovered around us, then he zoomed out the window and onto the capital's streets.

My eyes bulged, and I blinked a few times.

Trivan snickered. "You should see your face right now."

"He has shadow magic," Lander replied in a monotone voice, looking entirely unimpressed that Quinn had just *disappeared*. He ran a hand through his hair. Tangles met his fingers since his scarf had messed up the shoulder-length strands. If anything, he still seemed to be running through the scenarios of how the kingsfae had ended up in that forest.

"Shadow magic?" My eyebrows rose. That kind of magic was rare. "He's from Mistvale?"

Bowan shook his head and leaned back on the couch. "He has dual magic. Born and raised in Stonewild but blessed with magic from two kingdoms."

"Is he a stag shifter as well?"

Phillen opened his mouth to reply, but Trivan beat him to it. "How about we make her guess?"

Bowan rolled his eyes and laughed. "Don't be an arse, Triv. You've been enough of a cad for one night."

Trivan brought a hand to his chest. "You wound me. I wasn't trying to be rude. I was just trying to get some enjoyment from the night since all of our fun was stolen the second those kingsfae bastards showed up."

Phillen crossed his burly arms and ignored all of them. "Quinn isn't a stag shifter, lovely. He's the only one in our group who isn't. Instead, he's a *crowfy* shifter."

My eyes bulged when I pictured the shadow-magic male turning into a huge winged bird that was just as black as his swirling, inky magic. It was even more surprising because crowfy shifters were rare. And unlike the stags, crowfies usually were lone creatures, sticking to themselves. I wasn't surprised Jax had found other stags to band together with, but for a crowfy to join them was surprising.

My brow furrowed. "How did he become a part of your group?"

A sly smile curved Bowan's lips. "We helped his family once, and the tricky bastard managed to track us. It was back in our younger days when we still made mistakes. Anyway, when he confronted us, he blackmailed Jax. It was either we allowed him to join us, or he turned us in to the kingsfae."

My jaw dropped. "He threatened to turn you into the authorities after you helped his family?"

The feel of Jax shifting closer to me on the couch made my breath stop. His aura was so potent, and my body was so in-tuned to him. Every particle of my essence seemed to know when he neared.

Jax's low voice rumbled through the room when he replied, "As you can probably imagine, the first few seasons with Quinn were rather tense. But he's since settled in, and now we've all come to accept him as one of us. His magic has actually proven quite useful."

I could only imagine. Shadow magic allowed one to deform, similar to mistphasing, but fae with shadow magic could stay in that state indefinitely if they chose to. However, unlike with mistphasing, they were still able to see and hear when they existed as shadows.

"Do you think he'll be able to track down how the king learned of your whereabouts?"

Jax's brow furrowed. "I certainly hope so. That shipment would have fed a dozen villages for a full season with the wealth it carried. Fae were counting on us tonight, and we've let them down." He inched closer to me, his look softening. "But if it wasn't for you, we would never be able to help those fae again. My brothers are right." Jax's aura wrapped around me like a warm cloud, and my heart thumped. "We're all in debt to you, Elowen. You saved all of us."

CHAPTER 20

Jax's eyes were so intense that they sucked all coherent thought from my mind. All I could manage was a nod, and the group turned back to their drinks. The discussion quickly returned to how to find Bastian.

I was glad for the subject change. Emotions were pounding through me, and my collar decided to emit tiny zaps every time I breathed, despite its relaxed state, so I was in no state to offer any intelligent comments.

Not long later, Bowan headed out to the Wood to take Alec's place.

"Drink, Elowen?" Phillen asked after I continued to sit there silently.

"Please." I willingly accepted another glass of leminai and allowed its warmth to numb my mind.

I was on my second glass when Alec returned.

Jax, sitting next to me on the couch, shot to standing. "Any sign of him?"

Alec's lips thinned into a tight line. "No, I never saw Bastian, but there continue to be a lot of half-breeds here. Hundreds for sure, maybe even thousands." Alec cocked his head, his light-brown eyes looking like caramel in the fairy lights as he dropped onto the couch with the rest of us. "A group of them went into the barn about an hour ago, although I didn't recognize any of them. And that high up, I was able to see some of the competitors getting registered for tomorrow. Quite a few of them were half-breeds as well." He frowned heavily.

"So more half-breeds but no sign of my brother." Jax stabbed a hand through his hair.

Alec's jaw tightened. "No, I never saw Bastian, but I heard other troubling news from Bowan. He said everyone almost got caught tonight."

"We did. It was close," Phillen agreed.

"Too close," Lars replied quietly.

Jax tensed but nodded in agreement. "We're going dark. No more raids for several months, not until Quinn's able to find a way to explain what happened. So for now, we concentrate on finding Bastian and Bastian only. And back to my brother . . . You're certain he wasn't with any of the groups that you saw tonight?"

"I'm sure." Alec scratched his chin. The movement sounded like sandpaper since stubble had formed along his jaw. "I have to say, I did see something very strange. I saw a new group of half-breeds go into the barn tonight, and they were all acting peculiar."

My eyebrows slanted together, just as Jax's did the same.

"How so?" I asked.

Alec cocked his head. "They moved in a single file line, and none of them spoke to one another. Nobody made any gestures. Even if they've gained employment to help with the Matches and were fatigued following a long day's work, one would think that they'd at least speak to one another or move more casually, even if they were tired. But the way they were acting . . ." He made a disgruntled sound. "I don't know exactly. It was just strange. That's all I can say."

All of the males eyed each other, and the frustration leaking from Jax's aura grew.

The prince huffed. "We'll continue keeping an eye on the barn for now. Tomorrow, we'll go to the lake. There's supposed to be several Finals on it."

"And if we eventually find Bastian, and he says he wants to stay here, then what?" Lander asked, his look pensive.

Jax lifted his leminai to his lips. He took a sip of the green liquid, his throat rolling. But despite his bland expression, I could have sworn that hurt filled his eyes. "Then I'll respect his wishes. If he chose to leave us, without a goodbye or an explanation, then he's free to do so. I just want to make sure he's all right."

I nibbled on my lip. Once again, it was on the tip of my tongue to insist that I go to the Veiled Between. This was ridiculous. Five days had passed with nothing. The semelees could tell me exactly where Bastian was staying. And I still hadn't tested my loosened collar, due to Jax's insistence that I not even risk the chance of getting hurt.

Jax cut a sharp look my way, almost as if he knew what I was thinking. "No, Elowen."

I angled more toward him. "But what if I don't need your magic anymore? I could use another's magic and do a calling for them. What if I can find Bastian without your magic hurting me? Why are you being so stubborn about this?"

Lander arched an eyebrow and gave Jax a curious look. "What did I miss?"

I sighed. "The prince is still refusing to let me do a calling for him or anyone else, even if I could find exactly where Bastian is by venturing to the Veiled Between. But we still don't know if I can find him on my own without anyone's magic. I haven't ventured there since my collar's been loosened."

Alec cocked his head. "Ah, back to this."

Jax's nostrils flared. "With that collar in place, anything could happen to you."

"But I'd survive," I shot back. "I've never *not* survived a trip there."

Phillen shifted his large body to face Jax more, then said in a hesitant voice. "You know, she's right, Jax. It's been nearly a week with no sign of him. Who's to say Bastian is even still here? And if Elowen has a way to find him, don't you think we should take her up on that offer?"

Trivan rolled his eyes and muttered under his breath, "Here we go . . ."

No sooner had those words left Trivan's mouth, than the prince snarled softly at his friend. "No, Phillen. It's out of the question. Elowen doesn't know what traveling to the Veiled Between will do to her, even if she doesn't use anyone's magic. With that collar on, she could still be hurt. That possibility remains, because she doesn't know since she's never done it before. And I will not allow *anyone's* magic to hurt her again, so she's not doing callings for any of us." The prince stalked off before anyone could reply, and his aura left a cloud of malice hanging in its wake.

I released a breath and fell back onto the couch. "Is he always this stubborn? What if I'm *not* hurt when I try? He has to know that sooner or later I'll travel to the Veiled Between, with or *without* his permission."

Alec and Trivan shared a veiled look, then Alec replied, "No, Elowen, he's not usually like this. He's never been like this with any other female."

"It's true. Jax is very . . . protective of you," Lars remarked quietly.

Phillen nodded, then all of the males shared a look.

"What? What now?" I blurted. "Do you *all* think he has feelings for me?"

Everyone blinked mutely, and Alec frowned. "I'm beginning to think it's more than that."

"I think you might be right." Phillen sighed and leaned forward in his seat, his burly arms draping over his knees. "Jax's behavior around you, Elowen, isn't like him. It's making a few of us wonder about a few things."

I furrowed my brow. Magic stirred inside me, rising like a slow-growing flame. "What do you mean exactly?"

Trivan snickered. "I think I've already figured it out, but I'm waiting to see how long it takes the rest of you."

I didn't bother replying to him. He'd likely enjoy watching me guess what he meant.

Lander stood. "Let's all remember that Jax is stressed about Bastian. He's not himself right now, so perhaps we should all stop speculating."

I knew he was right. It was obvious Jax wasn't happy that we were no closer to finding his brother, with a botched raid on top of it, but as for why he adamantly refused to let me visit the Veiled Between again on his behalf, especially if there was a chance I *wouldn't* be injured . . . It was silly.

But it didn't sit well with me that Jax was in such a foul

mood. For some reason, an ache formed in my chest, and I burned to go to him, but I knew I couldn't. Jax wasn't mine despite the roles we were playing during the day, and even if he did have feelings for me, he was to eventually wed another.

Besides, I was still a lorafin. Still *other*. His realm and mine were never meant to collide.

JAX RETURNED to join everyone for a quick meal. A mountain of food was lined on the kitchen counters that the inn staff had brought up. Platters of grilled meats, roasted potatoes, fluffy rice and pitas, vegetables of every variety, and a range of sauces made succulent fragrances waft through the air.

By the time we finished, all three moons were high in the sky, and everybody began to disappear to various chambers for the night.

I began to walk to mine, but Jax stopped me. "Elowen?"

He stepped into my path, and his nearness immediately made my stomach tighten. He stood only inches away, his aura like a warm caress around mine. All week my magic had been responding to his more and more. Tingles immediately shot to my core, my belly tightening in his presence.

I tilted my head back. "Yes?"

"I never properly thanked you, for what you did in the forest tonight. You saved all of us."

"Oh . . ." I nodded quickly, my pulse leaping despite his innocent remarks. "It was nothing. I kept thinking about Cassim. I could never knowingly allow another child to grow up without their parent. Not if I could help it. I would do it all over again, not just for Cassim's sake, but for all of yours. But you're welcome." I made a move to step around him, but he stepped into my path again. Stopping, I gazed up at him, my head cocking. "Was there something else?"

His throat rolled, his aura spiking. "There's . . . one other thing I wanted to ask you. If you're willing, I'd like you to sleep in my chambers tonight."

My eyebrows shot up. "*Your* chambers?"

He tentatively reached forward and ran his fingers down my forearm, lightly caressing my inner wrist. "Yes."

A blast of shivers worked up my arm even though his touch was nothing new. He'd been doing things like that all week, even more so when we were in public, yet every time we made contact, my body practically convulsed with *want*.

"I heard several inn staff talking when they were leaving tonight after delivering the food," he continued. "One of them commented that she didn't think we'd been sharing a chambers at night."

My lips parted as his fingers continued doing those embarrassingly pleasurable movements. "But I've been so careful. Every morning, I make the bed, then cleanse the room of my scent."

His brow furrowed. "Apparently, it's not enough. They're starting to suspect that we're not sleeping together because your scent *isn't* in my room."

"How would they know that?"

"They're the ones who bring cleaning charms and new supplies for the bathing chambers. At least one of the staff come into this suite each day."

Alec's eyebrows rose just as he passed us in the hall, and Trivan muffled a cough from the living area.

I suddenly remembered that we weren't alone, and our conversation wasn't private. Flustered even more, I snatched my arm away from Jax's strong fingers while Lander watched us from his seat on the couch. Trivan was sitting right beside him, not even trying to hide his smirk.

At least Phillen and Lars had already retreated to their chambers, making two less fae to witness my flushed cheeks.

My heartbeat thumped, especially when Jax's focus never faltered. He continued watching me. Waiting.

Another second ticked past, and his gaze dipped to my chest, which was rising much too quickly for someone standing still.

"If you're willing?" he added in a soft voice. "I would like you in my chambers tonight."

I played with my fingers as the silence in the hall grew painfully quiet. "All right," I finally replied. "I suppose we could."

A flash of something shone in his eyes, but in a blink, it was gone. He stepped closer, and his mouth dipped to my ear. "Come." He hooked his hand around mine.

My heart began beating so fast I felt lightheaded, and I could have sworn that I heard Trivan snickering behind us.

INSIDE JAX'S CHAMBERS, only moonlight lit the furniture and decorations. It was a simple design with a large bed, several end tables, a cold fireplace, and a few couches. A large closet ran the length of the entire room, and of course, it had its own bathing chamber.

I hadn't seen the inside of his chambers yet. I'd been avoiding it all week.

I stood at the threshold, twisting my fingers. "Where should I sleep?"

His presence brushed up behind me, his chest like a wall of gravity that threatened to pull me in. "You can take the bed. I'll take the couch. As long as both of our scents are in this room, the staff shouldn't question our sleeping arrangements further."

A pang of relief, or perhaps disappointment, hit me. Not wanting to analyze *that*, I hurried to the bathing chamber and promptly closed the door.

But as soon as I was alone in the room, I groaned. I hadn't been thinking when I immediately retreated here. My bags were still in the other room. Not that it mattered, since I didn't own any pajamas. All week I'd been sleeping in my underthings, but there was no way I was leaving these chambers dressed only in that.

Huffing, I called upon my magic to whisk away the day's grime, then I cleansed my teeth and freshened my breath. Following that, I stood there, not sure what to do next.

My image stared back at me in the mirror. Wide green eyes. Pale skin. Long chestnut hair weaving itself around my shoulders. I'd taken out my braid hours ago, so my hair hung in waves down my back. The purple sweater I wore was slightly dirty from my crawl along the Wood's floor in Possyrose Forest, and since my magic was strong enough now to clean my clothes as well, I cleansed that too. But beyond that, there was nothing left for me to do.

Fingers twisting and turning together, I continued gazing at the mirror. I looked as I always did, minus the flush creeping up my neck just beneath my collar.

A soft knock came on the door. "Elowen?" Jax's voice was muffled through the door's thick wood.

I jumped. "Almost done!"

I made a few noises on the counter, just to make him think I was actually doing something other than delaying the inevitable. But after a few more minutes passed, I knew I had to face him.

My hand shook when I clenched the door handle. I had no idea what was spiraling between us, but as his friends implied, *something* clearly was.

I opened the door with a flourish, and my breath immediately stopped.

Jax stood before me.

Shirtless.

My traitorous eyes dipped down his chest before I could stop myself. Hard pecs, chiseled abs, a myriad of scars, and a very distinct V dipped below his waistline. *Stars and galaxy, why does he have to be so alluring?*

A rumble of magic clouded around him, and when I finally glanced upward again, I came face-to-face with a satisfied-looking crown prince who'd just watched me check him out.

Flustered even more, I gestured behind me. "The bathing chamber is all yours."

I slid past him, mortified that he'd just caught me ogling him. *But to show up shirtless?*

Before I got two steps past him, he clasped my elbow and swung me around. The hardness of his chest intimately met my breasts when he hauled me against him.

"What are you doing?" My words came out in a squeak.

"Why did you come for us tonight?" His question was muttered softly, but a razor hung in the air between us. One wrong move, and it would drop, slicing the tension that smothered us.

"I told you. I couldn't fathom a child growing up without their parent. Not if I could stop it."

His grip caressed my elbow, so subtly that if I wasn't hyperaware of every move he made, I would've missed it. "Is that the only reason?"

I swallowed, and his gaze tracked the bob of my throat. "Do you want there to be another reason?"

His expression grew stormy, his eyes blazing like liquid gems. "Would you tell me if there was?"

Our words danced around one another, and I'd never been more aware of a male in all of my life. But I couldn't allow this to continue. Attraction sizzled between us. I knew it. He knew it. It'd been growing since the very first day we met, and had become painfully acute in the week we'd been playacting.

But he was the crown prince of Stonewild. He was to eventually marry another of royal blood or of a pedigree that I could never claim. The reality was that I was a lorafin, which made me *other*. I could be an owned trinket or the scandalous lover of a royal prince, but any affair between us would always be kept in the shadows. I highly doubted his future bride would allow him to flaunt me in the open.

And I didn't want that. I wanted *more*, so if the bottom line meant that we could never have any future together in any capacity, that I could accept . . .

Our fate was already sealed, and it was best to accept that now.

I swallowed again, and Jax's aura rose like a swelling wave around him, growing higher and stronger, so large and powerful that I waited for it to crash all around me.

"Tell me what you're thinking." A muscle bulged in his jaw.

I licked my lips, and he watched the movement. "I'm thinking that someday you'll be wed to another."

He growled, and the energy around him soared. "I'm not wed yet, Elowen."

"No, not yet." *But I'll eventually have to watch you wed another, and if I'd already been with you . . . it would destroy me, which is why nothing can ever start between us. Don't you get that, Jax? I have feelings for you too.*

But I didn't voice that confession, and I didn't point out that his future bride would likely not stand for me lurking in her shadow. There was no point. Nothing could ever come of this.

His thumb moved in a languid circle on my arm. Goosebumps immediately sprouted. "What do you need? Just tell me, and I'll provide it."

I shook my head. "But that's just it. I don't *need* anything you can give me. What I want isn't possible, but thank you. You caring means more to me than I can ever describe, but I'll find a way to forge my own path with this new life I've been given."

I looked down slightly, still reeling that we hadn't come to any sort of resolution or agreement for what he would do with me. The fact remained that I knew their secrets. The Dark Raider's worry that a Mistvale fairy could pry those secrets from me still loomed. In all likelihood, I would forever be tethered to the crown prince. But still, I wouldn't demand things of him he couldn't willingly give. And he could certainly never give himself to me.

"You don't owe me anything, Jax."

His breath stopped, and his entire body turned to stone. A moment passed and then another before he rasped, "I do. Because of you, we know that my brother was here recently. If you hadn't gone to the Veiled Between for me, my search for him would still be entirely lost."

"You'll find him. I know you will."

His expression wiped clean, and it wasn't lost on me that I hadn't said *we'll find him.* I opened my mouth to correct myself, but Jax gave a brief nod, and then he turned.

He entered the bathing chambers and closed the door behind him, and it felt as if something inside of me died.

Heart feeling heavy, I shuffled away from the bathroom and removed my bulky sweater and breeches. Wearing only my underthings, I slipped under the sheets. I pulled the covers up until they met my chin. Since the lights were already out, I turned on my side to gaze out the window at the three moons.

A moment later, the door opened and closed behind me, but I didn't turn. I didn't make a sound. Rustling came from near the couch, and then the furniture creaked when the prince settled his heavy weight onto it.

Tension bled through the air until it congealed into a mass so thick I could've cut it with a knife. Yet neither of us said a thing.

Eventually, the pull of sleep became irresistible. Closing my eyes, I knew that no matter what tomorrow brought, I needed to stop these ridiculous reactions I was having for my former captor. He and I led two separate lives. As my guardian had pointed out to me time and time again, I was a lorafin. I was to be feared and revered, yet I would always be different.

And as Saramel had told me, and the queen had not so subtly hinted at by having all of the approved females on the royal ship when we'd ventured here, the prince was to marry a female of noble breeding next summer. A female that could never be me.

A pang fractured my stomach when that truth hit

home. But as much as that hurt to the deepest part of my core, I knew it was true. Jax would never be mine.

CHAPTER 21

I tossed and turned throughout the night, Jax's presence calling to something deep inside me. The urge to be closer to him was almost a physical pain, but I didn't allow myself to leave the bed.

Sleep came fitfully. Strange dreams came too. Dreams of my childhood. Dreams of being mounted atop a powerful black stag. And dreams of a masked male forever lurking in the shadows.

Something about being in the same room with Jax, with him so near yet so far, had my magic roiling and chilling within me.

The full moon was high in the sky when I finally fell into another restless sleep, but then a new dream began. An even stranger one.

A semelee swirled around me, crooning and wrapping

its strength around my soul. *"Daughter of Darkness, you've come to us again. What do you seek?"*

I spun in a circle, surprise filling me at the *realness* of this dream. The Veiled Between stretched in every direction. Shadows and ink. Mist and planes. Over a dozen semelees swam in my vicinity, their power enthralling.

But I ignored the semelee's question entirely and instead concentrated on my surroundings. *I'm dreaming, right?*

Confusion clogged my mind. I hung suspended in the shadowy mist. The weight of it felt heavy yet buoyant. The sensations I always felt when I traveled to this plane of reality pushed against me. Stars Above, but it felt *real*.

Reaching a hand out, I touched the back of one of the semelees. Its cool scaled skin met my fingertips.

My soul gasped. Its skin felt *very* real.

Eyes widening, I somehow managed to get out, *Am I actually here?*

Yes, Princess of Shadows, the semelee responded. *You've come to us again. It's been too long.*

I spun around again, and it hit me that I was truly here. I'd traveled to the realm between realms, yet I had no memory of detaching from my body and purposefully spiraling through space to reach the Veil. I had no memory of pulling on another's magic to perform a calling.

Surprise gripped me harder, and the semelees moved

faster, crooning to me more, sliding past my fingertips at increasing speed.

I waited for my growing fear to elicit a shock from my collar. The pull of its magic still anchored me to the fae lands, yet . . . it didn't come.

Another gasp shook my soul. The collar's hold on my soul was too weak. I couldn't follow it back, and I'd never been in the Veiled Between without it. I'd never learned how to exit this plane without the Veil within sight or my collar pulling me home.

I spun again in the darkness as genuine panic began to claw up my throat. *Which way? Which way do I go?* But my questions went unanswered. It was only me and the shadow creatures, the commanders of fate at my fingertips.

I wrenched on my magic, pulling more from the well in my soul, then demanded that the semelees come to heel completely. The nearest one eagerly surged forward, ready to do my bidding, but the largest coiled around me, seemingly content simply to touch me.

Stop, I commanded it. It paused, its massive weight stilling. *Return me to the Veil.*

But you belong here, it hissed.

Another pull from its massive body tugged me deeper into the Veiled Between, and the others, as though gaining confidence, began to do the same.

I fought the biggest one, my magic rising higher, and again it stilled. I was stronger now with the collar loosened, there was no doubt about that, and an idea suddenly struck me. If I was here, I could ask about my family. I could ask about Bastian. I could finally try to do a calling for myself and ask about Jax's brother even if the prince had been fighting me on it all week.

Release me. The semelee slithered back and bowed submissively. *Who was my mother?* I asked. *Tell me more about her. And where's Bastian? Tell me exactly where the prince's brother is at this moment.*

The large semelee lifted its head and slid along my thigh anew. *Are you trying to conduct a calling for yourself, Lorafin?*

I am. Tell me.

But it slithered against me more, not replying.

TELL ME, I said in a stronger, deeper tone, filled with my magic. An answering pulse came from my collar in the fae lands, but it was so faint, and I couldn't decipher which direction it came from.

But the semelee only spun around me more. *To conduct a calling for oneself or to command the fates, requires a queen, and you are not a queen, Lorafin. Not yet. You are still a princess, although you feel bolder. Stronger. Yet I do not feel compelled to bend to your will completely, so I will not answer your questions.*

I spun to the others. *Then you tell me. Or you!*

But one after another, the semelees refused to give me answers.

A crushing sense of defeat barreled through me. If they wouldn't respond, I would *never* be able to do a calling of my own. Ever. Not even with my collar diminished. Which meant, I could never uncover anything further about my past. And I couldn't find Bastian, not without Jax's magic or someone else's to assist me.

Aching under that realization, I turned away from the semelees and began to search for my way out.

A semelee slowly slithered at my side, not trying to ensnare me again, merely accompanying me. At least I had enough magic now to command it more readily, so it didn't try to take me away.

Where's the Veil? I asked it.

It's where it always is. It's where you entered it.

You're going to answer in riddles, is that it?

You should be able to find the way on your own, Lorafin.

So they weren't going to tell me, because an experienced lorafin didn't become lost here. Not like a caged one such as myself.

I swam through the shadows, searching for the Veil, but found nothing. I was in nothingness.

Genuine panic began to consume me. If I couldn't find the way out, I would never leave this place.

"Elowen!" someone called. The voice was so distant, so far away, yet I could have sworn that someone just said my name.

I swirled around as a bolt of magic flared on my collar.

I cried out. It came so suddenly but felt different. Stronger. Sharper. But its direction was clear.

It came from behind me.

The semelees whirled along my sides as I flew toward the Veil. Scales of darkness and shadows pressed into me, trying to encourage me to stay, but I held firm.

"Elowen!" the voice called again.

Pulses of magic elicited along my throat anew, strengthening with every second that passed. But it wasn't my collar's magic—it was something else. Something powerful, unique, and desperate.

Jax.

"Elowen, come back to me!" His growl rang through the cosmos, and then another shove of potent magic encircled my throat. Shocks ticked painfully around my neck, coming from the collar, and were so great that I cried out again, but I was thankful for his help.

I grasped a hold of Jax's magic. It felt different from my collar. More forceful. It was an entire realm of power spiraling against me and commanding all of my attention.

I followed the feel of it, grasping onto its essence.

The semelees hissed their displeasure, so I said, *I'll return again, but right now, I must go.*

Slowly, the Veil appeared, the mist growing thicker. I willed my soul toward my body, and with a burst of speed, I shot through the Veil and was barreling through the cosmos, flying through time and space as the strength of Jax's magic led me back home.

I returned to my body so hard that I gasped. Power sizzled around my throat, making my collar hum.

"Stars Above. Elowen? Can you hear me?" Jax's rasp came through the darkness. "Elowen, please, say something!"

The desperation in his words slammed my senses back to the present. I was lying on a large bed in my underthings. Darkness surrounded me. Heavy breathing came from my side. A large hand gripped my shoulder as another encircled my throat, magic barreling from the palm into my collar.

"Jax?" I whispered.

"Elowen? Yes, it's me!" His ragged breath followed. "Thank the gods." Jax's forehead pressed against mine, and the scent of his sweet breath puffed around me. "Are you here? Can you hear me?"

"Yes, I'm here now." A shiver hit me and then another. Terror made coldness creep into my veins. I'd been so close to becoming lost in the Veiled Between.

Another shuddering breath left him, filled with so much fear that it nearly encompassed me completely. "I thought I wouldn't get you back."

I pressed my palm to the back of his hand, needing to feel something tangible. "Thank you. I almost didn't. I was so disoriented, not sure which way to go, but you pulled me back." Frowning, I added, "But how did you know I was in the Veiled Between?"

"I felt it when you left."

"You did?"

He nodded. "I couldn't sleep. I was lying on the couch, staring at the ceiling, and then your aura shifted. A crackle of magic came from your collar, and then a huge release of magic came from your body." He sucked in another breath. His words were still too fast to be considered calm. "When I called out to you, you didn't respond, so I came to your side. And—" He huffed out another breath. "The magic around you felt exactly as it had when you traveled to the Veiled Between for my calling."

My lips parted, and my jaw dropped. Memories of the strange way my magic had been acting with Jax so near, yet so far, lingered. "I think I traveled there in my dream. My magic was being . . . strange."

"Has that ever happened before?"

"No, but I'm stronger now. The last time I traveled there so easily was before this was placed on me." I trailed my finger along the collar. "But I was definitely disoriented, and I was at risk of becoming lost. I don't have enough experience there without the collar to know my way back easily, but hopefully in time I will."

But another starker, and more resolute fact, barreled into my thoughts. I would never know anything more about my mother. And I could never ask about Bastian on my own. Both required being able to do callings for myself, and only a lorafin queen could conduct her own callings. But I would never be able to, because of the collar.

A breath shuddered out of me. Forever, I would be caged. There was no changing that, and the last thread of hope that I'd held onto that perhaps one day I could be the master of my own destiny, snuffed out of existence.

My lips quivered, and tears sprouted in my eyes.

Jax's palm skated gently over my cheeks. "Why are you crying?"

"Because I'll never know." I recanted what the semelees had told me, that I still wasn't their queen. "I can't do a calling for myself, Jax. They confirmed it. I'll never be able to do a calling without the aid of another's magic."

He lowered himself to my side, his weight dipping the mattress as his touches remained soft and gentle. "I'm sorry. I'm so sorry."

I shook my head, then dried my tears. "I kind of assumed as much, but to have it confirmed . . ." My hands were still shaking, but I forced them to still.

"I'm sorry," he said again. A tingle of his magic washed against my skin as he continued his soft, soothing motions.

I ran a hand along the cool metal encircling my throat. A flare of Jax's residual magic still penetrated it, and I turned my attention toward that, anything to keep from reliving what the semelees had revealed. "How did you use your magic to elicit my collar?"

"I blasted pulses of my sensory magic into it. It was the first thing that came to mind."

"I'm glad you did. It obviously worked."

He huffed in amusement, and for a moment, we stayed silent. In the dim nighttime lighting, our gazes locked together, and our breaths mingled. Slowly, he inched closer to me on the bed.

"You should go back to sleep. I'll stay close in case you accidentally travel to the Veiled Between again. I can help you find your way back if you need it." He lay only inches away in nothing but loose pants, and his large fingers curled around mine, holding my hand. A moment of bliss barreled through me. He was so warm. I curled into him more.

He scowled. "You're freezing."

He grumbled in displeasure, then wrapped his arms around me and pulled me against his chest. Hot skin met my frigid limbs. He swore silently under his breath and ripped the covers off the bed and encased both of us in them.

The heavy weight of the blankets settled around us as his hands ran up and down my back, using friction to warm me further, then a pulse of magic hummed around him.

His entire body heated to an unnatural level, and I knew that he'd pulled on his command of the elements.

The air in the room warmed too, and Jax's body turned into molten fire.

Closing my eyes, I sank into him even more. His skin felt like a burning rock. It was bliss, and some of the tension radiating through me lessened as my chilled skin began to warm.

"That feels so good," I whispered.

He didn't stop. His hands continued their wandering movements, and his magic settled into a constant cocoon of cloud-like warmth as though flames blazed from him.

Minutes ticked by, and slowly, the chill left me, but that only made me aware of how closely we lay to one another.

I felt every hard inch of him. Every sculpted line. Jax's body was huge and muscled, and I tentatively ran my fingers along his abdomen.

He stilled.

"Sorry." I snatched my hands back to my side. *What is it about this male?* Everything about him called to me.

But his hand glided down my arm until he cupped my palm, then he placed my hand back on his side and held it there.

"You don't need to be sorry." In the dim light, the bob of his throat was right in my line of sight.

My eyes snapped up. Fire rolled around him. A fire born of want and desire. His body grew harder in an entirely new way, and the room grew uncomfortably hot as a flush worked through my limbs.

In a breath, he calmed his elemental power, his skin and the air returning to normal.

I licked my lips, and he followed the movement.

"What is this . . . *thing* between us, Jax?"

His fingers sank into my hip, kneading the soft flesh there. "You haven't figured it out yet?"

And it hit me. What he was implying. And why he hadn't said anything sooner. My eyes widened as I finally accepted what had been right in front of me all along.

Tradition dictated that males wait for females to acknowledge the mating bond before acting. It was bad luck for the male to push the female into accepting the bond until she was ready. Some even said the bond was strongest when it was allowed to develop naturally.

My lips parted as panic threatened to engulf me anew. "No."

He growled. "Yes."

"We can't be fated. Fate means that you're my . . ." I didn't want to admit it. But the word brushed across my mind as though it'd been waiting to reveal itself, hidden behind a sheer curtain all along and only now peeking out to play.

Mate.

Another rumble filled Jax's chest, and he leaned down

to whisper in my ear. "I've been waiting for you to feel it too. This pull. This *want*."

My breaths sped up. "Oh Gods."

He was right. My magic certainly responded to him. Always seeking him. Always trying to join with his. Just tonight, it'd done it again, and I could have sworn that was the reason for my unrest and traveling to the Veiled Between in a dream. We were mates, but I'd been resisting it. My magic didn't like my resistance. It wouldn't ultimately stand for that, so it'd grown erratic. *That* was why I'd traveled to the Veiled Between in my sleep.

And there was a way to prevent that from happening again. My magic would calm if I accepted the bond.

I licked my lips as reality sank in more. Jax being my mate explained this pull I felt toward him—a pull created of the gods. It would also explain my undeniable attraction to him and why our magic sizzled between us. It would also explain why I'd been so captivated by him when he was my abductor and why he was so overly protective of me.

Of course. Fae males were fiercely protective of their females—to a point that it was unnatural. That was why Jax had so adamantly refused to let me do another calling to find Bastian. He couldn't stomach the thought of me becoming hurt, even if I would ultimately heal.

"What are we going to do?" I finally whispered. Because even if we were meant for one another, that was a feeling best kept behind locked doors in shadowed rooms in the dead of night. Come sunrise, I couldn't allow myself to acknowledge Jax as my mate. He and I came from different origins. Our lives were never meant to cross, even if the gods had forked our paths until they intersected.

"What do you want to do?" he whispered, his voice husky, his body hardening even more. He trailed his nose up my neck, and a smattering of nerves fired all along my body.

Shivering, I positively ached for him, but I shook my head. "We probably shouldn't—"

His lips collided with mine. He kissed me hard, his mouth claiming me. Strong arms entwined around me, as though he never wanted to let me go.

"We *should*," he growled into my mouth.

The second his taste flooded me, a low moan worked up my throat. My hands tangled in his hair, and I kissed him in return.

He was right. He was my mate. *Mine.* I wanted this so badly that I told myself the consequences didn't matter, even though a tiny voice in the back of my mind said that they did.

Shushing that worry, I dipped my tongue forward to dance with his. He tasted like spice and fire, sin and desire. I'd never tasted anything so good.

Growling, he deepened our kiss.

We kissed one another desperately, our touches raw.

Finally, my soul seemed to scream. *Finally*.

His fingers coasted down my thigh to crook behind my knee. Levering it, he hooked my leg around his waist, and the hard length of him pressed against me. A growl of satisfaction rumbled in his chest, but he didn't sweep my underthings to the side. His fingers stroked my skin, trailing along my sides, then cupped my breasts, all while he grinded against me.

Roll after roll of desire washed through me. He kneaded my soft flesh, claiming my body as though it belonged to him. Stars, but the male created a *want* in me that I'd never felt before. I was on the verge of coming when he ran a rough thumb over my taut nipple, and when I cried out, another satisfied sounding rumble came from his throat.

Goddess, I *wanted* him. Wanted him desperately.

"Elowen," Jax rasped and ripped his mouth from mine. Our breaths heaved around us. "If we keep this up, I'm not going to be able to stop. I need you to tell me to stop if you don't want this."

His body throbbed. Every line of him was taut and felt like a bowstring about to snap. My body was just as ripe, just as wanting.

My mate.

But in some dim part of my mind, it registered what he was saying. If we crossed this line now, there was no return.

Yet I knew I could do it. I could give my virginity to the Dark Raider here and now. I could become his mistress, his true lover, his *mate*. We could complete the bond, but come next summer, he would still marry another. Even if the gods had fated us . . . he was still the crown prince, and even princes weren't given everything they wanted.

I would have to watch him be with another. Marry another. Fuck another.

Cold reality swept through me, and I pulled back because just the thought of that made me sick. I didn't want a short fling with him even if it would give me something to remember for the rest of my life. I wanted more. I wanted him. *All* of him. Forever.

The realization that such a wish would never be granted hit me so suddenly that it was as if a stone brick had been thrown in my chest. "We shouldn't."

A pang of disappointment swirled around him.

"You're to marry another, Jax."

His nostrils flared. "I won't."

"You'll have to."

He huffed and tore a hand through his hair.

Tears threatened to spring into my eyes again, but in my next blink, he was there, cupping my cheeks, kissing away the stray tears that wanted to fall. "Elowen." He kissed me softly. Reverently. "I want you. Only you."

"We can't, Jax. Not with how things are."

His body stilled, and his breaths locked in his chest.

Energy swirled around him, meshing with my own. It called to me. Begged me to give in.

But Jax's throat bobbed, and he finally nodded. "All right. I won't bed you, if that's what you wish." He pressed his lips to my ears and whispered softly, "But let me give you release, Elowen. I can scent how much you want it. Just for this one night, let me give you that. I won't ask for anything in return. You owe me nothing. But I want to do that for you if you'll let me. Please, *mate*. Let me at least give you that."

A shudder ran through me. *Release*. From him touching me. I'd never experienced that with any male. Ever.

He waited. Waited for my consent. He'd *always* waited for me to say yes. He was the only male who'd ever given me that gift over and over, time and time again.

My chin dipped slightly, and warring emotions again blazed through me, but he'd said one night. Just once. Surely only one time wouldn't destroy me completely.

I finally nodded, affirming that I wanted what he was offering despite my better judgment.

A swell of satisfaction rumbled through his aura, even more so when I parted my thighs. Welcoming him. Wanting him.

A low growl rumbled in this chest, the sound possessive and raw. "You're mine tonight," he rasped.

In a flurry of his magic, my underthings were ripped

off and fluttered to the floor. I gasped when I lay naked and bare before him, the chilled night air coasting over my skin.

Jax's eyes heated, his gaze raking up and down my body, drinking me in. "So fucking beautiful." He cupped one of my bare breasts, his hand squeezing its weight. "So perfect."

Mouth finding mine, he kissed me again as his hands wandered freely. Boldly. He rubbed, caressed, explored, and owned every inch of me.

With each path his hands traveled, the heat in me built.

He inhaled deeply, my arousal clouding the air, and then his wandering fingers slipped through my folds, my breath catching completely as he played with my heat.

A low sound came from him that vibrated me all the way to my toes. My head fell back as his fingers fiddled and stroked, playing my flesh expertly with every swirl and caress.

His tongue ran along my lower lip, then he kissed along my jaw and down my throat. He slipped a finger inside me, filling me slightly, and I sucked a breath in.

All I could do was pant. Words wouldn't form. Only feelings. These *exquisite* feelings.

His mouth trailed down my chest to my breasts. He sucked one of my peaks into his mouth and slipped a second finger inside me, and then a third. He stretched me completely with his fingers, pumping them in and out, and the aura around him grew so potent that it commanded all of my attention.

His lips met my neck again, teasing me just above my collar, and then his thumb found my nub. He stroked me, rubbing my flesh expertly as he worked my body like a master craftsman carving a sculpture.

Throbbing need climbed in my belly with every pump of his digits and swipe of his thumb. I clung to him, feeling feverish with need. Moaning, I rocked against him. "Don't stop. Oh Gods, don't stop!"

"Nothing could make me stop. You're *mine* right now." His erection swelled near my stomach, growing so hard and big that I couldn't help but reach for it.

When my fingers closed around him, he hissed. But I didn't stop. The velvety steel of him had my fantasies blooming to an entirely new level. He was even bigger than I'd imagined. So hard and large. I ran my hand up him more, pumping him like he was thrusting into me.

"Elowen," he rasped. "Stars, *Elowen*."

I continued touching him as intimately as he touched me, clenching, stroking, as his length throbbed in my hands.

"Goddess Above, I want to rut with you," he growled.

My hand squeezed around him even more at that admission, and my earlier decision to not let this progress fizzled into non-existence. "Rut with me?" I gasped when his fingers withdrew, and he brought them to his lips.

He slipped his fingers inside his mouth, tasting me, and I didn't think I'd ever seen anything more erotic.

"You taste like honey." Eyes aglow, his gaze met mine. "My stag instincts are demanding that I bend you over and rut with you, but I promised not to take more than this." He moved lower, his mouth trailing down my stomach, forcing my hands away from his cock, and I knew exactly where his mouth was headed.

When his body settled between my thighs and his lips closed around my nub, my body arched off the bed. He rumbled low in his chest and positioned himself securely between my legs, refusing to let me lift again.

"You're going to take my mouth."

Short, sharp pants were all I could manage.

"Every lick." His tongue ran up my center. "Every suck." His mouth latched onto my clit. "Every part of my mouth you will take, do you understand?"

All I could do was nod.

He inhaled deeply. "Your arousal drives me mad. Did you know that?" He licked my nub again, then sucked it and fiddled it with is tongue. I slapped a hand to my mouth to muffle my scream. "Each time I've scented it, you've driven me crazy with need."

I gasped when he sucked me into his mouth once more. Words wouldn't form, and I couldn't get *his* words out of my head. *Every lick. Every suck. I want to rut with you.*

Everything he said sounded indecent. Wanton. And incredibly arousing.

He licked up my center, lapping and sucking me eagerly. I grabbed his head, tangling my fingers in the dark locks of his hair. A storm of desire unleashed within his eyes, the swirling power in them igniting a faint blue glow.

I nibbled on my lower lip, and the glowing in his eyes increased. "What if I *want* to rut with you?"

His eyes flashed more, and he pulled back from my core just enough to rumble, "Do you know what that means?"

I pictured him bending me over, taking me from behind, rutting with me until we both came undone. I didn't know if such an act would seal our mating bond, but if I held my magic back, I guessed it probably wouldn't. "I do."

The energy around him soared, heating the air around us. His throat bobbed. "And you . . . want that too?"

I thought again of what giving my virginity to the Dark Raider would mean. There would be no turning back. I could no longer look at him as though we were nothing more than friends in our endeavors. Even if he did release me, despite his fears about Mistvale, and we parted ways in the coming days or weeks or months . . . even if I never saw him again, a part of me would always belong to him and him to me. He would be my first, the first male to ever feel me on such an intimate level. *My mate.*

I found myself nodding. If I was going to give my virginity to anyone, I wanted it to be him. "I want that, Jax. So much."

He growled once more, and a flash of power rippled in the air around him. In my next blink, he was crawling up my body, his erection thick and heavy between my legs. He kissed my stomach, my breasts, everywhere his mouth encountered. All the while, the power around him grew and coiled, growing more dominant, more demanding.

"You're sure?" he rasped.

I nodded again. "Yes."

His eyes took on a feral look as his hard body hovered above me, and when his lips reached my neck, where my collar locked away the entirety of my power, his eyes flashed on the purple gem. A moment of anger stole over him, but then his mouth found mine.

"I don't know if I can be gentle," he said into my mouth, his kisses raw and desperate. "Rutting is primal, and my stag instincts have been demanding it for . . . a while."

"I don't want gentle," I replied in between kisses because if this was to be my only time with him, I wanted all of him, all of his magic, all of his cock, all of his power. I wanted it *all*. "I *want* primal."

His lips curved in absolute satisfaction, and he flipped me on my stomach, then lifted my arse in the air.

My arousal tripled from his rough movements, his uncensored desire flaming me to a spiraling peak.

"Goddess, look at you."

I glanced over my shoulder. Jax was staring at my core, at my round rump, my glistening folds. Leaning down, he licked me, his tongue parting my entrance before he sucked on my nub again.

A moan escaped me. On my hands and knees, I leaned forward, resting on my elbows and pushing my entrance against his face.

A strange sound came from his throat, part grunt, part growl, and it was entirely hypnotic. He lapped and kissed me again until he worked me into another fevered pitch.

"Jax, I'm so close to coming!"

A shudder ran through me as he lifted himself, kneeling behind me. "Not yet, my beautiful mate. You're to come on my cock."

His dominant demand had me aching so deeply, and the desperate need to be pushed over the edge had me ripping and clawing at the sheets.

He gripped my hips with both hands, and his stiff erection brushed against me.

My walls clenched, wanting him, seeking him, but he just brushed the head of his cock against me again.

My breath sucked in.

"You're sure?" he asked, his voice raspy and low. "You

want me to rut with you? There's no turning back once we do this."

My fingers turned into claws, and I shoved myself against him, but his grip held firm. "Yes, Jax. I'm sure. Rut with me. *Now.*"

That strange grunt tore from his throat again, and the head of his cock pushed into me. With each inch, the power around him increased. His magic collided with mine in the air, coiling and heating around us until everything in me swirled around everything in him.

He grunted again in that strange cadence. My thighs trembled, and his fingers dug into the flesh on my hips as he pushed into me more and *more.*

But then he hit a barrier.

He stilled. "You're a virgin?" he rasped.

"Yes."

Another strange sound came from him: pure satisfaction, pure male dominance. "Mine. You're fucking *mine,* Elowen."

"Yes, Jax. I'm yours. *Please.* Don't stop."

He hissed, and I cried out in need when his cock slipped another inch inside me, pushing against that virginal wall.

"All of it, Jax," I demanded. "I want it all. *Rut with me. Now.* Do what your instincts demand."

And those final words seemed to push him over the edge. In a barely controlled frenzy, he plunged his cock fully inside me, ripping through my barrier. The pain was sharp and brief, then it subsided.

He fit tightly, his erection large and throbbing. He filled every inch of me. I shuddered in bliss. Goddess, he felt amazing.

But he didn't give me any time to marvel. Another deep grunt came from him, and when I looked over my shoulder, his eyes were glowing brightly, and magic shimmered around his head.

He leaned over me, pushing me down more into the mattress as his hands anchored to my hips, refusing to let me wiggle away even an inch.

Power grew in his aura, swelling around him, and then he began thrusting into me, hard and deep. His movements grew faster, his cock swelling inside me, growing even bigger until his rough movements were commanding all of my attention.

I screamed in pleasure. He pounded into me, his movements hard, but I'd never felt anything so right.

I closed my eyes, growing lost to the sensations. With each shove from his pelvis, my body wanted to lurch up the bed, but his hands on my hips wouldn't allow it. He anchored me in place, demanding that I take every hard inch of him again and again and again.

"Jax! I'm so close!" I cried.

He didn't reply, but he grumbled a sound, and his slapping increased, and when I looked over my shoulder a second time, wanting to see what effects our carnal acts were having on him, I gasped.

Antlers had sprouted from his head, and his eyes were glowing blue orbs. The rest of him remained fae, only the antlers hinting at his shifter origins.

When our gazes collided, he curled over me, trapping me completely. All the while, he rammed into me harder and deeper, his thrusts never stopping.

I moaned again, more turned on than any male had ever made me. I was so close . . . *so* close to shattering all around him.

"Come for me, Elowen," he demanded. "Give me yourself. I want to make you *mine*." Magic swirled around him, coating me in his aura and power.

My magic threatened to join with his, but I wrenched on it, holding it back.

He pounded into me more, and I screamed just as my orgasm ripped through me. The realm crashed around me in a thousand dazzling waves and swirling sparks, soaring so high my vision swam and my core clenched.

He roared in victory when my channel spasmed around him, and then he slammed into me a final time, his cock pumping so violently that I felt every drop of his release as his seed flowed into me.

He curled himself around my body even more, his

pelvis jammed against my core as he emptied himself in hot spurts. Magic—hot, heavy, and pulsing—tingled my skin and electrified my senses. Jax's magic encased me. Protected me.

But I kept my magic in check so as not to fully enact the bond.

But I gasped when a searing burn flared on the back of my neck along my spine. It was gone so quickly, though, that I wondered if I imagined it.

All the while, Jax's hands stayed anchored on my hips.

I smiled as a thoroughly content feeling of being dominated by him completely overtook me. I loved every second of it.

I shuddered, and it felt like eternity passed before my orgasm and his pulsing cock finally, fully calmed. I felt spent . . . totally, completely, and perfectly spent.

I sagged beneath him, my body turning to mush as my brain fogged with bliss.

He moved with me, his body curling over me more, and his mouth slid just below my ear, his whispered words humming with immense satisfaction. *"You're mine now. Forever."*

I didn't know if I heard him correctly. I was too far gone from the effects of our love making to fully understand him.

But I was still a lorafin.

And he was still the heir to a throne.

We could never truly be together, but tonight, he was mine, and I was his. And I would take this one small gift and cherish it forever.

CHAPTER 22

I awoke to the feel of Jax's hard body pressed against mine. His naked chest was flush to my back, and his arm was wrapped around my waist, holding me close.

Sunlight streamed into the room, and one sniff told me that the scent of sex hung heavily in the air.

I blinked sleepily, a smile forming. Jax and I had done *many* activities throughout the night. A giggle escaped me, and I quickly slapped a hand to my mouth to muffle any further sound. But I couldn't help another small laugh because the crown prince of Stonewild had taken my virginity. His need through the night had seemed insatiable, but each time, I'd been just as ready for him.

Stars and galaxy, I'm not a virgin anymore. My heart felt so content that it took a full minute before reality began to seep in. Bittersweet reality. I'd given my virginity to my mate, but I could never truly claim him as mine. And that fact burrowed itself into my bones.

The room continued to brighten, but the light within me dimmed. My claim on Jax was coming to an end. We had this night, this one perfect night, but he was still the heir to Stonewild, and I was still a caged lorafin. Nothing could ever come of this, even if the gods had created us as fated mates.

Still . . . I smiled again. I could enjoy it while it lasted. I would forever savor the memory, and for this one delicious moment, he was still wrapped around me.

I snuggled closer to him. The prince's deep, rhythmic breathing continued, and I allowed myself time to memorize my mate—the feel of him, his strength, his tenderness, his unbelievably arousing aura that had commanded me completely. Everything about him I wanted to hold close.

I wanted to remember all of the best details, and the only regret I had was that we hadn't engaged in any positions other than him taking me from behind. Rutting seemed to be what he enjoyed most, but I cherished that too, and I would remember it forever.

Sleepily, I sighed against him.

Jax stirred on my next breath, and a tingle of his magic puffed in his aura. Still asleep, he tightened his arm, then his hand strayed lower, fingers dancing along my skin toward my—

The door banged open. "Jax, wake up!"

I started at the sound of Bowan rushing into the room, and a squeak emitted from me.

Bowan stopped halfway across the chambers, his feet planting to the carpet. His jaw dropped, and his gaze shot to the floor. "Oh, shite."

The emission left him just as Jax growled awake. The prince's arm locked around my waist, dragging me against him, and then a terrifying snarl tore from his mouth just as his magic speared toward the intruder.

Jax's magic hit Bowan at full force. Bowan twitched upright in a rigid board, his mouth opening and closing, but no sound came out. His entire body began to convulse, then his mouth opened in a silent scream.

Stars and galaxy, the prince was inflicting *pain*.

I shook Jax's arm, which was like trying to remove a steel band. "Jax, it's just Bowan!"

But the crown prince's arm just locked tighter around my waist.

Sleep was still evident in his expression, so I wiggled against him, hoping to snap him out of whatever sleep-crazed instinct had just overtaken him. "Jax, it's *Bowan*!"

In his next blink, the prince's eyes widened. "Goddess," he rasped. He released his magic, the power around his friend obliterating.

Bowan blinked and sagged, nearly crumpling to the floor. Somehow, he managed to stay upright, but the second his gaze snagged onto Jax's, he snapped his attention to the floor once more.

My heart beat frantically because *that* was quite the wake-up call, yet Jax just pulled me against his chest again, then gathered the covers around us to cover me completely.

"What in the realm are you doing in here, Bowan?" he growled. "And it better be an absolutely fucking fantastic reason. I almost killed you."

"I . . ." Bowan's gaze stayed on his toes, but slowly, he began to lift his head.

"*Don't look at her when she's not dressed.*" The energy around the Dark Raider soared as his Mistvale commanding magic speared his friend.

I gaped and whipped my attention upward to face Jax and demand to know why he would command his friend like that, but the prince's focus didn't waver.

Bowan immediately dipped his chin downward, then inhaled deeply. And even though he kept his attention latched to the rug beneath his feet, I couldn't help but notice his shocked expression. "I'm . . . I'm sorry, my prince. I meant no disrespect. I didn't know."

"What do you want?" Jax demanded. "And Galaxy Above, Bowan, never enter my chambers like that again when I have her with me."

"I understand now, but . . . well, I didn't expect to find her in bed with you or to know that you—"

"Enough." Jax snarled, and his body nearly curled around me. "For the last time, what do you want?"

"I'm here because I saw Bastian," Bowan said in a rush. "I saw him this morning in the Wood with a group of half-breeds. If we're fast, we can catch up to them."

JAX WASTED no time heeding Bowan's call. Within minutes, all of us were dressed and flying from the penthouse suite. Outside, the shifters transformed into their stag forms and took off through the capital's sleepy streets.

The realm moved in blurred speed around us. I sat in front of Jax, atop Phillen, as the other males kept pace around us. We'd been in such a hurry to leave that neither Jax nor I had spoken a word to one another about what we'd done during the night.

But the evidence of Jax coming inside me again and again had been a sticky mess between my thighs when I'd gotten dressed in a hurry.

I'd used magic to whisk his seed away, but I'd hesitated initially. It was stupid. It was just sex. We hadn't sealed our bond, and I took an annual contraception to avoid becoming with child, so it wasn't like anything would come of it, yet wiping away the evidence of what Jax and I had done had also felt like I was wiping away the memory too. And I didn't want that.

I wanted to remember each detail vividly, but regretfully, I made myself cleanse the remnants of our love-making away.

I nibbled on my lip as Phillen continued rocking beneath me. This wasn't good. Already, my heart was beating too fast at the thought of Jax taking me again, which he couldn't. This needed to stop. I couldn't allow myself to become attached any further. Even if he was my mate, reality wouldn't allow us to claim one another.

But despite knowing that, my heart was aching. Feelings were growing in me that I couldn't ignore, even though I *had* to ignore them because he was the *crown prince* who was to marry another.

Jax's arm hugged my waist, pulling me back to the present. He leaned down and kissed me on the neck, his lips warm, and the kiss seemed so easy and natural that I wondered if he was even aware that he'd done it.

My breath stuttered as his head slowly lifted, but instead of saying anything, Jax merely straightened and splayed his hand over my stomach again. His entire body was tense, his magic pounding around him. He'd been like that since we'd mounted Phillen and had taken off.

It seemed that finding Bastian was growing into a reality, and it was demanding all of Jax's attention even though his touches hadn't stopped, but all of his focus had shifted to finding his brother.

I'd known it would end this way, and it only reminded

me that last night was something I could cherish, but I would need to ultimately let go of it.

It was one night, Elowen. Only one night.

Bottom line, all of us were here for Bastian. We weren't here so Jax and I could begin a scorching affair that would ultimately end in heartbreak.

THE STAGS SLOWED MINUTES LATER. We were in the Wood. Soaring trees, colorful leaves, shrill bird songs, and chattering wildlings filled the space around us. Several pairs of eyes peered up at us from the brush when we finally slowed enough to see details again, and a few steps later, Bowan—who'd been leading the way—ground to a stop.

Jax slipped off Phillen, his hands automatically going up to assist me down, but I slid off before he could. He eyed me briefly, as though making sure I was steady, then turned his sharp eyes outward to assess the Wood.

I took in the prince's broad shoulders, powerful build, and commanding presence. My lower belly quickened despite trying to stop it, so I snapped my attention away from him. *Bastian. We're here to find* Bastian.

In a rush of magic, all of the males shifted back to their fae forms.

Bowan pointed at the wildling trail we'd just traveled

on. "He was on this trail, right here the last time I saw him."

"There's a stream just up ahead." I waved down the wildling trail. "This isn't far from Emerson Estate. I know this part of the Wood well. If Bastian got to the water, his trail might be lost."

Jax took off, running down the trail toward the stream before anyone could reply.

All of us sprinted behind him. Wind rushed through my hair, and the scent of the Wood, heavy and humid, filled my nose. It was such a familiar, comforting fragrance.

The sprint was quick, yet I was still entirely winded by the time we reached the winding ribbon of water. Of course, none of the shifters were.

Panting, I looked for a sign of Bastian. Rushing water, rustling leaves, and the chattering of wildlings in the trees filled the Wood. It all appeared normal, and there certainly weren't any signs of a half-breed anywhere.

Panic began to claw up my throat that we were once again so close to finding his brother, only to hit another dead end, because not even the distant sound of a fairy tromping through the Wood was evident. Instead, the only creatures within arm's reach were in the water. Colorful schools of tiny fish swam lazily at the stream's edge. The sound of bubbling water cascaded around them, and every now and then, one of the small fish would leap from the stream before splashing back down.

Jax crouched, his fingers going to the bank's soil. My eyes widened when I beheld footprints in the mud. Some were siltenite, and others were hooves and paws. I hadn't even noticed them.

"These are fresh." His gaze sharpened across the stream.

I gasped. There were footprints on that side too, only they were cut deeper into the soil and muddier, as though whoever owned them had trudged through the stream to reach the other side.

Jax stood and pointed. "They went that way."

My heart lurched that we hadn't lost the trail after all.

Before anyone could comment, Jax leaped across the stream, crossing the eight-foot span as though it was nothing. The other males did the same.

On the other side, Alec stopped and looked over his shoulder at me. "Sorry, Elowen, I'll come back and get you."

"No need to." I rushed back from the stream's edge and called upon my lorafin power to heighten my magic. Only a tiny buzz came from my collar, barely noticeable.

In a burst of speed, I took off running, and at the last moment, when I was about to launch myself over the water, I pulled on a segment of my power.

Magic heated my muscles and propelled me with increased strength. I flew through the air, catapulting across the water before landing on the other side. I only slipped slightly when my feet hit the damp soil.

Straightening, I grinned and ran a finger along my collar. "I couldn't have done that a few weeks ago because of this."

Alec laughed, then clasped my hand and pulled me with him down the trail.

The others were already well ahead, and we ran to catch up with them and nearly plowed into their backs. They'd stopped, standing immobile in a clearing.

A clearing that hadn't been here a month ago.

Jax's nostrils flared the second I neared. His gaze cut to mine, then to where Alec and I were holding hands.

Bowan's eyes rounded. "Um, Alec, you might want to release your—"

Before he could finish his sentence, Jax had Alec against a tree, ripping the male from my grip with a furious bellow.

"Don't. Touch. Her." Blue light glowed in Jax's eyes. "She's *mine*."

My mouth dropped in absolute shock at his menacing growl while the rest of the group of stag shifters released a collective intake of breaths.

Trivan gaped. "Holy shite, did he—"

"Yes," Bowan hissed. "Yes, he did."

I stared at all of them, my gaze traveling between them

rapid fire. "Did what? What in the realm is going on? Jax, *what are you doing?*"

But Jax ignored me, still holding Alec against the tree even though the noble held his hands up in surrender while keeping his eyes down. "I'm sorry, my prince," he said quickly. "I didn't know."

"Elowen?" Lander said quietly from behind me. "Can you lift the hair from the back of your neck?"

"*What?*" My chest heaved. *Seriously, what in the galaxy is happening?*

"Your hair," Bowan hissed. "Lift it up, so they can all know I'm not lying."

Shaking my head, I lifted my hair, showing them the nape of my neck.

The energy in the clearing soared.

"Fuck," Trivan said, then whistled.

"He seriously did it?" Lars whispered.

"He did," Phillen growled.

I dropped my hair and swirled around. "Did what?" I demanded, then ran my fingers under my hair, across my nape. Only smooth skin greeted me, but a memory stirred in my mind, of feeling something burning on my neck during the night. "What's on my neck? What in the realm are you all talking about?" I frantically thought back to my night with Jax. We hadn't sealed our bond. I was sure of it. *So what are they talking about?*

But nobody responded. Another snarl tore from Jax,

and my jaw dropped *again* when he appeared in front of me. Antlers had sprouted from his head, like those of a half-breed, looking exactly as he had last night when we'd rut.

My cheeks burned as those heated memories consumed me. "Jax? What. Is. Happening?"

But once again, he didn't reply, and nobody else did either. Everyone's attention stayed glued to the ground, and from the wild glowing light in Jax's eyes, I didn't know if his mind was functioning in a sane fashion right now. He inhaled, drinking in my scent, and more blue light flared in his irises.

Actually, I was pretty sure he wasn't of sound mind. *Yes, definitely insane.* He looked like a beast, and he was certainly behaving like one too given what he'd done to Alec.

Finally breaking the silence, Lander said quietly, "My prince, your brother . . . we were looking for him."

Jax shook his head, his huge antler rack swaying. In his next breath, magic puffed around him, and his antlers disappeared. Just like that. They *disappeared.*

"Dear Goddess, I'm hallucinating," I whispered.

"You're not," Alec said, still by the tree, although now he was in a submissive bow too. "But Lander is right. We need to find Bastian. We'll deal with . . . *this* . . . later."

I swung toward him. "*This*? What is *this*?"

Alec smiled feebly. "It's probably best if the prince explains."

I planted my hands on my hips and glared at Jax. "Explain what?"

Jax shook his head again, as though shaking off a spell that had been cast over him. His nostrils flared as he drank in my scent again, and then his look grew full of . . . satisfaction.

But before I could ask *again* for clarification, he ran a hand roughly over his cheek. "Sorry. I didn't mean to go all territorial . . ." He sighed heavily and glanced at Alec, who merely nodded. "Sorry," he added gruffly to his friends.

They all stood, casting him wary but understanding glances.

Baffled, I stood there immobile and once again wondered if I'd woken up in a new realm. *So he's apologizing for being so aggressive with his friends? Is all of this some kind of weird stag thing?* Shaking myself, I turned and lifted my hair. "Jax, what's on my neck?"

Silence was his only response. Dropping my hair, I spun around to face him, only to find the prince staring at me with another look of satisfaction spreading across his face.

I scowled. "Why are you smiling?"

"You don't know?" He cocked an eyebrow.

I blew a strand of hair from my eyes. "Know what?"

His brow furrowed, a heavy look descending over his features. "But you said—"

"My prince," Bowan hissed. "Bastian? We're going to lose him if we don't keep searching."

Hearing his brother's name erased Jax's heavy look, and he snapped his attention to the clearing.

"Right." He assessed the ground again. It looked as though someone had recently hacked down the trees, but there was nothing else to signify anything unusual besides the plethora of half-breed footprints.

But it was a reminder that we were here to find Bastian, and *that* was where our focus needed to be right now. *I'll ask him about my neck again later.*

"Where did the prints go?" Lander frowned, then crouched and touched the soil. All of the footprints, siltenite and wildling alike, stopped abruptly at the clearing's edge.

Jax inhaled, and magic curled around him. "Their scent is still fresh. They were just here."

Everyone circled the perimeter, listening, scenting, but . . . nothing. There was no sign of Bastian or any other half-breed in the vicinity.

"I don't sense him," Lars said quietly.

"Neither do I," Phillen agreed.

"Well, they didn't just up and disappear." Trivan threw his hands up in disgust, then prowled around the clearing's perimeter, inhaling deeply with each step.

But still, there was no sign of Bastian.

Jax dipped to the ground beside Lander and ran his finger along the prints. "What did you see this morning, Bowan?" he asked his friend.

I tapped my hands on my thighs and continued watching all of them.

Bowan's eyebrows slanted together. "That group of half-breeds that Alec saw enter the barn last night all left at the same time this morning, just before sunrise, but instead of heading back to the Finals, they all marched toward the Wood. I thought it was odd, especially if they're employed to work at the Matches, so I left my lookout point to follow them."

Bowan cleared his throat, then shook his head as his face became a mask of confusion. "At the Wood's edge, Bastian appeared, but he didn't really *look* like Bastian. He wasn't smiling, and he didn't say anything, and something about him seemed off. He turned wordlessly and led the group of half-breeds into the Wood on the trail we were just on. I followed them for a bit, but when they never deviated from the wildling trail, I left and came back to get you in hopes we could catch up to them."

Jax growled low in his throat. "But *where* did they go? Like Trivan said, they couldn't have just vanished in thin air from here."

"Unless they had portal keys?" I offered. "Even though that's unlikely. Or if a Solis fairy was with them, they could have mistphased them out of here. Or perhaps they went underground?" I thumped my foot on the soil.

"Underground?" Jax's attention snapped to me, and the second our gazes collided, that wild light entered his eyes, a blue glow appearing in his irises. But he shook himself, and in a flash, it was gone.

I stared at him warily. *What in the realm . . .* I didn't know much about mate bonds, but I was starting to wonder if that had something to do with his bizarre behavior. *But we're not fully mated, so how can that be?*

Shaking that thought off, I cleared my throat. "Um, yes, underground. It's common in this area of the Wood for wildlings to have extensive dens beneath the soil. There are also underground rock tunnels and caverns in this part. Some are quite large."

Alec cocked his head. "How do you know that?"

I shrugged. "On the days I wasn't doing a calling, I often spent my time in the Wood. My guards would give me space since there weren't any other siltenites nearby, and I've always found nature calming. The galaxy and the Wood are my solace. Even though my guardian and I had only moved here recently, I'm no stranger to this area of Faewood, and I've always made it a point to befriend local wildlings. A few of them told me about this area not long after we settled here."

They all glanced downward, and Jax ran his hand along the soil again, Lander doing the same. The rest fanned out, all of their nostrils flaring as they scented the Wood and perimeter anew.

On the opposite side of the clearing, Bowan put his hands on his hips, and a ray of sunshine shone upon his brown skin. "They definitely didn't move past this clearing."

"Agreed." Phillen stood opposite him on the outer circle, nodding. "I can't scent anything past the soil there." He pointed to where Lars and Trivan were both prowling.

Jax scowled. "But how would they have gotten underground?"

"*If* they're underground." Trivan drummed his fingers along his thigh. "Like Elowen said, if they had a portal key or were with a Solis fairy, it's possible they transported elsewhere from here."

Bowan laughed. "And when was the last time you saw a Solis fairy on this continent?"

Jax arched an eyebrow. "My fellow royal, Norivun, was here just last summer when we met about the Lochen's raids."

"But that was for a political reason," Phillen countered. "Surely, whatever's happened to Bastian isn't political. And nothing going on in this clearing would draw the attention of foreign royals."

My brow furrowed as I listened to them arguing about what could have happened, then I sighed in annoyance. "You know, I could simply ask my wildling friends what they know about this area. Or if they saw anything. They may be able to help."

Everyone grew quiet. Lander cocked his head, Phillen scratched his chin, and Jax eyed me with interest.

"Do you know them well enough to ask that?" the prince asked.

"I do. I'm good friends with a few of them."

"Well, then that would be quite . . . logical," Trivan finally stated.

"In that case, follow me." I turned away, intent on finding Esopeel. Of all my wildling friends in this area, she was most likely to know of any unusual changes made in this clearing.

Against my better judgment, I glanced over my shoulder at Jax.

His eyes were glowing again, and a slow grin spread across his face as he watched me.

My heart began to pound. *One night. We had one fantastic, amazing, mind-blowing night together, but he's to wed another. Calm yourself, Elowen.*

I snapped my attention away from the male who was fated to be my mate and tromped through the Wood.

CHAPTER 23

It didn't take long to find Esopeel. The *cerlikan* wildling had lived in this part of the Wood her entire life. Her den was only a short distance away, in a large burrow near the palace lands bordering Emerson Estate. I'd met her within the first week of moving to Faewood, and she'd been delighted that a local siltenite—one considered a lady nonetheless—had wanted to befriend her. Since most siltenites and other high fae of our realm viewed wildlings as lesser, her gratitude hadn't surprised me, but it still irked me. She was just as intelligent as me, so to think others viewed her as *less* always rubbed me the wrong way.

"Elowen!" she said brightly when I crouched near her den's entrance. She crawled along the dirt tunnel, parting the leaves that shielded it from the rain, and then emerged. "My dear girl, it's so good to see that you're all right!"

"Hi, Esopeel, I've missed you."

She hobbled to me, her short furry legs the color of the sky. The rest of her was a mixture of beiges, dark greens, light pinks, and blues. Her glossy fur perfectly blended into the many colors of the Wood.

"I've been so worried about you." She hugged my arm, and I patted her back. Our size difference made affection difficult, but Esopeel was one of the most caring wildlings I'd ever met. She straightened and looked me over. "Once the news reached me that you'd been taken, why, I don't think I've had a decent night's sleep since."

I gave her an apologetic smile. "I'm so sorry for worrying you. If I could have sent word to you that I was fine, I would have."

She inclined her head. "No matter. You're here now, and you appear well, but is it true? Were you actually abducted from the horrid guardian of yours?"

I winced. It was funny how everyone else had seen Guardian Alleron for who he was, but it'd taken me many moments over the past few weeks to truly accept that he'd never been a father to me.

Shaking that painful fact off, I replied, "I was, but that's a story for another time." I glanced briefly over my shoulder at Jax and his friends. They were concealed within the foliage, not moving a muscle. Turning back around, I smiled and settled myself onto the damp soil.

Esopeel glanced over my shoulder, and her eyes grew

wide when she spotted Jax and his friends standing a few paces behind me. They were still mostly hidden.

Esopeel's nose twitched when she scented the breeze. "I see you've met some brommel stag shifters."

I wasn't surprised that she guessed their shifter species since cerlikans had a sharp sense of smell. "I have, and that's actually why I'm here."

"Oh?" She sat beside me on the Wood's ground and folded her hands in her lap. "Does knowing them also explain why it's been weeks since I've seen you?" She tapped her chin. "I believe the last time I saw you was when you were riding that ridiculous carpet with your guardian. Had I known that day would be when you'd be taken, why I would have . . ." She let her words hang when it became apparent to both of us that there was little she could have done. While wildlings were quite aware of the comings and goings in the Wood, few siltenites ever paid attention to them when they tried to raise the alarm about something.

I nodded solemnly. "I know, but the fact that you would have tried to help me means the realm to me." I patted her hand gently, careful not to tap too hard since I was so much bigger than her. "Actually, my new friends are the reason I'm here. We're looking for someone and hope you can help." I quickly explained what Bastian looked like, then the clearing we'd just stumbled upon. "It was so odd because I could have sworn that clearing wasn't there a month ago."

Esopeel's eyes widened, and she clutched one of my fingers, her tiny paw wrapping around my knuckle. "It wasn't. There have been many strange things happening in the Wood lately."

"Really?" I frowned, cocking my head. "Are you referring to the Centennial Matches and how they cleared some of the Wood for it?"

She shook her head rapidly. "No, not that. Those were all approved clearings by the wildling mayors. I'm talking about the other activities. The ones that have nothing to do with the Matches."

A chill ran down my spine as though a gust of wind from the Solis continent had just rushed through the Wood. "What are you talking about?"

She continued in a hushed voice, looking around every now and then. "There have been strange occurrences in these parts lately. That clearing you stumbled across only being one of them. The mayors have gone to the kingsfae multiple times, trying to tell them what we've observed, but they keep brushing us off, telling *our kind* to get back in the Wood where we belong." She sniffed indignantly, and a flush of heat worked up my neck.

"How rude." I clenched my hands into fists.

"I know," she huffed. "But perhaps you could get them to listen."

I hunkered down closer to her. "Tell me everything."

By the time Esopeel finished recalling what she and other wildlings had witnessed in the Wood, it felt as though rivers of ice flowed through my veins.

"You're certain?" I asked when she finished. "Half-breeds have been seen regularly in these parts, and they've made homes underneath the soil?"

"I'm more than certain. I've seen it with my own eyes."

"And all of these half-breeds wear metallic anklet jewelry?"

"Indeed."

I frowned, wondering why they would all have matching anklets. "What about the half-breed we seek? The one with permanent antlers, have you seen him?"

She cocked her head. "It's possible. I've seen so many half-breeds lately, but I can't say for certain."

Jax's aura pounded into my back. Esopeel had flinched every time a pulse of it hit her, so I'd shifted my position and tried to shield her from Jax's power. "Do you know how we could enter the caverns beneath that clearing?"

She shook her head regretfully. "I'm sorry, but no. The usual tunnels we've used to access that part of the Wood had been sealed. But I can tell you whatever's occurring beneath the surface there, it's evil, Elowen. Magic pulses around it underground. Heavy, *dark* magic. Nothing good is occurring there."

My pulse turned thready. The chill in me grew. Dark magic. Hidden caverns. Matching anklets on the half-breeds. I had to agree with Esopeel. An ominous tone rang through everything she'd revealed.

"Thank you for sharing what you know." I squeezed her paw gently.

"Of course, you know I'm always happy to speak with you."

Jax stepped forward silently, the first move he'd made since we arrived at Esopeel's den. He crouched beside me, and Esopeel took a few steps back.

"He won't hurt you," I said gently.

Her tensed body relaxed slightly, but she still eyed Jax warily.

Jax extracted a few rulibs from his pocket, the coins nearly a quarter the size of her small body.

"Will you keep us posted if you see anything further?" He stacked the rulibs at her side. "You could dispatch a dillemsill to one of my friends if you learn new details." He gave her an address in the capital, but it wasn't his residence, and I had no idea where that location was.

Her eyes widened, and she glanced toward me. I nodded encouragingly, and she replied, "I suppose I could do that."

"Thank you. I will be in your debt if you're able to help locate the half-breed we seek."

Jax retreated back to the Wood, putting a safe distance between them, and Esopeel collected the payment, hefting the coins to the entrance of her den.

Once they were stowed away, she said quietly to me, "Is he the one that took you?"

My brow furrowed, my loyalty to her and Jax warring within me. I wanted to trust her with that secret and knew that I probably could, but I wouldn't risk Jax's safety nor that of his friends.

"No," I replied, the lie rolling off my tongue. "He actually rescued me from the Dark Raider."

But while I knew part of what I said was a lie, another part of me felt it wasn't. Because when Jax had abducted me, he'd truly been the Dark Raider, a stranger, a foreboding enemy, but that was before I'd come to know him. Now, he was Jax. My protector. My rescuer. My friend. My *mate*. My cheeks flushed when memories of last night brushed against my mind like butterfly wings, but it was the truth. He'd become so much more to me than the male who'd taken me from my guardian all those weeks ago.

Esopeel patted my hand, but if she suspected I wasn't being entirely truthful, she didn't push for more details. Instead, she said, "It was lovely seeing you again, dear Elowen, but please take care."

I nodded gravely. "I will. And, Esopeel? If you happen

to see Lillivel in Tassalee's Market, will you please tell her I'm fine?"

Esopeel's furry lips twitched into a smile. "I most certainly will. She's been as worried about you as I've been."

WE RETURNED to the clearing again, in search of a way to enter the caverns below. Now that we knew for certain that half-breeds were indeed under the soil, and Bastian was likely one of them, Jax had turned into a prowling beast.

His brother was here. Just beneath our toes. And all we had to do was get to him.

"What do you think that means, what she said about the dark magic?" Bowan asked as we all searched for a hidden entrance to the caverns.

Jax's aura pounded around us, yet the prince didn't stop his searches. "I don't know. Honestly, I'm not sure I want to know."

"And what about those anklets she mentioned?" Lander added. "That obviously has to mean something too."

Ever since Esopeel had released those details, a churning motion had settled in my stomach.

"Did you notice any unusual flares of magic around

them when you saw Bastian and that group this morning?" Jax asked Bowan. "And did you see anklets on any of them? Do you know what that jewelry is made of?"

The stag shifter swallowed, his throat bobbing. "No, but I wasn't scenting for magic, and I was too far away to feel any of their auras. And when I got close enough to clearly see them, I was only trying to discern their features so I could identify them. I wasn't looking near their feet."

Jax's nostrils flared, but he nodded sharply.

"We'll find him, Jax," Phillen rumbled for what felt like the umpteenth time as he dug through the soil across the clearing, searching for a door or tunnel or *something* that would allow us entry.

"He's right," Lars agreed. "We'll find Bastian, Jax. We won't stop searching until we do."

And now that we knew Bastian's disappearance from Stonewild likely was because of a nefarious reason, it suddenly seemed imperative that we did.

CHAPTER 24

Hours later, we were still in the clearing, yet we weren't any closer to finding an entrance to the hidden caverns. Everything we'd tried—digging, sending out magical pulses, thumping against trees' bases for hollowed doors— hadn't worked. We were no closer to discovering any entryway than we were when we'd arrived.

Yet a few times I could have sworn that I sensed something *off* in the clearing, as though something beneath us was repelling our advances. Just as Esopeel had described what she and the other wildlings had detected from within their tunnels, so did I. Something dark was definitely at play here, yet for the life of me, I didn't know how to get around it.

And neither did anyone else.

Jax slammed his fist into a babbo tree, causing a slight splinter to crack on its base. "Where is he?"

Instinctively, I went to Jax's side, laying a hand upon his shoulder before turning him toward me. He gathered me in his embrace, his arms locking around me as fear drenched his aura.

"Where is he, Elowen?" he rasped. "*Where?* And what's being done to him?"

I ran my hands up and down his back, tangling my fingers through the hair at his nape as the others watched on with mournful expressions. "I don't know, Jax, but we'll find him. Like the others said, we'll *find him.* Sooner or later, we'll know."

But hours later, we still had nothing to show for it. And when the sun shone high in the sky, and all of our stomachs were vengefully growling from being awake for hours upon hours without being fed, we finally conceded defeat for the moment and headed back to the capital.

Like the ride in, the males all shifted into their stag forms, save Jax, who once again rode behind me with his arm locked around my waist. He continually buried his nose in my neck, inhaling my fragrance again and again, and it struck me that he seemed to find my scent soothing. Because each time he did, the tension radiating through him lessened, if only a little, and that sweet gesture only created a pang of longing in me for something that could never be.

Whether or not I wanted to admit it, our time together last night had amplified my feelings for him, and our ruse to appear as lovers during our time in Faewood would have to continue. All of that only guaranteed a broken heart for me once this came to a crashing end.

The stags slowed, and the edge of Leafton appeared. Jax shifted in his seat, then whispered in my ear, "We'll have to shift back. My father doesn't like when we traipse around as stags in foreign kingdoms. If we're not careful, word could reach him."

Phillen slowed even more, the others doing the same, until they'd fully stopped.

Jax slid off his friend, helping me to do the same, and once everyone had returned to fae form, Jax threaded his fingers through mine.

The intimate gesture made my heart gallop, and I soaked up the closeness I could share with him while it lasted.

"Do you think your father will learn that you were all running as stags earlier this morning?" I asked him quietly as we walked toward the capital's streets. The long grasses surrounding the outer capital brushed against my thighs, and the soaring white palace in the distance rose higher than any other building in Leafton.

Jax shrugged. "Maybe, maybe not. We left early, so not many fae were about, but if anyone's inclined to gossip, it's possible word will eventually reach him."

"And if he were to find out?"

Jax tensed, his aura spiking. "Then I may have a few

new bruises to heal, if I let him land a few hits, that is. He doesn't beat me as much anymore, though, not since I outgrew his magic."

"He would . . . you mean he would try to physically hurt you?" My eyes widened as we strode into the capital. I wanted to ask Jax more, but a royal attendant standing on the street's edge noticed us and rushed to Jax's side.

The attendant bowed, and the pearly buttons running up his turquoise top sparkled in the afternoon sunshine. "Prince Adarian, good afternoon. I didn't realize you were about the capital on the west side. May I assist you in your visit in any way?"

Jax pulled a few rulibs from his pocket. "You can, actually. We're in need of an enchanted carpet. The faster, the better." He pushed the rulibs into the attendant's hands. "For your troubles."

The attendant's smile flashed wide as he pocketed the coins. "Of course, Your Highness. I shall have one here promptly."

BACK AT JAX's private residence in The Silver Hand, Lars called for food to be delivered from the inn's kitchens, and we all ate quickly, knowing that every moment spent away from finding Bastian was just another opportunity for him to slip away.

Jax sat beside me, eating rapidly and methodically as though lost in thought. Now that we were once again behind hidden walls, the royal mask he'd worn outside had dropped, and a starker one had taken its place.

I forced another bite of eggs into my mouth and swallowed, barely tasting it.

I wanted to help Jax or reassure him, but it wasn't like anything I offered would be more than empty words. None of us knew what bizarre situation was unfolding in the Wood outside of Leafton. If anything, the fact that each half-breed wore a metallic anklet, and dark magic clouded around that clearing, only solidified that Jax had been right to be concerned for Bastian.

Hoping to take his mind off that troubling matter until we could venture back to the clearing and search anew, I bumped the prince's thigh. "So are you going to tell me what all the fuss was about this morning about what's on the back of my neck?"

I was still puzzled by it. All of the males had seemed shocked when they'd looked at my nape, but even though I'd run my fingers across it multiple times, nothing about my skin felt amiss.

Jax cocked his head at me, as though coming out of a trance. "Do you not remember last night?"

A furious blush worked up my neck, and Trivan snickered.

"Of course I do," I hissed.

A sly smile lifted the prince's lips, the first genuine smile I'd seen on his face since Bowan had burst into our chambers this morning. "Then why are you asking?"

My brow furrowed, and I pushed my mostly empty plate away. "What do you mean, *why am I asking*? All of your friends seemed to find something on my neck surprising, yet I have no idea what's there."

His smile lessened, and he turned to face me more. Broad shoulders stretched when he also pushed his plate to the side.

"You told me you wanted me to rut with you," he said quietly, yet I still knew everyone heard him even though Phillen went into the kitchen, Lars following.

The others began talking to one another as if they were having normal conversations, except for Trivan, of course, who was blatantly staring at us, and I could have sworn that Bowan was hanging on our every word.

"Yes, I did," I replied in a hushed tone, but I didn't know why I bothered considering I was surrounded by shifters.

Jax's eyebrows slanted together until a wedge appeared between them. "And you said you knew what that meant."

"Right." My frown grew, and an unsettling feeling crept into my stomach. "It meant you wanted to take me from behind," I all but whispered and then wanted to die when Trivan snickered. "Goddess, do we have to have this conversation here?"

But if Jax cared that all of his friends were listening, he didn't show it. Instead, a storm of emotions unleashed upon his face. "Elowen," he said sharply, *too* sharply. "What is your understanding of rutting?"

"Um, you know, when a male stag shifter takes a female"—I mouthed the next words—"*from behind.*"

The smirk on Trivan's face died, a more troubling look taking its place, and a brooding scowl descended upon Alec's. He wasn't even trying to pretend he wasn't listening anymore.

The Graniteer House noble shot Jax an accusing glare. "Are you serious, Jax? She doesn't *know?*"

I scowled. "Know what?"

"Oh, shite, this isn't going to end well," Bowan said quietly before he raked a hand through his hair. Any mirth he'd shone earlier had vanished.

My chest heaved as I studied all of them, but as much as I tried to control my response at being left in the dark, I couldn't stop my growing sense of dread. "Will someone *please tell me* what you were all talking about in the clearing this morning?"

Jax scrubbed his cheeks.

Heart pounding, I demanded, "Jax, what's going on?"

The worry on Jax's face increased. "I . . ." He opened his mouth and then closed it. A soft growl rumbled in his chest. "We . . . Gods and Goddesses. I thought you knew."

"Knew *what?*" I swallowed the ball of anxiety that

threatened to work up my throat. "Jax?" I whispered. "Tell me."

"Oh, for stars' sake," Alec bit out, still across the room. "He claimed you, Elowen. That's what happened when you rutted with him. That's what rutting means. It's not just a stag shifter taking a female from behind. It's a male stag claiming his female."

Confusion swam through me. "*Claimed* me? But we didn't fully enact the bond, so how could you have claimed me?" But then the fact that Jax was a stag shifter hit me, and that maybe what Stonewild fae did was different from what Faewood fae did when a mate bond was formed. Maybe holding my magic back *hadn't* stopped us from forming the mate bond. All blood drained from my face. "You mean you . . ." But I couldn't say it. Because even if Jax was my mate, it still didn't change our future, yet if he'd claimed me . . .

I grabbed his hands. "Please tell me you didn't."

Devastation rippled across Jax's face, and in a sweep of his arms, he was carrying me away from the other males. He didn't stop until we reached his bed chambers, and then he slammed the door closed behind us.

He set me down and then paced a few steps back and forth in front of me. Finally stopping, he faced me, then scraped his fingers lightly across my nape. His touch made goosebumps shoot down my spine.

"Do you know what's here?"

I couldn't breathe. "No."

Nostrils flaring, he tugged me into the bathroom.

Inside the bathing chamber, he grabbed a mirror off the counter, faced me away from the large mirror above the sink, and held the handheld mirror up for me to see. He swept my long chestnut hair to the side, revealing my nape in the handheld mirror.

My breath sucked in.

A silvery-inked mark, like a tattoo that probably shone like stars in the sun, revealed a stamp upon my nape in the shape of a stag's antlers.

"Oh Goddess, you did. You claimed me as your mate." My fingers flew to the mark, but as before, I couldn't feel it, but I could *see* it in my reflection. "Jax, what have you done?"

The hopeful light in his eyes dimmed. "I thought you wanted me to."

I tried to rub it off, tried to erase it, but it was as though it was under my skin, as if it was a part of me.

A growl erupted from Jax, and he forced my fingers to stop their brutal attempts at smudging his mark away. "You can't wipe it off, Elowen. It's permanent. I'm mated to you, and male stag shifters mate for life, so you're it for me."

"*What?*"

"Male stag shifters mate for life, and I chose you. I can never choose another. And that has nothing to do with our mate bond. I chose you as a stag and claimed you. It's probably why you're so confused by this and why you don't feel the bond since you held your magic back when we were rutting." His eyebrows slanted together, and I realized he'd felt me suppressing my magic when we'd been fucking. Despite the fact that I'd suppressed our fated mate bond on my end, he'd claimed me as a male stag anyway because he thought I'd wanted that.

"You can't undo it? Truly?"

He growled anew. "I would never undo it. Once a male stag chooses his mate, even if they're not his fated mate, that's it for him. His choice is made."

"You're telling me that no matter what, it's permanent? But what if a male stag found his fated mate after he'd already claimed another female?"

His lips twitched in a humorless smile. "He'd be perpetually tortured. Male stags mate for life once they've made the claim, but if a male met his fated mate *after* already claiming another, his instincts would be perpetually torn between the two females. It's why most male stags choose very carefully when they claim a female. There's no undoing it." He looked down, his aura beginning to roll. "I tried to tell you that . . . once."

"When?"

"On our way to Lemos. When I told you that brommel stag shifters have extraordinary healing abilities and that we move like the wind. I was also going to tell you that males mate for life, but I stopped myself."

"But, Jax." I shook my head. "I didn't want this!"

His irises burst into a myriad of blue fireworks. "But I thought you did. You *consented* to it," he all but growled. "Last night, when I asked if you wanted to rut, you said yes."

"But I thought I was just consenting to sex. I thought that's what you meant by rutting."

He stilled, but a muscle in his jaw began to tick. "No, Elowen. That's not what I was asking. Rutting to a male stag shifter enacts his claiming bond."

My heart began to gallop in my chest. "But I didn't realize a male stag can still be bonded on his own. I didn't elicit any magic on my end, so I thought that would keep any bond from forming. I'd had no idea you can be bonded to a female just from rutting." I ran a hand over my nape, finally understanding what the burning sensation was I'd felt after our first time.

He tore a hand through his hair. "I thought you knew. Rutting seals the claim for a male. That's how it is with stag shifters. I thought you wanted me to."

My breaths grew so rapid that the room began to spin. "So what does this mean now? To shifters? Since it's obviously different in your kingdom than mine."

His jaw ground together. "It means that I claimed you as *my own*. You belong to me now. You're *mine*. I rutted with you, which means in the shifter kingdom, we're as good as married, because that mark carries more meaning than any wedding ceremony."

The realm tilted beneath my feet. Swaying, I reached a hand toward the wall to steady myself.

Married? Marked? He owns me? My mouth fell open. Then closed. Then opened again because those words chilled me to the bone.

"Belong to you?" My lips flattened, and my magic flared, then my lorafin powers swirled inside me, moving and spinning faster with every second that passed. A phantom wind billowed the towels hanging on the rack to my side, and shadows unfurled in the corners of the bathing chamber. "You said I would never again be owned by anyone."

"Elowen," Jax said sharply. "It's not like that."

"Oh, then what's it like?" The hairs on the back of my neck stood on end, and more of my power rose, swirling the air around us. The towels began to flap wildly as the room darkened.

"It means that I'm bound to you. I consider you mine, and I'll fucking kill *anyone* who tries to harm you or take you from me. But I don't physically own you. I would never claim that or do that to you. Please, Elowen." He cupped my upper arms. "It's not what you're thinking."

The breeze fluttering around us quieted, and the room brightened again as my magic calmed, but just as quickly, confusion hit me. "But when I consented to rutting with you, I thought it was only sex." His nostrils flared again, but I pushed on. "And what we had together was the most beautiful, amazing experience that I've ever had. I gave you my virginity. It was a moment I'll cherish forever, but I thought it was *only* sex, and now you're saying it was so much more." I canted my head, and the implications of what we'd done shook me to my core. "But that doesn't change my lineage. You're still expected to marry another even though you claimed me. Right? Saramel said your wedding will happen next summer to another royal or a noble." My stomach heaved. Just thinking about it made me feel sick.

Jax's jaw snapped closed. "No, Elowen. I can never marry another now."

"But your parents—"

"Are in for severe disappointment because I chose you."

"But what about what they expect of you?"

He sucked in a breath. "I know. It's going to cause some problems—"

"*Problems*? You'd be defying the *king and queen* of Stonewild Kingdom, Jax, and you only call that a problem? Even though you're the heir, you're still obligated by siltenite law to marry who they deem worthy of you. And I will never be worthy of you even though you've claimed me. You're the *heir* as much as you're trying to pretend otherwise. Oh Gods, Jax, what have we done?"

His nostrils flared so sharply that they looked like a knife's edge. "Don't say that. Don't ever say you're not worthy of me. It's *me* who's not worthy of *you*."

I laughed, the sound bitter. "In what realm do you live? I'm a *lorafin*. Yes, I'm powerful and have magic that others don't, but I'm not a shifter, and I'm certainly not of the same class as a royal. Your parents will never accept me."

"They'll have to."

It felt as though my heart stopped. Jax stared down at me, his eyes blazing, his aura pounding through him. He was gazing at me so intensely, achingly so, that for one moment, one *hopeful* moment, I pictured what that would mean if the throne considered me worthy. Jax and I could be together. We could actually marry instead of him being sold off to one of those horrible females I'd met on the ship. But just as quickly as that powerful hope came, it died.

My shoulders sagged, and my stomach turned into a knotted ball of sad acceptance. "They won't. I'm a slave, Jax. What king or queen would ever accept someone of my birth for their son? I was abducted in the Wood, taken from my mother, but I was still born among the poor. I'm not of royal birth or even of esteemed breeding. And your own father couldn't even accept his own flesh and blood—a male who *was* half royal by birthright—because he was a half-breed." I waved toward the door, to the capital beyond. "Bastian is here in Faewood, partly because of your father's unacceptance of him. Your brother was banned from your life and the Stonewild capital, yet you still think that the king and queen will accept me as an equal match for their son?" My heart clenched, as though a giant squeezed it between his fist. "I wish that was true. I wish we could make that a reality, but you and I both know that'll never happen."

Silence descended between us, and the only movement Jax made was the roll of his throat.

"You don't know that," he finally rasped, but some of the fierceness in his aura turned to something uglier, more jagged, as though the fear of our reality was catching up with him too.

"No, perhaps I can't know that for certain since I don't know your parents personally. But you made a comment back in the Wood about bruises you may have to endure if your father found out you were running in your stag form here. And you said something weeks ago in Fosterton, about abuse you suffered in your lifetime. Are they related, Jax? Is it *your father* who's abused you?"

He abruptly turned away.

"It is him, isn't it?" Something tugged at my insides. A sick realization that Jax had likely suffered abuse as I had. It made me feel physically ill. Because abuse behind closed doors, hidden away from prying eyes, cut one all the way to their soul. In all likelihood, Jax harbored achingly sharp wounds, just as I did. After all, he'd been banned from his own brother. And his father apparently beat him when he was displeased, or once had, until Jax had grown too strong.

"And your mother?" I asked quietly. "What role does she play in all of this?"

He sighed heavily, and in that sound, I heard the weight of all he'd lived with. "She agrees with his form of punishment. She always has."

I stepped closer to him and laid a hand on his arm. "I'm sorry."

He swung toward me, and in a move too swift for me to fully see, I was gathered in his arms, and he was holding me close, so close that his nose was buried in my hair, right along my neck near his mark.

He inhaled deeply, and even though I knew whatever had transpired between us last night couldn't be undone, for a brief moment, I was grateful for it. Rutting had forged the claiming bond for him, even if I hadn't allowed our mate bond to fully form. Regardless, his stag bond provided comfort to him.

And as he held me close and inhaled my scent . . . I could feel what it did to him. It provided a refuge. A place of security that hadn't been there previously.

We were irrevocably linked now because of his claim, and finally fully realizing that, and realizing what we had the potential to be . . . Jax's reactions to me all began to make sense. His overprotectiveness. His obsession. His terrifying responses anytime someone hurt me. His possessiveness. All of it was because he was my fated mate. And it was possible that since he'd also chosen me as his stag mate, even if he hadn't marked his claim before, his responses were exaggerated even more.

A memory flashed through my mind, like a million volts of lightning. It was the night in Fosterton when we'd been drinking in the booth, and what he'd said to me. *There's something about you, Elowen. Something I recognize in you is in me too.*

"You've known for a long time that I'm your mate, haven't you? Even in Fosterton, you knew."

His arms tightened. "Yes."

I held him close, running my hands along his back, across his broad shoulders.

His grip on me tightened. "That's why I was so angry in Fosterton that morning."

"What morning?"

"The night that male assaulted you and I insisted we share a room. That night was torture for me, and it wasn't because I'd slept on the floor. That entire night, I'd known my mate was sleeping in the same room with me, but I couldn't touch you. I was barely able to sleep with you so near, and it's why I woke up early. I wanted to stare at you and just soak up your presence. I knew it was likely the closest I would ever be able to get to you, but then your arousal started drenching the room. It made the fact that I couldn't claim you a hundred times worse. If you only knew how badly I wanted to rut with you even then, or the dirty thoughts that had been running through my head while you were sleeping, or the way you looked so damned sexy when you finally awoke that all I could think about was driving my cock into you . . ." He chuffed. "If you'd known all of that, you probably would have run."

"Doubt it." I laughed softly and bit my lip. "I can't believe that's what you were thinking. Did you know that I wanted to give you my virginity that morning? I'd had indecent dreams about you all night, but when you left in such a hurry, and then were so angry when I saw you again outside, I thought it was because you knew I was turned on by you, and it annoyed you."

"Annoyed me?" A laugh rumbled his chest. "Oh, Little Lorafin. How wrong you were. I was in a foul mood because I wanted to rut with you so badly, yet I knew I could never have you. I was the Dark Raider. Only a selfish bastard would try to pull his mate into that lifestyle. And I also knew what I'd have to do to you once we reached Jaggedston. I knew I'd have to take your sight and eventually your sound, and it was eating me up that I was going to treat you that way. So, between having blue balls and also knowing that I would have to hurt my mate, something that every instinct in me screamed not to do, *that's* why I was in such a foul mood by the time we finally left."

I released a breath and squeezed him. "That's why you were so mad?"

His throat rolled in a swallow, and he buried his nose in my hair. "It is. I'm sorry. You didn't deserve that, but I was still trying to do what I thought was best for you, and keeping you away from me and in the dark about my true identity was safer for you."

I lifted my shoulders. "I never held it against you, the way you acted that morning."

"I know you didn't. And that only made me feel like an even bigger arsehole."

"But what are we going to do now?" I asked quietly.

Slowly, he lifted his head, and that wild blue light shone in his eyes again. "I don't know. I tried once to let you go. I was going to free you after my calling even though I knew you were my mate. It would have been the smartest thing to do, the *best* thing, considering I'm the Dark Raider, and even being associated with me puts you at risk. But when you found out who I was, even though I felt terrified for what your future held, I also felt . . . relief. I wanted you to stay. I wanted to have you with me always. And after you found out, I had an excuse to keep you near."

I swallowed the lump in my throat, so many things aligning as he bared his soul. The way I'd also felt broken at the thought of leaving him behind now made sense. Or the fear he'd spoken of. I remembered seeing him look that way, but at the time I hadn't understood why.

He took a deep breath. "But the most important thing to me right now is how you're feeling. Are you angry with me? Since you didn't fully understand what rutting meant?"

My shoulders sagged, yet I kept my arms looped around him. "Angry? I don't know. I don't think it's fully hit me yet what's happened between us. Stars, I'm still not sure I fully *understand* all of the implications, but being connected to you—" I laid a hand on his cheek. Stubble met my palm when he pushed himself more into my touch. My insides tightened. Even that simple caress seemed to soothe him. "Even before your mark, I felt connected to you, Jax. You took me from a male who spent his life abusing me. You tried to free me in every way your ability allowed. You protected me when others couldn't or wouldn't. You made me feel—" I cut myself off and swallowed the thick lump that suddenly formed in my throat.

Intensity smoldered in his gaze, and he dipped his forehead toward mine. "Yes? What have I made you feel?"

Tears sprouted in my eyes, and against my better judgment, I choked out, "Loved. You make me feel *loved*, Jax, and that's something I've never truly felt from anyone."

His aura abruptly spiraled through the room, coating the walls, soaking into the towels, and bathing me in its richness. His chest heaved. "It's because I *do* love you, Elowen."

A stab of disbelief nearly cracked me in two. "But . . . why? Is it just because we're fated?"

He kissed my eyes, brushing away each escaped tear,

then trailed his mouth across my cheeks, pressing soft kisses along my skin. His touches were gentle. Reverent. Solidifying.

"It's not just because you're my mate. But because you're *you*. You're brave, resilient, kind, beautiful. You're everything I could have ever wanted in a mate and more. And just because something in you calls to me, that's not the entire reason I want you. I can't explain it, Elowen. It's a feeling I have when I'm around you. An instinct. A need to be with you. To hold you, protect you, love you. It feels like I can't exist anymore without you."

"Even though I'm a slave?"

He growled. "You're not a slave. You'll *never* be a slave again, and someday, you will see that you're worthy of everything in this life. I know you doubt yourself, that you have insecurities, but you are worthy of every goodness that comes to you, Elowen. *You are*."

I shuddered when his lips met my throat. "You truly believe that?"

"Of course I do. I only wish you did as well."

My heart thumped, but instead of plaguing self-doubt thoughts creeping into my mind, they stayed at bay. Instead, a tentative bridge grew in my chest, connecting me to a new sense of confidence. Maybe Jax was right. Maybe I was worthy.

"How did you first know I was your mate?" I asked quietly.

A wry smile tugged at his lips. "All shifter males are taught from boyhood what happens when they meet their mate. Like other male fae, shifter males usually recognize the bond first, before the female. It's a feeling. A sense deep within us that grows the more we're in our mate's presence. I felt it with you from that first morning you awoke in my tent and had even gotten inklings of it from the weeks leading up to us taking you, when I'd been watching you from afar. But I didn't know for certain until we were in the Ustilly Mountains, and I felt the absolute rage and need to murder Lordling Neeble and his guards for what they'd done to you. The feeling overtook me completely." He paused. "I've never felt the absolute need for vengeance as I did when I saw him abusing you on that domal. It's why I was particularly brutal with him. I don't usually carve up fae like that."

A chill ran through me when that horrific night reared, and the lethal brutality that Jax had shown Lordling Neeble punched through my mind.

"Yet all along," Jax continued, "I'd known something about you was different. Special. And since being with you, getting to know you more, that feeling has only grown. I've barely been able to stand it. Being around you and not being able to touch you, when all I've wanted to do is hold you, consume you, fuck you, *love* you," he added on a low growl. "And when Alec kept flirting with you on that fucking ship, I could have . . ."

I laughed lightly. "He did that on purpose, you know."

He rolled his eyes. "I know. He told me the other day. He even apologized for it." His gaze bore into mine, and he cupped my cheek, brushing his thumb over my skin. "Suffice to say, you're *mine*, Elowen. And I'm never going to let you go as long as you want to stay at my side."

Something in me shattered at his raw declaration. It was real. Heartfelt. *True.* Everything he'd just shared had come from the depths of his soul. I knew that as truly as I knew the sky was green.

Before I knew what I was doing, my arms were around him, and I was tangled in his embrace, feverishly kissing him.

He hauled me to him and kissed me just as fast.

Loved. Jax loved me. Nobody had ever loved me, not really. Yet with Jax, I *felt* it. Every word he'd spoken had called to something inside me, an ancient bond, a fated link. If anyone else had said to me what Jax just had, every insecurity I'd ever felt would probably have come rearing back. But not with Jax. Not after feeling this.

He seemed to know the second I fully accepted our bonding. His aura swelled, and a fierce tide of his magic consumed me.

And then I was sitting on the bathroom counter, hauled up on it so quickly that my head spun. Jax was peeling my clothes off, his coming free just as fast. The need inside me grew stronger, more urgent. Jax was my mate. *My* mate.

His lips met mine, our tongues clashed, and my fingers raked down his bare skin, relishing the feel of his naked chest.

In a blink, his antlers emerged in a tidal wave of potent magic. Their huge span brushed the walls. Breaking our kiss only long enough to see what I was doing, I tentatively touched an antler, not even knowing I was going to until my fingers curled around the right one and then, with my other hand, the left. They felt textured. Rough. In a way, his antlers felt like stone.

I caressed them, running my fingers along that part of him, marveling at their width and feel.

"*Fuck*, Elowen." A wild grunt came from Jax's throat as my feathery touches cascaded over his antlers, and then in a flurry of speed, we were both entirely naked, and his hard length was parting my folds as he entered me with a single thrust.

He plunged himself inside me so swiftly that I arched against him, grabbing a hold of his antlers to steady myself. My grip only seemed to heighten his frenzy, so I held on fully and ran my hands up and down them, crying out with each buck of his hips.

He pumped into me hard and fast, with so much force that my entire body shook, and the counter groaned beneath me.

"*Mine*, Elowen," he grunted and slammed into me again. "You're fucking *mine*."

"And you're mine, Jax," I replied as my bottom squeaked against the counter. "Forever and always."

The wildness around him grew, and then his magic simmered in the air, coasting over my mark, heating my blood. Something cracked open inside me, and tendrils of my magic surged forth. But instead of trying to stop my magic from colliding with his, I let the well to my power burst open, knowing there was no going back after this, but with the bond gaining hold of me, I was powerless to stop it.

Magic slammed out of me, heading toward Jax until our powers collided. Spirals of our magic swirled around us, entwining, embracing, and tangling together. My magic coated him as his did to me, and that was when I fully felt our connection solidify. The fated bond within me fully, finally connected with his.

A shattering of power melded our souls, and his mark burned on my neck just as light flared on his wrist. The skin near his palm, shone with a twist of shadows and the eye of a semelee. A lorafin's mark. The same mark I bore upon my lower stomach. My stamp was now upon him, just as his was upon me.

Jax growled in pleasure when my mark settled on his skin, enacting the final acts of our bond.

He slammed into me even harder, and our souls

blended and became one. Finally, the instinct he'd been feeling all along, the deep throbbing need to claim another as their own, fully awoke within me too.

The need to be with this male, own him, claim him . . . it nearly overtook me.

And in that moment, when Jax did a final thrust inside me, and we both came together, our climaxes shooting through our bodies in a final blazing light, I realized that he was right. He'd been right all along.

I was his fated mate.

And he was mine.

And somehow, we would figure out a way to forge a path together.

CHAPTER 25

Jax carried me from the bathing chambers, my body limp and sated. Internally, a new bond hummed inside me. Golden, beautiful strands danced within me, linking my soul to my mate's. We were mated. Bonded. This was more than just a stag claiming a female, and there was no going back. I'd heard that mate bonds allowed you to feel the other, but I'd never known it would be like *this*.

I felt Jax's presence, his very being, and his emotions strummed into me. Love. Satisfaction. Possessiveness. The ultimate victory.

Back in the bedroom, he set me down on the cool sheets, his eyes glowing like twin sapphires. He crawled in beside me and gathered me in his arms.

Soft kisses were pressed to my mouth, throat, cheeks, eyes, breasts, stomach . . . everywhere Jax's mouth traveled,

I felt his love filling me up, rolling through me like a warm spring coming to life after a harsh, cold winter.

My bond vibrated in contentment.

"We'll figure this out," he said softly. "I don't care if my father and mother disown me. I don't care if I'm dishonored among the Houses. I won't give you up."

I laid a hand on his cheek and nodded. "I'm not giving you up either."

A soft knock came on the door, and Jax immediately growled and whipped the covers over me. Possessive energy strummed from him, and my insides curled as the extent of his protectiveness washed over me.

So this is what it's like to be mated.

It was the only thought I had before Jax called, "Enter."

The door opened, but Lars didn't step over the threshold. The mid-afternoon sun shone on his scarlet locks, vibrantly highlighting them as he kept his face firmly positioned toward the floor. "We were going to head back to the clearing, and the others are wondering if you plan to join us?"

Jax nodded. "Yes, we'll be out in a few minutes."

But just as Lars was about to close the door, I called out, "Wait."

The guard stopped but didn't remove his gaze from his toes.

I clasped Jax's hand tighter. "There's so much going on

here, Jax. So much we don't understand, but we need to if we're going to save your brother, and I don't think returning to the clearing to continue our search is going to provide any further answers than what we found this morning."

I let my words sink in, the inner meaning of them hitting Jax, then Lars.

"No," Jax growled just as Lars's breath sucked in.

"*Yes*," I emphasized just as sharply. "I need to do another calling for you. It's the only way to truly understand what's occurring and find Bastian."

Jax's jaw locked, the muscle in the corner sharpening. "Absolutely not. I'm never doing again to you what I did back at the palace—"

I brought my fingers to his lips. "But what if it's different now? We're *mated*. Bound by the very stars in our galaxy. And I'm stronger. My magic is freer because of the loosened collar, and I wasn't adversely affected when I ventured to the Veiled Between in my dream. I firmly believe that it won't be like last time." I removed my hand from his mouth and coasted my finger over the mark on his inner wrist. "Please trust me."

A shiver racked his entire frame when I touched my mark on him. "But is it too soon to demand answers of the semelees?" he asked.

I shrugged. "It's close to two full weeks since your last calling, so it may be okay, but regardless, we're mates. A bond lives within us that's born of the gods. I no longer know what rules are at play."

Warring emotions surged across Jax's face, and I could practically feel Lars's trepidation at the thought of me venturing to the Veiled Between again.

"Please," I added quietly. "Let me help you. Let me find Bastian. Do it for me?"

I felt it the instant he surrendered to my wishes, as though a power greater than himself demanded that he please me.

A low rumble shook his chest, but eventually he nodded. "All right. We'll try it one more time, but if it's anything like the first time, that's it, Elowen. I'm never allowing you to do a calling for me again, and please"—his voice turned hoarse—"don't ask it of me again."

I nodded, my brow furrowing. "I won't. You have my word."

I LAY ON THE BED, similar to how I had the first time I'd done a calling for Jax. The others all stood around me. As soon as I willed it, my magic rose, and my soul detached from my body and shot me through the stars.

Amazement filled me at how easy it was to call upon my lorafin powers, but I also knew it'd only been days since my collar had been loosened, and sooner or later, it would tighten again and lock down my magic with chained suppression.

But at the moment, I was mostly free.

I shot through the galaxy, spiraling amidst the stars as I traveled to the very edges of the universe and reached the Veil.

The Veil parted like a mist, a shadowy curtain that opened only for a lorafin.

On the other side, the semelees stirred, sensing my presence as I entered their domain and ventured farther into the plane between planes.

She's come, one of them crooned.

A large one slithered forward, its cool scaled skin gliding past me. Power surged through me, stronger and sharper than it ever had been before, and deep within me, I felt my mate bond burning bright.

The semelee paused, then dipped down, nearly bowing at my feet. *What do you seek, Lorafin?*

Where's Bastian? I called upon Jax's magic, feeling his hand still wrapped around mine even though eons of time stretched between us. Our mate bond heated and glowed.

An image of Bastian readily appeared in my mind, and I showed it to the shadow creatures.

The one nearest me slid around my legs. *Ah, the same one you sought last time.*

Yes, tell me where he is and how we can reach him.

The semelee was quiet and twined around my legs. *You feel different, Lorafin. Stronger.*

Hope surged through me. *Tell me where he is and how we can reach him,* I repeated.

You and your mate want answers. That's the added power I feel in you.

Yes.

But that's not a simple demand, Lorafin. The half-breed you seek is under the power of another who's commanding him as we speak.

How are they commanding Bastian?

With a gem.

What gem? And who's commanding him?

The gem in his anklet.

A chill ran through me, but my magic heated more. *Tell me about the anklet he wears. And how that came to be on him. And where it comes from. And I need to know why so many half-breeds are in Faewood and how Bastian got caught up in it.*

More semelees drifted to me, moving like shadows and ink. Their hold on fate stretched around me. One touch from their all-knowing bodies and the threads of time would shift, bowing before them, altering the essence of the space and time continuum. Altering fate.

A new semelee drifted around me. *There are many answers you seek today, Lorafin, but despite that powerful bond within you, you're still a princess. You are not a lorafin queen. You demand too much.*

Annoyance flashed through me, but I held firm and called upon more magic to rise inside me, tethering the semelees' power to me more forcefully. But just as I was about to demand obedience, my collar stung.

The flash was fleeting and subtle, but my magic twitched, and a wave of horror washed through me that it just activated on its own. It wasn't quite as loose as it'd been previously. What Guardian Alleron had stated would inevitably occur. The collar would eventually rein me back in, and it had just manifested, if only a little. Who was to say how many more days or weeks I had before it fully suppressed me again.

Nearly panicking, I shouted at the semelees, *Tell me!*

But the semelees inched back, and my hold on them slipped. *You seek too much for a lorafin princess, but we shall grant you two questions today for the male you're bonded to, but that is all.*

One of them *tsked. To demand more answers for the same fairy so soon from the last time is not something we normally grant. Choose wisely, Lorafin.*

My soul ignited in frustration that I still wasn't strong enough to make them completely submit and never would be able to because of my damned collar, but I also knew it was fruitless to fight them.

But I had to be smart.

They were allowing me two answers and two answers only.

I knew immediately I had to ask them to explain how we could reach Bastian, but as for the second . . .

Someone was commanding Bastian with a gem. The semelees had willingly revealed that much, so I could ask who was the culprit, but then my thoughts shifted to what Esopeel had revealed. All of the half-breeds she'd observed wore anklets.

My thoughts whirred, because the semelee had said the gem was in Bastian's anklet, similar to how my collar held a gem. If so, it was possible the anklets were responsible for the strange behavior the semelees had commented on and Bowan had witnessed.

The anklet might be more important than uncovering the identity of whoever was behind it. Because if the gem in his anklet was controlling Bastian, it was imperative that we remove it.

Forcing myself to calm, I took a deep breath and hoped I was making the right choice. *Tell me how to get to Bastian, and then tell me how we can remove that anklet from him.*

As you wish, Lorafin.

I SLAMMED BACK into my body with so much force that I bowed off the bed. Jax's magic streamed through me, stabbing me and making my teeth grit. Ironcrest magic muffled my senses, and the sounds around me slowed as though coming through water. But as the seconds ticked past, everything began to clear.

Relief barreled through me when I felt my arms, legs, and toes. Excruciating pain never came. I wasn't burning in Jax's fire or being stabbed by his psychic Mistvale magic as I had been the first time, when the aftereffects of his calling had scorched me with intensity. And even though soreness plagued me, it was manageable.

I became more aware of my surroundings with every breath I took. The bed I lay on had smooth sheets and a soft mattress. Scents were present too. Pine and spice floated around me. *My mate.*

"Elowen?" Jax appeared in my line of sight, hovering above me with pinched eyes and tousled hair. Worry strummed out of him like a vibrating instrument's chord. "Are you okay? Can you see me? Hear me?" His hand held mine gently, but I felt the power he kept in check, his panic like a brewing storm ready to pound the shore.

"She's not bruised like she was the first time, Jax," Phillen said from my other side.

"And her eyes are almost fully open," Lars added in a hopeful tone.

"She's not moaning like last time either," Lander said.

"She's going to be fine, Jax. See? Her fingers are squeezing yours." Trivan grinned from the end of the bed, arms crossed over his lean chest. "Welcome back."

I nodded briefly, knowing that I needed to get up and moving. Opening my eyes wider, I gave Jax a small smile. "Hi."

"Are you all right?" Fear cascaded through him, around him, over me. *Stars*, over us all.

Each raider winced when Jax's potent magic hit them, but my lorafin powers and our mate bond rose, cocooning me. Amazingly, my magic wasn't as weakened as it usually was following a calling. I felt tired, stiff, and sore, but not spent and not entirely depleted. *Our bond protected me.*

"Where does it hurt?" Jax demanded.

"It's not that bad." I forced myself to sitting, and Jax immediately reached out to assist me, but I brushed him away. "I can do it. Truly, I'm fine. It's not like last time." Despite the fatigue plaguing me and a dull headache swimming through my mind, I wasn't lying. I didn't feel like death, not as I had before. "It's easier with my collar loosened so much, and I think our bond has helped too."

Relief flared in his aura, and he didn't question me, maybe knowing on some level that I wouldn't lie to him.

"And the semelees?" Lander asked, cocking an eyebrow. He stood beside Phillen, his face a mask of brown stone as he assessed me shrewdly. "What did they reveal?"

"I know how we can get to Bastian and why he disappeared. Someone's controlling him with a gem in that anklet he's wearing. That's probably why you never heard from him, but I know how we can remove it, but we need to venture to the anklet's origins to do so. It will be an extensive journey."

Jax's energy rose like a wave. "But we can save him?"

"I believe so."

A spike in Jax's aura filled the room, and his lips pressed into a hard, determined line. "Then let's find my brother."

CHAPTER 26

Since I didn't feel at death's door, and I knew time was of the essence, I insisted that we all get moving *now*.

Evening had arrived, and what the semelees had shown me of where Bastian was being held meant we couldn't delay. Every minute counted, considering what was happening in the Wood.

Consequently, Jax and his friends all dressed in their black raider attire, masks in place, while I slipped into my ebony clothing. I didn't know who we would encounter in the Wood when we attempted to rescue Bastian, and it was wisest if nobody could identify us, because we still didn't know who was behind it all.

Once dressed, we all gathered in the living area.

"Are you sure you're strong enough?" Jax's intent gaze wouldn't relent.

I grabbed a ribbon to tie my hair with. "Yes. Besides,

you need me. I have to show you how we enter the underground tunnel in the Wood. I can't stay behind."

A groove appeared between his eyes, but he nodded.

"Thought you could use this, Little Lorafin." Bowan handed me a black mask. "Best to keep all of our identities concealed, yours too."

Smiling tentatively, I took it and put it on. The silky material draped over my face, hiding my nose and mouth. Surprisingly, it was easy to breathe through.

The entire time I was securing it, Jax watched me, and I could have sworn that the worry that'd been emanating from him only moments ago turned to pride.

"Shall we use a portal key to get there?" Phillen dipped several short swords into sheaths at his waist. And Lars, Bowan, Trivan, Lander, and Alec were all busy clipping daggers and knives to straps hidden beneath their clothing.

"We'll have to." Jax grabbed the jar off the table. "Nobody can see us leaving here or returning dressed as this. I could weave an illusion over us, but it would still take time to travel back to the Wood, and since Quinn brought back so many keys, we should use them when it's truly needed."

I eyed the jar. Someone had placed all of the keys back into it following the night I'd spilled them everywhere. They were now sealed with a lid, but I was reminded of the last time I'd used one—when Jax and the others had been so close to being caught in Possyrose Forest—a capture that the king had supposedly initiated.

My brow furrowed, and I wondered again how the king had known that was where they would be. The semelees would of course know, but only a lorafin queen could demand that answer of them.

I brushed that thought off because at the moment, rescuing Bastian was all that mattered.

"Has anyone heard from Quinn?" Mask and braid secured, I bent down to tighten the laces on my boots.

Alec shook his head. "No, although that's not unusual. Our crowfy friend typically stays in the shadows until he has something worthwhile to report."

I straightened, and Jax held out his hand to me. "Back to the clearing then?"

"No, we're not going back to the clearing."

"We're not?" Phillen asked in a gruff voice.

I shook my head. "It's a decoy. That's not how we can reach Bastian." I took the portal key from Jax, then threaded my fingers through his as everyone began to link up. "I'll show you where we need to go."

WE REAPPEARED IN THE WOOD, over a half mile from the clearing we'd searched earlier today. I'd taken us to the exact location the semelees had shown me, and the second the realm stopped turning, the portal key fizzled out of existence, crumbling in my hand.

Around us, the nighttime insects and birds, chirping and singing, grew quiet in the growing twilight.

In the surrounding Wood, wildling eyes peered at us from inside dens, logs, or from their perches on the branches in the trees. I searched in the foliage, wondering if anyone was about that I knew, but the wildlings all withdrew from sight, and it struck me that none of them were near us. All of them were stationed at least fifteen paces away. In the area I'd taken us to, no creatures were about.

Jax grumbled quietly. "Do you feel that?"

A few of the males nodded, and the hairs on the back of my neck rose when I sensed it. Magic crackled in the air around us. Strong magic. Potent power.

Everyone spun in a slow circle, a few reaching their hands outward.

I did the same, and near the tree to my right, I encountered something heavy. "There's a spell cloaking this area."

"It's a repulsion spell," Jax replied. "I can sense it with my Mistvale magic."

Phillen placed his hands on his hips. "No wonder the creatures are staying away."

I pulled my hand back, recoiling when my fingers brushed it more. Similar to what Esopeel had shared, it felt . . . *wrong*.

"They're using dark magic here, just like Esopeel told

us, and it's hiding what's underground." I surveyed the forest floor and searched for the door. My eyes alighted on the small blue marker barely visible amidst the colorful leaves coating the soil. "There."

I hurried to it and crouched. Vines and dirt covered the small latch that stood only a finger's distance above the ground, and I began to brush the foliage around it away. The handle was small, easily hidden, and as I swept more plants and dirt to the side, what it was attached to was finally revealed.

A trap door appeared.

"Galaxy and stars." Bowan whistled. "We never would have found that."

The door was large, easily able to accommodate full-grown siltenites, and according to the semelees, a staircase was hidden beneath it, and at the stairs' base, two guards waited.

"Is anyone picking up any scents?" Jax asked.

All of the males inhaled sharply, but when they all shook their heads, I knew they hadn't scented Bastian or anyone else in this area.

I brushed more of the soil away until the door was fully exposed. "The semelees said it's the only entrance to what's been created underground. The clearing we found earlier is a decoy. All of the half-breeds that Bowan followed were whisked here to enter the tunnels and caverns beneath. They never entered at the clearing."

"But how did they get here?" Lander asked, his eyes narrowing to slits.

"They rode *malingees*. Whatever's happening here has also extended to some of the local animals."

"Malingees?" Lars's eyebrows shot up. "No wonder we couldn't track them past the clearing. Those beasts carry no scent."

I nodded. "Yet they're big enough and strong enough to easily carry two to three half-breeds each, not to mention they're gentle creatures, probably doing whatever is being demanded of them by whoever created this place."

Jax's jaw locked. "If there's only one way in and one way out, and it's right here, we must keep that in mind when we search below."

"Do you still have the escape portal key?" Lander asked shrewdly.

Jax patted his pocket. "Right here."

Phillen leaned down and wrapped his massive fist around the trap door's handle. "Only two guards, correct, Elowen?"

I nodded. "There are two fusterills at the bottom of the stairs. Be prepared."

Trivan grinned and withdrew two blades. "Fusterills. Excellent. They're always worthy opponents."

"Put your blades away, Triv. There'll be no fighting if we can prevent it," Jax said in a low tone. "I'll be removing their eyesight and ability to speak the second that door opens. We knock them unconscious and move. This rescue is going to be fast and efficient. No one is to make a sound."

Trivan sighed but sheathed his weapons. "You're always ruining my fun."

Bowan laughed lightly, and Lars slugged him in the arm.

"Behave," the redhead hissed.

Phillen rolled his eyes, and it once again struck me how they all seemed to thrive off this type of danger.

"Elowen?" Jax said quietly. He gripped my arm gently and pulled me away from the door. "You're not trained, my love. You need to stay behind me."

My heart squeezed at how easily he called me *my love*. "I know. I'm not stupid. I'll stay out of the way if any fighting occurs. I'll stay safe."

His hand traveled down my forearm to clasp my hand. Heat from his palm wrapped around me. After giving me a single squeeze, he let go.

"Ready?" he asked everyone.

Everyone's heads bobbed, hands on their weapons just in case.

Jax nodded at Phillen. "Go."

CHAPTER 27

Phillen grasped the door handle and with a mighty wrench, tore it open. Before I could inhale my next breath, Jax was down the hole, leaping from the forest floor to the bottom of the stairwell in blurred speed.

My heart lurched, but nobody hesitated. In seconds, the entire band of dark raiders were underground, and I hurried to race down the stairs after them.

The sounds of the Wood quickly fell behind me. Stone slid beneath my soles. Musky, damp scents assaulted me. Solid rock walls met my fingertips when I reached out. It was exactly as the semelees had shown me.

Torches lit the stairwell, and my eyes widened when I beheld two massive fusterills lying at the bottom, already unconscious. Jax hadn't been kidding. He'd made quick work of them, and given the strength of Jax's magic, I highly doubted the guards had even known what hit them.

"Elowen, which way?" Jax asked quietly.

It took me a second to realize I'd frozen and was staring at the guards. Snapping myself out of my shock, I got my bearings.

Three tunnels branched out from this stairwell, all carved from stone. Water dripped from the ceilings of all of them, a steady *drip, drip* filling the quiet.

"That way." I pointed at the right tunnel.

Jax took off, leading the way, with me closely behind him, and the others silently padded at my back. The tunnel snaked downward, and heavy pulsing magic emanated from the walls, making a sickening throb grow inside my head.

Several times we reached intersections, and I kept a firm grip on the information the semelees had shared with me. *Take the right tunnel from the stairwell, past three intersections. At the fourth go left. Look for a cell on the right, sixth door down.* I'd already told Jax that, but he didn't have the visuals the semelees had given me, and they'd warned me that magic cloaked entrances to caverns in this labyrinth. I not only had to remember the directions they'd shared, but I also had to assess the *feel* of each tunnel.

A few steps past the second intersection, Jax raised his hand in a silent gesture. I stopped just in time to prevent myself from smacking into him.

Male voices came from down the tunnel.

"Move that group to the training cavern," a deep voice said in the quiet, his tone reverberating on the walls ahead. "They're starting training today. And those females there, take them to cavern eight. They're to be bred tonight."

My stomach twisted as I hovered behind Jax. *Training? Being bred? What in the realm is happening down here?* How I wished I'd been able to demand more answers of the semelees.

Jax didn't move a muscle as we waited to see which way the males went. Not that it mattered. If whoever was ahead happened to venture our way, they'd spot us immediately. The tunnels were too narrow to hide anywhere. But I also knew Jax could coat us in illusion magic at the last second, hiding us from view.

Footsteps finally drifted farther away, and then the males speaking grew quieter.

My heart thundered.

Jax crept forward, his steps silent. The only sound I heard was my own breathing through my mask and that constant *drip, drip* from the water.

Jax took off again, moving swiftly now that we were in the clear. Moments later, we reached the third intersection, and a branch of four new tunnels appeared. Moans came from down one, banging from another.

Jax was about to continue onward, but I reached out and grabbed his waistband. He stopped and peered over his shoulder at me.

I closed my eyes. Something about this intersection felt different from the others. I paused, sensing the magic around us.

"It's this one," I whispered.

He cocked his head, knowing damned well that we hadn't reached the fourth intersection yet, but this one felt right.

"You're certain?" he asked, speaking just as quietly.

I nodded. "The third one must have been cloaked. It's this one."

He inhaled sharply and turned left. The tunnel cut steeper downward, and the moans ahead increased.

Every fiber in my body turned on high alert, and it felt as though my heart would leap into my chest. Behind me, the others crept silently, so quietly that I looked over my shoulder several times just to ensure they were still there.

The tunnel abruptly ended, and a huge cavern emerged. Jax's breath sucked in, and I nearly squeaked.

Torches flickered higher up, dimly lighting the huge space. A huge circular room lined with solid doors waited. Thumps came from behind the door nearest me, as though whoever or whatever was in it was banging its head against it. Moans came from another. Scratching sounds emitted from one farther down. But the rest were silent.

"Stars and galaxy," Bowan whispered so quietly that I almost didn't hear him.

Jax inhaled sharply but let out a frustrated growl, and I

couldn't help but wonder if whatever magic contained this space was masking scents too.

But this cavern looked exactly as the semelees had shown me. "He's in that one." I pointed to the sixth door, and within seconds, we were all surrounding it.

Lars and Phillen immediately covered our flanks, turning outward and watching the entrance to the cavern.

Jax grabbed the door handle and shoved.

The door didn't budge.

He shoved his shoulder into it, and the door creaked but still refused to open.

"Let me try." Before he could attempt muscling his way through it again, I whispered the most powerful unlocking spell I knew.

Potent lorafin magic swirled around me, billowing the air around my mask and clothing.

An unclicking sound followed, and the door opened.

Jax's eyes crinkled in the corners, and I knew he was grinning at me, but before any of us could celebrate, an alarm blared.

My breath sucked in just as Jax shoved the door fully open.

A male with antlers appeared on the other side, sitting on the floor. Dark-blond hair covered his head. Muscular arms were visible in his thin tunic. He sat upright, legs sprawled out in front of him, his back to the stone wall, but he didn't move. He didn't even flinch at our violent entrance.

Jax's entire body tensed. "Bastian?"

Bootsteps sounded in the distance, running through the distant tunnels as the shrill alarm continued to wail, and two things hit me at once.

Guards were coming, and the male who sat despondently in this cell, as though completely unaware of us, was Jax's missing brother.

CHAPTER 28

"Bastian!" Jax crouched and shook his brother by his shoulders. But Bastian continued to sit against the cell's wall, unmoving. His eyes were open, his chest rising with each breath, but he made no move to rise.

Large antlers rose from Bastian's head, and they swayed every time Jax shook him, but unlike when Jax's antlers appeared, Bastian's couldn't be magically whisked away.

"Jax!" Lander barked. "They'll be here in seconds!"

Jax growled. "Dammit, Bastian, get up!"

But his brother still didn't move.

My eyes flashed wide just as the first shout hit my ears.

"Cell six's door is open. There are siltenites here!"

Jax whipped away from his brother and plastered me to the wall in the same breath. Before I could so much as squeak, he was flying through Bastian's cell door as the sound of steel meeting steel met my ears.

Clanging weapons clashed, and shrieks of fear followed.

"My eyes!" someone wailed. "I can't see!"

Another screamed. "I'm blind!"

"Get Bastian," Jax snarled.

Phillen was suddenly through the door, Lars at his side. The two of them wrestled Bastian up and off the floor, but Jax's brother remained completely unresponsive.

I plastered myself to the wall to stay out of the way.

Bastian appeared lifeless. Comatose in a way, and I recalled what the semelees had initially told me. *Something's not right.* It matched what Bowan had seen of Bastian in the Wood this morning as well, but at least then he'd been walking.

Now, he was entirely lethargic.

"We'll have to carry him," Phillen grunted. He heaved Jax's brother over his shoulder and looked at me with wild eyes. "Go, Newole. I'll follow you."

It registered that he just called me by the same nickname as he had one time earlier, and a brief moment of hysteria wanted to rise in me that he hadn't called me *Gorgeous* as Alec had teased on the ship, but I locked down my response and leaped through the door.

My footsteps nearly planted to the cavern's floor when I beheld the scene outside Bastian's cell.

A dozen guards lay dead on the floor. Blood pooled around them, and I had a feeling this *wasn't* an illusion.

Jax and his friends' eyes were all filled with wild, manic energy. Nobody uttered a word.

Before I could blink, Jax's hand was encircling my arm. Everyone else connected hands.

But when Jax gripped the portal key and said the magical words, nothing happened. Only an answering pulse of magic emanated from the walls.

Jax seethed and shoved the key back into his pocket. "The walls are spelled. The magic surrounding this place must be suppressing the key's ability to transport us. We'll have to go out on foot."

"Go," Phillen rasped. Bastian's dangling body was still draped over his shoulder. "I got him."

Jax's grip on me tightened, and then we were flying back through the tunnels, toward the way we'd originally come.

All the while, the alarm continued to wail.

More bootsteps came from the distance. Yells sounded too, but they were farther away and deeper within this rocky labyrinth, as though the other guards stationed within this terrifying enclosure were too far away to reach us in quick succession.

None of us stopped to find out.

Jax lifted me at one point, carrying me as fast as the wind. The others moved just as quickly and silently behind us, even if Bastian's antlers scraped along the walls the entire way, and it struck me just how formidable this group was and why they were so feared.

They functioned as one. Stealthy. Silent. Deadly. And with Jax's potent magic rendering anyone they encountered obsolete, it was no wonder they'd remained uncaught as a band of raiders.

We reached the stairwell to the Wood only minutes later. Phillen grunted when Bastian's antlers caught alongside the narrow passage, catching in the rocky indents.

I quickly worked them free, and Phillen nodded his thanks.

We all hurtled upward on the remaining steps and out of the trap door, then the musky damp air from the caverns fell away, and the Wood's fresh breeze swirled around us.

Nighttime had fully set in, the three moons appearing in the sky.

Once free of the stairwell, Lars slammed the trap door closed, and I hastily whispered a spell to lock it.

"Join hands!" Jax barked.

Everyone gathered around, linking together physically, and in a flurry of whispered words, the realm disappeared from around us as the portal key whisked us away.

CHAPTER 29

We slammed back into the prince's private residence at The Silver Hand, everyone appearing at once. Phillen still held Bastian draped over his shoulder, but he released him and set him on the nearest chair.

Bastian fell onto it in a heap. His eyes remained open, and he bounced a few times, but it was as though he was unseeing. Not even aware of his surroundings.

Jax tore his mask off and kneeled in front of his brother before I could blink.

"Bastian?" he said urgently, smacking his cheek lightly.

Nothing. No response.

"Bastian!"

I undid my own mask, the others doing the same, and I pulled my bottom lip into my mouth, gnawing on it in serrating motions as I watched my mate try to rouse his brother.

Jax continued calling and shaking Bastian, but no matter what he did, Bastian didn't respond.

I kneeled at his other side, then lifted the bottom of Bastian's trousers. A flash of metal gleamed in the light.

The anklet that Esopeel and the semelees had told us about was indeed around Bastian's ankle. "Jax, look at this."

The prince stopped his frantic movements. A low growl rumbled in his chest, and when his finger ran along the anklet's metal and stone, a chill ran through me.

Because the gem staring back at me—the gem the semelees had said was controlling Jax's brother—was a purple stone. It was encased within the anklet, and it appeared to be the exact same stone that was locked within my collar.

"WHAT DO YOU THINK IT MEANS?" Jax paced in the living room. All of us had changed out of our dark clothes and were sitting together in a circle.

For the past hour, we'd tried everything we could think of to rouse Bastian, but it was no use. Whatever that anklet was doing to him was like my collar. No amount of effort could disengage its suppression. Magic held it in place. Powerful magic from the feel of it.

Bastian had sat numbly through everything we'd tried, and he was still unmoving. Still despondent. He lived physically, but it was as though he no longer existed, and even though he was with us, it was like he wasn't there at all.

I knew Jax's heart was breaking. It was as though his baby brother, the male he loved and cherished, was no more.

And the semelees warning that he was being controlled by another chilled me to the bone. There was nothing to say that Bastian wouldn't suddenly become animated and try to kill us.

Jax placed his hands on his hips and eyed my collar and then the anklet on his brother. "Elowen, what did the semelees say about Bastian's anklet?"

"When I asked how we could take it off, they said we would have to venture to where it was created and have the creator remove it. That doing so was the only way, and that we couldn't remove it ourselves."

Bowan sighed. "Please tell me they gave you more details than that."

"They did. The gem comes from the mines of Harrivee's floating meadows on the Solis continent, and they showed me what its creator looks like. A female Solis fairy forged Bastian's anklet."

My mate's aura flared, and his attention fixated on my collar.

I knew he was thinking the same thing I was. I'd been thinking it ever since I saw Bastian's anklet.

I raised a finger to my collar, and a pulse of magic emitted from it. "The gem on Bastian's anklet looks identical to the gem in my collar."

Jax's throat bobbed. "It does."

Tears threatened to spring into my eyes. "Do you think the fairy who forged Bastian's anklet also forged my collar?"

Jax's eyes gleamed, and our mate bond hummed with his heightened emotion. "We can only hope they did."

Magic swelled inside me. Potent, powerful magic. The semelees had shown me the face of a female who resided in a land far away. A female with silver hair, crystalline blue eyes, and small black wings. She was the female who had forged Bastian's anklet, and we needed to find her. She was the only one who could remove it.

And a part of me, a trembling, hopeful sliver of my soul, hoped it was possible that she'd created my collar too.

I didn't want to get my hopes up, though, and I knew that we needed to focus on Bastian, not me. Yet a part of me couldn't help but dream.

Bowan arched an eyebrow. "Does this mean we're going to the Solis continent?"

The aura around Jax grew, and for the first time since learning the depth of my guardian's betrayals, a flash of possibility ignited inside me.

A fierce look of determination stole over Jax's face. "That's exactly where we're going. Because if someone is mining magical gems on the Solis continent to control my brother and other half-breeds on our continent, then we need to stop them." His attention flickered to me, his eyes burning like sapphires. "And since Bastian's anklet looks strikingly similar to Elowen's collar, then it's possible that many summers ago, the same fairy forged Elowen's necklace, and maybe, just maybe they'll know how to remove it too."

DON'T MISS THE FINAL BOOK IN
FAE OF WOODLANDS & WILD

Elowen and Jax travel to the Solis continent, knowing it's the only way to save Jax's brother, but what they discover catapults them into a string of events that threatens to destroy the fated love they've only just found.

ABOUT THE AUTHOR

Krista Street loves writing in multiple genres: fantasy, sci-fi, romance, and dystopian. Her books are cross-genre and often feature complex characters, plenty of supernatural twists, and romance in every story. She loves writing about coming-of-age characters who fight to find their place in this world while also finding their one true mate.

Krista Street is a Minnesota native but has lived throughout the U.S. and in another country or two. She loves to travel, read, and spend time in the great outdoors. When not writing, Krista is either chasing her children, spending time with her husband and friends, sipping a cup of tea, or enjoying the hidden gems of beauty that Minnesota has to offer.

THANK YOU

Thank you for reading *Veil of Shadows,* book two, in the *Fae of Woodlands & Wild* trilogy.

To learn more about Krista's other books and series, visit her website. Links to all of her books, along with links to her social media platforms, are available on every page.

www.kristastreet.com